The Single Feather

Ruth F Hunt

Published 2015 by Pilrig Press, Edinburgh, Scotland

A CIP catalogue record for this book is available on request from
the British Library.

ISBN 978-0-9927234-2-2

www.pilrigpress.co.uk

Printed in Great Britain by Imprint Digital

'Rachel flees her past to build a new life for herself. But living a lie isn't easy. She struggles with a guilty conscience and the fear of being exposed. Eventually, she has to decide: tell the truth and risk all, or say nothing and betray everything she has ever believed in. A stunning debut novel written with intelligence and clarity. Rachel's efforts to belong exposes our prejudices against those more vulnerable in society while shining a light on the power of friendship and the importance of being part of a community.'

Marianne Wheelaghan, bestselling author of The Blue Suitcase and Food of Ghosts

'An intense, bittersweet story for anyone who's ever doubted themselves.'

Louisa Dang, author of The Rain Catcher, winner of Duke University Writers' Workshop Fiction Prize

Cover photo by Sally-Ann Tatlock

Acknowledgements

I want to thank the following people for their help and support during my journey to publication.

Anne Hamilton, Chris Marshall, John Wilson, Katrina Hart, Louisa Dang, Sally-Ann Tatlock, Marianne Wheelaghan and Pilrig Press.

I would also like to thank my family for being so patient and listening to me talking about The Single Feather for two years. This novel is dedicated to them.

R.F. Hunt is a writer and artist. The Single Feather is her first novel published by Pilrig Press.

'When you meet somebody for the first time, you're not meeting them, you're meeting their representative.'

Chris Rock: Bigger and Blacker tour 1999

Four Months Ago

The guards were in the living room watching television with the back door open, the mid-June heat, still oppressive in the early evening. One guard was sprawled on the sofa; her vest top straps were pushed down her arms, which revealed white strips of skin in stark contrast to the rest of her mahogany coloured tan. The other guard lounged on the armchair, noisily chewing gum in his open mouth. His body was half turned, with one leg at the front, the other dangled over the arm of the chair.

I shut the living room door, and told them I was reading before I moved into the kitchen and pulled out the letter from under my bottom. I heard my cue, the start of the theme tune for Coronation Street, and took one last look around me. When I first arrived in the bungalow, I worried about the area, with kids posturing on street corners and reports of anti-social behaviour in the paper, only to discover the risk was indoors.

After placing the letter from the solicitor on the kitchen table, I heard a faint stirring from the living room followed by a muffled voice. I sat completely still. My heartbeat felt like a bird inside my chest, flapping about, trying to break free.

The sound of my mum's car pulling up outside prompted me to quietly move to the doorway of the kitchen and I strained to hear the guards in the living room. I wheeled myself carefully until I was at the front door. Here again, I heard a voice and seconds later, a thud. I stopped breathing. When all I could hear was the television, I took a deep breath in.

'Just going out for a cigarette.' My voice wavered with nerves.

'Two minutes. You know the drill,' shouted the male guard.

By then I was almost out of the door, Mum shut it while I sped to the car. She helped me in, pulled the footplates off my chair and threw the rest of it on the back seat before running around to the driver's side.

She was just about to put the key in the ignition when I heard the guards; one had run around the back and one through the front door. The male guard, his face purple and contorted, was trying to pull open my locked car door and the female guard was bending over the bonnet, her arms outstretched and her pendulous breasts in full view.

'Get out of the way,' Mum yelled.

There wasn't any response from the guards who remained in position.

After a sidelong glance to me, Mum revved the engine and tried a different tactic.

'It's been approved, the letter's in the kitchen.'

For a second, the female guard stood up straight and half turned towards her colleague.

At that point, Mum reversed, throwing me forward, before she swerved past out of their way, the car screeching as she put her foot down. In the passenger wing mirror I could see both of them standing in the middle of the road waving their arms before they disappeared out of view.

A few minutes later, my stomach flipped over and a wave of nausea flooded my mouth with bile. 'Mum, I need to stop. Quickly, I'm going to be...'

She did a sharp left turn into a side road, prompting other motorists to sound their horns in protest.

When I'd finished being sick in the gutter, Mum handed me a wet-wipe. Her eyes fixed ahead while she raked her fingers up and down her forehead. I reached over to hold and squeeze her hand and in reply she gently put her other hand on top of mine.

'We'd better get a move on. They're probably on the phone to the police right now. You don't still feel sick, do you?'

'No, it was just...'

'I know, love. OK, Carthom here we come. I need to get back onto the road for the junction.'

'We've done the right thing haven't we? I tried to swallow, a foul taste in my dry mouth.

'Course we have. You did put the letter in the kitchen, didn't you?'

'Yes, on the kitchen table. I just hope they can't... I mean, could they get me back in and..?' I felt a tight pain in my chest.

Mum interrupted me. 'The solicitor said it would just be a case of getting you out of the door. They'll find it hard getting you back there now.'

'I can't go back, I'd...' I opened my mouth but the words wouldn't come out and the discomfort in my chest was getting worse.

We stopped at red lights and she half turned towards me. 'Don't worry; as long as you're sensible, you'll be fine. Now, I know you said no before, but I'm alright to stay with you in Carthom for as long as you need. I really am.'

'I think it's going to be hard but if I'm going to be independent again, then I'm better doing it from the start.' I half turned towards her. 'I don't want you as a carer, I want you as my mum.'

'OK, as long as you promise me you'll call if you need me.'

I nodded then put my head against the window, and for a minute closed my eyes.

'I had to put my bank details down at the estate agents, and act as guarantor; mainly because they're not happy you're on Benefits.'

I stared ahead, images flashed through my head of what would've happened if they'd managed to stop me from escaping.

'And legally, it's going to be alright?'

'We've been through all this. He said he couldn't foresee any major problems. The only issue we're going to have is in daily life. I say 'we' as this affects both of us now, but in a sense it's you who's almost going to have to reinvent yourself.'

'Again,' I said grimly.

'You won't have any problems here; it's something like sixty percent of residents are over the age of fifty. It'll be good to get some independence back, won't it?'

I made a 'hmmm' sound in my throat. She was making it sound so easy and, as usual, was treating me as if I were seventeen or eighteen, not a thirty-one year old woman.

We were stationary and in a queue to get onto the road linking Weston to Carthom. A sign for Carthom said it was eight miles away.

'You don't think they're going to be waiting at the house with the police, do you?'

'Who?' Sweat bubbles were lined up in rows on Mum's brow and top lip.

'The guards waiting for us, with the police.'

She lifted her right hand temporarily off the steering wheel, and held it out. 'How'll they know where you are? They won't be able to find out your new address that quickly. They're much more likely to be waiting at my house, and if they are, I'll call the solicitor, so don't worry.'

We were moving again and soon reached the rural and affluent neighbourhoods on the edge of Carthom, with expensive looking barn conversions dotted along our route.

As we drove closer to the centre of Carthom, we passed farms, and rundown agricultural buildings. A few minutes later we pulled into my new road and stopped outside number four. The 'to-let' sign was still up and hadn't been changed to 'let-by'. It looked like a red brick, terraced house Lowry would've painted.

When we got out of the car, Mum gave me my new house keys. Just the fact I had my own keys felt deeply symbolic.

'Open up, it's your home.'

The first thing I saw was the stair lift and I could smell fresh paint.

'Your lightweight chair's upstairs,' Mum said, reading my mind.

I turned right into a large wooden-floored room and through a wide door into another big space; one half was a kitchen, with some of the units, including the sink at wheelchair height and low plug points as well. The other half had plenty of elbowroom to manoeuvre myself around.

'It's perfect, Mum.'

'It should be for the money.

'I'm sorry, all this money, all of this.' I gestured towards the front room. 'I do appreciate it and I'll try to pay you back.'

'Don't be silly. Let's look at the bedrooms. Onwards and upwards.'

With my voice breaking with emotion, I repeated, 'onwards and upwards.'

One

As I sat in my doorway, trying to get the courage to propel myself forward, I listened intently to the sounds of Carthom. Due to it being a much more rural and open location than Weston, with a bird sanctuary only two miles down the main road, it was the sound of birds singing, and in particular, the blackbird's song, with its melodic, mellow tone, which supplied the sublime soundtrack to spur me on. If I listened carefully, I thought I could hear the high pitched screams and shouts, from schoolchildren, giddy as they ran around at mid-morning break. Periodically, I could also make out the low rumble of trains as they weaved around the tracks that circled Carthom. Above all of that, I heard the wind, as it flowed past through the trees and picked up then scattered the leaves in my path.

It was both comforting and terrifying being alone. I didn't have the guards shouting and swearing anymore, but with only my thoughts for company, I was very aware this wasn't how I wanted my life to be.

In the four months since I moved to Carthom, I'd only ventured as far as the end of my road by myself. Even though I was free from the guards, I was still under their shadow, which meant this short trip felt like it was illicit, as if I were going to be punished later for simply going out.

I was trying to find the library, to find out what groups and other activities took place in Carthom, so with trepidation I set off, armed with only a minuscule map I'd downloaded from the internet.

As I wheeled, I was aware people were staring or smiling at me. Not friendly smiles but condescending, and full of pity. No surprise there. It's disconcerting, even though I'm used to it. I wanted to unnerve them by staring back. Instead, I lowered my eyes and counted the paving slabs as they disappeared under my wheels.

At the lights I crossed the clogged main road that cuts through the centre of Carthom. I stopped to quickly check the map. Before long, I was on the road, which had a signpost pointing to the police station and the library.

Halfway down, I found it. The door and windows were boarded up. The remnants of a large poster were stuck on one of the window boards. The only words visible were, 'Hands Off.'

The building next door caught my attention. It was Carthom Community Centre and was nestled in between the library and police station. It was an ugly, one storey structure with dirty grey-bricks, which looked out of place, squeezed in between the two more traditional, older buildings.

Despite its uninviting appearance, I knew if anywhere in Carthom had activities to do, it would be in there. It was even better than my original idea to find groups advertised in the library. Ideally, I would've wanted an art connection but I was close to the stage where I'd accept anything. Since I escaped from the bungalow, I was struggling to find things to do.

I started to wheel towards the main door but nerves got the better of me and I turned back. For the next few minutes I dithered. I was like that a lot then. My confidence evaporated while at the bungalow and I knew it would take a lot for it to come back. I gripped the sides of my chair and after a deep breath in; wheeled up a second time.

Inside, I could just about see into the reception desk, and a man with a crumpled up face, appeared.

'Can I help you, love?' The man spoke loudly, and very carefully, enunciating his words as if I were five years old.

'Do you have?' I ran my tongue across my lips and tried to swallow. 'Do you have anything to do with art here, like a group, a gallery or maybe a wall where I can display my paintings?'

'In a word, no. Oh, hang on, did you mean for people like

13

you?' He pointed down at my chair, before using the same hand to scratch at his greasy, grey hair. 'Or did you mean generally?'

'Generally,' I growled.

He disappeared for a minute and I tried to calm down my breathing.

'Right, love, this might be what you're looking for,' he said, when he returned. 'There's a gallery inside Garden and Crafts for You. The woman who runs it might be able to help you. It's just on the edge of Carthom, towards Weston in that direction.' He pointed over my head.

I glided out of the centre and made my way back home. As I turned into my road, I stopped for a moment and dried my fingers, which were cold and wet from the autumnal leaves on the pavement.

Further down my road I saw Janine, my dinnertime carer, already on my doorstep. She was blowing into her cupped hands and stamping her feet, the Concerned about Care uniform, with its short sleeves and cotton trousers not suitable for the October chill.

'Where've you been? I was ready to send out a search party.'

'Sorry. I decided to go out for a bit,' I said, as I unlocked the door.

Janine froze, one foot inside, one outside and her mouth dropped to form an 'O'.

'On your own?'

'Yeah, to go to the library but it was closed down. Then I found the community centre and they told me about a gallery where I can display my paintings.'

'Really? A gallery? Around here?' Janine rubbed her eyelid and picked up a couple of letters from the mat in my hall and put them down on my coffee table.

'If it's not far from here I reckon it'll be quite posh.' I pictured somewhere like The National Portrait Gallery or The Tate, but on a much smaller, more intimate scale.

Janine perched on the arm of the chair and nodded encouragingly.

'I just hope it means I'll soon be meeting people and won't be stuck on my own as much. Listen to this.' I wheeled over to my bookshelves and after I picked out the small paperback book, an image from my eighteenth birthday party flashed in front of me with Paul, my boyfriend at the time, reaching across the table to hand me the book for my birthday present. Thirteen years later and the powerful words still resonated with me as much, if not more, as they did then. I opened it where I'd folded down the corner of the page.

'With friends you grow wings. Alone you are a single feather in disgrace...' My voice trailed off as I saw her check her watch.

'Lovely, Rachel. Now, do you want me to do your bedroom today?'

'You better had. Actually, see this box next to my bookcase. 'Would you be a star and take it up to the study for me?'

Janine bent down to pick up it up. As she stood up she briefly lost her grip. She balanced the box on her bent leg, before grabbing it again. 'God, what's in here?'

'The old Rachel.'

She scrunched up her nose. 'I don't get you?'

'I just meant papers, rubbish really,' I mumbled. 'At some point it needs shredding.'

When Janine finished upstairs, she joined me for a cappuccino. She was meant to be my dinnertime carer and provide personal care. However, she'd agreed to do housework in the allotted time. As she'd been so flexible, I didn't mind giving her a break if she wanted one.

Before she sat down, she handed me her phone and showed me a photograph. 'See, that's what I looked like before I toned the makeup down.'

I squinted at the picture, but couldn't see much difference. She still had the jet black hair, which had a blue hue in the light.

Her purple eye shadow, thick black eyeliner along with the black or dark blue lipstick was still evident and if anything, looked more dramatic than in the photograph.

'Who said to tone it down?'

'My narky supervisor.'

Janine collapsed onto the blue chair and slurped her drink, tipping up the mug to finish off the dregs before putting the black lipstick stained mug on the coffee table and wiping her mouth with the back of her hand.

She'd found out we were both thirty-one, our birthdays only being a week apart. This was significant as she believed in astrology and now wanted to compare our weekly activities for similarities. However, due to my embarrassment at my lack of social life, I'd already started to lie about this.

Janine delved into her tunic pocket and pulled out a scrap of newspaper. 'It's not much good this one, I'll check my magazine when I get home see if it's any better. It says this week's all about meeting new people who'll be important in our lives, though it might not turn out to be positive. We can also expect a complication with money.'

'Oh, I could do without money problems.'

Janine nodded as she gazed out of my living room window. 'Are you off out at the weekend?'

'Yeah, just with a few friends,' I lied. 'What about you?'

'I might stay in with my fella, give him some attention.' Janine twisted the gold ring that hung from a gold chain around her neck.

The visit to the garden centre was the only thing I'd planned for the weekend, apart from being with my mum. Since I'd moved to Carthom, the novelty of being on my own had been replaced by loneliness and anxiety. Even though the guards were abusive they still formed a layer protecting me from the outside world. Now the layer was stripped away, I was exposed and on my own.

In anticipation of the visit, I got out my art materials and sketched a picture but by the weekend I'd put it straight into the bin. At least, keeping occupied with the sketch meant the weekend came around quickly. If I was busy, time didn't drag as much as it usually did.

On Saturday, I half-watched out of my living room window and waited for my mum to arrive. I'd unsuccessfully tried to find Garden and Crafts for You on the internet, which made me suspicious as to whether it was still open or had been one of the many businesses to fold during the recession.

'Taxi for Miss Aspinhall,' my mum said, in a put-on posh voice when she arrived. 'May I take your bag?'

She started to fold up my wheelchair, putting it in the boot. 'Your foot plate feels a bit loose – does it need fixing?'

'No, it's alright.'

'Let's see if we can find this garden centre. Eyes peeled.'

Carthom was a small picturesque village, overshadowed at one end by a large supermarket, the red and blue lights more visible than the two churches. At the other end of the village, the residential area petered out leaving acres and acres of farm land. If you carried on the road, travelling north you'd meet a junction which led to a busy 'A' road, linking Carthom to Weston.

We travelled in silence on the road for a few minutes. When we turned a corner, we passed a llama, enclosed in a grassy area to the side of a large house, as well as farm shops with wooden painted signs on the side of the road, offering jumbo eggs, pony carrots and fresh manure.

We turned right and in the distance I could see hills and moors across from the fields. Being so close to open countryside was one of the main attractions of Carthom. After the house arrest in Weston it felt like I could breathe again.

'Blast, it was on the other side. We've just missed it. Damn, I'm going to have to find somewhere where I can turn around. Didn't you see it?'

'Nope.'

The car park was empty and before Mum got me out she checked the lights were on inside.

'Is there anything you're after, Mum?'

She scratched her ear. 'I'm pricing up water fountains, that's all.'

I nodded. 'OK, I'll try and see if I can find this gallery.'

We went our separate ways around the shop; I was amazed by the variety of stuff inside. There were tables all around the perimeter of the shop, and more in the middle making a long island. As well as the usual garden supplies, at the end of the island there were lots of different coloured cards and papers and on the floor, a mountain of cheap-looking loo paper.

As I negotiated my way around I managed to knock over a stack of Christmas crackers. I lifted my head up and felt myself blush, but the man on the till hadn't moved, let alone registered that most of the Christmas crackers had now been squashed by my wheels. By the time I rejoined my mum, I'd passed hanging baskets, plant pots, bulbs and seeds as well dog food, tatty second hand books, and an assortment of cleaning materials. The only artwork I could find were the bland, dust and cobweb decorated paintings dotted around the walls.

'What do you think, Rach? Have you found it?'

'No, not really, not unless these paintings are what's meant by a gallery.' I pointed up to the wall. 'It's a bit of a weird place, isn't it? What've you got?'

Mum produced some tea lights, gardening gloves and a strip of sticky Santas and then wanted to know if I'd share a six pack of kitchen towels with her.

We decided to stay on for a drink in the cafe so whilst she went off to pay, I wheeled towards the cafe near the back of the shop and ordered two hot chocolates.

When the drinks eventually arrived, I sniffed at the dark brown sludge in my cup and overheard her tell the man on the till my disability was due to an accident. Over the years, this is what we've said. Even I called it an accident now.

Mum joined me in the cafe and after sipping her drink she bobbed her head around the side and over my head.

'What is it?'

'There's the gallery, opposite the kitchen.' She pointed behind me.

I turned myself around and wheeled towards the handwritten sign. Inside the gallery, which wasn't much bigger than a box room, there was an interesting mix of artwork with watercolours, oils and acrylics on display. The favourite subject matters seemed to be flowers, animals and buildings. It was all a bit safe, with nothing adventurous or abstract, but I'd certainly seen a lot worse. A closer examination of the prices made me whistle. Who'd pay two hundred pounds for a small painting in the back of a shop like this? In fact, I couldn't see any art for sale less than seventy-five pounds.

When Mum wandered in, she pressed her finger on a piece of card half-way up the wall. 'Do you want to display your paintings here? Leave your details at the cafe.'

'I don't know, it's not exactly The Tate, is it?'

'It's better than nothing, Rach.'

She pulled out a biro and after groping in her bag, found a piece of paper which had a few items from a shopping list scribbled on it.

'First name and phone number?'

I nodded.

We set off back to my house. My mind was on the gallery at Garden and Crafts for You. I wondered what my dad would've said if he was alive. I had one vague, sepia coloured memory of him before he joined The Butterfly Collective. It was in a gallery that can't have been much bigger than the one at the shop. I must've only been three or four, young enough to sit on my dad's shoulders but old enough to be proud of him.

We pulled into my road. Mum turned the radio off. 'Are you going to try and find out if there are any groups around this week?'

I shrugged.

She glanced at me. 'It'll get better. It really will. Once you get a bit more involved in the life of Carthom, it'll improve.'

'I hope so.'

Mum parked opposite my house and helped me out and into my chair. 'Do you need anything else?'

I glanced up at her and shook my head and in reply she affectionately ruffled my hair.

The following evening, my carer told me there was a message on my answering machine, a call I must've missed during the day. It was from the lady at the gallery. She said she could come over to my house to discuss how I could display my artwork. She spoke in a soft voice and sounded young. I rang back only to get her answering machine, so I left my address and suggested the following evening at seven o'clock.

The next day, I couldn't concentrate or even eat. Apart from the women from the care agency, my mum and the man to read the meter, nobody else had been inside my home.

I didn't know whether I should dress more smartly but nothing was ironed, so I left it. I hoped the dishevelled look would indicate an artistic nature

An hour before she was due to arrive, I'd started to put out my artwork. I put my best painting, a large monochrome landscape, on the coffee table in the living room, so it would be one of the first things she'd see. I also moved one of my large art books from the bottom of my bookcase next to my TV, so if she sat on the blue IKEA chair, this book would be on her right hand side. In the kitchen, I'd put some of my smaller ink and watercolour paintings on every bit of my surface area.

With fifteen minutes to go, I boiled the kettle again and

checked everything was OK. I went back into the kitchen, opened the back door and gulped down a cigarette to steady my nerves. I rifled through the cupboard trying to feel for the air freshener. It was empty so as a last resort I got my hands on some furniture polish and used that instead. As I did, I managed to get some in my eye. I was about to look at my watch when there was a knock on my door. My mouth was dry and I tried to swallow.

I made my way to the front door and whispered to myself, saying, hi, I'm Rachel. And you are?

When I got to the front door, she knocked again. Flustered, I pulled out my keys from my back pocket. 'OK, OK, just unlocking the door.'

I was taken aback to see a tall lady, in her late fifties, I guessed, wearing a duffle coat, with a royal blue woolly hat and matching gloves.

'Oh, I'm sorry, I didn't realise. Are you, Rachel?' She looked crestfallen.

'Yes, do come in, er.'

'Anne, Anne Wilby'

An awkward moment followed, as she didn't give me time to move away from the door. Due to the stair lift and my wheelchair, space was limited in my hall, which meant she had to squeeze past through the gap. It didn't help she was plump. I followed her into the living room where I could see her bend over the coffee table and look at my painting.

'Do you like it?' I tried to moisten my lips with my tongue.

'Who lives with you?' Anne sat down on the edge of blue chair and took off her woolly hat to reveal light brown and greying hair, cut into a helmet style haircut that framed her face. Her features were etched with wrinkles and looked as if they'd been barbecued by the sun.

'Nobody.' I nodded towards the coffee table. 'That one took me a month to complete.'

'A month? I can sometimes spend months and months on just one painting. It's marvellous that with everything you can still paint and nobody looks after you, not even your parents? The woman who lived in this house before, her husband looked after her. She was crippled with the nasty form of arthritis. Mind, it was in her arms and hands, as well. In the end, even her husband couldn't look after her. They both ended up in separate homes. It's probably because of the nursing home fees why this place got sold. I suppose with the stair lift and everything, it's perfect.'

I listened as this woman wittered on. She'd said my most hated words, wheelchair bound and crippled and I started to feel defensive.

'Would you like a coffee? I've got some more of my work in the kitchen, if..?'

'Coffee?' Anne interrupted. 'No, I'm alright. I'd a cup of tea at home. I can't stay for long.' She shook her sleeve so she could look at her watch, 'I'm helping my friend, Marjorie, with some packing. You can't have lived here very long. Where were you before?'

'I actually sold one of my paintings to the pub when I first moved here.'

'The Vines?' Her eyes narrowed.

'Yeah, the landlord's wife bought it.'

Anne folded her arms. While she was quiet I took the opportunity to ask more about the gallery and how it worked.

'If I were to put paintings up in the gallery, how much does the shop get?'

'Like commission? We don't do it like that. You have a wall for your paintings. Then, for only five pounds a week you can display them there. So, no commission.'

'How many artists do you have? Is it a wall for each artist?'

'If you had three paintings this size.' She gestured towards the painting on the coffee table. 'Or one large and either one or two smaller ones. It depends how many you can fit in the space. I ask for the first weeks rent to be paid in advance. After that, it's every Monday you pay.'

'Are you getting many sales?'

Anne picked up her handbag and placed it on her knee. 'I only set it up properly a few weeks ago, and it's not been easy at all. Before, we all had our paintings up around the actual shop, but nothing sold. Mind, you couldn't see anything and the shop's such a mess. It was my idea, the gallery. I'm there three mornings a week and I organise the rents. It looks good, doesn't it?'

'Yeah, great, but what happens if you aren't there and someone wants to buy something?'

She brushed the air with her hand. 'Oh, Rob sees to all of that. I've known him since he was a nipper. I reckon, over the years he's had at least three businesses go under. He's a typical man, hopeless with money. His poor wife is the one I feel sorry for, mind. Problem is, if it goes under so does the gallery.'

'Do you reckon it'll be closing soon then?'

'Closing? I don't know for certain its closing. Don't say anything to him about it. I've seen him on lots of occasions, looking over his account books.' She held out both palms. 'I've tried to offer him help, we all have, but he takes no notice, not at all. You won't say anything, will you?'

I shook my head.

The blue chair creaked as she leant forward. 'What's wrong with you?'

'I was in an accident.' I felt myself blush again.

'Accident? Do you mean a car accident?'

'Sort of. When can I put my paintings up?'

'Just give me a ring. You know my number. I can put them up for you, if you want. Are you able to drive?'

'No, but I could get a taxi up.'

'Well, give me a ring anyway. I must go; Marjorie will be wondering where I am. Don't get up. Sorry, I mean, I can see myself out.' Anne stood up; the corners of her mouth pushed out to the sides and into a flat, forced smile. With her bag on her forearm, she'd a final look around the room, without making eye contact.

'It was lovely to meet you. I really think you're brave, very brave.'

I cringed and felt myself tense up.

I followed her to the front door and for a minute watched her make her way to her car. Just as she was about to get in she turned to look at me, as soon as she did, I banged the door shut. When I went back into my living room I wanted to throw the bloody paintings against the wall.

Two

It didn't take much to convince me to put my paintings in the gallery. It's not as if I had lots of activities to do, or friends I could call on. Don't get me wrong, I did have friends at one point, people who I worked with and the odd school friend who kept in touch, but like an abusive partner, the guards needed to isolate me in order to control and abuse me. They made sure people weren't made welcome. I was so embarrassed about what my life had become, I didn't want visitors either.

I'd dreamt for so long about being free from this situation, and perhaps unrealistically, I expected to be suddenly active with my new life and friends. Now this hadn't happened, I knew I'd be mad not to try out the gallery. Even though I felt I couldn't tolerate Anne for any length of time, I banked all my hopes on the other artists at the gallery.

I phoned Anne and we agreed we'd meet on Thursday

morning. I did what she had suggested and took five paintings; three medium sized, two smaller. The first was a painting of a simple fishing boat at sunset. Although the subject matter wasn't challenging, it'd been a tricky one to pull off. As I was mostly self-taught, my paintings were experiments with some turning out better than others. The second painting was a country lane with a large tree on one side and red and blue flowers in the foreground. The third was a farmhouse in ink and pencil, with a track, stone wall and hills in the distance. The two smaller paintings both featured water, one a canal scene, the other a waterfall.

We arrived at Garden and Crafts for You at half past nine on a sharp and squally morning. We expected to find the shop open so Mum helped me out of the car. As I sat in my wheelchair she piled the wrapped paintings onto my knee. Although the shop lights were on and the sign on the door said 'open' the door was shut with no opening times shown. After five minutes shivering outside, we packed everything back up, and waited in the car.

A few minutes later, the same large bloke who'd been on the till, unlocked the door. He yawned, followed by a long stretch with his arms above his head. His shirt came adrift from his trousers and exposed his flabby, hairy paunch.

Mum helped me out again and when we were inside I spotted Anne as she tottered out from the gallery, carrying a mug in each hand.

'Rob, here's your tea,' she shouted.

He lumbered off towards her and I whispered to Mum, he wasn't simply a shop assistant but instead, the owner of Garden and Crafts for You. By then, Anne had seen both of us.

'How lovely to see you again. Is this your..?'

'Yeah, this is my mum, Joan. Mum, this is Anne.'

My mum outstretched her hand, but Anne ignored it. Instead she lifted the paintings off my knee. She had a quick peek at the top one, before she put them all under her arm and traipsed through the centre aisle towards the gallery.

I was hoping the space allocated to me would be one where my paintings would be visible from the corridor, but instead it was next to the door on the left inside wall.

For a moment I sat in front of the wall and sighed, before Mum tapped me on the shoulder wanting to get on with the job in hand. I watched as she hammered in the nails and then I helped her put the paintings into position. We both decided whether they were straight and then I found the price label and Blu tack, which she put on. We made a good team.

When two of the paintings were up, Anne walked back into the room and put on her glasses, her 'eyes' as she called them. She screwed up her face as she squinted.

'Is that all you're charging?'

I started my spiel. 'Yeah, it's a fair price, I like the fact someone who...'

'Fair? It might be fair on the buyer but not on all these other artists.' She made a dramatic sweeping gesture with her hand to include the entire gallery and glanced at my mum as if to try and get her agreement.

I'd heard all this before. 'Surely if I'm paying my money each week I can charge what I want.'

Anne stood with her arms akimbo, before she started to point with short jabbing movements. 'Not if you hog the sales and don't allow the other artists a chance, no.'

'Well, I'm not stopping them charging lower for their paintings, not if they want sales, that is.' I knew the tone in my voice had changed and my mum gave me a dig in the side and glared at me. Anne, by then, had walked out, lightly shaking her head.

'Stop it, Rachel.'

'Come off it, she can't tell me what to charge.'

'Yes, but there's no need to be nasty. No need at all.'

Anne strolled back in, with a small, red notebook and I

realised she needed the money. I saw her write my first name in the book before she paused.

'Aspinhall; my surname's Aspinhall.'

As we sorted out the money, Mum had wandered over to a large watercolour painting of golden sunflowers, set against a dark green background. 'Who painted this one?'

'That one? That's Fiona's. Lovely, aren't they? Mind, she's professional.' Anne turned to me. 'You'll like her.'

'You should have some blurb to say who each artist is,' Mum said. 'Where they're from and what they paint.'

Anne nodded. 'I'm just starting. It takes an awful lot of organisation, you know, and there's so much to do. I don't like having the responsibility of it all.'

'You wouldn't mind helping out would you, Rachel?'

'Actually you mightn't be interested in this but we're going to have a meeting next Wednesday at 2 o'clock just to think about how we can improve the gallery and talk about recent developments. I can pick you up if you want to come.' She whispered, 'it's about Rob and his debts.'

'Yeah, I'll come, thanks.'

We'd just about finished, so while Mum went to the outdoor section looking at the plants and shrubs, I found myself alone in the gallery with Anne.

'Did you get a lot of money then?'

'What for?'

She put one hand on her hip. 'The accident. I know this woman, at my line dancing group. Now, she got left a pile of money in a Will. Her family won't ever want for supper, as my mother used to say. She can do what she wants with no worries. Mind, if you've got your compensation money.'

I examined my nails. 'I didn't get any compensation. Anyway, it was a long time ago.'

Anne gestured towards the door of the gallery. 'Rob said all accident victims who are left like you get...'

'Not everyone does,' I snapped.

Thankfully, a stocky man sauntered in, dressed in cycling gear and carrying a helmet. Anne spun around on her heels.

'Eddie, look who we've got here.' Anne pointed towards me. 'It's Rachel.'

Eddie dropped his head slightly in deference, and smiled as he silently scanned the walls. When he saw my paintings he stepped forward onto the toes of his right foot to look more closely, his hands clasped behind his back.

'Is this your work?' He turned his head towards me for a moment.

'Yeah.'

'Have you ever tried cartoons? I used to be an architect at the council so plenty of time spent with a pen, plenty of time for doodling. I can see my work in yours, in how you use ink.' He pointed at the wall behind me as he said this.

I wheeled around. Like me he used black ink with watercolours but unlike me, his paintings were very proficient. One painting of a road in Weston stood out from the rest of his artwork. He'd captured a night scene with the pale light from the full moon picking up some of the cobbles and the golden glow of the streetlights illuminating the brickwork and architectural details of the buildings.

'This one's lovely.'

Eddie walked up to the painting and with a groan he lifted it off the wall. He held it in front of me and spoke quickly. 'I'll let you have fifty pounds off, if you want it. It's an original and framed professionally.' He rotated the painting so I could see the sticker from the framing shop on the back as well as his signature in the bottom right hand corner.

'It's lovely, I just don't have that kind of money, sorry. I'm broke at the moment.'

'OK, I'll do you a deal; you can have it for seventy pounds. It'd look impressive anywhere, in a lounge, dining room, bedroom, office or perhaps a gift?'

'I'm really sorry, maybe another time. I've got my rent to pay soon.'

He put the painting back on the wall. 'Is that straight?' He took a step back, then a step to the side holding up his hands and making a square shape with his fingers, his head at an angle.

'Yeah, it's fine.'

'Is that a Westonian accent?'

'Are you local?' I replied with a side step of my own.

'Me? Oh I'm Weston way, that's why I'm on the bike.' Eddie stood with his legs wide apart.

'So you're a Westie, my mum's a Wally.'

'From Wallaston? As youngsters we used to say how do you get from Weston to Wallaston? The answer is to thumb a lift from a car. Do you get it? Car-thumb?' He held up his fat thumb.

I laughed along with Eddie. He'd a booming guffaw, followed by a snort. I guessed he'd be about fifty-five if not more. His eyes were wide-set, which drew you to the middle of his face, and the start of an oily and bulbous nose. I'd not seen a nose like that before, violet and dark purple in colour like a plum in the middle of his face. When he laughed it seemed to go a deeper colour and it was obvious, with his salient features, he'd make a good cartoon character.

I realised I was staring at his face and felt relieved when Mum appeared at the door. I introduced her to Eddie and after saying 'hello' to him, she explained we needed to go.

'Oh, you need to get a wiggle on then,' He joked with a laugh and snort.

'Quite.' Mum raised an eyebrow to me.

We made our way out. 'What do you think of them?'

'They seem nice people.'

'And Anne?'

'Yes, she's pleasant enough. Sometimes, Rach, you can lose friends before you make them, with the tone of voice you took in there.'

I raised my eyes to the ceiling and sighed. It wasn't worth arguing, so I remained silent.

The spinal unit was set at the back of the general hospital in Wallaston. For my yearly check-ups, I usually managed to be in and out fairly speedily. I'd see my consultant who had the rather unfortunate name of Mr Walker and if nothing had changed, he'd check my medication and ask if there were any problems.

To get to the outpatient waiting room we had to go along corridor 'D'. I always thought there was a whiff of disinfectant, along with a sense of despair that permanently hung in the air. At one end of the corridor was the door that led to the mortuary, next to that was the Intensive Care Unit and opposite a ward where some with the most serious and grave injuries would never leave. The close proximity to death and life-threatening disability was always a reality check and if I ever felt miserable about my own condition I had only to spend five minutes on this corridor before I felt better.

In the waiting room, a quadriplegic man around my age was staring at the wall while biting on his bottom lip. He sat next to an effusive young woman, who had her dark brown hair in a messy top knot. She was reading the Grazia magazine and seemed oblivious to her surroundings as she held a one sided conversation about bags, boots and the importance of being bang-on-trend. I played with my phone while Mum was reading Doors Open by Ian Rankin. All four of us were lost in our own worlds.

The guards were with me when I had my last appointment at the unit. They answered every question Mr Walker asked me. He would answer them, while staring at me, as if he was trying to say why on earth are you letting them do this? I would just squirm with embarrassment. It was the same with every hospital or GP appointment; they would take over and answer for me.

'Miss Aspinhall to see Mr Walker, please,' a female doctor

said in a perfunctory manner. She peered down at her clipboard, and made what sounded like an exasperated sigh as she turned the top sheet over.

I followed the junior doctor in; she was very slim with cropped short blonde hair and reminded me of a young, albeit short tempered, Mia Farrow.

Inside the consulting room, I sat in front of the desk and told them how I was feeling, and about how I thought my pain was getting worse and my back was more bent since the last appointment.

Mr Walker nodded slowly while I was talking.

'There's evidence of increased Kyphosis, as well as natural wear and tear, of course.'

'Kyphosis?'

He swivelled his head as he spun around in his chair to face the computer. 'What I'm saying is here's the source of your pain.' He pointed at a dark patch on my x-ray.

'It's a posture problem,' he added. After stroking his neat grey beard he spun back round to face me. 'Realistically, the only thing we can offer you is pain management.'

'Can't you do something about it, operate maybe?'

'The risks of surgery could mean you could lose the use of more of your body on the operating table and I wouldn't even consider it at present. Frankly, I don't think you'd find a surgeon who would.'

He caressed his beard again and picked up his Dictaphone. 'I'll refer you back to the pain clinic and perhaps see if wheelchair services can look at your posture in your chair. I just need to ask, is everything alright at home?'

'Yeah.'

'You moved to Carthom. Are you still with..?'

'No, living on my own.'

Mr Walker mumbled something under his breath to the junior doctor.

'The pain you're experiencing you don't think is linked to anything emotionally?'

It was my turn to lightly shake my head with an added look of derision.

'As long as you're keeping out of trouble, that's the main thing. Now, I'll send a letter to your GP and do the referrals.'

I was led back out to my mum, who was tidying up the magazines on one of the tables in the waiting room.

'What did he say, Rach? Can they do anything?'

'It's all to do with my posture. But he doesn't want to operate, doesn't think anyone else would either.'

'Did he mention anything about the move?'

I scrunched up my face. 'Not much.'

'What did he say?'

'Nothing really, just was I keeping out of trouble.' I puffed away outside the unit. A no smoking notice was above my head. The cigarette butts on the ground indicated it was a popular spot.

'In here,' Mum held up a magazine she'd stolen from the waiting room, 'they talk about learning to walk with exoskeleton walking aids, and electrical stimulation for your muscles. I just wonder whether he's up to date on all these advances in treatment. I really do think in your lifetime there'll come a day when you're up and walking.'

'I don't. Anyway, he's meant to be one of the leading spinal surgeons. If he'd got a way of getting me walking he'd have mentioned it by now. Sometimes, things just aren't going to change.'

Mum helped me into the car.

'I just wish sometimes you'd be a bit more positive. Honestly, I remember when you were first injured the surgeon said positivity was...'

'... key. I've heard this about a thousand times.'

'I'm only saying, stop being so defeatist. Now, while you were in with Mr Walker I remembered what I needed to tell you.

Do you remember Brian, who lives near to me? I introduced you to him one time while we were at Tesco. He always wears a hat, runs the charity Inspire and...'

'...Support?'

'Support, yes. Anyway, I met him the other day and the charity is on the lookout for people to do befriending and he wanted me to ask whether you'd be interested.'

'I suppose it's not paid.'

'No, it's not, but I think what Brian's wants are people who've actually got a disability. It sounds a great idea. When you were in hospital, it would've been superb if someone took you under their wing; a friend who understood what was happening and helped you cope. Just think, you could be a friend to people who are now trying to cope with a disability. You do need things to do now, don't you?'

I half turned in my seat and held out both my hands. 'How can I work with someone who's just been in an accident? They're bound to ask me what happened with me. So what do I say? If I lie, it's not really setting a good example is it? What if someone asks what I've been doing recently? See, it just wouldn't work.'

'It's not always all about you. But if you're certain then I suppose I'll have to say no to Brian. I think he was really keen on having you as well.'

'I need to get more settled here first. This gallery might be something I can get more involved with. Anne's invited me to a meeting next week and any time now I'm going to get a sale so I'll need to start churning out some work. So tell him I'm interested, but not right now.'

For most of the journey back we both sat in silence. Half an hour later, we were parked outside my house.

'Should be hearing from the gallery soon.'

'I hope so, love. Do you need me for anything now?'

'Nope, I think I'll start doing some painting at least now I've actually got somewhere to put them. It makes me feel more motivated.'

'If you did this befriending the same would happen.'

'Maybe,' I conceded.

Three

As I waited inside for Anne to pick me up for the meeting at the gallery, I could see the morning frost hadn't had chance to melt away, leaving some of the parked cars in my road still cocooned in a glistening canopy. Across the road, a man balanced on a pair of steps, and directed by his rotund wife below, put up fairy lights around the perimeter of their front door.

Anne pulled up and helped me into her car.

'The car's a bit messy. I haven't had chance to clean it what with all the fuss organising this meeting and the gallery.' She glanced at me before peering into her rear view mirror.

'It's OK, I've seen worse,' I lied. I tugged on an empty crisp packet I was sitting on, but couldn't pull it out. The car was full of mud, wrappers from sweets, crisps, chocolate and it was all making me feel queasy.

'You don't drive at all?'

'No, I'm on morphine, which makes me really...'

'Morphine?' Anne interrupted. 'You won't be on that; they only give it to people who're dying. My brother begged the nurses at the hospice for morphine. They only ended up giving it to him the day before he died.'

My hands were curled up into fists on my lap.

'I'd be lost if I couldn't drive, it gives me freedom, stops me being isolated. Do you know what I mean?'

A 'hmmm' sound in my throat was my reply.

We waited at a red light and the conversation changed from being casual to pointed questioning.

'How do you manage? Like getting out and about?'

'My mum helps a lot.'

'Nobody else, just your Mum?'

I turned my head to look out of the passenger window and didn't reply.

'I remember when my ex-husband first taught me how to drive. He drove a Ford Anglia and used to think he was Jack Brabham racing around the village.' Anne's car screeched as we turned a sharp right into the empty car park of Garden and Crafts for You.

There was no sign of Rob inside, so we both went into the gallery. I was glad I'd put my thick jumper on because it felt chilly. Anne left the room and on return carried a small electric heater, the cord and plug trailing behind her.

'It won't take long to heat up. Now, are you alright sitting there for a minute?'

She didn't wait for my reply as she darted back out.

I wheeled around the gallery trying to find out how many artists were actually involved. I could spot Eddie's artwork and the loose watercolour paintings of flowers, which were Fiona's. I was looking for Anne's paintings when she came back dragging four small chairs into the room.

'Is there anything I can do to help?'

'Help? No, I don't need any help, just need to arrange these, like this, and that's it, we're done.'

She arranged the chairs into a circular shape around me. By now I started to feel warmer and also had begun to relax. I'd been quite apprehensive about meeting the other artists but when I realised only four artists were coming, and I'd already met Anne and Eddie, I felt less anxious.

In the distance I could hear Anne say 'hello' to Eddie and in a quieter voice she said, 'Rachel's in there, you know, the one in the wheelchair.'

I breathed in and snorted out through my nose.

Eddie and Anne trudged slowly back in carrying a round table between them. They positioned it in the middle of the circle of chairs. Eddie said a quick 'hello' before going back out of the room to bring in his rucksack. When he returned he pulled out the chair next to me and sat down. I could hear his knees creak and was concerned the small wooden chair wouldn't bear his weight.

'So, what have we been up to?'

I struggled to think about what I'd been doing, aware I hadn't done anything which would be of interest to him.

A woman strode through into the gallery.

'Fi-Fi!' Eddie jumped up.

Fiona was tall with bouncing brown curly hair and had attractive if slightly equine features. She wore skin tight jeans and knee high boots. Around her arms she had on a leaf-green coloured cape and carried a large Radley leather bag. She didn't look much older than me.

She held onto Eddie's shoulders and air kissed him first on his left cheek followed by his right. Each kiss accompanied with a loud 'mwah, mwah' sound. They embraced and despite the age gap, looked like lovers rather than friends. Fiona then turned to Anne. Silently the two women hovered in front of each other before they hugged, swaying from side to side as they held each other.

'You must be Rachel?' Fiona stood over me. 'I've heard a lot about you.'

Before I'd time to reply, she indicated towards the door and all three of them left the gallery. I couldn't make out what they were whispering about in the corridor, but it was making me feel paranoid. My hands were sweaty, and as I clenched them into fists, I had the sudden urge to leave but without money to get a taxi home I knew I was trapped.

Instead, I got out my notebook and whispered out loud my ideas for the meeting. I'd just finished when a lady came in, who was around the same age as Anne.

'Hello, you must be Rachel. I'm Lena. Gosh, is it me or is it hot in here?'

She took off her grey overcoat and sat beside me. She wore black trousers with a dark grey jumper and had a friendly face, temporarily flushed, with grey and white straggly hair cut into a messy bob just below her chin. The dainty gold-rimmed reading glasses perched on the bridge of her nose reminded me of my old French teacher at school.

Anne, Fiona and Eddie walked back into the room. Anne winked at Lena while Eddie carefully eased himself down onto the chair and squeezed the top of Fiona's thigh, making her smile.

'Remember to be quiet everyone,' Anne whispered. 'Rob said he was going to do a stock control, so he might be in the office sometime this morning. I said to Eddie stock control? He's never done a stock control in his whole life. Anyway, we need to talk about this gallery and what we should do about it if it does close.'

'Fi-Fi and I were talking and we were wondering whether we should ask Rob, that if the centre is sold, we'd like to carry on renting this room.'

'I'm not sure, Eddie,' Anne replied, frowning. 'It's not exactly been a money spinner, has it?'

He gestured towards the paintings on one wall. 'I'm sure if we concentrated on getting more sales, it could be.'

'I agree. We should at least aim for that.' Fiona's eyes glinted as she stretched with her back arched in the chair.

Eddie smiled and mirrored Fiona, with his back stretched and arched as well.

Lena leant forward and with each word tapped on the table. 'I agree with Anne.'

'If it stays as a garden centre,' Fiona said, 'whoever buys it may be glad we are making use of this room?'

What sounded like a man coughing outside made us all turn towards the door.

Anne placed a finger over her mouth and walked with big exaggerated footsteps, raising one foot high after the other. After poking her head outside, she walked back to her seat and shrugged.

Lena frowned. 'I'm sorry, but we don't know what will happen when this is sold or even that it's going to be sold. Nobody has heard him talk about selling it, have they?'

'Not directly, but when he's in debt so much, I can't see what else he's going do,' Eddie replied. 'What we're saying is it's likely to remain a garden centre, so if he does sell up, we need to think about what we would do. I say we make this gallery the best it can be, and we rent this from whoever takes over.'

'I know what you're saying. I just wouldn't have the money to rent.'

'I couldn't afford it either,' Anne said. 'Not when we hardly get any sales.'

All eyes were now on me and I realised I had the casting vote. Suddenly my mouth was dry.

'I don't really...I mean, I'm not sure.' I stared down at my knees.

'I think we should do as Anne suggested a few days ago.' Lena said. 'Become an art group and bide our time. You never know what may come along in the future.'

Eddie turned to Fiona and shrugged.

'My kitchen's big enough we can meet in there.' Anne nudged me in the ribs. 'You could fit in there as well.'

Fiona looked up at the ceiling, with a slight shake of her head.

'But even if we have a group,' Eddie snapped. 'Surely it's worth trying for one last push here, to try and increase sales.'

'I'm not disagreeing with that,' Anne said. 'I've got a few ideas and you've got some, haven't you, Rachel?'

I nodded slowly.

'The problem isn't the gallery, it's the centre itself. What hope is there if people are put off as soon as they arrive?' Fiona held up her hand and shrugged her shoulders.

'We should have a sign on the door about the gallery. I'm sure most customers don't even know we're here,' Lena replied.

I re-read my list of ideas and cleared my throat. 'My mum said it'd be good if some information about each artist was put near the paintings,' I said.

'Information? I'm not sure putting information up would help. It may put the likes of me and Lena at a disadvantage, as we're only amateurs. Being able to put you're professional, like Eddie, Fiona and Johan sounds much better.'

'I'm not professional.' I could feel my hands begin to tremble.

'Yes, but even you could say you're handicapped. Information like this can give people the edge. I think we should just leave it as it is now.'

I tried to keep my jaw rigid and not cry.

'Surely we don't have to put whether we're professional or amateur, and Anne, I really don't think you can say being disabled is an advantage.' Eddie had folded his arms with his foot tapping.

'I can't say anything right these days, can I? All I meant to say is we're all so different. I just didn't want amateur artists put at a disadvantage.'

I gave a half nod.

'Well, I'm sorry, but I'd want to let prospective buyers know I'm professional,' Fiona snapped. With her finger she pointed at one of her paintings. 'I want to bring up how we price our paintings. If we're all to be the same, as Anne says, then we can't have such disparity in prices. Someone walking around will naturally be going to go for the cheaper options. I don't have any other form of income so I think we should have a shared pricing system.'

'Shared pricing system? That sounds a good idea. We all need the money, so I think there should be no deliberate underselling of work.'

Anne turned to me. 'Do you have anything else?'

I looked down my list and shook my head. I had five more suggestions but every time I opened my mouth I was shot down. I knew the last remark and the emphasis on deliberate was for me.

'Is this what we're saying then,' Eddie queried. 'Try and maximise sales and then if it closes, concentrate on an art group.'

'I think we should meet as an art group anyway, whether it closes or not. We'll have to meet in my house because we can't run a group in here and have customers milling about as well.' Anne replied. 'Does anyone else agree?'

One by one we all said 'yes' apart from Fiona who made a grunting sound.

'We'd better call it a day, time's getting on.' Anne said. 'Thanks for coming everyone.'

Anne stood up and with a wince, rubbed her back. Lena spoke to her and soon they occupied a corner of the gallery chatting to each other. Next to me Eddie was deep in a discussion with Fiona, the two of them continuing to mirror each other. While nobody was looking, I wheeled out of the gallery, through the shop, and waited for Anne outside.

It had been snowing while we were in the meeting. The car park had a glistening, crisp and crunchy coating of snow and ice.

I watched the flakes swirl down in great flurries over Carthom. For a moment, I could picture myself as a solitary figure inside a snow globe, being shaken up and down with my loneliness and position in life, permanently fixed by forces beyond my control. I shivered and yearned for the safety and warmth of my home.

Anne eventually joined me and appeared to be in good spirits despite the heated nature of the discussions we'd just had. When we were waiting to get out of the car park, she briefly turned towards me.

'What does your father do?'

'He's dead. I was only twelve when he died. My mum had to manage on her own with me and my brother.'

She didn't reply and for a couple of minutes there was an uncomfortable silence. The traffic was slow moving and the cars in the opposite lane had ground to a halt. When she eventually managed to pull out onto the main road, I asked her about her own situation.

'So are you married, do you have kids?'

'I'm divorced and, I had...' She hesitated. 'I had a daughter. Mind, I don't have a relationship with her like you have with your mother. Your mother's lucky, really lucky.'

I didn't know if she'd fully understood what I'd said; after all, my mum could hardly be described as lucky. I asked her what she meant.

'My daughter stopped speaking to me when her father split up from me. He, he twisted things,' she said quietly.

'That's awful.' I turned my head to face Anne, but her eyes were fixed on the road.

I looked out of my window at the tiny red and silver lights in the trees that lined the main road, and the impressive Christmas themed window displays in every shop. The blurred headlights from the cars contrasted with the iridescent lights in the trees, all providing a superficial image full of joy and excitement.

Anne pulled up outside my home. I turned to undo my seatbelt, and saw her eyes were glistening with tears.

'Oh, Anne.' I wanted to reach over, maybe touch her leg to show I cared. Instead I opted to rest my hand for a moment on her shoulder.

'It's nothing, nothing.'

'Do you have grandchildren?'

'The only grandchild I know about is Katie; she'll be nearly sixteen soon. There could be more. I just don't know.'

'I'm sorry, it must be awful.'

'It was for the first few years. I'd be going to the shops, turn the corner and suddenly see Theresa stroll straight past me, as if I was invisible. For a while I didn't see sight or sound of them. When I asked around I found out they'd all moved hundreds of miles away. After that, not a dickey bird. Nothing, nothing at all.' She looked down as she twisted her clasped hands. 'As for my granddaughter, I don't even know if she knows who I am.'

'Come in for a coffee please, better than sitting out here in the cold.'

Inside, once the drinks were made, Anne sat down at my kitchen table and nursed her cup of tea.

'I knew soon after I married Andrew I'd made a mistake. I got wed far too young. It was my fault, I suppose, I thought I'd be secure with him. When...um. I mean when Theresa was born, I wasn't very well. Andrew made out I was a bad mother.' Anne paused to sip at her drink. She was rocking in her chair with her eyes downcast.

'Couldn't you leave him, or divorce him earlier on?'

'In those days, it wasn't like it is now; you just had to get on with it. In the end, though, I had to divorce him. I thought Theresa was old enough to understand my side of the argument.'

'How old was she?'

'Fifteen, but as he'd done such a good job of brainwashing her, she wanted to live with him. That was the last time I had a full conversation with her. I heard from a neighbour, she'd given birth to Katie. Mind, she was born out of wedlock but all the same, I want her to know me, I doubt there'll be any chance of that now. It hits me, Rachel, hits me right here.' Anne tapped her chest three times. As tears bubbled up she put her head in her hands.

In my wheelchair I moved closer.

'I'm sorry, here's me moaning and you...'

'You're not moaning. Do you know where they live now?'

'The last I heard they lived in a village called Ellsford, not far from Cornwall. For all I know they could've moved again. They could be anywhere.' Anne stared at the table and took a laboured breath in. 'If I'm honest, this is the reason I turned to art. I took myself off to college and I've done two certificates with the AINAB. I suppose it filled a hole.'

I thought I could almost see the depth of her pain, amongst the wrinkles and lines on her face.

She eased herself up, using the table for support. After carefully placing my cup in the washing up bowl she turned around and leant against my sink unit.

'I think an art group would be a good idea. We've got to try in this life, haven't we?'

'What's the AINAB?'

'It's a scheme for pensioners to try out courses at colleges and universities. It's all free. It stands for Age is Not a Barrier. Going back to what I was saying, if you ever need a lift, I can give you one. I'd like to help. It must be hard what with not being able to, um... I just want to help, if I can.'

I smiled cautiously at Anne. 'We can help each other.'

'I just wish Theresa had been more like you. Mind, I don't mean crippled. Well, you know what I mean.'

I smiled and understood exactly what she meant.

Four

The first art group was arranged for the week before Christmas. Although I was excited at the thought of being in a group, when the morning of the meeting arrived, I was in a mess. The night before I'd barely slept, worrying about how the group members would react when they met me. When I looked in the mirror in the morning and saw my face, I resembled the figure in the painting 'The Scream' by Edvard Munch.

When Anne arrived she appeared to be even worse, with red eyes and dark lines running downwards from her tear ducts. As she folded up my chair, she began to talk about her back.

'You see, I've started this line dancing group and I think I've pulled something. The pain's unbearable. I need something stronger to take.'

I listened while I scratched my jaw. Anne wanted sympathy for a bad back, from me?

'Speak to your doctor, Anne. Honestly, I can't really give you advice on this.'

'Doctors?' She huffed. 'They treat me as if I was a dotty old woman.'

Silently I sided with her GP.

We were now in the affluent part of Carthom, with large detached houses, high gates and intricate topiary. We started to slow down and passed a young woman pounding down the pavement like a catwalk model, with drainpipe jeans and skyscraper heels. She dragged along a miniature poodle wearing a tweed jacket.

'Have you spotted my little bungalow yet?'

I couldn't believe there would be anything described as 'little' on this road.

'There it is!' Anne pointed across the road to a huge house.

'That's your place?'

'Next to it, look next door.'

Next to it was a smaller detached bungalow.

It's a granny flat. Mind, it belonged to the bigger house at first, but it was then sold separately. Perfect for me.'

I looked closer. 'Is it all on one level, or do you have some stairs?'

'No. No going up and down the stairs for me. I should be able to stay here until I die. I don't want to end up in some awful nursing home, with smelly, incompetent people.' Anne screwed up her nose.

I didn't reply. I knew what she meant and was tempted to describe the difficulties I had in just going to the toilet. The nerve damage to both my bladder and bowel rendered them useless, which meant I had to use catheters, suppositories, laxatives and pads.

I heard the boot door slam as she got my wheelchair out and I couldn't help but notice she didn't complain about her back as she bent down and put it together.

Up close the bungalow was much bigger than the one in Weston. A giant Christmas wreath was attached to the glass panelled, front door. Below the wreath were two stickers, one about CCTV being in use the other about it being a neighbourhood watch area, along with a picture of a burglar wearing a black and white striped top, a balaclava and carrying a swag bag.

Inside, I found it unsettling to be back in a bungalow. I half expected a guard to appear out of one of the doors. In the hallway, was an ancient looking grandfather clock and next to it a coat stand, which was so laden down with coats, hats and scarves, it was a miracle it was still standing. I was still following Anne and for a moment she stopped by the living room, where a real fire crackled away, alarmingly close to a fully decorated, large fir tree. She turned towards me with a quick smile.

'Do you like it?'

I nodded. 'It's lovely. I used to live in a bungalow, but not as big as this...'

'Bungalow?' She interrupted. 'You went from living in a bungalow to where you are now? Surely you would be better off all on one floor, with your, erm...needs?'

'Which room are we in, Anne?'

'In here, we're in the kitchen.' She kicked open a door.

I was surprised to see around a large pine table, not only Lena, but also a man who must've been about my age. I was relieved I wasn't the only one under sixty at the group. Two other ladies who were about the same age as Anne and Lena were also at the table and they both were staring at me.

'And heeeere's Rachel,' Anne announced, as if I was the next act up on stage.

There was nowhere obvious for me to sit, so I wheeled over towards the man, who was called Johan. When he spoke I detected a slight foreign accent.

'Are you, are you,' I stumbled over my words. 'Are you German?'

Johan blushed. 'Close, I'm originally from Holland, but I've been over here since my early teens. What about you? Let me guess, Weston?'

'Sort of, yes.'

I was struck by Johan's lanky, angular frame, which perfectly matched his symmetrical features. His high cheekbones jutted down to give an inverted triangle face shape. In addition, he had a dreamy, coffee-coloured complexion and luscious, long eyelashes. I found it almost hypnotic when he blinked slowly; his eyelashes sweeping me up and off from my wheels. For a brief moment, which felt much longer, it was as if we were the only ones in the room.

'Rachel,' Anne called out. 'Meet Pauline and Elaine. They saw the card in the gallery just like you.' Anne pulled away a kitchen chair and put it at the side. 'Are you OK sitting there?'

I nodded and as I slotted into place. I said 'hello' to Pauline and Elaine and in less than two minutes learnt they had both worked in the NHS as Occupational Therapy Assistants and that Pauline's daughter was expecting a baby. They'd both taken early retirement and like Anne and Lena they'd completed the two AINAB courses in painting and drawing. As close friends often do, they had a habit of ending each other's sentences.

'Are you in pain, dear?' Pauline asked.

'She must be.' Elaine replied.

'Yes, I am. I take MST,' I looked over at Anne. 'I suppose pain is one of my main problems. Though MST comes with a lot of side effects.'

'Constipation,' Pauline whispered.

'And tiredness,' Elaine and Pauline said together.

For a few minutes, everyone got out their art materials, and sketch pads, canvas boards or paper. I looked down at the uninspiring photograph of a bunch of roses I was planning to paint and grimaced.

'If Eddie's going to be coming to this group, Anne, it's going to be too tight. We're cramped as it is around this table; it's just fortunate nobody's working on a large scale painting this morning,' Johan said, looking around the table.

Anne sighed. 'I thought we'd have enough room in here. Maybe, we'll have to use the gallery.'

Pauline and Elaine turned to each other. It was then I saw how alike they both were. They both had light grey hair, with much darker eyebrows that looked as though they'd been tattooed on. Their eyebrows framed laugh-lined eyes with Roman noses leading to thin pursed lips and a dour expression. Even their glasses appeared to be a similar make or design. It was as if their close friendship meant their features had morphed into one.

'In Garden and Crafts for You?' queried Elaine

'For the time being. If it's still a garden centre when it's sold we can ask the new owners if we can carry on meeting there.'

Pauline pulled a face and Elaine raised her eyebrows. 'You say it, Pauline.'

'No you say it.'

'Say what?' Anne snapped.

'Do you know Cathy, Rob's wife? She told us the outhouse at the back's going to be converted and used by Sam...'

'Sam? As in their son, Sam?'

'Yes, because his girlfriend is expecting. The baby's due in February, so they need their own place.'

'What's that got to do with the shop?' Anne's brows were as one, her lips just a line.

'Apparently, Rob was asking around to see if anyone would be interested to buy it. Dickinson's Carpets were interested. They've a big store in Weston and wanted another one this end. All the legal stuff is going through. They didn't get what they wanted for it, but I think they just wanted to get rid.'

I didn't know all of this. Are you sure about this? How do you know Cathy anyway?'

'She used to work in our department and each year we meet up around this time for a meal. So we're sure it's true, aren't we, Pauline?'

Pauline nodded. 'Yes.'

'We're going to have to think of somewhere else then.' Anne got up and opened the kitchen door. 'Just getting some painkillers, my back's killing me.' As she left the kitchen, she patted my head.

'Damn.' Johan muttered. He put down his pencils and charcoal.

'What's up?' Lena replied.

'I was just doing this.' Johan lifted up one corner of his sketchpad so Lena could see.

I wheeled over to Johan, and he showed me his drawing. In pencil and charcoal he'd drawn Anne's face and neck, including the collar of her blouse from a three-quarter view position. He'd emphasised her helmet style haircut, and her glasses perched on top of her head, but apart from that he'd been very generous towards her.

'It's really good. I reckon you did it in less than ten minutes. Is this your thing, portraits and caricatures?'

'Not really, I prefer to do large acrylic paintings. I actually turned professional last year.'

'You're really talented,' I gushed. 'Whereabouts in Holland are you from?'

'Haarlem, but I've not lived in Holland for many years now.'

For the next five minutes I talked to Johan. It wasn't a surprise to find out his mind was as sharp as the angles on his frame and face. He'd studied Philosophy of Art as well as Fine Art at University. While I was talking to him, my body tingled and I felt warm and relaxed and soon forgot my disability. It was like the seventeen year old, pre-accident Rachel was back again.

I needed to catheterise so went out to find the bathroom. I wheeled down a hallway and tried the door at the end. It would open but only partially. I poked my head inside and could see a mountain of junk. The rubbish was up to the ceiling. At my level, I could make out a broken, naked Barbie doll and on the tiny bit of floor space still visible there were old photograph frames and a mangy looking teddy bear.

I peered down the corridor, nobody was watching so I quickly shut the door. I could've questioned why in a fairly well ordered home Anne had a room like this, but I knew I had secrets I didn't want exposed and no doubt Anne was the same.

I turned around and wheeled back towards the kitchen. I passed the living room and saw Anne, as she warmed her hands over her fire.

'Is everything OK, Anne?'

She frowned, the deep grooves on her forehead like an intricate maze.

'We're going to have to find somewhere else to meet. I was hoping we wouldn't have to pay.'

I nodded and tried my best to muster a look of concern.

'Are you alright?'

'Just need the toilet, please?'

Anne walked up the hallway and opened the bathroom door. Inside it had grab rails and a hoist above the bath. The shower was also designed for someone in a wheelchair.

I couldn't find the toilet roll so I opened the cupboard next to her bath. Inside it was stuffed full of empty bottles, toothpaste, flannels, razors, pill bottles and right at the back there was a toilet roll. With the contents of the cupboard now on the floor, I tried to put everything back. Each time, I crammed a bottle into the cupboard, another product would tumble out. Eventually, everything was back in, bar one pill bottle. I picked it up to put on the side. As I did, I read the name of the tablets and they sounded familiar.

Back in the kitchen, Johan was showing the caricature to Anne. She held it with her arms outstretched.

'I can't see it. I've haven't got my eyes.'

'Here borrow my spare pair,' Lena said.

The glasses started on their journey to Anne, but before they got to her, Pauline tried them on. As she was doing this, Elaine put on Pauline's spectacles. This encouraged Lena to put on Elaine's pair. Pauline then passed the glasses onto Elaine before she swopped spectacles with Lena. Eventually, they were passed to me and I gave them to Anne. She put them on for a second then pulled them off.

'I can't see in them.'

'They're not mine, that's why,' Lena exclaimed. 'Where's my bifocals?'

'Oops, sorry,' Elaine said. 'Here they are.' She passed them back up the line to Anne.

Still squinting, Anne grinned at the picture. 'Oh, I do like this. Can I keep it?' She held Johan's drawing at arm's length for a moment. 'This is getting framed.'

While Anne still had Lena's glasses on, she then held up her own painting. 'What do you think? Have I got the perspective and the colour right?'

Anne showed her painting to the rest of us, and everyone murmured praise. The glasses went back down the line, and the brief break encouraged everyone else to show each other what they were doing. I put the front cover of my drawing pad down, grabbed my coat and went outside for a cigarette.

As I sat in Anne's driveway, I found myself thinking about Johan. Although I barely knew him, he provoked in me a strong visceral sensation, with my heartbeat pounding, my breath quickening and a strange sensation that made me warm as well as light headed. Apart from the two year relationship with Paul when I was able-bodied and at college, I'd always been on my own. In the intervening years, I'd been searching for someone who was on the same wavelength as me, who I was able to confide in, and who wasn't fazed by disability.

I wheeled back inside and shivered. Before I went into the kitchen I sat near Anne's fire to warm up. I could hear the laughter and chatter from the kitchen and found myself smiling. There were positives; I'd got my artwork in the gallery. I'd sold a painting to the pub and now I was part of a group.

Anne poked her head into the living room. 'Are you coming back in? We need a name for the group.'

In the kitchen, I tried to think of something clever to call the group but was getting nowhere

Lena screwed up her face. 'I can't think of one at all.'

'Never mind, has everyone else got one?'

Elaine and Pauline shook their heads at exactly the same time.

'I could probably think of a better one, if I had a bit more time.' Johan said. 'So, the only one I can think of is, Art for You?'

'Art for You. Oh, I get it, like it's come from the Garden and Crafts for You shop,' Lena said. She grinned at Johan. 'It's great.'

'If we ever needed posters or flyers we could do a take on the First World War poster, the one with the picture of Lord Kitchener saying "Britons Lord Kitchener Wants You." For our group, we could have an artist with a beret. Instead of a finger pointing, he could be holding out a paintbrush.' He quickly started to sketch out his idea, and while he was doing this, the phone rang.

Anne popped out to answer the call. While she was gone, Johan passed around the quick sketch of his idea for the poster.

I looked down at my art pad. It seemed to be buildings and local scenes, which proved the most popular. I'd planned to do a floral painting and brought all the paints and equipment for it. Instead I packed away the paints and concentrated on sketching out the railway station in Carthom, using a photograph from the local paper, The Carthom News.

Anne walked back into the kitchen, and stood by the table leaning on her hands which were placed palm down. 'That was Fiona, she wanted to tell me a couple of people who I know, have also expressed interest in joining this group. So this means, three more people including Eddie. We'll have to find somewhere now. Does anyone know of anywhere?'

'There's always the community centre by the police station?' Johan said.

'Carthom Community Centre? I go to a couple of groups there. Mind, they're all pricey. My line-dancing is three pounds for only an hour and a half,' Anne said.

I cleared my throat. 'That's where I first heard about the gallery.'

'Who was it, Rachel, who put you on to us?'

'I don't know his name. I reckon he was in his fifties with greasy grey hair.'

'Greasy grey hair? It could be Jack, the caretaker. I'm

surprised he pointed you in our direction. I've always found him a bit of an odd fish.'

'I heard a couple of years ago it was struggling finance-wise,' Elaine said.

'It's strange, set-up, isn't it,' Lena said. 'The Council runs it, but don't they have a committee as well?'

'And you know who's on the committee? Rob's wife, Cathy.' Pauline winked at Lena.

Anne leant forward. 'Cathy? Oh, I didn't know she was on it. Do you think on the hush-hush you could find out how much they charge, Pauline?'

I glanced at my watch. It was now five past twelve.

'Do you want to go home, Rachel?' Anne asked. 'I can drop you off if you want to?'

I nodded and started to pack up my art materials. Johan was doing the same.

'Hopefully next time we meet, we will be in a new venue,' Lena said. She walked towards me and crouched down. 'Have a lovely Christmas, Rachel.'

'Ah, happy Christmas, Lena and to everyone else as well.'

I wheeled out to Anne's car and waited for her. Johan was next to come out. The hem of his long leather coat skimmed the top of his paint splattered boots. Despite our earlier conversation, he didn't speak to me. He stopped at her gate and put his rucksack on, peeking out of it were rolls of paper and in a mesh pocket at the side were paintbrushes and pencils.

He was a lot like Paul, serious, erudite and cosmopolitan. I stopped staring at him. It was disappointing he didn't want to speak to me, so I watched Anne's door instead. After a couple of minutes, I was aware Johan still hadn't moved. I glanced at him and saw him blush as he lowered his eyes. He then fumbled with his rucksack strap and for a moment our eyes met. He blushed again, and gave a quick smile before he turned on his heels to stroll down Anne's road

At that point, Anne marched out and helped me into the car.

'Do you think it's the right thing to do?' Anne asked, on the way to my house.

'What is?' I put my hand into a fist and when I'd turned it towards me I examined my nails.

'Carry on with the group idea?'

'Yeah, why not?'

We pulled into my road.

'What are you doing for Christmas?' Anne asked.

'I'm just going to my mum. What about you?'

'Me? I try to keep busy; it's not my favourite time of year, so I try to spend it with friends. I might see Marion and Albert; they're the ones who want to come to the group. You've not met them yet, have you?'

'No.

'I knew Marion first. Mind, in those days, I tell you, she was at the end of her tether.'

'Why?' I tried to sound interested, but I was cold and bored in the car.

'When Marion's husband died her son, Simon, went completely off the rails. He stole money from her, and basically treated her like dirt. I took her to one of the courses where she met Albert. He got Simon back into work, into his own flat, and warned him not to scrounge from Marion anymore. Next thing, secretly, they started to go out with each other. Now they're married.'

'What about, erm...Is Lena married?'

'No, she's widowed. Why?'

'And Johan? Has he got a wife or girlfriend?' I stared out of my passenger window, aware I was blushing.

'No, I've not seen him with a girl and I've known that family for a long, long time. I think he might be the other way inclined, if you know what I mean. Mind, I've not seen him with a man, either. Why do you want to know?'

I tipped my head to one side. 'Just interesting finding out about the other members of the group, that's all.'

Anne glanced at me for a second, her forehead hanging over her eyes, before she buttoned up the top of her coat, and got out.

I opened my car door. The icy air made my scalp tingle and tighten. Anne put my wheelchair together. When she pushed it towards me, she stretched her back, placing a hand on the bottom of her spine.

'I'll need one of these soon.'

I transferred in and was just about to go up my path, when she called out.

'I said to Eddie wouldn't it be good if you had a little job to keep you busy. Oh and have a happy Christmas, Rachel.'

I wished I'd the confidence to give a one-liner to shut her up. Although, I could occasionally understand where she was coming from, most of the time I was mystified. It was clear she'd got no understanding of me or my situation. The more I got to know her, the more things drove me mad. I banged the front door shut.

I didn't expect to hear any more from Anne until the New Year. So when she rang me the weekend before Christmas she took me by surprise.

As she spoke very softly and often mumbled, I couldn't make out what she was talking about, so I asked her to speak up.

'Pauline said we could use the community centre. The problem is, so far, apart from you and Johan, everyone's a pensioner, or heading that way. We just think it might not be suitable for you.'

'Are you saying I can't come?'

'It's not just me saying it. Anyway, I'm sure there are some nice groups and clubs you could join, that might be better for you, considering your, erm...Well, you know, your needs, if you know what I mean.'

'I don't want to sound too desperate, Anne,' I pleaded. 'I

really enjoyed the group and it's not as if I do a lot of activities.'

'What can I do, Rachel? I'm sorry. I'll drop a Christmas card in tomorrow.'

I banged the phone down. Did it mean I was going to have to find something else? I knew already, during the day there were hardly any activities for adults my age. I didn't want to have to travel and I certainly didn't want to go back to just sleeping my way through my days. As I considered the alternatives, I could feel my mood sink.

Five

As I waded through a more than substantial Christmas dinner, I was preoccupied with memories from my last Christmas in the bungalow. By then, I was running out of hope anything would change, and the thought of another year in the bungalow meant I was seriously contemplating suicide. The worst part of it all was how rapidly and with such ease, my life had been blown apart. The guards, like insurgents in the night, had taken away all that was precious to me. My independence, something I'd fought so hard for and any pride I had left, went up in smoke. I barely recognized myself at the end.

It was hard to comprehend the enormity and significance of the changes that had taken place in the past year. I wiped a rogue tear away with my sleeve and as I did, I sensed Mum was staring at me. I finished my mouthful, gripped onto the edge of the table and straightened myself up.

'Is everything OK?'

Her orange coloured paper crown had slipped onto the side of her head. 'I was just thinking how different things were last

Christmas.'

'Same here. Last Christmas was a nightmare.'

Mum stretched to stroke my arm. 'I'm really proud of you. You've done so well.'

Through the window I saw a tiny Goldcrest bird fly on to my mum's fence. The distinctive black and orange striped head, like a Mohican hairstyle, with a green and grey body provided a brilliant flash of colour on a dull day. For a moment it looked in my direction before flying away.

'I just wish I was free from everything that happened.' I stared down at the table. 'Do you know what I mean? I don't want to always be thinking about it.'

Mum didn't reply instead she fiddled with her napkin.

'It's on my mind nearly all the time, Mum.'

'When you start to make some friends with people in the art group, it'll help and soon, it'll just be a distant memory.'

I felt myself go hot.

'What's up?'

'It's the group; it doesn't look like I'm going to be able to be part of it.' I picked up my fork and twisted it around with my fingers.

'Since when?'

'A few days ago. They're now saying, it's just open for older people. Presumably, Johan can't either.'

Mum put her elbows on the table and adjusted her paper crown so it was straight on her head, the sides tucked behind her ears.

'Oh, what a shame, you enjoyed it, didn't you?'

'I told Anne I wasn't doing much else, but it seems the decision's been made.' Another tear meandered down my cheek.

'Well, if you can't go to the group, I'm sure there'll be other things to get involved with.'

I pulled a face.

'Did you get his phone number?'

'Are you talking about Johan?'

'Yes. Did you get it?'

I rolled my eyes and sighed. 'There's no point, Mum.'

'Why not?'

'He's not going to be interested. I like him but I really doubt he'll want to be my boyfriend or anything like that.'

'Can't he just be a friend?' Mum collected our plates together and stood up. 'Have you got room for a piece of chocolate Yule log?'

'A small piece, thanks.'

She walked into the kitchen. I could hear the clatter of plates before she came back in carrying two bowls.

'Here you go.' Mum passed me my bowl. 'This should sweeten you up.'

Later in the day, we were in the living room talking about my brother who was spending Christmas with his girlfriend, when my mum stopped mid-sentence and started to fiddle with her skirt, and hands.

'What's wrong?'

She stared at the floor and took a deep breath, before she lifted her head to look at me. 'I don't want you to get worried about this but I think you should know that a couple of weeks ago I got a phone call. I've been unsure about whether to tell you, as I didn't want you to get upset.'

'Who from? Not the gu..?'

'Yes, one of them, I couldn't work out which one she was.'

I put my elbow on the side of the sofa and covered my eyes with my hand. For a minute I stayed like this before I lifted my hand up slowly, like a visor. 'What did she say?' I covered my eyes again, my heartbeat thudding in my ears.

'It was a rant. A rant about how many jobs had been lost as a result of what we'd done, apparently five of them were made redundant. She said I'd been irresponsible, that what we'd done would be challenged. She said you'd no right to leave and so on. All this was shouted. I tried to reason with her but she shouted over me.'

'Oh God, what did she mean it would be challenged?'

Mum slowly shook her head. 'I really don't know. I did speak to the solicitor, and he didn't know either.'

'Do they know where I am? I suppose they must think I'm living with you?'

'I thought that at first but then I assume she would've asked for you rather than me. She didn't mention Carthom, so I think maybe for the time being they don't know. I've been getting silent calls for a while, it was the same number.'

'Oh, God.'

'So I'm going to change my phone number and go ex directory and let's hope that'll be the end of it.'

I glanced across at Mum. 'They know your address.'

'And I know how to call for the police.'

'I feel really angry at them for taking it out on you.'

'See these,' Mum pointed to each shoulder, 'they're broad enough, darling.'

I sank into the sofa. This was the last news I wanted to hear. I wasn't ever going to be free from them.

Mum switched on the TV to watch a special Christmas edition of Songs of Praise.

I pulled out my book, The Corrections by Jonathon Franzen, out of my bag. Before settling down to read, I put the novel on my knee and wheeled through to the kitchen and sat by the back door to have a cigarette.

Hearing a guard had phoned my mum unsettled me a lot, not so much the content of what she said but the fact she'd been shouting. The anger and venom from the guards towards my mum worried me, and my dual anxiety was what would happen if the guards turned up at my mum's house, or what would happen when they found me?

As I was smoking, I ran my finger over the cover of my book. This was one of the novels I bought for a second time after having to leave the majority of them at the bungalow.

I used to use books as shields, covering my face so they couldn't see me getting upset or embarrassed. Reading also provided a temporary means of escape. It meant I could climb over the wall and watch how other people managed life. It was transformative even if only for ten or fifteen minutes, a brief period of bliss unconnected with the boredom and abuse in the bungalow. The guards hated me reading, it was one act they couldn't control, though they did do their best to interrupt or disturb me. I became an expert in speed reading in brief snatches of time.

I looked down at the cover of the novel again. I wanted to be free from the guards, and able to live my life without constantly thinking about them. All the time, they were there in the background, a constant threat to suck me out of normal day to day life and spit me out, back under their control so they can humiliate and threaten me again.

Back in the living room, Mum had one of her fixed smiles on as she listened to the carols. It was her 'everything is alright' smile though the fact she was deploying it meant everything wasn't alright at all.

Six

On the second of January I was resting on my sofa when I saw Anne's face squashed up at my living room window, hands cupped on either side of her eyes. By the time I opened the door, Anne had started to pace up and down my path.

'Are you coming then?'

'What? To the group?'

'It isn't a proper meeting; it's really to make sure everybody's OK about the new arrangements.'

'So I can come now?'

She put her hand on her hip. 'Yes, we had a think about it. We'll open it up to anyone, except children, of course.'

'And Johan? Is he going to come?'

'Let's get you in first.'

For a moment I paused, did I really want to go to back to this group?

'Stop dilly-dallying; they're all waiting for us.'

I followed Anne to her car.

'Johan said he might come every now and then,' Anne said, as she drove up my road. 'He prefers to work on his own, anyway.'

'What about Fiona, isn't she interested in coming to a group?'

'During the week, she's very busy. She's also just a young woman, I doubt sitting around with a bunch of old folk is her thing.'

I stared out of the window and wished I'd stayed at home.

We pulled into Anne's driveway. There was an assortment of cars parked on the road and Eddie's bike was propped against the wall at the side of the bungalow.

Inside, everyone was crowded into the living room. Pauline and Elaine were there, squashed up on the sofa alongside Lena. Marion, the new lady was sitting on the armchair with Albert, her husband, by her side.

Standing next to Albert was Eddie. When Anne started to talk, I saw Albert who was a good few inches shorter than Eddie, start to size him up. He started from his boots. Albert was dwarfed by Eddie but when he'd looked up and down at him, he squared up and seemed to gain an extra inch.

Anne was standing in the middle of her room. The chairs and sofa formed a circle around her.

'Well, most of you know this but for those who don't, I've managed to get us a new venue. We're going to meet every Wednesday morning at the community centre here in Carthom.'

Eddie started to clap, but Anne nodded and made a small movement with her hand to signal to him to stop, as if she was the keynote speaker at an important conference.

'We were going to make it a club for pensioners. However, as Eddie pointed out, if we want as many members as possible, we should open the doors to anyone, including the handicapped.' She gestured in my direction.

Eddie nodded. 'Old people and the disabled have a lot in common.'

'Now, Johan can be a bit of a loner sometimes. He said he might come once in a while. He's still going to do the flyer for us.' Anne bent down and after a fight with various objects in her bag; she pulled out a crumpled A5 piece of paper.

'This is a sketch of what he's going to paint.' She held it up.

'Can we see it, Anne?' Marion asked.

'Pass it around.'

When the sketch was handed to me, I was amazed at how good it was. He'd drawn an artist with a paint splattered smock. He had a black handlebar moustache and in one hand, he held his palette. In his other hand the artist was pointing a paintbrush like a finger. The Art for You lettering was at the top, with a space at the bottom where the details of the group could be added. I passed it up to Eddie.

'When will Johan have finished?' Eddies voice boomed in comparison to Anne's soft tone.

'He said it was nearly done. Why? Could you print them off?'

'Yes, I could do say ten posters and fifty flyers. Would that be enough?'

'Enough? Oh yes, that's plenty.'

'So when will be the first meeting?' Lena asked.

Anne pushed her glasses from the top of her head down onto the bridge of her nose and peered at the palm of her hand. 'It'll be on the ninth of January. Ten o'clock until midday. If it's just us it'll be three pounds each, but if we get more people involved, it'll go down. They don't have any staff in on a Wednesday, so it means we've to lock and unlock the doors.'

'We could ask David next door to do a piece on us, couldn't we love?' Albert said, looking down at his wife.

Marion shook her head. 'He only sells advertising space at the paper, he isn't a reporter.'

As I listened to Albert and Marion it struck me how different they were. He had an Irish accent and also spoke with a rising intonation, which made each statement sound like a question, whereas, Marion had a deep, deliberate drawl. She was large and broad with dark grey hair. Albert was small and slight, his hair wispy and white. When I glanced over at them again I saw a little terrier dog, yapping and running rings around a faithful old Labrador.

'I think what Bertie means, is we have this contact with Carthom News. We could always advertise the group there, to get more people involved.'

'Advertise? Yes, I think that'd be a good idea once we've got started, because in time we might want to have an art exhibition.'

Albert was now telling everyone about David's ambition to be a Fleet Street reporter. Marion looked fed up as if she'd heard the story many times before. She glanced at her watch before she started to gather up the cups to take into the kitchen. I followed her in just as she was putting the cups into the washing bowl.

'So what do you do? Rachel, isn't it?'

'Yeah. I do watercolours with ink mainly.'

Marion dried her hands slowly, and as she turned around to face me she smiled incongruously.

'No, I mean what you do for a living, for a job?'

Anne walked into the kitchen as well.

'I used to work for the Council, in a scheme, but when all the cuts began, the scheme folded and I lost my job, I've not been able to get anything else.'

'Don't let Bertie hear that. He's not keen on people who live comfortably off the State. Not keen at all.' Marion raised an eyebrow to Anne.

I turned my chair away from Marion towards Anne. 'This has all happened quickly, the group and everything, and thanks Anne for including me. I really appreciate it.'

Anne swiped the air with her right hand. 'I couldn't stand hanging around not when I knew the garden centre was closing. So getting this art group up and running should be good.'

'How many groups are you in now, Anne?' Marion asked. 'You must be in four at least.'

'Groups? I go to bingo on Saturday evening with fat Harry. Scrabble on Tuesday morning and in the afternoon go to a craft and sew group. Sometimes, I go to line dancing on Thursdays, if my back can take it. On Friday I go to a discussion group. Mind, the other week the topic was the Middle East. Why would I want to talk about that? It's not as if a group of pensioners can wade in and make everything right. Anyway, you know me; I do anything to keep me busy; I can't stand having nothing to do.'

'I couldn't think with all that going on. Bertie's like you, he has to be busy, busy all the time. He can't bear to be on his own.'

'I don't want time to think. By the way, how's Simon these days?'

'Oh, you know, I hardly hear what's going on with him. All I do know, is he's been at Taylor's for five years now,' she replied. After a sidelong glance at me she added, 'working.'

Eddie stepped into the kitchen. 'I'll be off now, Anne. Let me have the poster and I can do them in a day, ready for you to pick up.'

I wheeled outside for a much needed cigarette.

Anne followed me out. 'Rachel, I've just thought on. We've

got to take our paintings out of the gallery. If you want, we can go once everyone is gone. Is that alright? Eddie, Fiona and Lena have already taken theirs.'

'Yes, OK thanks.'

Pauline, Elaine and Lena strolled outside, closely followed by Albert and Marion.

'You've done really well getting this off the ground.' Lena said. 'Hasn't she, everyone?'

'Hear, hear,' said Eddie. He bent down to put his cycle clips on his trousers

People started to drift off home.

'Ready to go, Rachel?'

I nodded.

On the drive to Garden and Crafts for You, Anne talked about the new group. I could sense she was really excited and I had to admit I was as well.

'Ooh, look, they're not hanging around, are they?' Anne cried out.

A large sign was now outside the garden centre that read 'Dickenson's Carpets Coming Soon'. The front window was completely bare.

'Eddie said over Christmas, Rob has been in here, getting stuff sorted out.'

We parked up beside a big lorry, which was open at the back and full of stock. In the shop, all the tables that were in the middle had been moved and were folded up at the side, alongside tea chests, crates and more bags of stock. It looked vast. Rob was working at the back with a man I hadn't seen before who was ticking off items on papers on a clip board. Every now and again he would stop to photograph an item before putting it away.

Inside the gallery, most of the walls were bare and the little room was a lot more spacious than I originally thought. My paintings were still up, as well as a few of Anne's, which were dotted around the room. I started to take down the paintings I could reach.

Anne brought over some bubble wrap. 'You wrap them and I'll take them down.'

When the last painting was wrapped up, Anne, for a moment, leant against the wall, her head down.

'It's sad isn't it? I expected this to last longer.'

Anne looked across at me and nodded slowly. 'I was so excited about this gallery. I just hope the group's not a lot of effort for nothing, like this was.' She brought out from her bag the piece of card my mum had first spotted. 'I can remember writing this. I was so excited. Can you tell what this card's from?'

I shook my head.

'It's from a pack of tights. Every time I look at it, I see myself as a young woman. I used to wear miniskirts, American Tan tights and have all the boys from the village chasing after me.' Anne walked over to the window. 'Mind, I used to stare at my mother when she put on her stockings and think she was the most glamorous person I'd ever seen.'

With one hand she brushed some hair away from her eyes as she walked back over to me, her eyes watery and red. She took one last protracted look at the now empty gallery before she sniffed and lightly shook her head.

We moved through the shop, which was now unrecognizable from when I first visited. Anne called out to Rob, to wish him a happy new year. He was perched on the edge of a tea chest and with a vacant expression he held up his hand in a silent reply.

Seven

In the village, Art for You flyers were popping up. I spotted one on a parked car, one in the charity shop window, one in the betting shop window, and two on the glass covered notice board outside the Catholic Church.

Anne had dropped ten flyers at my house, with a message telling me to distribute them between friends and family. I didn't see any point in having one at Mum's house in Wallaston so apart from the one I stuck on my living room window, the rest I concealed carefully in the middle of some newspapers and put them into my recycling box.

While I waited for Anne, I fastened up my art bag and watched out of my living room window. The blue-rinsed elderly lady from across the road was slowly watering various potted plants in her front yard. Her overweight black and white cat was watching her from the doorway before it plodded out and collapsed on the pavement with its paws in the air. Even the sound of Anne's brakes, clattering and banging, didn't disturb it.

Anne had already been into the centre and put the tables into position, the heating on and the tea and coffee out. With nothing left to do we sat in a tense, nervous silence while we waited for everyone to arrive.

A man limped in; his straggly long brown hair tied by a red elastic band into a pony tail. He walked with crutches and introduced himself as Mike. He was around thirty-five years old, perhaps a couple of years older. For the next fifteen minutes it was just the three of us and before long, bad back stories were the subject. Mike spoke of his slipped disc and sciatica. Over the holiday period, Anne's back complaint had also developed into sciatica, even though she hadn't yet seen her GP.

At some point during the discussion, Anne told Mike about my 'dreadful car accident' before she walked off towards the toilets. Mike turned to look at me and there was a brief flicker of a smile. He limped towards me and talked about his artwork. He said he often painted dog portraits and showed me an example on his mobile. The framed painting was on an easel, and a diagonal shaft of light from the top left corner to the bottom right illuminated it, picking out the tones and shadows.

'Is this in watercolours?'

'To get the hairs right, I use watercolour pencils and then stick watercolour paints on top. What do you think?'

'It's really good, very lifelike. Great photograph of it as well, very effective.'

'Thanks, I like doing ph...' His voice trailed off as he turned at the sound of the main door being shut.

Out of the corner of my eye, I saw the swaggering frame of Eddie appear, this time with no cycling gear as he'd given Lena a lift in his car. He looked good in dark blue jeans and a red and blue check shirt and when he ruffled my hair, I could smell his pungent aftershave.

Pauline and Elaine wandered in next, deep in conversation. Behind them was another new member, who introduced herself as Kate. She was in her early thirties, I guessed and was very pretty and tanned, not in a fake tan, gaudy way but instead had a healthy, and no doubt, expensive glow. Her blonde hair was styled into a sharp bob, which accentuated her high cheekbones. She wore a white shirt and designer jeans with a smart navy jacket and a floral scarf.

Kate was using two crutches and I overheard her tell Eddie she was born with a deformed spine and as a child had numerous operations, which left her with a permanent stoop. This meant she was in pain as well as having mobility problems that increased over time.

Eddie began to talk about his art, every now and again giving a self-conscious guffaw and snort.

Kate glanced over at me and for a moment flashed a wide smile and raised her carefully plucked and shaped eyebrows. I smiled back and noted that even her teeth were perfect. I was annoyed at myself for not changing my jumper when I spilt some coffee over it before the meeting.

In the minute or two before the start of the group, I saw how those who'd already arrived gravitated towards Kate and formed a circle around her. Even Mike who'd been at my side wandered over to her. Seeing them side by side, I'd underestimated Mike's age. He was more like forty.

Just after ten, Marion and Albert arrived. While everyone was piling into the kitchen to get a cup of tea or coffee, Anne took me to one side.

'See these walls.' She gestured towards them. 'Wouldn't it be great, if we could put a few nails in and put our paintings up?'

'Can we just do it, or would we need to ask someone?'

'Ask? I think I'll have to ask Rob's wife, but I might see if Pauline can do it for me.'

I was about to reply when I saw Albert leap across the room. He grabbed Anne by the waist and spun her around.

'How's my most beautiful girl today?'

Anne blushed and was saved by a bleep from her mobile. As she untangled herself from Albert's arms she passed it over to me to read the text.

'It's from someone called Sebastian and he says he's sorry but can't come during the week.'

'Oh, he did mention something about looking after his grandchildren.'

We all began to take our places at the table. As I turned to go up the hall, Albert got hold of my wheelchair handles and started to push.

'Don't push me.'

'Where are you heading?' Albert leant over my shoulder, his hot smelly breath was on my face and his hands were still on my handles.

'Albert, she can push herself,' Marion shouted across to her husband.

It seemed to be when he was in trouble Marion called him 'Albert' and when not he was 'Bertie.'

'I was only trying to help.' Albert raised his arms before

flopping them back down. He walked over to sit with Marion who was glaring at him.

With a cough to clear her throat, Anne pulled herself up and stood with a small piece of paper, fluttering in her fingers.

'Hello everybody, I was going to make a speech but I've gone and forgotten my eyes.'

The piece of paper floated gently to the floor, landing next to my wheel. I picked it up to give to her later.

'So instead, I'll just say a few things. The plan for these groups is just to bring along a painting or drawing you're working on, and we'll paint together. The rent here is quite high, so with ten of us, it means three pounds each. Mind, it'll get cheaper as we get more members. Put your money in the cup on the hatch, please.'

I don't think anybody expected the speech to end there but when Anne scraped her seat back and plonked herself down it was to the sound of Eddie hurriedly crying out, 'hear, hear' and a ripple of applause.

After this introduction, the group started to paint and draw. The more confident artists showed off their work to each other and multiple conversations stopped and started up and down the table. Kate moved up a seat as she was working on a large canvas and needed a bit more room.

For a few minutes, it appeared there were two groups within one; the older people on one end and the disabled at another. However, when the conversation included everyone, this split wasn't as noticeable.

The piece of paper with Anne's notes was still in front of me but when I turned to her she was engrossed in a conversation with Lena. I toyed with putting it in her bag but eventually put it in my art bag to give to her another time.

Elaine nudged Pauline. 'Your mobile, is it on?'

'It's on!' Pauline beamed and blushed. 'My forty-two year old daughter's expecting her first baby. If she isn't in labour by the weekend then she'll be induced. I've been told to have my mobile on at all times.'

Up and down the table there were murmurs of congratulations before conversations started about babies and grandchildren.

I'd been working on a poppy painting using watercolours. The colour was right; I mixed together scarlet lake with rose madder and completed two poppies, but it was time consuming work. My back was starting to ache from bending over to paint so I grabbed my coat from the back of my wheelchair.

'You're not going, are you?' Mike asked.

'Nope, just nipping out for a cigarette.'

'Thank God, I didn't want to be the only one. I'll just get me coat.' Mike put his painting down and pulled on a thin cagoule jacket.

Outside, Mike limped over to the bench, and took out a cigarette, tapped the end of it two times on his packet and cupped it into his hand to light it. I saw his sore looking fingernails along with the dark brown stains on the inside of his first two fingers on his right hand and how he smoked fast and inhaled hard. It was a struggle to get any conversation out of him.

'Are you from Liverpool?'

'Near Birkenhead area, but I've been over this side of the country for ages now.'

'It's always a bit nerve-wracking, the first group, isn't it?'

Mike stood up and started to pace up and down the car park. 'It's alright.'

I tried a different approach. 'Did you do art at school or somewhere else?'

'I've always liked drawing, but it wasn't until...um... later... I was in hospital; they had this Occupational Therapist who said I should do some painting, to calm me down. I was mad then, y'know, angry at everyone and everything.'

'Were you in hospital over your slipped disc?'

'Nah, it wasn't that. It was...' Mike looked at me, as if he was undertaking a quick evaluation of my character to see whether I could be trusted or not. He stared down at his feet. 'It was just the usual, y'know.'

For the next couple of minutes we smoked in silence.

'We'd better go in, they'll be wondering where we are,' I said eventually.

Mike's weary eyes met mine again. For that brief moment I could see a flicker of pain and anguish in them, like dark, stormy clouds passing in front of a full moon.

I wheeled behind Mike and as he turned left into the hall, I carried on ahead to the kitchen where Kate had made a drink. I realised she wouldn't be able to carry it in with two crutches, so took it from her and put it in between my legs.

'Don't do that, sweetie, you'll get burnt.' She tried to take the mug back from me.

'It's OK; I can't feel my legs.'

'So, even more reason why you shouldn't do it.'

'It's alright, Kate. I'm used to it.'

I put her coffee down near to her canvas and looked at her work. Her painting was in acrylics and showed a fence with daisies and multi coloured flowers all painted in a quirky way. Most people in the room were copying from other paintings but here Kate was using her own imagination.

As I made my way back round the table I examined all of the paintings and drawings. It made me feel very insecure about my own work as the standard of the artwork in the group was high.

For a while, more people got drinks from the kitchen and soon a packet of Hobnob biscuits was passed up and down the table.

I felt pleased; this is what I wanted, a chance to get to know more local people and do my art. It was slow-paced and safe, but coming from the bungalow, it was probably what I needed. I glanced across the table at Kate and at Mike next to me. Here were people who understood what it was like to live with a disability and I wondered if they and maybe even some of the others could go on to be proper friends.

Due to what happened at the bungalow, I tried not to get too carried away. After all, when I first met the guards I thought they seemed friendly and open, and although I knew actual friendships would be unlikely, I did expect the predominantly female staff to be friendly towards me. How wrong could I be? The smiles when I first met them were fixed and false, and it wasn't long after that the abuse started.

Eddie tapped on the table, which made me jump.

'Why don't we hold maybe one or two exhibitions each year to display our paintings and to sell them too?'

Anne nodded. 'Excellent idea, Eddie, we could invite some other local artists like Johan and Fiona to have a table as well, so this whole hall is full of art for people to buy.'

'I haven't got enough work to fill a table,' Lena moaned.

'Yes, but if we held it in April or May,' Anne held out her hands and weighed them in the air, like imaginary scales, 'everyone should have some work to show. It's enough time to prepare. What about everyone else? What do you think?'

Those who spoke up said it was a good idea.

I glanced down at my poppy painting; if the exhibition was going to be in April then I'd have to produce some more work. I'd have to get a move on especially if I needed them to be framed.

There was less than an hour to go before the end of this first Art for You meeting. Albert had captured everyone's attention again and told a story about a friend in the war being decapitated, which was merged with a tale about his role in a local production of 'West Side Story'. He stood up, and I saw his chest rise as he launched into song with added gusto.

'Maria! I've just kissed a girl named Maria.'

I swallowed the urge to laugh. I was amazed everyone seemed to be enjoying Albert's performance as he warbled his way through the lines.

Kate tapped her finger on the table and I turned to face her; she was red faced with a mischievous twinkle in her eye. I pulled my sleeve down and tucked it into my mouth, tears running down my face. I couldn't look at Kate in case I giggled.

When lunch time arrived we all started to pack our things up. I turned to Mike, and then to Kate and wished them both all the best. As Kate limped out of the hall, she was humming 'Maria.'

I heard noises in the corridor so wheeled towards the door. There was an elderly woman dressed in a pink leotard. She was much older than Anne and when I stretched my neck, more women in vibrant coloured leotards came into view. Anne walked up to me and explained it was the pensioners disco dancing, keep fit class in next.

I started to pack up my art equipment.

'I don't have enough stuff for an exhibition,' Mike said. 'Do you?'

'Not at the moment, no. I guess we'll both need to get a move on.'

'I'd better get off or I'll miss me bus. See you next week.'

We all said goodbye.

Pauline and Elaine stood up together and immediately linked arms. I was amazed how they managed to stand-up and sit down at exactly the same time.

'See you next week, kiddo,' Eddie chirped, as he tossed his car key to Lena.

I went to the toilet and when I came out, everyone had gone, bar Anne. Dancing Queen by Abba was being played by the disco dancing group. They'd stuck dark paper across the door so nobody could see into the hall.

'Did you enjoy it today, Rachel? I thought it went really well.'

I nodded. 'Definitely, I really enjoyed it.'

'I hope we get some more people coming. Mind, I don't think there'll be anymore handicapped members.'

When the wheelchair was in the boot, and we were both in the car, I turned to her. All the enthusiasm in my voice had gone.

'Can I just say something, Anne? Nowadays, you say disabled not handicapped. Sorry, it just annoys me.'

While we waited to get onto the main road, Anne glanced at me. 'I don't understand why it's a disability and not a handicap. What's the difference?'

'Handicap's old fashioned, now and some see it as offensive.'

'Back when we had black and white TV, everyone said handicapped,' Anne muttered. 'It's not meant in a nasty way.'

We pulled into my road.

'Back when there was black and white TV, disabled people were treated like scum, like outcasts. Saying disabled, is just more politically correct,'

'Politically correct? I hate political correctness, I mean who's got the right to tell you what you can and can't say. In The Daily Mail they'd got this campaign...'

I interrupted her. 'That's The Daily Mail for you.' I pretended to shiver. 'Can I get out now, I'm getting cold?'

Anne had put her arms over the steering wheel, her head rested in the middle. After a moment of silence, she sighed and got out of the car, came round to my side and flung open the passenger door.

She bent down and hissed, 'I can't do anything right today, can I?'

My wheelchair bore the brunt of her anger towards me as she threw it together.

'See you next week, Anne,' I called out and tried my best to sound informal and friendly.

Anne didn't reply. She got into her car and banged the car door shut.

Inside my home I felt myself get increasingly annoyed. Her nuanced view of life was at variance with most people and it left me wondering if she was misguided, or was being deliberately offensive. There was a knock on the door. I opened the front door so hard it banged against the hall wall, and Janine immediately reacted.

'God, have I done something wrong?'

'No, no. Sorry.'

'Did your group go well?'

'Yeah, it's just I've gone and annoyed Anne, the woman who runs it.'

'Why, what did you do?' Janine bent down and was searching for my bin bags in the cupboard below the sink.

I knew Janine read the horoscope section of the same paper. Oh, it was just.' I shrugged.' You know - nothing really.'

'Oh, right.' Janine said, with a nod. She tossed the can of polish from one hand to her other hand.

I slotted myself in at the kitchen table and watched as Janine cleaned the kitchen.

'You're really confident, aren't you, Janine?'

'I wasn't always.' Janine turned around and leant against the fridge. 'Why do you ask?'

'I was just watching you and comparing myself to you. I can't imagine you'd get pushed around by someone like Anne.'

Janine folded her arms, and peered at me with her head slightly tilted to one side.

'You always look confident to me.'

I stared at my hands. 'There was a time when I was really confident, but when I had my accident, everything changed. I really want my time in Carthom to be different.'

Janine nodded slowly.

'I'm putting all my hope in with the art group but I've got this sinking feeling it's not going to work out, especially friendship wise.'

'You're not going to believe it but our stars in the paper say just that. It's all about trusting your gut feeling.' Janine pulled out her purse from her tunic pocket and gave me the tiny piece of newspaper.

'Thanks.' I tucked the piece of newspaper into the side of my wheelchair.

'I'd better get on, get this floor mopped. I've got a double after you and I'm doing it with the boss.' Janine pulled a face.

I wheeled into the living room. When I was with the guards it was impossible to meet new people but the struggle to find and keep friendships started as soon as I had my accident. When I left hospital I found I was no longer invited on nights out or holidays and some of my school friends didn't keep in touch at all. I watched as they went to university, began careers, got married and had children. It was hard not to be jealous or view my life as anything but substandard.

Whether it was protective layers or wings, the starting point always seemed to be friends. If I'd people who I could trust, I might get my confidence back and perhaps would feel more comfortable when I was on my own. The problem was if anyone knew what I'd done or where I was before Carthom, would friends desert me leaving me ostracised like I'd been before?

Eight

When I got the call from Anne to say I could put up a painting at the centre, I thought about my watercolour of a canal scene. It was traditional in terms of subject and style, which would make it perfect for the centre. The problem was finding it, so with two days to go before the next meeting, I enlisted Janine's help to try and locate it.

We both sat in my study that doubled up as a studio. Janine had emptied a plastic crate onto my desk, which held over twenty hard backed journals. In them, I had my own system to keep track of completed paintings and any sales I had, which was usually unfathomable to anyone else. While I was working my way through them, Janine had stacked together a collection of framed paintings. She sat cross legged on my carpet and examined each one. If she liked the painting, she would make an approving noise, if she didn't like it, the grunt would be lower in pitch and she'd quickly move on.

When she'd finished going through the paintings and still hadn't found the elusive picture, she crawled on the floor to reach inside a brown box that had a pile of art books on top of it. Along with a cloud of dust she pulled out a framed watercolour of a beach scene with a busty young woman in a red swimming costume sitting on a towel and looking out at the sea.

'Loving this one, Rachel.'

Janine blew some more of the dust off from the painting, which made me cough and splutter. I took it from her and turned it over to see when I painted it.

'It's years old. I did this a couple of years after my accident.'

'Your early twenties?' Janine stood up and perched on the window ledge.

'Yeah, around twenty.'

'God, it feels a long time since I was twenty.' Janine stretched out her legs in front of her.

I shook my head. 'It doesn't for me. My twenties were pretty awful.' I started to chew the end of my pen

'Why?'

'I should've been at university, working, and living independently maybe living with someone. Instead I was stuck at home with my mum.'

'You get on with her though, don't you?'

'Yeah, but at twenty who wants their mum helping them go to the toilet, or have a bath. I want her as my mum, not a carer.'

'At least she helped you. I doubt my mum would've even had

78

me at home in the first place, let alone do all that.' Janine stood up and put her hands on her hips.

'What were you doing in your early twenties?'

'You're not going to believe it, when I tell you.'

'Go on.'

'I wanted to be a hairdresser like my mate, but when I was meant to be watching this woman who was having her hair dyed, I messed up. She ended up with a burn on the top of her head nearly this size.' Janine drew a circle with her finger on her palm. 'The boss gave me such a bollocking I ended up walking out.'

Janine glanced at her watch. 'I'll do downstairs and after that, a cappuccino?'

While she was making her way down, I used the sleeve of my hoodie and cleaned the painting and frame. As I did this, memories of my time living with Mum drifted into my brain. I ended up with her for most of my twenties. Every weekend my brother would come for a meal, telling us about what he'd been doing in work and about his relationships. The more he succeeded the more I failed. I knew my life had been put on hold, and at times was scared it was over before I'd even had chance to be an adult.

I held the beach scene painting out in front of me and then placed it on a shelf with my head tipped sideways. If Janine liked it, it was worth putting up at the centre. I hadn't a clue where the canal scene painting had gone.

I also unwrapped my watercolour painting of Staithes in Yorkshire. It could be used to go on a flyer to promote my own work and hopefully get more commissions.

When the group met, each of us had one painting, apart from Anne who'd brought three.

As soon as Marion realised this, she turned to Anne and banged her fist on the table. 'Is there any point you phoning up and telling us to only bring one painting, when you don't do it yourself?'

Albert nodded and Elaine, who this week wasn't with Pauline, also muttered something under her breath.

'I just didn't want the room to be bare. It looks good now, don't you think?'

'I do, Anne,' Lena quickly replied. 'It looks so colourful and vibrant.'

Elaine put her hand up. 'Can I just make an announcement? Pauline's daughter had a baby girl, Rebecca, at the weekend. They should be coming home tonight. They're all staying with Pauline for a week or two.'

'That's great news, Elaine,' Lena said.

'Anne, do you think we should get Pauline a card, some flowers or chocs?' Eddie said. He half stood up. 'I could pop down to the village, if you want?'

'Thanks, Eddie.'

Anne and Eddie walked out of the hall together, and had a conversation near the kitchen.

Kate limped over to me, and after a wobble sat in Anne's chair. She talked in a quiet voice not much louder than a whisper.

'Do you know the restaurant in Richmond Way?'

'Is it near the butcher?'

Kate nodded. 'So, the owner, Gary, doesn't have any artwork up, but he's got plenty of wall space and he's interested in having some paintings up for sale.'

'I was thinking about this, but if we put paintings up in Carthom what'll the others say?'

'So, we'll deal with that when the time comes.' She held out her hand. 'It's not that I'm saying nobody else can join in. It's a free world. I just think it'd be better if it was the two of us. Gary...'

Kate turned her head as Anne walked back into the hall. She leant on the table for support as she stood up, and before going back to her own seat she whispered, 'write down your mobile number, sweetie.'

'What was she saying?' Anne walked up towards me stiffly,

her hands clamped to her side. She stood next to my chair as she waited for my reply.

'Just talking about painting.'

Anne snorted through her nose; she sat down and put her arms under the seat of the chair to move it closer to the table.

Mike was quiet next to me. He was drawing the outline of a Labrador. The photograph of the dog was next to his paper.

'How are things?'

'Crap.'

'Why? What's up?'

'I got one of those forms about me money. It's really worrying...'

'What's this you're worried about?' said Anne. She leant across me so that she could speak to Mike.

I answered for Mike before he could speak.

'It's nothing, Anne,' I insisted. I tried to get my arms out from under her body.

'It's about me sick money.'

I heard someone tut.

I immediately suspected this was Albert so I glared down the table at him but he appeared to be deep in concentration. The tutting had stopped but one by one I examined each face around the table, in an attempt to find the guilty party. Everyone was painting or chatting and didn't seem to be taking any interest in what'd been said. It didn't appear as if Mike had registered anything either, so I quickly changed the subject.

'Do you know when the exhibition's going to be, Anne?'

'The exhibition? Oh yes, quiet please.' She paused until the whole group was watching her. 'I know we wanted a Saturday but it isn't possible due to the bingo, with fat Harry. April is completely out as there're Farmers' Markets and attic sales going on throughout the month. So the only date we can have is on the Sunday before Easter in March, erm...Hang on.'

Anne put her glasses on and bent down to pull a diary out

from her bag. She licked her finger before flicking through the pages. 'Right, here it is. It'll be on the twenty-fourth. Mind, as this is our first exhibition, I really do think we should try and get the papers to do a spread about the group and the exhibition.'

'Why don't we call it an art sale? Some folk may think because it's exhibition, nothings for sale. We want them to get their wallets out,' said Albert.

'Good point,' Anne murmured.

Eddie wandered in with the card and chocolates for Pauline, and soon the card was being passed around for members to sign it. When Mike had passed it over to Kate he tugged on my sleeve.

'Fancy a ciggie?'

'Yeah, go on.' I grabbed my coat.

Outside, Mike leant against the wall, tapped his cigarette two times before lighting up.

'You could easily sell dog portraits.'

'I would, but with this review hanging over me, I'd better not. I don't want someone grassing me up, saying I'm earning.' Mike was biting down on his bottom lip.

'You'll be alright with your review. Honestly, you will.'

'Haven't you seen all the stuff in the papers?' Mike was red faced and his voice had gone up an octave. 'People like you in wheelchairs; they're being chucked off their money. So I've got no chance, no chance at all.'

Mike was smoking quickly, and as he inhaled he wheezed.

'Yeah, but half what they print isn't true, and anyway, even if you do get a bad decision you can always appeal. Apparently, loads of cases are being won on appeal.'

'Have you had your one yet?'

'No, so I'm worried like you,' I lied. I didn't want to tell Mike the decision from my review meant I'd more money.

'The problem with me is on top of all that I've got a pile of debt as well. When me ma died, the funeral was going to cost a packet. So when I saw the advert for loans through me door.

I filled it in straight away. It meant I could give the old girl the send-off she deserved. They were good, like. They lent me what I asked for. The problem's paying it back.'

'They gave you a loan, even though you weren't working?'

He gazed towards the police station. 'Me mate helped me out; he'd just started work as a caretaker, so I used some of his details. Don't think these places do many checks, anyway.'

'What about the interest? Some of these payday loans are...'

Mike crinkled up his nose. 'Numbers make no sense to me. All I know is I'm finding it hard to make the payments. So, on top of all that, I've got all this review business.'

He turned around and started to kick the wall. 'I go to bed each bloody night, and I know it's wrong to think like this but I'm hoping God will take me in my sleep. I dread the postie coming. If it's a brown envelope, I nearly have a heart attack.'

For a moment I sat and watched him hobble back into the centre. I didn't know what I could do apart from finding out some information about managing debt. I wheeled back inside and wrote on the palm of my hand in black pen 'moneylenders – help?'

Kate signalled to me just as I'd finished writing. She pretended she was drinking from a cup and then pointed to me. I gave a half nod and dutifully followed her into the kitchen.

Kate leant against the fridge. 'So, I'll send you a text during the week. I think it'd be helpful if we meet Gary to discuss arrangements in person. Let him see an example of our artwork. It's just so he's got idea and he's happy with it.'

'Yeah, no problem, I've been thinking a lot about putting my work up in cafes and galleries – being a bit more professional in my approach. I'll let you know if I find somewhere.'

'And I'll do the same. I'll send Jonathon over to give you a lift. So, whereabouts are you?'

I gave her my address and asked what time it would be.

'It'll be later in the day, Jonathon usually finishes work at half five, so it'll be after then. Is that OK?'

'Yeah, brilliant, thanks, Kate. What time does The...?'

'Oh, not until quite late,' Kate said, interrupting me. 'Do you want a drink, sweetie?'

'Nope, I'm OK, thanks.'

Later on, Pauline walked in with an expansive, and no doubt, cheek-aching smile, accompanied with red eyes and blotchy skin, as if she'd been crying. In that one expression, I thought it must illustrate the pride and relief that comes with a healthy newborn baby. With her mobile she went around the group showing the photograph of her new granddaughter, Rebecca, with her daughter.

When she'd done her rounds, Eddie stood up.

'Everyone in the group wanted to say congratulations to you and your daughter and baby Rebecca, of course.' He handed the envelope and chocolates over to her.

The group burst into applause and Pauline's face now matched her crimson top.

'Ooh, thanks everyone. Hopefully, they're coming out later on today. They're going to be staying with me for a bit.' Pauline sat down and cleared her throat. 'Their house really is far too small but they just can't find anywhere suitable.' Pauline looked around the group, in a conspiratorial manner. 'I'm not racist, but I tell you, in this country everyone would have somewhere decent to live, if we just didn't accept all these foreigners in.'

I was really shocked at what she'd just said, and then dismayed when there was murmurs of agreement. I wanted to challenge them but my nerves held me back, even though my silence made me feel as if I were complicit.

It occurred to me where I used to live in Weston, with all its deprivation, might have been more diverse and more accepting than an area such as Carthom. I thought Carthom collectively had a 'not in my back yard' attitude. Maybe that attitude was amongst the residents and meant they didn't accept people who were different from the white, British majority. Maybe that even extended to those who were poor or disabled.

Thankfully the conversation changed as Pauline showed everyone some more photographs of Rebecca. As the group members chattered around the table, I felt very much on my own and my back was throbbing.

I turned to Anne. 'I know we've got another half hour, but can I go now? I haven't got any painkillers on me and really I need them.'

'Painkillers? Oh, OK. You want to go now?'

'Mike, I'll try and get some stuff together for you.'

Mike shrugged and for a second he looked up at me with a sad, almost tortured expression before he started to paint again.

'Are you ready, Rachel?' With her foot tapping Anne was glancing first at her watch and then at the clock in the centre.

As soon as we were out of the centre, Anne dropped her bags and stood still, her hands on her hips.

'What's this you need to find out for Mike?'

'Just an address, that's all.'

'An address?' Anne's eyes narrowed. 'Is everything OK?' With an inquisitive gaze she waited until I replied before helping me into the car.

'Yes, fine. No problem at all.'

We set off back to my house. Anne was silent and at the lights was biting on a thumb nail. When she parked outside my home, she gazed across to the house opposite mine, without taking her seatbelt off.

She turned back to me, and jolted slightly as if she'd forgotten I was sitting next to her.

'Do you know Dot who lives in number three?'

'I'm not sure.'

Anne gestured towards the house. 'She has a blue rinse, a very nice lady, very kind.'

'Oh, I think I've seen her watering her plants but I've not

spoken to her yet. I haven't really talked to any of the neighbours yet, apart from a quick hello to the couple next door and their little girl.'

Anne stared down at the steering wheel in silence.

I took my seatbelt off and cleared my throat.

With an audible long sigh, Anne finally unclasped her seatbelt. She turned to me and opened her mouth as if she was going to say something before she shut it and turned back this time, staring at her knees.

'Let's get you out, then, Rachel,' she mumbled without making eye contact.

As soon as I was in my kitchen, I took some painkillers and while Mike was fresh in my mind, tried to find out some information online. The morphine made my vision blurred, which made the whole process much longer than I envisaged. After two hours I was in the process of printing off fourteen pages all about debt management.

I was also gradually getting my artwork ready for the visit to The Richmond. I didn't know how many paintings to take, so opted for more rather than less.

On Friday, when Kate and Jonathon arrived I was ready with my paintings priced, wrapped and piled up on my knees.

'Would it be OK if I put those with Kate on the back seat?'

As Jonathon stretched out to pick up my paintings, I could see what looked like a very expensive watch under a crisp white shirt sleeve. I approached the silver Lexus and through the tinted windows, could just about make out Kate on the back seat, waving at me. I transferred into the front seat and could smell the leather seats. I started to explain how to dismantle my chair, but he said Kate had been in a wheelchair for a while and as such, he 'knew the ropes.'

Kate tapped me on the shoulder. 'Hi, sweetie.'

I turned my head towards Kate. 'I love your car. It's very luxurious. Is it new?'

'It's Jonathon's rather expensive birthday present for his fortieth.'

'Come off it, forty? No way!'

'So how old do you think I am?'

'I don't know, around my age, thirty-one, thirty-two?'

Jonathon laughed. 'You've got a friend for life now. She's the big four '0' as well. In fact, I'm your toy-boy, aren't I?' Jonathon winked at Kate. 'Two months younger. Not that I want to rub it in.'

The Richmond restaurant was empty apart from a couple of young mothers with toddlers. One of the children was bawling, which made conversation a battle. The walls were completely bare and painted in a magnolia colour. Gary explained if the paintings were to go up, they should be changed each month and he'd need our details in case of sales. He didn't ask to see our work, but while the child was screaming and being taken outside by his mother, Kate indicated with her eyes to unwrap some paintings.

Gary stood up. 'Excuse me for a minute.'

He quickly walked over to the door and spoke to the woman with the toddler. He walked back, and slightly shook his head.

'Sorry, it's my partner and my little boy; he's a bit cranky today.' He looked for a moment at our paintings. 'Right, OK then. Are we agreed four paintings each? Did you say your husband would..?'

Kate poked Jonathon's side to stop him reading a copy The Times from the counter. 'So, Jon, Gary wants to discuss how we do this.'

The two men talked about where the nails would go on the wall.

'I don't think he's going to look at these paintings anymore, sweetie,' Kate whispered. 'So we might as well wrap them up again.'

Gary and Jonathon walked back over to our table. The nails

were going in on Tuesday, and any time after that we could display our paintings.

We were ready to leave, when the door swung open. Gary's partner, her back bent, had her legs either side of the young boy. She held his hands and walked one foot then a pause, followed by her other foot, as the young boy toddled towards Gary.

'He's gorgeous' Kate gushed. 'What's his name?'

'Jacob,' Gary said. At which point the little boy smiled and gurgled 'da-da.'

Gary's partner lifted Jacob up with his bottom resting on her hip.

'Hello, Jacob,' Kate said. She smiled at him, but he buried his head in his mother's chest.

With that, we said our goodbyes.

'Oh Kate, thanks so much,' I said outside. 'It went like clockwork.'

'Sweetie, I wanted a partner so really it should be me thanking you. So, if Jonathon puts the nails in on Tuesday, how about we go after art?'

'It'll have to be after my cleaner has been. What about two o'clock?'

'Super. I'll pick you up then.'

In the car I tried to take it in. I couldn't believe soon I'd have four paintings in The Richmond, plus the paintings I'd sold at The Vines. A painting was on sale at the centre and before long it would be the exhibition/art sale. I half turned in my seat towards Kate and smiled. I was aware a key element of settling into Carthom life, was the growing friendship with her.

The more I got to know her, the more I harboured the desire to come clean. However, the plan to escape from who I was and guard diligently my past was already in motion. Each time I spoke to Kate, Mike or any of the others, I was strengthening this false image. Admitting I'd been less than truthful could risk everything, and I knew as a result I'd no choice but to keep up with the deception.

It made me upset that the only real chance to make friends wasn't built upon acceptance and truth, but a cover up and lies.

Nine

The atmosphere in the centre was bleak and matched the weather outside. The water droplets had been getting bigger and falling more frequently. What had been a light trickle when I'd woken up was a torrential downpour by 10 o' clock.

Inside the hall, I was nervously arranging and rearranging my pens, while Anne was pacing up and down clutching a hardback notebook to her chest. Her mouth was downturned and the dark sacks under her eyes contrasted with the grey, pallid skin and the garish orange-red lipstick. It was the first time I'd seen her with make-up on but rather than enhancing her features it looked like a ghoulish mask.

I'd asked if everything was alright in the car and her response was all was OK.

However, as the group members arrived, it was clear that she wasn't alright at all. Eddie gave Anne a long hug, as did Lena, Marion, Albert and Pauline. I felt excluded and again was aware of a split between the older members of the group, and the disabled.

Once everyone had sat down, Anne stood up.

'To make sure everyone pays, I'm going to do a register each week. When I call out your name, bring me your money.' Anne opened the hardback book at a blank pager, and pressed the paper down, before reaching for her biro.

By the time the register was completed, twenty minutes had

been taken up, and there was an eagerness around the table to start doing some art work. A knock on the door minutes later made Pauline, Marion and Albert groan out loud.

'Johan,' Anne called out. 'Can you find a seat? There's one here next to Kate.'

Johan sat down and put his rucksack on his knee. He brought out an A4 piece of paper in a clear plastic wallet that he placed face down.

Anne cleared her throat. 'I asked Johan to come up with a flyer for our art sale. For those of you that don't know, Johan was one of the original artists at Garden and Crafts for You.'

'With the limited amount of funds,' Johan said. 'I thought a good solution would be to come up with a printed sticker, which then can be put on the original flyer like this.' Johan pulled out a flyer from the wallet, which was then slowly passed around the group.

When I saw it, I was amazed at how simple it was. The man with the paint splattered smock now had a sticker across his body with the details of the art sale. Before I handed it to Mike, I pulled out of my bag the envelope, which had the debt advice notes inside and surreptitiously gave it to Mike.

'What's this?' Mike whispered.

'It's all about managing debt.'

Mike passed the flyer over to Kate and she gave him a folded piece of paper to give to me. In it she asked if I was still alright to go to The Richmond that afternoon.

In reply, I held up my thumb.

Johan put a pile of flyers on the table. 'I've done twenty for you already and there's fifty stickers on these sheets.'

'That's great, Johan. Really great,' Eddie said.

'We're going to have to replace all the flyers that are out there with these ones, aren't we?' Anne said grimly.

'I think you're better just concentrating on the main road, places like the post office, supermarket, The Vines and so on.'

Johan was fastening up his rucksack. 'Do you need me for anything else?'

'No, I don't think so,' said Anne. 'Thanks, Johan.'

Johan put in his head phones and looked as if he could stroll off without even a glance in my direction.

On impulse, I started wheeling. As he sauntered, I picked up my speed. I was first through the double doors.

Johan joined me. He seemed surprised to see me sitting in the foyer area.

'Hi Johan.'

He took out one of his headphones.

'Hi Rachel.' He lowered his eyes to his feet as he shuffled on the spot.

A second later, Anne opened the door.

'Thought you were still here, Johan. I just need to look at the original sketch for a minute.'

While Johan took off his rucksack, I went back inside the hall, annoyed my plan didn't work and concerned he still didn't seem interested in me.

Later in the morning, Kate limped over to Anne. With one hand on the back of her chair to steady herself, she slowly bent down.

'So, I was thinking, whether it would be a good idea to have a website now we're having an art sale.'

Anne turned pink as she laughed nervously. 'Website?' You're going to have to forgive me, I know nothing about them.'

Eddie arched his back. 'That's a great idea, Kate. You know Fi-fi and how good an artist she is? Well, how she gets her sales is through her website. You can't buy directly from it but instead she puts up a calendar showing when the next exhibition is and what they can buy at it.'

'It does seem like a good idea,' Anne said cautiously. 'Could you find out some more details about how it can be set up?'

Kate nodded.

A period of silence followed as everyone started to draw or paint. Mike was hard at work doing the pencil work for a painting of a Jack Russell dog.

'Is this for the art sale? 'I asked.

'It's for me mate.'

'I know I've said this before, but you really could make money from these.'

Mike shook his head.

I tipped my head to the side. 'Do you fancy a..?'

'Yeah, just a quickie.'

We put on our coats as it was still raining outside.

'How many tables are you having at the sale?'

Mike was yawning. 'One, I was going to say two but me main problem is transport. I can only bring three or four small paintings in me rucksack. I can't drive cos of me epilepsy.'

'I can't drive either because I'm on morphine. Anne gives me a lift; she might give you one too. Where do you live in Carthom?'

'The Windmill estate, but it's Weston not Carthom.'

'I'm sure Eddie would give you a lift then, he lives somewhere in that direction.'

I pulled up my hood because the rain was getting heavier.

'I'll ask him about it later.' Mike tried to pull up the collar of his jacket as high as it would go. 'I haven't heard nothing about me money, by the way. Me mate said if they're OK with what's written on the form then you don't have to go for an assessment, is that right?'

'I think so Mike. Do you want to go in because you're..?'

'Thing is, I won't survive with less money. It's not fair, I see these young girls at the jobcentre, no fella, but a couple of young kids. They get loads of money, and a house too, and what for, to watch daytime TV all day. It gets me bloody angry.'

Mike started to hobble back indoors. When he was in the reception area, he bent his head down and started to shake it like a dog.

I held back for a minute not wanting to get soaked. His rant against young mums reminded me of how divisive welfare reform had been, pitting one vulnerable group against another. I was worried if my secret was ever to come out I would be moved from the box labelled 'deserving poor' into the 'undeserving poor' box.

I was doing the preliminary sketches for an ink drawing of my street, and soon became completely engrossed. When my concentration was broken, I shot a quick glance at the clock and was surprised it was midday.

I took my coffee cup to put in the sink. Just as I was coming out of the kitchen, Kate was limping out of the toilet.

'Still alright for two'o clock, sweetie?'

'No problem.'

I got my art materials together and put them in my rucksack. A few minutes later

Anne sidled up to me.

'Ready when you are, Rachel?'

Anne walked with me to her car; she was still subdued and seemed to be unhappy.

She helped me into the car, and when she eased herself into the driver's seat, for a moment she didn't do anything. I put my seatbelt on and Anne glanced at me.

'What do you think of the art sale flyer?'

'I suppose it saves us having to have another flyer just for the sale. Why? Don't you like it?'

'No, not at all, I was hoping he'd do one just for the sale. Having a sticker on it just looks scruffy.' Anne put her seatbelt on and after a glance in her rear view mirror, started to back out.

We passed the boarded up library and crossed the main road.

'Are you OK, Anne?'

'Today is just an anniversary, Rachel. I'll be alright when

tomorrow comes.'

She parked up outside my house.

'Do you want me to take a flyer, one with a sticker on, so I can change it with the one on my living room window.'

'That would be helpful. Let's get you out first.'

After I had my lunch, I changed over the flyer in my living room window and looked up at the sky. The weather was improving, with some patches of blue sky appearing. By the time Kate was due to pick me up there was a rainbow that looked like it straddled the length of Carthom. I sat with the front door open, my wrapped and priced paintings by my side.

I was concerned Kate wouldn't cope with my wheelchair on her own, but between us, we managed.

When she sat down, she fed her crutches through the gap between the driver's and the passenger's seat into the rear foot well, before driving to The Richmond.

'Anne said you're fairly new in Carthom.'

'Well, not that new now. I've been here for about eight months.'

'Where were you before?'

'On the far edge of Weston. I never planned...' I let my voice trail off.

'So, what, you didn't plan living there, in Weston?'

I needed to change the subject so I peered outside for inspiration. 'I think we came to this restaurant when we were searching for a suitable house or flat. '

'Really? The Richmond? I thought it only opened about four months ago. Are you sure it was this one?'

As my chest tightened I felt an acute stabbing pain. 'It must've been somewhere else. We couldn't quite believe it when we found number four. It was fully accessible; we didn't need to involve the Occupational Therapists at all.'

Kate nodded with her eyebrows raised. 'It was so lucky you found it. Did you buy it or..?'

'I rent it though it's quite expensive compared to other houses the same size.'

Kate checked the visor mirror and tilted her head. 'So, you know you may be paying more simply because it's accessible? They always say having a disability is more expensive, than being able bodied. I think I remember seeing your house online for sale a while ago.'

'Why, are you looking to buy a house?'

'No, it's one of my husband's obsessions, checking house prices. So, who's your landlord?'

'I've no idea, the estate agent acts for him or her.'

We pulled into a parking space and Kate unfolded her blue badge. I felt I could breathe again. I took my paintings in on my knee, whereas Kate was a lot more professional carrying a large portfolio case.

Two middle aged women were sitting on the sofa with their backs against the wall where our paintings were going to be. Kate offered them other seats but instead both women helped Kate put the paintings up. While she fussed over what should go where, I ordered two cappuccinos from Gary. As I waited for the drinks, Kate came up and tapped me on the shoulder.

'Tra-la,' Kate called out. She put both hands together in front of her before opening them out like a curtain. She closed her mouth and made her own trumpet sound.

My paintings looked alright but Kate's with their vibrant colours, quirky characters and smart, expensive frames were impressive. I wheeled over to the wall to examine one piece. It was an acrylic painting of a ginger kitten stretching over a wall and hitting an insect with its paw. Next to the kitten was a shrub with purple flowers. The level of skill required to pull off such a painting successfully was high, yet Kate was, like me, mostly self-taught.

'Wow, they're superb, Kate.'

Gary came out from behind the kitchen and walked over to

look at the paintings. He whistled, before fishing out his mobile and taking a photo.

'This is going on Facebook . He put the two mugs of cappuccino on our table. 'On the house girls, cheers.'

I tapped on the table with my finger. 'Wouldn't it be better if we had a Facebook page for the group?'

Kate nodded. 'Great minds think alike. We could have a central page for the group, and then each of us has our own page. It could work. Though I imagine quite a few of them will need assistance.'

'Yeah, I'm not even sure if the likes of Anne or Lena have got computers.'

Kate gazed out of the window. 'Why did you decide to move to Carthom?'

'This might sound a bit mad, but I wanted to live somewhere quiet, rural and preferably with older folk. I thought it might be a bit easier.'

Kate frowned, with her head tipped sideways. 'So, sweetie, did you have some trouble in Weston? Was it about your disability?'

'It was and it wasn't.' I swallowed hard. 'Everything's OK now.' I felt uncomfortable.

'I hope you don't mind me saying this, but you're quite guarded in what you say, aren't you?'

My heartbeat was thumping and all I could hear was that pulsating beat.

'Maybe I am. I just don't think everyone will understand. I'm not saying you'd gossip but I have come across some people who do and I just think it's my business, nobody else's.'

Kate nodded. 'Like Anne? She's already told me you were in a massive car crash.'

I held out my upturned hand. 'It's my business and it was years ago. I don't want to have to talk about it everywhere I go.'

Kate placed her hand momentarily on my forearm. 'I

do understand, sweetie, I really do. I found disclosing key information regarding my disability such as the cause and how it can affect me, meant there was less space for anyone to speculate or gossip. Do you understand?'

'Surely people would gossip anyway?'

Kate shrugged. 'Perhaps, but if the information is 'out there' it makes it harder for anyone else to come up with an alternative scenario.'

'What if the reason I give leads to more questions and so on? I just can't do it, Kate.'

'So, is it can't or won't?'

'A bit of both,' I muttered under my breath.

'I'm not criticising you or saying you have to do exactly what I did. I'm just saying talking about my disability, not only helped me in coming to terms with my situation but also helped others to understand and ultimately, empathise.'

'When did you stop work? It must've been difficult to leave your job as a manager?' I stopped talking and put my hand on my forehead, slowly dragging it down to cover my right eye. 'Oh, God, that's me, being nosy now.'

'Nonsense. You can ask me anything, sweetie. It was actually only the start of last year, when I left. Retirement on medical grounds was the official reason. It was hard, very hard indeed, and not just for me and Jonathon and but also Jeremy.'

'Oh, I thought it was a few years ago. I didn't realise.'

'It feels like years ago, now. At the time though it was a tough decision as Jeremy's at Duncan House College and we were worried we might have to take him out.' Kate paused as she got out her mobile. 'Give me a moment, here it is.' Kate passed me her phone.

A tiny head was barely visible, swallowed up by an extremely large blazer with purple and brown stripes.

'Is this Jeremy?'

'Yes, he hates this photo. When he started at the school, I

bought a blazer he'd grow into. I've got a petulant teenager on my hands these days. When he was younger he was quite precocious but now all I get out of him is 'nah' this and 'nah' that. I'm forever saying, enunciation Jeremy, enunciation.'

I smiled as my mum used to say this to me when I was younger.

Kate pushed both sides of her hair back over her ears. 'What I was saying, the College were great, and there was a bursary in case of illness or disability, which meant we were able to keep him at school. Any money we're able to save will go to giving him a hand in the future.'

'Do you get help with your car?'

Kate glanced out of the window at her car. 'So, at present we do but we're worried now it might get cut as they tighten up who is eligible. I seem to spend all the time worrying about money now.'

'Same here.'

'What are you worried about?'

'The Independent Living Fund is one I'm worried about and Disability Living Allowance has been replaced by Personal Independence Payments and so I'm worried by that as well. Over the last couple of years, so many changes have taken place. It does feel like I'm being hit from all angles.'

'Yes, P.I.P is one I've been worried about, if I lose that, I lose the car.'

'If I lose it, then I doubt I'll afford my rent.'

'It's terrifying, isn't it? Jonathon's been trying to get me to relax a bit more. In fact, Jonathon has been a lifesaver, ever since I gave up work. Do you have anyone special, like a boyfriend or..?'

'No.' I interrupted. 'Nobody at the moment.' I was thinking about Johan and felt myself blush.

Kate stared across at me, a smile slowly spreading across her face, lighting up her features.

'Oh, sweetie.'

'I don't even know if he likes me.' I lowered my eyes as my face continued to burn. For a moment we both were silent, the only sound the slurping of drinks.

Ten

Janine tried to convince me that the reliance on both my mum and the agency was decreasing due to our favourable stars, but I knew it was due to the art group, the need to produce paintings for The Richmond as well as my growing friendship with Kate. It reminded me of the quote from Henry VIII by Shakespeare, 'to climb steep hills requires a slow pace at first.' My dad used to repeat it when he talked about The Butterfly Collective taking on the art establishment, but the quote could equally refer to my battle to be accepted and independent.

With the next group meeting only a day away, I received a phone call from Lena. She told me Anne was incapacitated with a cold and she was going to take over for the week. My first reaction was one of relief. Despite the art group playing a large part in my quest to be accepted and more independent, the downside was dealing with Anne each week.

Eddie picked me up on Wednesday morning with Lena in the back. He wasn't his usual jaunty, buoyant self and was uncommunicative in the car. I'd not seen Eddie as subdued as that before; usually his ferocious joviality had been all I'd encountered.

When we arrived at the centre Eddie rubbed his temples.

'I've got to take Misty to the dreaded, 'V E T.' She's been very poorly overnight.'

Lena helped me out and as we made our way to the main door, I turned my head towards her.

'Is Misty his cat?'

'No, his dog. After the divorce, all he was left with was Misty. He's worried now he's going to lose her.' Lena unlocked the main door. 'Hopefully he'll be back by the end of the meeting, if not we'll have to make our own way home.'

The tables in the hall were all out ready for us. I put my rucksack down and turned to Lena who had begun to unpack her bag.

'Have you worked with wheelchair users before?'

Lena sat down on one of the chairs and put her hand over her eyes. 'Not exactly, Jim, my late husband, had a neuropathic ulcer on his heel, which then got infected.'

'Oh, I'm sorry.'

'It doesn't end there, I'm afraid.' She fumbled with a finger and thumb down the collar of her blouse, eventually retrieving the silver cross on a chain around her neck. As she talked she held on to it, rubbing it between her fingers.

'The infection spread into his heel bone and ankle, which was when they decided it wasn't viable. Nine months later he died.'

Tentatively, I put my arm around her shoulders. 'Oh Lena, I'm really sorry.'

'What I'm trying to say is I understand how challenging it can be to live with a disability. Nearly every day someone would say to Jim, "What's wrong with you?" Do you get that as well?'

'Yeah, all the time it drives me mad. Those who just stare bug me as well. I call it the two heads treatment.' I stared at Lena with wide eyes and dropped open my mouth and let my tongue hang out.

With a sad smile, Lena let go of her cross and fished a tissue out from her sleeve to blow her nose. 'He used to get annoyed about that too.' She peered at her watch. 'I'd better just get the kettle filled and mugs out.'

Lena boiled the kettle and brought out mugs and the tea and coffee. When she'd finished she leant into the hatch and spoke to me through it.

'What I underestimated was bereavement. Jim and I got married just after I left school. I was only seventeen. So for all my life I was known as Jim's wife. Being without him I felt lost, totally lost.'

She walked back into the hall and sat back down at the table.

'So how did you? I mean, how did you cope?'

'I tried to do it all on my own but that was a disaster. I went to see my GP and thankfully, he could spot immediately what was wrong. He said he could give me antidepressants but was only going to do that as a last resort. He referred me to a counsellor, specialising in bereavement. She really taught me to concentrate on the here and now, and do things to make me feel good about myself. I ended up doing the AINAB courses and got involved in the gallery with Anne.'

'You've done really well. I know it's hard, I lost my dad when I was twelve, so my mum had to try and cope on her own.'

'Twelve's very young to have to deal with bereavement.'

'Yeah, it was harder on my mum, though, I think.'

Lena glanced at the clock on the wall. 'What else do we need to do, Rachel?'

'I think that's it. Oh, do you have the money tin and the register?'

'Sorry, they're in my bag over there. Don't worry, I'll get it.' She walked over to the plastic chairs stacked up at the side of the hall and brought out the register and tin. Before she put them down, she stood next to me, her hand resting on my shoulder.

'Before the others arrive, Rachel, I just wanted to add I was so pleased this group started. Having this each week is something to look forward to, isn't it?'

I gazed up at Lena and it was obvious she had potential as

a leader of the group with her kind, tolerant and thoughtful nature.

After five minutes, Albert and Marion arrived. Albert collapsed onto the chair, and groaned.

'We've just been around the supermarket,' Marion explained with a wink.

When Albert had recovered, he jumped up and gave Lena a kiss on the cheek.

Lena squirmed and with a spare hand wiped the side of her face. She was almost purple in colour and glared at Albert but he ignored her discomfort and for a moment, looked as if he was heading for me. Thankfully the arrival of Kate, followed by Pauline and Elaine distracted him enough to allow me to slot back into my place at the table.

Lena cleared her throat and then gave a gentle tap on the table.

'As you can see, Anne isn't here today; she's got a cold and has left me in charge. Eddie had to take his dog to the vet and will be back later. Does anyone know where Mike is today?'

We all shook our heads.

Albert chuckled to himself. 'Absent without leave ma'am,' he said.

'Thank you Albert. We have a pile of these flyers still to be distributed. I know Eddie and Anne have been putting some up, so if you can all take a few that would be great.' Lena pulled out of her bag a bundle of flyers held together with an elastic band. 'Ok, I'll quickly do the register before we start.'

Half-way through the register, Mike limped in, using only one crutch. With his spare hand he held a framed painting. When he sat down, I turned towards him, ready to smile, but he was examining his dirty fingernails. The painting he'd brought in was the black Labrador/Retriever dog.

After the register had been taken, I turned again to Mike. 'Where's your painting going? Are you giving it to your friend?'

'Nah, I wanted to swap it with the one up there.' He pointed to his watercolour painting up on the wall.

'That's no problem, Mike,' Lena said. 'Do you need a hand changing it over?'

'Nah I'm alright, ta,' Mike muttered. He ambled over to the side of the room.

Marion rapped her knuckles onto the table and asked for quiet.

'We've got news about the paper. We spoke to our neighbour who gave us the phone number of the community news desk. A reporter is coming, not next Wednesday but the Wednesday after.'

'Ooh, that's marvellous, isn't it Pauline?' Elaine said.

Pauline was staring at the painting Mike had just put into position. 'Look at his painting, it's as if it was a photograph.'

Elaine squinted up at the painting. 'Ooh yes, and I do love your frames too.'

Mike shuffled back onto his chair and gave a quick nod in response to the praise.

Marion now banged her fist on the table, her nostrils flared. 'What do you all think of us arranging for us to be in the paper? Or aren't you bothered at all?'

'I think we all want to say a big thank you to Marion, and Albert,' Lena said quickly, 'don't we?'

'Yes, brilliant news.' Kate turned to face me with an arched eyebrow raised.

Lena picked up her paintbrush. 'We'd better get down to some painting, folks, otherwise we won't have anything to exhibit.'

Albert leant across to Marion and whispered a comment behind his hand. When he'd finished Marion glowered down the table at Mike, and then behind her hand, she whispered her reply.

I turned to Mike as he hadn't got any of his art materials out yet.

'What are you painting today?'

'Do you want a ciggie?'

I really wanted to get on with my painting but instead I pulled on my coat. By the time I was ready, Mike was already outside. The smoke from his cigarette led me to him as he paced up and down at the side of the centre.

'Is everything alright, Mike?'

'I can't stay today. I'll have this and get off.'

'But you've paid your money so why don't you just stay for a bit?'

He stood still. 'I didn't pay me money last week. Anyway, I've got to go into Wallaston. I've got an appointment with Cash Today, No Fee or Fuss.'

'Is that who you borrowed money off, for your mum?'

Mike shook his head. 'Nah, that lot have sent me a legal letter. If I don't pay them back, they're taking me to court. So I need to get some money somehow. I'm going to try this other moneylender's place in Weston, to see if they'll give me enough to cover what I owe.'

I held out my hand. 'But that means you'll just be replacing one debt with another. Couldn't you contact the people you've got the debt with and suggest a weekly amount to pay them back, explain your situation to them?'

Mike pulled a face. 'What with? I'm not exactly managing at the moment. I don't know about you, but I'm in arrears now with both me rent and council tax.'

'I know what you mean; it's a lot to deal with.'

'I've not been behind on me rent for ages, but now it's just getting too difficult. There's hardly anything left for eating or keeping me place warm as it is. On top of it all, I've got the review hanging over me head. I'm having seizure after seizure.' He lit another cigarette. 'If this lot give me some money, it'll help a lot.'

'You might be better talking to someone. You know, like a debt charity or C.A.B?'

'You've not told anyone, have you?'

'Course not.'

'I'll come in now and say I've got to get off to see me GP, alright?' He pushed some hair back from over his eyes and tucked it behind his ear. This exposed a red and purple lump at the top side of his forehead.

'That looks sore.'

He self-consciously pulled some hair over to cover the lump. 'I'd a seizure the other day and whacked me head on the side of the cupboard.'

'Are you on tablets for that?'

'Sort of, but they make me really knackered, so I don't always take 'em. Anyway I'm going in to get me stuff, OK?'

He threw his cigarette near to the fence between the centre and the library and walked back into the centre. I followed him in, and as I wheeled past Lena, I heard him say he needed to go to his GP appointment.

'Good luck, hope you get it,' I whispered, as Mike grabbed his bag.

'Ta, Rachel, see you next week.'

On his way out Lena asked whether he wanted one or two tables at the art sale.

Mike held up his forefinger.

Lena turned to me, 'Rachel, how many tables?'

'Only one thanks, Lena.'

Lena pushed her glasses up the bridge of her nose. 'Right, so everybody wants one table apart from Eddie, Anne, Johan and Fiona who all want two. Now what's happening about the website plan, Kate?'

'So, I've been thinking about it. The best way to do it would be through Facebook. I would set up a central page for Art for You, and then everyone would join this page by doing one of their own. Now, I know some will need a bit of help. I can assist and Rachel has offered to give a hand too.'

'I've avoided computers as much as I can, but my daughter and husband are on Facebook so they can help me and Elaine.' replied Pauline.

'I'll help with Marion and Albert, and Eddie if he needs it,' said Kate.

'What, do you want me to do the rest?' I asked.

Kate nodded. 'We really need this to be done ready for the art sale. It only takes a few minutes to do.'

'You can't buy paintings from this?' Marion mumbled.

'You can put a price on them, but no, someone wouldn't be able to buy straight from the page; they'd have to get in touch with you by email or you'd need a PayPal account. Logistically, it could be a nightmare, a real nightmare.'

'Have the grocery shop and the Post Office got the new flyers up?' Pauline said. She dangled her paintbrush in a glass of water.

'I don't think so. Anne was trying to get as many places as possible covered but I think this cold has been putting her a bit behind schedule. The Vines could do with one as well,' Lena explained. 'You could always take some up there yourself.'

Pauline whispered behind her hand to Elaine before she leant over the table towards me.

'Would you like to come with me, Rachel?'

'Me?' I pointed at my chest.

'Yes, what do you say?'

For a moment I was silent, and tried to work out why she'd asked me, but eventually agreed making it clear I couldn't get into The Vines without help.

'Great, here you are then.' Lena pulled a few flyers out from the bundle and pushed them across the table to Pauline.

I put on my coat and waited for Pauline to get ready.

'Are you OK, do you want me to push?'

'Nope, I'm fine. I might need a push on the way back.'

'So how long have you been painting, Rachel?'

'Since school really, but after my accident I've found it to be a life saver. What about you?'

'I only started after a nasty incident at work; it helped me cope, and to relax.'

I was getting tired and momentarily stopped wheeling.

'Do you want to stop for a breather?'

'Thanks.'

'Can you manage to get to the estate agent's cross the road? Then I can sit on the bench with you.'

'Fine,' I gasped.

The wooden bench had a bronze plaque, the inscription now too worn to be legible.

Pauline perched on the end and stretched out her legs. With the side of her forefinger she rubbed underneath her nostrils.

'The nasty incident I was talking about was when one of my clients, a woman not much older than you, killed herself.'

As she talked she started to rub the top of her left arm up and down.

'It affected me dreadfully and I don't think people realise working in public services you see or deal with terrible things.'

'It must've been awful.'

'It was. I keep on going over what I said, whether I was to blame.' Pauline stood up and stared at the traffic. 'I didn't know she was so troubled. Nobody shared that information. All I knew was she was recovering from a broken hip. It was dreadful. For months I could hardly speak. I had nightmares, everything. I still sometimes wake up in a panic about it.'

'I'm sorry.'

'If it wasn't for art and for Elaine, I'd be in a right mess.'

I didn't know what else to say, so gazed out at the traffic, where an old tractor was spitting and spluttering as it chugged down the road.

'I'd understand if someone like you felt like you'd had

enough. The woman who killed herself didn't have half the problems you have.'

'Shall we both go in?' I asked, desperate for a change of subject.

Pauline nodded; we went straight to the counter and found we were behind five other people.

'So art was something you and Elaine could do together?'

'Yes, it's been a hobby really. Both of us are a bit unsure about selling our work. What to put in the exhibition? What price to put paintings at and so on?'

'I get into trouble because I don't charge a lot for my paintings. I think art should be for everyone and available to anyone, whether you're rich or poor.'

At the checkout, Pauline confidently held out her hand and started to shake the young assistant's hand in an exaggerated manner. The assistant looked baffled and uncomfortable.

'Hello love, we're having an art sale, with most of the paintings done by older people and younger disabled people.' Pauline gestured in my direction and would've hit me if I hadn't ducked.

'Do you want it on our community notice board?'

'Yes, super.'

'Do you want to buy anything?'

'No, just to have this up on the notice board would be fabulous, thanks.'

'OK, give it to me, I'll do it later.' The assistant took the flyer and then leant to one side. 'Who's next?'

'I wish I was as confident as you.' I immediately regretted the sarcastic tone, but Pauline didn't pick up on it.

'Thirty years of working with the public and I've not lost my touch.'

I stopped for a moment and stretched my hands. 'Is it The Vines next?'

'Yes, and then cross the road to the Post Office, cross back over and then we're done.'

We carried on down the main road. When I stopped to catch my breath, I pointed across the road, to my street.

'I live down there.'

Pauline bent down. 'Anne told me the house was already adapted when you moved in?'

I concentrated on adjusting my wheelchair gloves.

'The Local Authority would've probably paid for most of the adaptations. Didn't you know that?'

'Yeah, but it would've taken ages. I needed to move in quickly, it seemed the best way to do it. It's never happened to me before, finding a fully adapted home for rent, so I had to act quickly to get it.'

'Surely, you've got some of your compensation left?'

We reached The Vines.

'I'll wait outside and have a cigarette,' I said, pleased I'd avoided answering her question.

'OK, see you in a minute.' Pauline bounded up the steps.

A couple of minutes later she walked back down shaking her head.

'No joy there. They only put flyers up advertising groups who meet in the pub. Come on; let's go to the Post Office, before we get soaked.' She looked up at the low level, dark grey clouds that hugged the length of the high street like a rippled blanket, and threatened to smother us in mist, fog and rain.

We waited to cross the main road.

'You've sold paintings, haven't you? Do you enjoy selling?' Pauline asked.

I was just going to reply when my blue-rinsed elderly neighbour, appeared and over my head spoke to Pauline.

'I do think she's marvellous and so brave.'

'Oh, hi Dot, yes she's super, really super.'

I cringed. In my mind this was pity, just expressed in a different way.

When we crossed the road, my neighbour turned right, as we turned left to go to the Post Office.

'I'm sorry but that really does my head in. She doesn't even know me. Just because I'm in a wheelchair she thinks I'm amazing. If she thinks that why hasn't she spoken to me?'

Pauline shook her head, 'I never get it, why someone like you doesn't just take a compliment for what it is. All Dot was saying was how much she admired you. You had some brute ruining your life in a car crash, you don't moan about it you just get on with it.'

'You don't know me and neither does Dot.'

'What did you say?'

'Nothing.' My mood was plummeting.

'OK, I'll just nip in to the post office, are you all right here a minute?'

After two minutes I saw the woman from the Post Office display the flyer in the window, Pauline walked out with a beaming smile. 'She's lovely, put it in the window straight away. Can you see it?'

I nodded.

'Right let's go back. Are you sure you don't want me to push?'

I shook my head

'See you are brave, just like Dot said. I know you said you didn't like being called that, but there are folk out there, making out they're sick when really they're pulling a fast one. I suppose it's why I agree with the government over welfare reform. For too long people who are playing the system haven't been challenged. Just like these health tourists.'

I didn't reply, so we made our way back to the centre in silence. I started to get tired and my back was hurting but I didn't want to ask for help from Pauline. I couldn't imagine ever being friends with her. The only thing we had in common was art and even that was tenuous at best.

'Have I upset you?'

'I just think sometimes people have no right to judge.'

'All I'm saying is there are some who're genuine and some who aren't. An assessment will weed out the ones who are making stuff up. Come on; don't get moody with me just because I spoke my mind.' She stopped walking and had one hand on her hip.

'I'm not getting moody.'

'Let's not go in there like this. I'm sorry if I offended you. I wasn't talking about you anyway. I was talking about those who are playing the system. We were talking about art, who's your favourite artist?'

I wanted to be able to say my dad but it might result in questions I didn't want to answer. Instead, I said one of my dad's favourite artists.

'Adolf Wolfli'

'I've not heard of him. Is he German? I suppose he is with a name like Adolf.'

'No, Swiss.'

'Oh right. Well, I think my favourite is Sir Anthony Gormley. I think his men on the beach at Crosby in Merseyside are wonderful. I've got a theory that the men represent all of us, lonely souls wanting to connect.'

We were just about to go back in to the centre.

Pauline opened the door for me. 'Pals again?'

I looked at my knees.

We rejoined the group. Eddie had returned and seemed to be more relaxed than when I saw him this morning.

Pauline carried on this topic of favourite artists and least favourite artists. It was all back to being good natured and I took part in the discussion.

'Who's your favourite artist alive or dead?' Pauline asked Eddie, who was just sitting down.

'I think I'd have to say Cezanne.'

'Right, so we've got Eddie with Cezanne, I like Sir Anthony Gormley. Lena, what's yours again?'

'I'm in Eddie's era, I like Gauguin. I love the Post-Impressionist period.'

'And yours, Rachel, again?'

'Adolf Wolfli.' Out of the corner of my eye I saw Kate write something on her hand.

'I know Elaine's without even asking, it's Van Gogh.'

'How did you guess?' Elaine said with a grin.

Pauline turned to Kate. 'Kate, who's your favourite, alive or dead?'

'It's got to be Andrew Marr.'

'From the TV?' Eddie asked.

Kate nodded. 'He's very talented.'

'Marion and Albert, who do you like?'

'I'm a big fan of Cezanne,' Marion said.

Albert puffed out his chest. 'I never used to rate this chap but over time I've got more into his work, he is, of course, our very own David Hockney.'

'Gosh, imagine if all those artists were in our group?' Lena said laughing. 'Maybe one day the Art for You group will be an art movement talked about by other artists.'

As conversations began up and down and across the table, I wished I'd been able to mention my dad and the Butterfly Collective, though I hadn't got that many memories of the group as a whole. One memory was when they'd arrive at our house. I used to be going to bed around the same time. On more than one occasion I was woken up when they left, as doors slammed and voices were raised. Whenever my dad mentioned the Collective he'd add the tagline 'out of something ugly something beautiful will appear.' Each time he'd say it, the look of disgust on my mum's face would grow more pronounced.

'Are you alright, kiddo?' Eddie said, as he ruffled my hair. 'What's going around that head of yours?'

'Just thinking about the art sale, that's all.'

'Are you alright to go in a minute? Get yourself ready and I'll have a quick word with Lena.' He patted down my hair.

'How's Misty?'

'She's alright thanks, she'll live another day. My fault, I shouldn't share my curry with her. Do you want to see a photo of her?'

Before I'd chance to reply, Eddie fished out his phone and after locating a photo passed it to me. I stared at a mangy, underweight, old dog and attempted a smile.

'She looks, erm, looks...' I was lost for words.

'Beautiful. I know. She's just had a haircut in that photo.' His face was flushed with pride.

Eleven

In my study, Janine was helping me photograph my paintings for my Facebook page. I held out my hand so it was flat and raised it up.

'Higher, try to have it so it covers your face.'

She held the painting up but I could still see her eyebrows and forehead.

'Just a bit higher.'

She lifted up the painting with one leg in front bent slightly, the other leg straight behind, as if she was a weightlifter.

'Brilliant, just hold it there a minute.' I took a photograph. It looked comical; the body of a woman with a painting instead of a head. Her Concerned about Care tunic was visible but I hoped once it'd been cropped it wouldn't be too noticeable.

'How many more have we got to do?' Her face was now nearly cadmium red, the colour of the poppies I'd painted.

'Only four. Are you OK, do you need a break?'

'No, let's push on.'

When I'd photographed five paintings we went back downstairs. I uploaded the paintings and sent a 'Friend Request' to the Art for You site Kate had created. While I waited for her response, I examined her page and then looked at Eddie's.

Janine leant against the living room wall, excavating with her finger inside her left ear.

'Have you got a couple of minutes?' I asked.

She straightened up. 'Why? What needs doing?'

'What do you think about these paintings? They're Eddie's, a guy from our art group.'

Janine sat next to me on the sofa as I showed her Eddie's Facebook page.

'I really like that one.' She pointed to his painting of a street in Weston, the same painting I'd admired at Garden and Crafts for You.

'That would easily sell, if he put it just a bit cheaper.'

On Eddie's page there was a link to Fiona's website, which was very professional and included a diary of classes and workshops she did. It also included a blog called 'Fiona's Fantasy.'

'I'm not being funny, but that doesn't half sound like a dirty book,' Janine said, with a grin.

'You must have read one to know that.'

'I've read Fifty Shades of Grey, but it wasn't anything special. What about you? Have you read it?'

I shook my head vehemently.

In amongst Fiona's pictures of paintings, I found a photograph that appeared to be completely out of place. It was a small speedboat and had been sent to Fiona from Eddie. The caption read, 'I'll never forget the ride in your boat, Ed xx.' I nudged Janine and silently pointed it out.

'This is like a private detective, snooping to try and work out if that guy and her are an item.'

'What? You think I'm snooping?'

'No. So do you think they are, y'know..?'

'I don't know, not for sure, anyway. If they're together, I reckon there must be at least a twenty year age gap.'

Janine stood up and swiped the air with her hand. 'That's nothing; one of my mum's boyfriends was nearly thirty years older than her. Listen, Rachel, I'd best be off soon. The time just flew, didn't it?'

Janine let herself out and for a moment I relished how she seemed to be becoming more of a friend than a carer. It was such a contrast to how life was at the bungalow where I couldn't confide in any of the guards. Anything I said was written down and shared with managers. It meant I became increasingly paranoid and nervous.

The ping of my mobile brought me back to life in Carthom. The message said my friend request had been accepted by Kate and I couldn't help but smile as I wished real life friendships could be made as easily as that.

I spent the afternoon doing individual price labels and signs for my art sale paintings, using my calligraphy pens. When I finished, I wheeled into the living room and momentarily glanced out of my window. Anne was standing by my gate, her arms wrapped around her body. Her presence unnerved me, as I wondered how long she'd been there. I opened the door just as she was about to knock, her fist poised mid-air.

She wanted to drop off some extra flyers for the art sale so I reluctantly invited her in. While I made the drinks, she coughed and blew her nose.

'How's the cold?' I asked, as I handed her a cup of tea.

Anne sat down at my kitchen table, and nursed her drink.

It's a bit better, thanks.'

'Anne, are Eddie and Fiona more than just friends, they seem rather close.'

She grimaced and bent down, bringing her bag onto her knee.

'Close? Yes, you could say they're more than close.'

'Are they seeing each other then? I thought Fiona was married?'

'She's married, but they do have history.' She put her hands under the seat of her chair and using her feet and bottom shuffled closer to me.

'If I tell you something, you must promise not to breathe a word.'

'I don't gossip.'

'Well, you know when Eddie says he's retired or was made redundant? That's actually codswallop because he was sacked. The truth is, in his office there was a lot, and I mean a lot, of drinking. Eddie's one of those people who can't say no.' She paused for a moment and then added in a whisper, 'Where someone might have one or two drinks, Eddie would have five or six. They'd be doubles, as well.' Anne stretched out her hand and tapped with her forefinger on my kitchen table. 'After this was going on for a while, his poor wife had enough and walked out. This was quickly followed by him losing his job. I think all that must have given him the shove he needed to go to Alcoholics Anonymous. While he was there, who does he meet, but Fiona? She acted as his sponsor and ever since then they've been 'friends'.' Anne made air quotes with her fingers.

'So are they just friends then?'

'I'm not sure. It looks like more than friends from where I'm standing. Why? Have you heard something?'

'No, I was just checking Eddie's Facebook page.'

Anne wagged her finger at me. 'That's what I wanted to talk to you about. How do I get my paintings into this Facebook? What do I need to do?'

'I just need to help you set up an account. You've got email, haven't you?'

'I don't want to have to pay, if I can help it.'

'No, it's free but you do need an email address.'

'Email? Yes, I've got email. Well, I pay for it, I think, but I don't use it. I pay for everything on my electric bill.'

I held back a smile. 'Do you know your email address? It will be Anne at something mail, dot, com or dot, co, dot, uk.'

'I think it's in my diary.'

'OK. When I set up the account, you use your email and a password and then you start transferring photographs of your paintings, which I'll do, onto your Facebook page and then you'll join the Art for You page. It'll only take about ten minutes. I'll need to come over to your place.'

'Is it safe? I watched a programme about cyborgcrime last night.'

'I think you're safe from Cyborgs but Cybercrime is what most people are worried about these days. If it's only going to be your paintings and no other personal details bar your name, then I don't think there'll be a problem. Kate and I are both on Facebook, but if you need more time th..'

'Time?' Anne interrupted. She shook her head. 'No, I don't need any time; I just need to know how to do it. I did try to learn about computers and had a lesson a while ago. The teacher was hopeless. He did everything so fast. There I was, sat like an idiot, not being able to follow him.'

I could see her mood switch before me, her gloomy, grim expression a warning for me to wrap the conversation up.

'So can I come round this evening? Or tomorrow?'

'What about tomorrow? I could pick you up before tea and I'll cook you something nice when we've done it, and bring you back home.'

'That sounds great, thank you.'

The next day I cancelled my tea time carers and got ready to go to Anne's. Along with my catheters and painkillers, I put my iPad, notebook and pen in case she wanted anything written down on paper.

With my bag packed and my coat on I waited in my hallway

for the toot of Anne's car. She arrived on time and before long, I was in her living room, warming myself in front of her fire.

Without the Christmas tree, her living room looked huge and without the decorations, I noticed how chintzy the decor was. Flowers were everywhere, on the wallpaper, rug, cushions, throws, and even on the lampshades. In the corner of the room by the French windows, I saw her desk with an ancient computer and printer. When the sunlight moved, I could see a layer of dust on the computer and managed to resist the urge to write 'USE ME' with my fingers.

'I hope you're going to go easy on me. I feel quite nervous about this.' She passed to me a mug of coffee, before she brought in her own cup of tea. When she sat down, she picked up a small blue diary from a side table.

'The email address is in here. I put all the important things down in here. My bank account number, everything.'

'Good. Do you want to see the Art for You Facebook page while you have your tea? Just to look at it, you don't need to do anything.'

'On this?' Anne waved her hand towards her computer.

'No, I'll show you on my iPad.' I pulled it out from my bag, quickly logging on to the Art for You Facebook page.

'Aren't those things terribly expensive?'

'They're not as expensive as they used to be. I was lucky I got this for Christmas from my brother, Colin.'

'Colin?' She frowned. 'You don't talk about him much do you?'

'I don't see him that much that's why,' I said brusquely. He's busy with work, and where he lives isn't very accessible either.'

'What does he do?'

'He works for an advertising agency.'

'Doing art?'

'No, he's more into designing. He works a lot with computers.' I looked down at my iPad. 'Right, I've got the page.'

Anne half stood up, and carefully took the iPad from me. 'Oh, there's our flyer, and there's the one about the art sale. So that's Eddie. Oh, hang on what's happened? I've lost it.' She quickly thrust the iPad back on to my lap.

'It's OK, it does that sometimes.'

As I began to log on again, she walked over to me and crouched down.

'If you tap where it says photo album, you can see my paintings.'

She put on her glasses from where they were sitting on top of her head and squinted at the screen. 'Where?'

I moved the iPad closer to her and tapped on the album.

'Oh my goodness, that's excellent. Who's that, holding your paintings?'

'Janine, my cleaner. What I'm showing you is what I can do for you. So, after our drinks I need to photograph your paintings.'

When we'd finished our drinks, I followed Anne to her spare room, which was opposite the room with all the rubbish. All around me were framed paintings, some stacked up on the floor and above me were shelves with boxes and frames. There was a drop leaf table at the side that had on it canvas boards, paper and paints. Next to it, on the floor, were five small brown cardboard boxes on top of each other. Above them on a shelf were ten greeting cards each with a flowery design on the front apart from one with a Christmas design.

'Are these your cards, did you paint them?'

She slapped her palm on her forehead. 'Don't ever make them, Rachel. They hardly ever sell and cost a bomb to get them printed. See those boxes below them. Open the top one and you'll see what I mean.'

I carefully opened the top box, nervous I would knock the tower over. I peeked into it and saw a pile of cards with a crease in the middle.

'Are these all cards?' I pointed to the other boxes.

'I got one hundred printed of each design. I've not broke even yet.'

'You should take some to the art sale; sell them alongside your paintings.'

She leant against the drop leaf table. 'I'm not sure. They don't sell. Do you think six paintings are enough for the Facebook? You'd put five or six on it, didn't you?'

'I put on it the ones I was most pleased with and the ones I was going to take to the art sale.'

Anne, in all, chose ten paintings, which she took to the lounge. Most of them were acrylics apart from one or two watercolour landscapes. I recognised a couple of them from the gallery at Garden and Crafts for You.

When we'd photographed them all, I uploaded her photographs and asked her to sit at her computer so I could show her how to get onto Facebook. After each step I wrote what I was doing onto a piece of paper. When we eventually got to her page she was taken aback by how good it looked.

'Rachel, I just can't believe it!' She wiped her forehead. 'My paintings on the wide world web at last. Thank you, so much. Do you think my Theresa or Katie would see this?'

'If she put your name in, she would see it. It might be easier the other way around and you put your daughter's name into the search engine. Do you want to have a go now?'

'Now? No, not now. I'll have to think about it. If I need help I'll give you a tinkle.'

'No problem. All we need to do now is send a friendship request to the Art for You page. Kate's looking after this. Go back over to there.' I showed her what to do. 'When Kate's got it, you'll be on the Art for You page alongside Fiona and Eddie Now, do you want me to show you anything else while I'm here?'

'I think that's enough for today, I'm hungry now, are you?'

'Yeah, fairly hungry.'

'Normally I just put everything into my slow cooker, but

today I haven't been out to the shops. Is a chippy tea OK?'

'That'd be lovely but I didn't bring my purse. I can give you the money when we...'

Anne shook her head. 'Don't worry, you've just got me on the internet, I was going to make your tea anyway. I'll go now, are you OK for ten minutes or so?'

I nodded. 'No problem.'

After a few minutes I wheeled over to her French windows. The weak sunlight glimmered through the branches of the trees, and illuminated clumps of grass, in a hopscotch-like pattern on her lawn. There was large weeping willow tree at the back, which reminded me of my garden when I was young. It was about the same size, with a large ash tree at the back. I could picture myself running up and down, doing cartwheels and having water fights with my brother. For a moment, I smiled at the memories, but when I saw my reflection in the window, I turned away.

On her wall there were nine framed photographs. A black and white photograph of a chubby baby and another of a girl in pigtails wearing a school uniform stood out. I assumed they were photos of Theresa.

There was also a photograph of Anne when she was probably about my age, leaning back on a fence. It must have been in the seventies as she was wearing an all in one purple jumpsuit with long collars and flared trouser legs. Another photograph showed her a bit older, this time she was holding hands with an elderly man but she seemed tense.

The key being opened in the lock made me jump. I got out my mobile and pretended to look at it when Anne put her head around through the living room door.

'Do you want salt and vinegar on this?'

'Yes, do you want me to help?'

'No I can manage. I'll be back in a jiffy.' She disappeared back into the kitchen.

Anne brought the two plates in, so we could eat our tea on

our knees. I needed a cushion to help me do this, which she provided.

'You were asking me about Eddie and Fiona earlier? Well, if you were to put me on the spot, I'd say there's something going on. He's very, what's the word? He's always touching her.'

'Tactile?'

'Yes, that's the word. Eddie has nothing to lose now, nothing at all. Fiona's different, mind. She's got two gorgeous little boys and her husband's lovely. Alright, good for them to have given up drinking, they don't need to celebrate in bed, do they? They don't think about the cost? It's left to the likes of you and me to worry about the damage they're causing.'

I nodded.

She picked up two chips with her fork. 'I think it looks as if Eddie's on heat, squeezing her legs, stroking her hair. It makes me very uncomfortable, like it's some great big secret between them.'

'Albert's a bit like it too isn't he? He's a bit touchy-feely over women.'

'Yes, but the difference is he's like it all the time, with everyone. Eddie's only like this with Fiona. I told you Albert wanted to go out with me, didn't I?'

'I think so.'

'You won't tell a soul, will you? Eddie can get awfully cross, especially if he thinks folk have been talking about him.'

'I don't goss...' I stopped speaking mid sentence as I knew I'd initiated the conversation about Eddie and Fiona.

We finished our tea and Anne wanted to know if Lena had done a Facebook page.

'Lena and Mike both need one doing.'

'Lena won't be able to do it because she's not got the internet.'

'She's not online at all?'

Anne shook her head. 'No, so she won't be able to do it, will she?'

'The only way she could do it is if I took some photographs of her paintings and then put them in a separate album on your page or mine, saying they are Lena's paintings. Just like we used to have albums for different holiday snaps, you can have different albums on Facebook.'

'You've lost me a bit, but I could ring, if you want, see if we could do it once we're ready to go? It would save a second journey for you. She only lives two minutes away, down the road and round a corner, as my mother used to say.'

'OK, ring her then.'

Anne spoke to Lena and after finding out she was free, told her we would be over soon. As she was chatting away, I thought about Mike, if I was able to set up his Facebook page, it might be a good opportunity to talk about the help available regarding his debt.

'Right, she doesn't want many up, just three for the time being. It won't take long, will it? It's a big week; we find out who really killed her.'

'Who's been killed?'

She giggled. 'It's on Corry! You thought it was real life, didn't you? Mind, I must admit, there's times when I'm so taken up by the story that I feel it's real life.'

'By the way, did you know the week after next there will be a reporter from the local paper at the group?'

Anne nodded. 'Yes, Marion phoned me on Wednesday night to let me know. They've done well, haven't they? I was also thinking we haven't got many tables left, so should it just be our lot and say, Fiona and Johan but leave it at that. What do you think?'

'Yeah, if it was just Art for You members and friends, yeah, that makes sense.'

'I'm really hoping I make a few bob at it. I think we've got a good chance. Do you?'

'I hope so. It's always a bit of a surprise when you've not had one before, in terms of who comes, and who doesn't. So, yeah, fingers crossed.'

I'd finished my food and I could see my mobile flashing.

Anne nodded towards my mobile. 'Who's that? Kate?'

'Yeah, you've been accepted as a friend for the Art for You page.'

She eased herself up from her armchair. 'Are you ready now? Shall we head off to see Lena?'

Lena lived in a large sheltered housing complex on the edge of Carthom. From the outside it had the appearance of a private clinic or small hospital, with pretty gardens at the front. A sign near the main door said, 'Beech Hill', despite the lack of Beech trees and the area being completely flat. Inside, the blue carpets were well-worn and the cream walls needed a fresh layer of paint. The temperature was unbearably hot and I soon found myself sweating. They'd tried to make it look more comfortable with easy chairs clumped together in twos or fours at the end of corridors, and photographs and paintings on the wall.

I followed Anne as we meandered down the long corridor and before long we encountered an old lady wearing odd slippers with her stockings gathered around her ankles. She wanted to pat and fuss over me.

Lena opened her door and before we had chance to speak, the old lady grabbed Lena's forearm.

'Is that your daughter?' The old woman peered at Lena and pointed directly at my face.

Lena shook her left arm. 'Vera get off me.' With her right arm she pointed down the corridor. 'Go back to the lounge. These are my visitors.'

'Isn't she your daughter?'

She hurriedly ushered us through her door and shut it with a bang.

'I'm so sorry, but she's just had me up to here today.' Lena indicated above her head. 'Do either of you fancy a drink?'

'Drink? No, I think we're alright, aren't we?' Anne said, glancing at me.

I nodded. 'I'm fine Lena, thanks. Have you got the paintings you want to use?'

All I could see in her tiny living room was Poole pottery. It was on every surface possible; even the bookcase had one shelf free from books and instead was used to display the blue and white pottery. It made me nervous in case I knocked something over.

Lena walked slowly over to behind the television where she'd put a sheet over some paintings.

'These are the three I want put on it,' she said, as she dragged off the sheet.

'OK, let's photograph the first one.'

She pulled out a frame with a delicate watercolour painting of dark pink, yellow and blue pansies.

After I'd taken the photograph, I looked up at her.

'What do you want to call this?'

'Can you just put pansies and then my name?'

On my mobile I entered the details. Next was another floral picture, this time pink roses painted in acrylics on canvas. Finally she dragged out a large painting; this was painted in watercolours and the style was so different it could've been painted by a different artist. It was framed and showed an elderly man sitting near a window. His face was illuminated by the light, the reflection evident in his grey-blue watery eyes. She'd even picked out the light brown age spots and purple veins on his hands, as well as skilfully painting the folds in his clothes.

'This is brilliant, really brilliant. What do you want me to call this?'

'Can you just call it Jim please?' Lena pulled out her cross and chain from under her blouse and started to rub it between her fingers.

'Is this..?'

'Yes it's him. This one's not for sale. It usually goes there.' She pointed to a hook on the wall behind her sofa. It was obvious where it'd been because the un-faded area was the same size as it.

Anne stood in front of the painting, then with one step back she leaned to the left, and then to the right.

'You're lucky you were able to do this.'

Lena's face clouded for a second before giving a half nod to Anne. 'Yes, yes, I suppose I was. One day, I just thought I needed to do it.' She wiped her eyes with the back of her finger.

I wheeled closer to photograph it and then checked the image. 'Did he sit for you, or did you use a photo?'

Lena shook her head and interrupted me. 'Jim wouldn't have let me paint him. It was bad enough trying to take a photograph of him, without him protesting. No, it was after he died, I used a photograph and grid. It took me months and months to finish it.'

I carefully wheeled up towards her French windows and shook my mobile but was still losing the connection. 'I'll have to add these to Anne's site when I get back home, as the signal here isn't very strong. Is that OK?'

She put the paintings back behind the TV and draped the sheet back over them.

'That's fine, Rachel. Thank you.'

'We'll have to leave you and love you, as I want to get back in time for the soaps starting. You're finished now, aren't you, Rachel?'

I nodded.

Lena showed us out, first giving Anne a quick peck on her cheek, before she crouched down and hugged me.

On the way back to my home, Anne was very quiet. I broke the silence first.

'The painting of her husband, it was in a totally different style. I've not seen Lena do watercolour paintings in the group

126

yet.'

'She used to do watercolours all the time, but since her eyesight has got worse, she's been doing acrylics. When I first saw her painting of Jim, I went straight home to try it myself. I tried to paint my daughter but I couldn't do it. It wasn't my painting skills, mind, it was emotionally, and something mentally stopped me from painting her. I don't know how she managed it, I really don't.'

'I saw the photographs in your living room, are those photos of your daughter?'

'Photos? Oh, I know exactly what you're going to say. How can I look at photos of them?'

'I'm only asking because I find it really hard to look at pictures of when I was younger.'

'If I didn't have them up, it would be like that part of my life had just disappeared. I think it would make me feel even worse. Just say, my daughter turned up on my doorstep. Can you imagine what she would think if I didn't have photographs of her up? And they're almost a comfort at times. It helps me remember. Mind, there are times I stop and I do just break down and cry.'

Anne gripped the wheel, her white knuckle bones looked as if they could pierce through her translucent skin.

For the rest of the journey we sat in an uncomfortable silence. I wanted to be able to hug her and tell her everything would be alright, but I didn't think she was ever going to find peace or even closure on this issue. The intensity and depth of her sadness was familiar and frightening at the same time.

Twelve

Out of all the art group members, I thought Mike was the artist with the most chance of making his Facebook page work. It only took five minutes of looking at other pages on the site, to see how many people were posting photographs of their pets. If he priced them reasonably and set up a way of getting sales then I thought it might help his financial situation. I only had his page left to do, so while the art group members were arriving for the next meeting, I loitered near the main door ready to persuade him to do it. I knew he was reluctant to have his work online, but hoped to convince him over a cigarette. When he arrived, I pointed to the bench.

'Just got your Facebook page to do Mike. Do you want to do it at mine or..?'

Mike interrupted me. 'I don't want anything online, Rachel. I'm sorry but I just don't.'

He limped to the bench and after retrieving a crumpled up packet of cigarettes from his back pocket, eased himself down. He gazed ahead and pulled out a cigarette, tapping it two times before he cupped it in his hands to light it.

'Why? You're really talented. Everyone thinks so.'

'I don't think I am. Anyway, I'm not online; I haven't even got a computer.'

'Lena isn't online but she's put paintings up. As for your artwork, I reckon your dogs could prove to be really popular.'

Mike pulled a face. 'Maybe, but I can't see the point of having me artwork up, OK?'

We both turned to stare at the road at the same time. Two refined looking ladies with haughty smiles and long blonde manes were bobbing up and down in the saddles of almost identical dapple grey horses.

As they trotted past the centre, I turned towards him. 'It's another world, isn't it?'

He ignored me and continued to puff on his cigarette.

'Is it because of the Benefits situation that you don't want your paintings on..?'

Mike shook his head and interrupted me. 'Nah, it's because I just can't see the point.'

I shrugged my shoulders. 'Alright, alright, I won't ask you again.'

For a few minutes we sat and smoked in silence.

'You didn't tell me how you got on with your loan,' I said eventually.

'I got it, though it didn't cover what I owed but at least it stopped them going after me in court.' Mike stretched out his legs and with one hand massaged his knee. 'I haven't heard a dickey-bird about my Benefits either, so I reckon it means I'm OK.'

'Oh, that's good.'

'I think everything had been making me a bit stressed, but thank God, things seem to be improving. Are you coming in?'

Even though I didn't believe he was calm at all, I didn't press him further. I followed him in but as he turned left to go into the hall, I wheeled straight ahead and joined Kate in the kitchen as she made a cup of coffee.

'Are you OK?' I whispered.

'Why are we whispering?'

'Because, I've tried to get Mike onto Facebook but he's still saying he doesn't want to be online.'

'He may change his mind when he sees everyone else has done one.'

'I don't think he will, to be honest.' I was ready to take her mug. 'Do you want a hand?'

'No, I'm OK thanks.' She lifted up her arm to show me she was only using one crutch.

I wheeled back into the hall and slotted into my place just as Marion and Albert were revealing their strategy for the art sale.

'What we're going to do, is take fourteen paintings each, so we can put seven out on each table and as each one sells we can then replace it with another one.'

Pauline frowned. 'I was only going to take six paintings.' She turned to Eddie. 'Do you think I should take more?'

Eddie sat up straight. 'It's better to have more and not sell than know if you'd brought more you'd have sold more.'

Anne stood up. 'Today, I'm going to do the plan where all the tables will go. Basically, they'll be around the sides.' She made a few illustrative gestures with her hands. 'Though, we can't put tables or chairs across fire doors, or, for that matter, across the door into the small hall. If anyone wants a particular spot then come and ask me.' Anne bent over the table and put on her glasses as she read from her notebook. 'Marion and Albert have managed to get a reporter to come and do an article about us. I imagine they'll want a group shot of us, so if we all bring a painting for next week. OK, that's all for now.'

Elaine looked across at Eddie. 'How do you know what price you should sell your paintings? Some folk are still hard up.'

'I find it helps to think about what the minimum and maximum you'd charge for each piece of work, then adjust it within that range depending on how rich or poor your customers are.'

'I usually try to have a mix of prices,' I said. 'So there's something for everybody.'

'Something for everybody?' Anne gave an exasperated sigh. 'Rachel, you undersell your work. OK, everybody might be able to buy it, but it means other paintings look expensive compared with yours.'

'All I was saying was there's a good way to meet all price brackets by having a mix of prices.' My hands had started to tremble.

'Hey, time out you two,' Eddie said with a nervous laugh. With his hands he made a 'T' sign. 'Pricing's a very personal subject, for some here art is a hobby for others it's their main income. We have to respect that in each other.'

Eddie's intervention brought peace and calm back to the group. After a few minutes, I could hear Albert talking to Anne about where he wanted his tables. After Albert, I saw Eddie point to the back of the hall and ask Anne if his tables could be next to Fiona and near to Johan. I didn't think there was going to be any point in saying where I wanted my table, I was sure it wouldn't make any difference where it was.

Later in the morning, Anne got up and walked around the table, handing out to each member a copy of the plan showing where the tables would be. As the details of this were being absorbed there was silence in the group.

I got my sheet of paper and found my name first and then looked to see where everyone else was. Anne had put her table in front of the hatch so anyone buying a drink or a cake would see her work. I was near the back next to Mike and Johan, opposite to me was Kate. So, overall, I was happy with where I was.

Eddie was the first member to express an opinion. He got up and leant over her shoulder and with his pencil pointed at the sheet of paper in front of her.

'I said I wanted to be next to Fiona. Why can't you put someone else where you've put Fiona and put her tables by mine?'

'I'd prefer it if Marion and I could be together and not be between a fire door. There's nothing I want to have between us, my love, especially not a fire door!' Albert blew a kiss to his wife.

'It's not like you've not got the best place, Anne,' Eddie grumbled. He picked up his sheet of paper and sat back down.

Anne had visibly slumped in her chair with her head between her hands as she stared down at her plan.

'If you're moving people around, I think Elaine and I, well, like Albert we've got this door keeping us apart.' Pauline pointed at the door leading to the small hall.

Kate turned to Pauline with a quick smile. 'So, it's not as if it's the Berlin Wall is it? After all, it's only a door.'

Pauline scowled. 'Yes, but if we're sitting there all day we want to be sitting next to each other.'

Anne pushed her chair back and stood up. She picked up her piece of paper, and in what seemed like an act of both despair and defiance crumpled it up and let it drop it into the small bin near the door. She went into the kitchen, slamming the door behind her.

When no one went to see if she was alright, I wheeled into the kitchen and found her leaning against the cupboard with her head down.

'Are you OK, Anne?'

She remained silent.

'Anne?'

She breathed in deeply and slowly exhaled. 'I could swing for Eddie, I really could. If I move him, I have to move everyone.'

'Is it because of 'you know what' why you want Eddie there?'

Anne hesitated. 'Not really. It's more because I'm doing Fiona and Johan a favour allowing them to have tables. Mind, Eddie's always like this, he just wants to have everything his own way. He really does.'

'You're just going to have to go in there and stick to your plan. I mean, people aren't going to be glued to their seats, are they?'

'I didn't think anyone would make a fuss. I tried to put friends together, like you and Mike, Pauline and Elaine. I don't know what else I can do.'

'Go back and stick to it, Anne. You're organising it, after all. Put your foot down.'

She nodded and together we went back into the hall.

Anne stood next to Albert. 'Listen everybody, I know some

of you aren't happy but the reason I've got seating in the middle as well at the sides is I hope we all do move around and talk to each other. Mind, it's only when it's very busy you need to be next to your table. When it's quiet you can sit where you want, do you understand?'

Eddie screwed up his face but said nothing and because he kept quiet the others did as well.

'Now, I've asked my friend Marjorie to do the tea and coffee,' she said brusquely. 'We'll get one free drink and then for us its fifty pence, for outsiders it'll be a pound. Marjorie said she's going to do a Victoria sponge and fruit cake as well. I think that's all for now.'

Beside me, Mike had got up and was putting his coat on. He nudged me and indicated he was going out for another cigarette.

I followed Mike outside, and lit my cigarette.

'Are you looking forward to this, Rachel?'

'Sort of, but I think people are being quite optimistic about sales. If all these big stores are being closed, would an art sale on a Sunday in a community centre, in a back street really be that busy? I'm not convinced.'

He nodded. 'I think it's going to be a waste of time. I've done loads of exhibitions now, and you never get many sales.'

'Where did you do them, the exhibitions?'

'I told you I did art in hospital, didn't I?'

'Yeah.'

'Well, I wasn't on me own; there were a few of us. When we left hospital, some of us carried on meeting, as a group, and we had art exhibitions. Years before that, I joined this group near Wallaston, they did exhibitions every few months. But, I'm not messing when I say they were stuck up.' Mike pressed his nostrils upwards with his finger. 'I ended up having such a row with them; I walked out and never went back. Anyway, the exhibitions they did never got many sales either.'

I sighed. 'Hopefully being in the paper might mean we get

more sales.'

'I don't even want to be in the paper.'

'Why not?'

Mike walked over to the bench and as he sat down, he pulled up his jeans. With one hand, he ran his fingers through his hair.

'Just with me review on me Benefits. I didn't mention art or any money I get from it. Not that I do get much from it, but I don't want the paper making out I'm this successful artist, just in case.'

'I'm sure the Benefits people wouldn't be looking at the Carthom News. It's not exactly the most exciting of reads, is it?'

Mike lowered his voice. 'But other people could. I just don't want to take the risk.'

As soon as he mentioned risk, I thought about the guards. Would any of them, or their families or friends read the paper? It was strange because part of me would've liked to be able to show them how much I'd achieved since I left. However, after the phone call to my mum, I knew they wouldn't be bothered; instead uppermost in their mind would be retribution. They'd been very manipulative when I was with them, and openly lied about me in meetings so I knew their capacity for trouble-causing. One part of this would surely be to let everyone know who I was and what I'd done.

'Are you ready?' Mike stood up, his weight shifting from foot to foot.

I followed him in and met Kate as she limped towards me.

'You've seen the painting, the one below Mike's dog?' Kate whispered.

I frowned. 'Pauline's?'

'I reckon there are at least four paintings that are copies. Pauline's is the most blatant as it's a very recognizable Monet copy. We should have cards or a sign to indicate our work is original? What do you think?'

'I don't know, Kate. I don't want to get them annoyed and

I've been at plenty of art sales where I've recognised a piece of work.'

'Yes, but are they described as 'original'? That's the problem.'

Anne eased herself up again. 'Don't forget to bring a painting next week, so we can show off our paintings to the reporter.'

Out of the side window, I could see the dance instructor arrive and get a large tote bag out of her car. Around the table there was a real buzz as we packed up our art materials.

When everyone had left, Anne passed the key over to the dance instructor and turned to me with a quick smile.

'Didn't it go well in the end?'

'Yeah, I know. Everybody was OK about the plan after all.'

'Mike seemed happier. I asked him if he was alright and he said he was now that everybody was off his back. What does he mean? Who was on his back?' Anne asked, lifting my bag into the boot.

'I think he just means family,' I mumbled.

When Anne sat down she checked her rear view mirror and then gave me a sidelong glance. 'I assumed he was talking about his Benefits. Put your seat belt on, Rachel, time to get going.'

'How many paintings are you going to put into the sale?'

'I'm thinking of doing what Marion and Albert are doing, but I'd take about twelve. How many are you bringing?'

I screwed up my face. 'Seven hopefully, I haven't got any more. In fact I'm going to have to get a move on or else it'll be just six.'

As we pulled into my road, I got my key out of my back pocket and threw it gently into the air, catching it.

Anne parked in front of my house.

'The disco dance group might be finishing soon. The official story is numbers are down.'

'Oh, I got the impression it was a busy group.'

'I know, I thought it was too.' After waiting for the traffic to pass, she got my chair out from her boot.

Anne followed me up my path, with my bag. After I unlocked the door I reached out to take it from her but she was crouching down.

'You've got a letter here,' she said. She tugged on a white envelope stuck on the bottom of my wheel. When she pulled it free she examined it, before eventually handing it to me.

When I turned it over I saw the Inspire and Support logo on the front.

'What is it?' Anne twisted her head to try and have another look.

'Just a bill. See you next week, thanks.'

I closed the door and before I even took my coat off, I ripped open the envelope and read the letter inside.

Dear Rachel,

Inspire and Support Information Day for the Befriending Service.
Thank you for your interest in the Inspire and Support
Befriending Service.

It is with pleasure we'd like to invite you to a drop-in Information
Day. Here you'll have a chance to meet our inspirational staff,
service users and befrienders as well as finding out more about
the services Inspire and Support offer.

If you want to apply to join the service and you are successful in
this application, we'll invite you to a training day before starting
with the team. Reasonable travel and out of pocket expenses will
be paid.

Please complete the attached form to confirm your attendance.
If you have any further questions contact Andrea Mulligan on
the number or email above
Thank you once again for your interest.

Brian Taylor C.B.E.

I read the letter and form attached again, aware my hands were trembling. When volunteering had first been suggested I was much more diffident and insecure. It certainly seemed like a different proposition now and perhaps was an indication that my self-confidence was growing.

I phoned Mum, still wearing my coat and as I waited for her to answer, I re-read the letter once more.

'Why have I got this?'

'You told me to tell Brian you might do it at some point. I think it's great news. When is it and what time do you need to be there?'

'Third of April between eleven and three o'clock.'

'I could take you in if you want, I'd have to come for you at about ten 'o' clock, it'll take about an hour, I reckon.'

'It says it's just a drop-in information day, it's not an interview or anything like that. I'm sure I don't have to be there as soon as it starts. It's on a Wednesday so 'I'll go to the art group for an hour first.'

'Have you looked at all job descriptions on the website?'

'Yeah, it does seem interesting. Do you know why he set the charity up? Is he disabled or is someone disabled in his family?'

'I've no idea. I don't know him that well. Does this mean you fancy doing it?'

'I'll go to this Information Day and then see what I think.' I knew in my mind my view on this subject had changed but didn't want to sound too enthusiastic in case it didn't work out.

My mood certainly seemed to lift with the news of the Information Day, but for the time being I had to concentrate on the coming art sale. For the rest of the week I started getting my paintings ready. My priority was the Carthom Street Scene. Rather than buying an off the shelf frame I had it professionally mounted and framed. When it was ready, I was certain it was one of the best paintings I'd completed and would be perfect for the next art group meeting with the reporter.

Thirteen

As soon as I opened the door, Anne's perfume hit the back of my throat. It was then I realised instead of wearing trousers, or 'slacks' as she calls them, she was wearing a very long velvet-like plum coloured skirt and a pale pink blouse with a pussy bow. To match this outfit, she wore a purple and pink wool cardigan, black shoes and bag.

'Wow, you look good, today'.

'Good? I did try to make an effort.'

'I don't think I've seen you in a skirt before,' I said, as Anne helped me in the car.

She eased herself in, put her seatbelt on and glanced at me. 'When I was your age I wore skirts right up here to my thighs.' Anne turned the key in the ignition and her mood went down a gear.

'Andrew was the one who put an end to all of this. I'm sure he just didn't like the idea other men could find me attractive. He was a wrong 'un. The silly thing is I knew it, but stayed with him. Sometimes, I look back, and all I see is... ' Anne's eyes flicked towards me again before she pulled onto the main road. 'Anyway, I think it's why I need my art to be successful. I know Andrew and the rest of my family won't read the article, but if I know in my head I've made something of myself then it'll be something.'

'What time's the reporter coming?'

'Time? Marion told me it was going to be around eleven o'clock but it could be later. At least, it means we can have a discussion about the group ending.'

'Our group?'

As we waited to turn onto the main road, she let out a nervous giggle.

'Not ours silly. No, I mean the disco-dancing keep fit group.'

'I can't believe it finished so quickly?'

'I think I know why. I heard on the grapevine, Doreen, the leader of the group, is going away. Between you and me, I've heard it's her son who's poorly again. Mind, he's always been a bit on the slow side, even as a child he was backward.'

I wanted to be able to challenge her language and attitude, but felt it wasn't the right time or place to discuss it with her.

We drove past the police station where I saw a large group of people outside, a couple wearing imitation police helmets, and some with placards saying, 'Protect You're Local Police Station', with a criminal howler.

'Anne, slow down, look. I didn't know it was closing.'

'It was in the local paper last week. They're saying the station would be better based nearer to Weston.'

'We'll be in between two empty buildings if it closes'

'Oh, I doubt that'll affect us. I'm more concerned about what would happen if there was a mugging or a murder. Right, let me get my art materials together and then I'll get you out. Oh no, is that Mike? It's Mike, isn't it? Over there?' She pointed towards the library.

I couldn't see anyone at first but when I was in my chair I could see him pacing up and down.

'At least you're not the only one who isn't dressed up. He looks like he got dressed in the hedge.'

I pulled a face as I glanced down at my attire, suddenly seeing my sweatshirt and jeans in a different light. I wheeled over to Mike. His shirt was grubby, half tucked into trousers, which were baggy on him. Every so often he would hitch them up and I could see how thin he really was. With his gaunt and haunted appearance, I began to be more concerned for his general welfare.

'You alright, mate?'

'I got this. I don't know what to do. I don't see why I should go, I don't see the point.'

Mike retrieved from his back pocket a crumpled brown envelope and thrust it towards me without saying anything. I quickly skimmed through the letter; a request for him to attend an appointment for an assessment for his Benefit.

'At least you've not got Atos doing the assessment. They did mine. You know why they're called Atos because people say they couldn't give a toss.'

Mike stared at me, his face impassive.

'You've got to go, If you don't you'll lose your money.'

Mike shook his head. 'I don't see why. It's at the other end of bloody Weston as well, how am I expected to get there? I get more fits when I'm stressed. I've had two big ones this week.'

Anne walked out to us, gripping her cardigan around her shoulders. 'Rachel, can you come and give me a hand, please?'

Before I answered her, I turned to Mike. 'Are you coming in?'

Mike glared at me. 'I thought you said you hadn't been assessed.'

I felt myself blush. 'I just meant. Erm, I meant...'

He gave me a withering look and had started to pace without waiting for my reply.

Inside the centre, Anne waited in the hall, her arms folded and her foot tapping on the floor. 'What on earth is the matter with him now?'

I shook my head. 'It's nothing, Anne; just think he's got a few things on his mind.'

'His money, I suppose? Can you tell him to talk about it later, when the reporter's gone? I don't want her to be reporting about Mike and all his problems.'

Mike was just about to limp in, so I wheeled into the foyer to speak to him.

'Listen, Anne's flapping back there. She's nervous about today, with the reporter coming. If you want you can call me and we'll have a chat about what you can do.'

He bent down to my level for a second and hissed. 'You haven't gone and told her what's wrong? I told you, I didn't want people to know.'

'All I said was you had things on your mind. Can we talk about it later?'

'Whatever.' Mike pulled a face and hobbled into the main hall.

Through the door I could see him look at the paintings on the walls. Anne walked in and briefly said something to him. She was pulling more tables into position, while he dragged chairs to the tables using just one crutch.

I concentrated on getting the mugs out of the cupboard and tried to fill the kettles. In an attempt to save time, I tried to move four mugs on my lap at once. As I turned round in the small kitchen, one mug fell off and smashed into pieces onto the unforgiving, tiled floor.

'Oh, shit,' I called out.

Anne jogged into the kitchen, and stared at the floor.

'Oh dear. We're all a bit nervous today.'

'Sorry, I tried to move too many at once. I'll pay for it.'

'Pay? Oh, don't worry, you won't have to pay. They won't miss one. If you come out of the kitchen, I'll sweep it up, there's a dustpan and brush somewhere.'

Most of the tables were now out, and Mike dragged the last chair into place.

'Do you two want a drink? Mike?' Anne held up a mug.

Mike shook his head without straightening up. He was standing against the wall, his hands on his knees as he bent over.

With the mug still in her hand, Anne pointed at me.

'No thanks.'

Mike walked over and sat next to me. For a minute he stretched out on the table, his head down and arms over his head. His spine, like a crooked wall, was visible under his shirt and divided up the sweat patches under each armpit.

Eddie was the next to arrive with Lena. They both had made a considerable effort to look smart with Lena in a pastel blue skirt suit and cream blouse and Eddie in dark jeans and a crisp white shirt.

Eddie stood, his legs wide apart, his hands on his hips. 'It appears we're not the only story today. Did everyone see the protest next door? Sometimes I wonder why people bother to strike when a decision's already been taken.' He turned towards the window and pointed towards the police station. 'What's the point of standing outside with a placard? You see the same lot of protesters each time. They were the ones trying to keep the library open. Didn't do much good, did they?'

'I feel sorry for the police, they can't strike, so now they've got all those people outside,' said Lena.

'I just hope the reporter doesn't spend all her time covering the strike,' Anne replied. 'We're just as much a news story as them.'

'He'll probably do both,' Lena said, putting a mug on the hatch. 'Eddie, there's your drink.'

'He's a she, the reporter. It's a woman called Lizanne, she does everything; interviews people as well as taking the pictures.'

Mike was getting his art materials out. The brown envelope was on the table in front of him.

I picked it up. 'Give me a ring afterwards about this.'

'I've got four weeks anyway before the appointment.' He snatched the envelope from me and stuffed it into the pocket of his jeans.

Marion and Albert staggered into the centre, both glowing red from exertion and out of breath. Marion clasped two paintings, one in each hand, and placed them side by side on the table, while Albert trudged into the kitchen to make the drinks.

'Hello everybody,' Marion said. 'Are we all ready for stardom today?'

I stared at the paintings. Anne had with her a watercolour painting of a dramatic Prussian blue and Indian red evening sky above a rural landscape, which I had to admit, was rather good.

Eddie had brought the painting of the street in Weston I'd admired at the gallery. Lena had her watercolour portrait of her husband. Marion's acrylic painting of a basket of wild flowers was so detailed and realistic, I wanted to reach into the painting, lift it out and carry it home. Albert, like Anne had brought a watercolour painting, which featured a Picasso-style woman's face.

I looked down at my street scene painting and then compared it with Mike's watercolour painting of a Labrador with twinkling eyes. All the past week I'd spent getting my work ready and was sure I'd done enough but the standard of work was high. All of a sudden I felt ill-prepared.

'Eyeing up the competition?' Eddie said.

His voice made me jump.

'Sorry, shouldn't have crept up on you.'

'I was just thinking how good all these paintings are. I know I've said this before, but I do love your picture of Weston.'

'If it's not sold by this time next year, you can have it, kiddo.'

'You'll sell it, no problem. I reckon you've got a good chance of doing well.'

'I hope so. My ex-wife has got an unrealistic opinion about what she should be getting from me at the best of times.'

Anne glanced at her watch; Pauline, Elaine and Kate weren't here yet, but by the clock in the centre it was only just ten o'clock.

I wheeled into the kitchen, and filled a paper cup with some water for my paints. Just as I was slotting back into my place, Kate limped into the hall.

'Hi everyone, sorry I'm a bit late.'

When Kate sat down, Anne cleared her throat.

'Before Lizanne the reporter comes, I've just got something to discuss. The dance class that usually meets after us has had to close as they didn't have enough people attending. So I was wondering whether we'd like to meet for longer. I was thinking maybe until two-ish?'

As Anne discussed the plan with the rest of the group, I sneaked a peek at Kate's work. It was painted in acrylics and featured horses and donkeys in a field. I could imagine it on the wall in a child's bedroom.

Kate tapped her finger gently towards me and whispered, 'Are you OK?'

I nodded and smiled. I pointed at her painting and mouthed, 'Love it.'

Anne shot me a stern look. 'What do others think?'

'I agree, Anne,' Eddie said. 'When we have stuff to sort out, it all takes time away from when we could be painting.'

'What I was thinking, mind, was just making it free and easy, so people don't have to stay until two o'clock. Just let folks know it will be open until then. Can I have a show of hands of those who agree?'

Every hand went up bar Mike's.

'Mike?'

Mike jolted in his seat and looked quickly around the table. 'What? Oh sorry, yes.'

'Right, well we can start today, as the group has finished already.'

'Lizanne, the reporter is due here in about half an hour or so, so let's get some art going.' She picked up her paintbrush, and we all settled down to paint.

Ten minutes later, Pauline walked in holding two floral watercolour paintings, one in each hand, closely followed by Elaine. I looked at the paintings they'd brought in. They were very similar, not just in terms of the subject but style as well though I had to admit they were accomplished and beautifully framed.

As we were painting and drawing it was hard not to notice

the intermittent 'beep' from car horns, followed by cheers from the protestors next door.

'They must have one of the signs up saying, if you support the police sound your horn,' Eddie said.

For a second Anne closed her eyes, and rubbed her forehead, with an impatient sigh. 'Whatever it is, it's driving me mad. How on earth are we meant to concentrate?'

Anne scraped her chair back and wandered over to the window. She leant on the ledge straining to peer at the police station. As she stood there silhouetted in the light from the window, she looked completely different. She reminded me of myself when I was at sixth form college; sometimes I'd wear long skirts down to my ankles which made me appear taller and slimmer than usual. I used to really be preoccupied with looking my best.

Kate waved her hand in front of my face. 'Earth to Rachel, do we have a connection.'

'Sorry I was just thinking.'

Just as I said this, the door swung open and a young woman bounded in.

'Hello everyone,' she said in a sing-song voice. 'I'm Lizanne Oltermann from Carthom News. Is this the Art for You group?'

'Hi, I'm Anne, I run the group.' Anne shook her hand vigorously. 'We've been expecting you.'

Lizanne looked down at her mobile. 'Um, my notes say it's a 'Marion' who contacted the paper.'

Marion stood up and pointed at her chest. 'That's me. I'm the one who phoned in.'

'Yes, but I run the group, don't I?'

'Yes, Anne runs it,' snapped Marion.

Anne stood in front of the reporter, her weight shifting from foot to foot.

'So do you want a group shot of us first? We've all brought a painting in. I thought we could stand with our paintings for a photograph, Maybe at the back of the hall. Mind, you need to know about the times, and date of art sale and...'

Lizanne held up her hand in a stop sign. 'Can I stop you there and be cheeky. I'm dying for a coffee. Then I can sit down and find out about your group and meet the members. You see, I've been stood outside for half an hour covering the protest next door, so I just need a minute or two to catch my breath.'

Eddie jumped up. 'Sugar, milk?'

'Three sugars and just a drop of milk, thank you.'

She took her coat off and underneath had on a grey hoodie and jeans. She was pint sized and with her long brown dreadlocks in a ponytail she could easily pass for a teenager despite probably being in her early twenties. From her messenger bag, she brought out a tiny Dictaphone as well as a digital camera.

When Eddie came back, with a mug of coffee, Anne pulled a chair over for Lizanne and put it next to her.

Lizanne blew over her coffee, before taking a sip. She smiled at Anne.

'So tell me, how long has this group been going?'

Anne spoke with an accent pitched somewhere between the Queen and Margaret Thatcher.

'Officially as a group since just before Christmas. Before then, was a smaller group of us: Eddie, who just made your coffee, Lena here, and Johan and Fiona who are not members of this group, oh and me and Rachel. Aren't you taking any notes?'

'This is recording what you say.' The reporter showed Anne the Dictaphone.

Lizanne took hold of her mug and for a moment, sat back and gulped it down.

'So there was a smaller group and since Christmas it's grown?'

'Smaller group? No, we didn't meet as a group. We just had our paintings up at Garden and Crafts for You. It's Dickenson's Carpets now. So when I knew it was closing, I came up with this idea to have a weekly group.'

'Right, now, when and where is this art sale and is it your first?'

'Our first art sale? Yes, it's the first one as a group; hopefully we'll have more. It's on Sunday the twenty fourth of March. Fiona and Johan, who were original members of the gallery, are having tables as well.'

'What time is it?'

'It's on from ten o'clock until four o'clock. All the details are on this flyer.' Anne picked up one of the flyers which seemed to have a life of its own as her hands trembled.

'How many members are there in this group?' Lizanne asked, looking at the flyer.

'Everyone you see here today.' Anne made a sweeping gesture around the table. 'Ten in total. Shall we do this group photograph now?'

'If you don't mind I'd like to go round and meet everyone and take a few photographs and then we'll do a group shot at the end. OK?'

'Oh right, at the end. OK.'

Lizanne asked her when she first started to paint and eventually got to the point when she wanted to take a photograph of Anne.

'Can you just sit there with your painting in front of you while I take this?'

Anne posed, paintbrush poised in her hand.

'Right, OK, are you ready? Smile. That's great. Thanks, Anne.'

Lizanne and Anne stood up at exactly the same time. As Lizanne tried to go one way, and interview Lena. Anne blocked her path, her weight shifting from one foot to the next. From my position, it looked like the pair were performing an odd pas de deux.

Lizanne dragged her chair over so she was between Eddie and Lena. She swung it so it was facing the other way, and sat on it like this, with her chest against the back of the chair, her legs dangled on either side. Anne hovered behind her.

With a change in tone, Lizanne turned her head towards Anne. 'I'll just speak to these two people. You can sit down now because I'll talk to everyone.'

Anne huffed and muttered under her breath as she sat down.

Mike nudged me. 'Do you fancy a..?'

'Yeah, go on.'

I grabbed my coat and followed Mike. He was surprisingly calm and had an almost indifferent attitude.

'I've decided it's not worth me working myself up about. They can do their worst. I really am past caring.' He trudged over to the bench. 'It seems like every one of them is taking a part of me away. Soon there'll be nothing left.'

I wheeled over to him. 'A lot of these cases are won on appeal. I think it's something like forty percent of them win on appeal. So, even if it doesn't go your way, there's still a good chance the decision will be overturned when you appeal.'

'Yeah, me mate won his on appeal.' Mike glanced at the protest at the police station. 'This country is going to the dogs.'

He looked despondent. I changed the subject and asked him if he was going to let the reporter take his photograph as part of the group shot.

'Nah, I won't.' He dropped his cigarette butt onto the ground. 'Come on, we'd better go back in.'

Back inside, Lizanne was talking to Albert and Marion. I wheeled past and heard Albert mention D-Day. I felt sorry for this young reporter having to listen to all of his war stories.

After a few minutes, Marion and Lizanne had got Albert off the topic of war and back onto art. I listened in as Lizanne steered the conversation to a conclusion.

The reporter moved along and crouched in front of Pauline and Elaine.

Anne got up. She seemed jittery and didn't know what to do

with her hands. All the time her head darted back to the reporter like a bird bobbing up and down. She walked up towards me and leant on the back of my wheelchair.

'Lovely, Rachel, maybe put a bit more shading there.'

I bristled with annoyance at Anne's suggestion.

Lizanne stood up and after taking a photograph of Elaine with Pauline; she joined Kate, crouching down by her left side. Anne followed her and stood next to Kate on her other side, her hand resting on the table.

'This is one of our handicapped artists,' Anne said.

Kate grimaced in response.

There was a brief trace of a smile from Lizanne, before she adopted the polite, professional persona of a journalist again, and carried on with the interview.

'How did you get interested in art, Kate?'

'It was after I gave up work; by chance I went to an arts based workshop and discovered my love of art.'

'And you have a really quirky style. I love this. Can you just hold it up for me while I take a photograph? OK, now, big smile. Great.' She looked at her digital camera. 'Thanks, Kate.'

Lizanne walked across to Mike.

Mike stood up and took a quick step out of her way, holding up his hands.

'I don't want to be interviewed or have me photo taken.'

'Oh, OK. Are you sure?'

Mike nodded. He leant forward and pulled his chair out, offering her his seat.

'You can sit here and talk to Rachel. I'm just nipping out for a smoke.'

Lizanne sat down. 'Hi Rachel, how did you become interested in art?'

'After my accident, I'd a lot of time on my hands recovering and that's when I started painting again. I find it helps distract me from pain as well.'

'What happened? Was it a car accident?' She scratched the top of her scalp with her biro.

'I don't like talking about it, too traumatic.'

Lizanne twisted her head to peer down at my painting. 'I like this one. I used to live in this street, near here.' She pointed at the betting shop. 'Many moons ago, of course. Is this going in the sale?'

I nodded. 'Yes, I got it ready especially for it.' As I talked there was silence in the room.

She picked up her camera. 'Rachel, can you pretend to paint and then look to the side at me? OK, ready, smile.' She peered at her camera. 'One more Rachel, look at me, and then smile. That's it, that's great.'

'OK, folks. I'm just going to take a group photo of you all working, so in a minute all pick up your brushes when I say, OK, everybody ready? OK, everyone look at me and smile.'

The camera whirred, as she took three pictures in quick succession.

For a second, she squinted at the images. 'Yes, perfect,' she purred. 'Cheers everyone. The article will hopefully be in next Thursday's edition of the Carthom News, in time for your art sale.' She grabbed hold of her coat and bounded out.

'I don't get it?' Anne frowned. 'Why's she only saying hopefully?'

'I suppose it's whether there is space,' Lena said.

'Well, if it all goes in, I think there's enough to fill a page. It'll really help in getting people to come,' Anne replied.

I peered down at my watch and swallowed a yawn.

Anne turned to me. 'Do you need to be off? Do you want a lift?'

'Yes, please.'

When I'd said my goodbyes to the group, Anne skipped with me to her car. Her good mood was infectious.

'All my life I don't think I've ever been in the paper, apart from my wedding notices. What about you, have you ever been? Oh, I suppose when you had your..?'

I interrupted her. 'It's exciting, isn't it?'

'Exciting? I'm really excited, and so looking forward to this sale. It's been hard work to organise it, but it's all coming together now.'

'Yeah, you've done a really good job, Anne.'

As soon as I was home and back alone, I fantasised about the guards reading the article and feeling sorry for what they'd done. In reality, I knew if they read it, they wouldn't notice how independent I was or even that I was painting again. Instead, I knew how vindictive they could be and how they'd want to make life uncomfortable for me. They'd want revenge. My main concern was what action they'd take. I had no doubt an element of it would be to expose me. I was finding the more I settled into life in Carthom, the more I had to lose.

Fourteen

Despite Carthom being a relatively small village with a population of around ten thousand there were two local newspapers, The Carthom News and The Carthom Advertiser. The only difference between the two was one had jobs advertised in it, the other didn't. They weren't the most riveting of reads with a typical week having articles about fly-tipping, farming news or the latest fund raising activities for the bird sanctuary. In stark contrast, the Weston paper, which the guards used to get at the bungalow, would be full of crime reports, court appearances and drug deaths.

Reading about the various crimes in the Weston paper

didn't help me feel secure in the area. However, it was an honest reflection of what was happening locally. The Carthom newspapers felt as though they were deceiving the public, hiding tensions that must surely exist.

The week after the reporter had been to the group, I heard the papergirl stuff the newspaper through my letterbox. As I pulled it out, I hoped the article would be in and if so, it promoted the sale well. On the front cover, there was a report of the protest at the police station, along with photographs. My eyes drifted to the right-hand column where I saw a box with text in bold. It said: 'Local Artists hold Art Sale, Sunday 24th March, see page four for details.' Trying to breathe calmly I struggled to get to page four. The paper fell to bits and all I'd left in my hands, were pages four and thirty-four. I didn't need to look closely as I could see a huge photograph of myself along with three smaller photographs. I felt sick, my mouth full of bile, and the newspaper was shaking in my ink stained hands. Underneath the photograph it said: 'Rachel, disabled artist, who specialises in painting local scenes.' Alongside my photograph, was a smaller photo of my painting, which read 'Street Scene in Carthom by Rachel Aspinhall.'

'Oh God,' I said out loud.

Underneath my picture was a small photograph of Anne, the text read: 'Anne Wilby, group leader.' Next to this was the group shot, but as the photo was tiny it was hard to make out who was who.

With a feeling of dread I started to read:

Carthom Art Sale

There's a new cultural event to put in your diary this spring, as a group of Carthom artists called 'Art for You' would like to welcome you to their first art sale and exhibition. It's for one day only, on Sunday 24th March at Carthom community centre, so

don't miss this opportunity to purchase quality, original artwork
with prices to suit everybody. There'll also be a delicious array
of homemade cakes as well as other refreshments available.
Admission is free.

Art for You was founded by Carthom artist, Anne Wilby.
Originally it was based in Garden and Crafts for You
(Dickenson's Carpets) but the group now meets every Wednesday
in the Community Centre.

Art for You caters for every artist from the beginner to the
professional and anyone over the age of 18 can join.

Top up on your culture and come and visit them. They'd all love
to say hello as well as show you their artwork.

'Oh God' I said again. I folded the paper up into as small a piece as I could, and then placed it on the coffee table where it unfurled. The rest of the paper, which was still on the floor, went into my bin.

Momentarily, I imagined my dad's photograph being where mine was. I could clearly remember my mum shouting one time, 'It's good for you but not for the family,' when his photograph was in the paper. Very easily, I could replace my mum's voice with Anne's, with her shouting, 'it's good for you, but not for the group.'

I should've been excited, pleased my photograph was in the paper, along with a photo of my painting, but instead I was worried about Anne's reaction as well as the growing concern the guards would find me as a result of the article.

I phoned Mum and told her about the article.

'What's the problem? Which paper did you say it was in?'

'Carthom News, though it's probably in the Carthom Advertiser as well. Do you think it's safe for my picture being in?'

'Do you mean with Anne?'

'Nope, she'll be fuming. No, I'm talking about with the guards.'

'It's a risk you're going have to take, Rach. You can't live your life constantly worried about them. What made you think of them, just this article?'

I murmured a response not wanting to admit I thought about the guards nearly every day.

Later on in evening I picked up the article again. There was still no word from Anne. She was due to pick me up on Saturday afternoon so we could start to get ready for the art sale. Why didn't I follow Mike's example and refuse to be interviewed or be photographed? I'd taken a big risk and it was one easily avoided.

Saturday arrived and Anne still hadn't been in touch. I didn't want to phone her, so planned to get a taxi up, if she didn't turn up. However, with five minutes to go, Anne arrived. As she got me into the car, neither of us spoke. The tension made me feel nauseous. She slammed my passenger door shut and drove to the centre, and again, we were both silent. Even though I was only inches away from her in the car, it felt like a gorge was between us and was getting deeper and more treacherous by the minute.

When we pulled into the car park, I started to take my seatbelt off.

'I'm assuming you've seen the newspaper article,' Anne said, with a menacing tone.

I held onto my seatbelt and kept my eyes fixed on the 'no ball games' sign on the centre wall.

'I don't know why I bother reading that rag. It's full of rubbish, people showing off saying I've done this or I've done that.'

I remained silent. Anne got me out but prevented me from moving, as she leant over me, one hand against the car.

'She must have felt sorry for you. That must be it.'

Anne stormed towards the centre and forcibly turned the key to get inside. As she marched through, she let the main door swing back into my path. I wanted to be strong, challenge her, but instead I could feel a rush of tears threatening to fall. I swallowed, then slowly exhaled, determined not to cry.

As I wheeled into the hall, Anne stood waiting, her right foot in front of her, her left hand on her hip and the manner in which she spoke was clipped and abrasive.

'Not everyone's coming today. I think Marion, Albert, Lena and Eddie are all leaving it until tomorrow, so you can go once you've put your paintings up, but if you want a lift from me, you'll have to wait until everyone else is finished.'

I nodded.

'Fiona's coming today as well but Johan's setting up tomorrow. He's going to do caricatures for visitors. Mind, I think it'd be a good idea if the entire group had one done, to support him.'

'I don't even like getting my photo taken, let alone having someone draw a caricature of me.'

I heard Anne snort through her nose.

All the tables had been set up in the right places and on each table was a piece of paper with a name on. I immediately went over to my table and just by looking at it, didn't think I'd fit all seven paintings on it. I was beginning to regret not going for two tables.

As I unpacked my bubble wrapped paintings, I heard the outside door bang and seconds later, Fiona strode in carrying a large portfolio case.

'Anne, darling, you couldn't just get a couple of paintings from my back seat?'

'Pass me the key.'

Fiona tossed her car key to Anne. When Anne was out of the hall, Fiona spun around to face me.

'Lovely photo in the newspaper, Rachel, Eddie sent me the link.'

I made no comment, not wanting to aggravate the situation. She walked a couple of steps closer to me. The smell from her perfume was so intense my head started to throb.

'I hear Anne isn't too pleased?' Fiona had her hand on her protruding hip bone, which was visible due to her low slung jeans.

'It's OK, don't say anything, please.'

Anne walked in carrying two heavy paintings, both with ornate, and in my opinion, ostentatious frames.

'They're absolutely gorgeous, paintings, Fiona. You are talented.' She carefully placed them on Fiona's table. 'Are you all right here, on this table?'

Fiona walked back towards her table. 'Yes, thanks. Wasn't it a good article in the paper? It should translate into a decent footfall if nothing else. The photos were lovely.'

'Lovely?' Anne's forehead hung heavily over her eyes. 'The reporter took photos of everyone. I know why it ended up like it did and all I can say, is it's not fair.' She glared across at me.

Fiona chuckled. 'There's always rivalry where painting is concerned. Never mind, Anne, come and have a chat with me.'

She put her arm around Anne's waist and walked with her into the corridor near the kitchen and offices. I couldn't hear anything but could see Anne's hands were on her hips and Fiona was doing something with her finger, before pointing to me. Our eyes met and she turned back to face Anne.

I'd managed to fit all my paintings onto the table. The only one I wasn't sure what to do with was my Carthom Street Scene. I couldn't decide whether to have it lying flat on my table or hang it on the wall. Until I found a place for it, I decided to leave it wrapped up. When Fiona and Anne came back in the room, I went out for a cigarette, my coat on and my rucksack still on the back of my chair.

For a couple of minutes I smoked outside, and was getting increasingly upset. I didn't want to go back inside. I put my coat on my knees and on impulse wheeled off towards my home, trying to hold back my tears.

Mike stepped in front of me. 'Where are you going? Have you put your paintings up yet?'

'I've upset, Anne. It wasn't even my fault. I didn't say to the reporter to put my photo there.'

'Hang on, I haven't seen the paper. What's happened?'

'The reporter put a big photo of me, not Anne at the top. She's in a right mood.'

Mike was struggling carrying his paintings. He had a bulging rucksack as well as carrying a painting in a carrier bag.

'Do you want a hand?'

'Ta, it's been a bloody nightmare getting here. Don't worry about Anne, she won't mean anything by it,' he said, putting the carrier bag flat on my knee.

I turned around and accompanied him back up the road to the centre.

'You know with your Benefits? I read somewhere you need to get together some medical evidence for your assessment.'

'It's OK, Rachel, honestly. I'm trying not to think about it.'

We were now at the centre and before going in, Mike took off the rucksack, and dropped his crutches on the floor. He put his arms out, placing his hands flat against the wall and then leant with his back bent, his ponytail falling over the top of his head. For a moment he was completely still, the only sound was his laboured breathing

'Are you alright?'

He nodded and slowly straightened up. 'If I have to take this lot home again I'll go spare.' His face was now a deep violet colour.

'You should've come tomorrow and got Eddie to give you a lift.'

Back inside, Anne cornered me.

'I thought you'd gone so I took the bubble wrap off the

painting on your table.'

Trying to keep calm, I went over to my table and checked she hadn't sabotaged my artwork in any way, before helping Mike to set up.

He'd brought six pieces: five were dogs, including a large golden Labrador painting; the dog had a twinkle in its eye and with its mouth open and tongue out, it looked as if it was smiling. Mike reached over and put a 'not for sale' sticker on the Labrador.

'Why not for sale? This would be snapped up.'

Mike brushed some wispy strands of hair from out of his eyes, revealing dark shadows under each eye. He appeared to be jaded, his dogs' eyes having more life in them than him.

'It's me neighbour's dog. Sandy. She's the only one who bothers about me. She's not well herself but she always has a friendly smile and says hello, so I'm giving it to her.'

'She'll love it, Mike, that's really thoughtful.'

I picked up an abstract watercolour with a marble effect. 'If this hasn't sold by dinnertime, I'll buy it.'

'You don't have to, you know?'

'I'm not doing it just for the sake of it, Mike. This would be lovely in my bedroom.'

Kate had now arrived, followed by Pauline and Elaine. Mike had finished and wanted to get home before it got too dark, so instead I sat by Kate's table as she unpacked her paintings.

'Wasn't it an excellent article in the paper, Rachel?'

'Don't say anything about it.'

'Why?'

'Anne's fuming.'

'It was a good article, concise, accurate and the photographs were clear. If I stare into my imaginary, crystal ball, I predict your street scene painting will be one of the first paintings to be sold.'

'After that article I honestly don't want many sales. What I was going to say, is do you think we should change over some of the paintings at The Richmond? I was thinking, some of the ones on my table could go up there if they don't sell.'

'So, let's see how things pan out tomorrow and then look at what we've got to go up. Have you put anything on your labels about your work being original?'

'I was thinking maybe just putting a piece of paper on my table saying all my paintings have come from my own ideas. Why? What have you done?'

Kate smiled as she gave me one of her price labels. Along with the name of the painting, price and medium, she'd added all her work was original.

'What do you think the others will say about it?'

'So, what can they say? We're competing for sales now.' Kate picked another painting out from her portfolio case and then stood up and placed a hand on the small of her back. 'I'm beginning to wish I'd kept my two tables. I didn't want to have all my work bunched together.'

I left Kate to get on with putting her paintings out and wheeled over to Elaine's table to have a look at her artwork. The paintings were all acrylics with a floral theme. I wheeled over to Pauline's table whose paintings were floral acrylics. Since Kate told me about the Monet-copy, I couldn't look at their work without feeling everything was faintly familiar.

A memory from school floated up to the surface of my mind. It was when a girl in my class had painted a bunch of daffodils and my art teacher had called it 'unimaginative dirge'. What would she say if she knew I was part of an art group, made up of mostly retired women, with half of them painting the type of insipid artwork she hated so much?

'Are you ready, Rachel?' Anne said behind me. 'Everyone's nearly finished, so get your bag.'

Pauline and Elaine were pulling on their coats, talking to Fiona. Kate was outside talking to Mike by her car. I followed

Anne as she turned off the lights and closed the curtains in the centre. In the dark, she paused and turned around to me.

'Sometimes, I wish I wasn't the one organising this. It's a lot of responsibility and I'm not going to be able to please everyone all of the time.'

'I stared down at my clenched fists.'

'Let's get home then. We've got a big day tomorrow.'

Fifteen

While I waited for Anne to arrive, I gazed out of the window. Despite it only being seven o'clock, it was sunny, the sky ultramarine in colour with no clouds visible. From my window, even the dirty white van parked across the road now appeared to be pristine as the light bounced off the paintwork.

For a moment, the sultry heat took me back to the last few days at the bungalow. The instructions from my mum and the solicitor were clear and simple; all I had to do was act normally. I did try to do this, but when emotionally I swung from feeling scared to being jubilant, acting as if nothing was happening was hard.

Although my emotions weren't as extreme as they were then, I was feeling excited about the exhibition, but at the same time felt anxious. I hoped Anne wouldn't be as cross as she was the day before and I prayed it would attract the people of Carthom and not the guards.

As I heard the banging breaks and toot from Anne's car, I put my rucksack on the back of my chair, and after locking my door, pushed hard on my wheelchair and sailed down my path.

Before Anne started the car, she turned her head towards

me, without any obvious animosity.

'Let's go. A few of them are arriving early to set up. I've already been down to the centre first thing this morning.'

We pulled into the car park. Johan was leaning against the wall reading with his headphones on. Behind his legs were three very large paintings. Anne saw me looking at him.

'I knew he'd be the first to arrive.'

When I got out, I wheeled over to where Johan was standing. He took out one of his white headphones and smiled.

My heart pounded and I felt light-headed. I smiled back, and was going to say 'Hi' but Anne spoke first.

'Is that all you've brought, Johan? You've got two tables.'

'Mum's coming soon and she's bringing some other bits and pieces. All the stuff I need now is in here.' Johan pulled out his portfolio case from in between his paintings.

'I have a gut feeling we'll be celebrating our many sales this evening,' Anne said triumphantly. She kicked the door open.

I gave a shrug and smiled up at Johan.

'Come on you two, we haven't got all day.'

Anne opened the hall door. 'My mother used to say for an added bit of luck, you should touch a piece of wood.' She tapped on the door frame three times.

Eddie arrived soon after us, and declared he was in a 'tizz'.

'I trust the Lord's looking down on us today and giving us his blessing, despite the fact we're having this sale on Sunday.' Eddie leant into a shopping bag and brought out two small abstract oil paintings.

'Are you a Christian? I've heard you mention a couple of religious things now?'

'Well spotted, Sherlock,' Eddie replied, with a grin.

'So do you go to church?'

'Not church as in choirs and hymns.' Eddie put his painting down and turned to me. 'I do pray though. I believe God helped me during a very dark patch. If I hadn't found God then, well, I

161

don't know what would have happened to me. What about you?'

I shook my head. 'No, I used to be, not now though.'

Eddie sat on the side of his table. 'I don't want to stick my foot in it, kiddo, but surely you must get days when life is hard. Would a belief in something higher help?'

'I doubt it. Anyway, I stopped going to church when the vicar told me a story about a paraplegic girl who when prayed over, got up and walked back down the aisle. I felt like asking him if he was on drugs.'

'Prayer can be powerful.'

'I tend to believe science more,' I muttered. I didn't want to get into a religious debate.

'It's your call, kiddo.' Eddie stood up and stretched. 'Phew, this is hard work.'

Kate arrived along with Marion and Albert with Pauline and Elaine following, arm in arm, a couple of minutes later. Fiona's sports car screeched and swung into the car park. There was half an hour to go, and in the hall there was a real buzz. Mike appeared and after he'd thrown his bags under his table, he nudged me and pretended to light an imaginary cigarette.

I nodded and followed him out.

As I was lighting my cigarette, a large lady, who I guessed was Marjorie, arrived. She balanced three cake tins on top of each other.

'You OK, Mike?'

'Not bad, are you staying all day?'

'Why? Aren't you?'

'I don't know, all the exhibitions and sales I've done have been crap with hardly any sales. It's a long day with nothing to do'

'Was this with the group from the hospital?'

Mike cocked his head as if he hadn't heard. 'Hospital?' He leant back against the wall. 'Yeah, when we did one of these short art exhibitions we only got about five sales.'

'Oh God, I hope it's not like that today. I've only got a book with me.'

'I've got nothing that's why I might get off early-ish'

As we chatted, a petite, bohemian looking lady with cropped silver hair walked past. She was carrying a large canvas and was dressed in a flowing purple skirt and matching cotton jacket, an Amnesty International badge positioned prominently on her lapel.

'That must be Johan's mum,' I whispered.

'Are you ready, Rachel? I'm gagging for a drink.'

Inside there was a queue forming for the kitchen with everyone in it bar Johan and his mum. So I took this opportunity to wheel round the tables. On my knee was my phone, I knew I'd want to keep a record of the exhibition, so at each table I tried to take at least one photograph.

I wheeled back past Pauline and Elaine's tables, and noted they'd already put their chairs together in front of the fire door, before I moved over to look at Mike's paintings . As I wheeled forward, I saw Johan's mum step backwards into my path.

'Oh, sorry, are you Rachel?'

'Are you Johan's mum?'

'Yes, Eleanor.' She thrust out her hand for me to shake it. 'Pleased to meet you.'

Eleanor wandered over to my table.

'Lovely artwork, Rachel. Really lovely. Have you been painting long?'

'Quite a few years now.'

'Well, I hope you get plenty of sales.' Eleanor placed a hand on my shoulder as she walked back over to Johan.

While Johan was talking to his mum, I went over to his tables. One table was set up for portraits and caricatures, the other selling his acrylic paintings. One painting was lying flat on the table, the other three were standing up behind. All of them featured rows and rows of perfectly painted circles, which made my eyes dance. One was painted in black and white and would be a great birthday present for my brother. I peered at the price label and tried not to react at the nine hundred pounds he was asking for the piece.

His other table was neatly laid out, with two examples of caricatures – one of Mick Jagger and another one of Woody Allen. A chair had been placed strategically at the side of his table ready for his subjects.

He was still talking to his mum so I wheeled back over to my table, every now and then taking a furtive glance at them. I had to admit I wasn't overly pleased with his reaction to me, even though he was friendly and polite. It was becoming obvious he just saw me as a group member, nothing else.

Everybody was now filing back into the hall and soon were either sitting by their tables or putting the final touches to their table displays.

'It's ten, I'm opening up,' called out Anne.

Anne opened the door and then walked back into the hall, her glasses on as she checked the time on her watch. I pulled out a book, The Studio Game by Peter Burnett, which I'd secreted behind one of my frames. Johan was drawing in a sketchpad. Mike leant with his elbows on the table and his head resting in his hands. Anne hovered, one eye on the door, another eye on her watch. In the kitchen Marjorie was putting onto the hatch a three tiered display of cupcakes.

After a long fifteen minutes, a lanky young man, with a crew cut, wearing a Nirvana t-shirt and battered jeans sauntered into the hall. He was in his mid-twenties and in one hand hung a car key from his thumb and the other hand a mobile. He spoke quietly to Anne who pointed over in my direction, with a scowl.

'Rachel?'

I nodded and gulped.

The man stared at the Carthom street painting and after stuffing his mobile and keys into his back pocket, he picked it up. He stretched out his arms and held the painting at eye level, his head on one side. He then loosened his arms and examined the painting, his eyes squinting. After this he'd a quick glance at the price sticker on the back.

'Can I erm..? I mean, do you..?'

'You met my girlfriend the other day, Lizanne Oltermann, she works for Carthom News. She really liked this.'

He took a couple of steps until he was next to me and pointed to one of the shops on my painting.

'She was born there. It used to be a house, a two up, two down. It's our third anniversary today, so I decided to get her this. Has it been this quiet since you opened?' He took a quick panoramic look around the hall.

I nodded.

With the painting under his arm, he stuck his heel out and moved his foot from side to side.

'You should put a sign near the main road; let people know you are down here.' He opened his wallet and pulled out two grubby twenty pound notes. Without making any eye contact, he passed it to me.

'Here's the money, love. Keep the change.'

'Thanks, that's great. Do you want some bubble wrap?'

'Nah, I've got the car out front. Cheers, love.'

With that, he was gone without looking at any other paintings or any other table.

Anne strode over to me, hands on hips and with an accusatory tone demanded to know if I knew him.

'No, he's the boyfriend of Lizanne the reporter. He said we ought to put something near to the main road, to let people know we're here. We could attach a sign to a lamp post or something?'

'A lamp post? Let's just see who comes. As long as we don't get more like him. He wasn't bothered about looking at anything else.'

Kate limped over to me. 'What did I say? My crystal ball was right, for once.'

'She isn't impressed.' I nodded towards Anne who was walking down the hall.

Kate arched her back and rubbed it with her fingers. 'She'll be all right once she gets a sale.'

When it was nearly eleven o'clock, more visitors arrived. They included, Pauline's husband, a couple of Anne's friends, a woman who knew Johan, and Jonathon, who after a quick word with Kate, walked over to me.

The woman who was talking to Johan, wandered over to me. She was very masculine looking, with unruly brown hair, a square jaw and bushy eyebrows. She took a cursory glance at my paintings before reaching for my book. She glanced at the back cover and then flicked through the pages.

'Do you do a lot of reading?' she asked in a gruff voice.

'Yeah, a fair amount.'

'I'm Janet, by the way.' She put my book down and stretched out her hand, to grip mine and shook it so hard my arm was jerking up and down.

'I'm starting a book group in the village after the summer and I'm trying to find out who'd be interested. We'd read a book a month, and then meet to talk about it. Would this appeal to you?'

I nodded enthusiastically.

Janet pulled out some yellow post-it notes and a biro from her shoulder bag.

'Put your email or phone number down, and I'll be in touch.'

After I wrote down my details and handed it back to Janet, she shook hands with me again, this time with a wink, before she made her way around the other stalls.

Meanwhile, Anne sold a painting of an owl to one of her friends and Pauline's husband had his caricature drawn by Johan. Half an hour later we were back with an empty hall.

Eddie sidled up to me again. 'I wasn't trying to indoctrinate you earlier, kiddo. I just imagine you have some tough days?'

'I do, but getting more involved with things like this is helping.' I made a vague gesture in front of me. 'I was getting quite lonely at times, but the art group has made a big difference.'

'Oh, I know that feeling. Loneliness, I mean. Christmas this year was especially tough as the friends I usually spend Christmas day with were away and I didn't make alternative plans in time. I spent Christmas on my tod, eating scrambled eggs and an apple pie that I cremated in the microwave. At the end of the day, I tell you, I felt like microwaving myself.'

'I'm sorry, I didn't realise.'

'It's alright, kiddo. It was my fault for not sorting something out sooner.'

'Do you have...erm...a lady friend?'

'I have a good friend in Fi-Fi over there.' Eddie nodded his head in the direction of Fiona. 'But as for romance, it's a big, fat no. I don't even know how to go about it nowadays. I don't want to seem like a dirty old man, but when you've been comfortably married for a long time, in my case twenty-two years, you get out of practice. Fi-Fi keeps threatening to set me up with one of her friends or their relations. I wouldn't mind as long as they were genuine.'

Eddie scooted back to his table as another group arrived. This time it was members of the public with no connection to anybody. They spent an inordinately long time over at Fiona's table but the only sales were from one couple who bought a small ink and pencil drawing from Marion and a woman who bought a small acrylic abstract painting from Kate. An elderly man wandered in wearing a sweat band around his bald head and full running gear. He wandered around looking lost and left without buying anything. After him, a middle aged couple poked their heads into the hall, but soon turned away. At midday, the members who hadn't yet sold anything weren't happy.

Mike signalled to me, and I followed him out for a cigarette.

'I knew it would be like this,' he said, lighting his cigarette. 'I'll give it until one o'clock and if nothing has gone by then, I'm off.'

Anne walked out of the centre, armed with a couple of posters and wide masking tape.

'Just putting a few of these up. I thought about putting one on the pedestrian crossing pole, what do you think?'

'Yeah, as long as it isn't obstructing anything.'

Anne nodded and started to walk up the road.

'Is it still alright for me to buy your painting, Mike?'

'You don't have to buy it, you can have it.'

'Come off it. I'll buy it, Mike, it'll...'

Mike interrupted me. 'Do you think Anne will mind if I go soon?'

'It's up to you when you come and go Mike; it's not up to her. What will you do, pick up your paintings later on? You could always leave them here. I'll get Eddie to put them away in the store cupboard, when the sale's over. You could pick them...' I stopped talking as I spotted a group of five people walk into the centre.

'Yeah, I could do that,' Mike said. 'I'll just take me painting for Dot.'

'Ah, I bet she'll be really pleased with that.'

'Actually, I might as well go and get off now, before Anne gets back.'

I followed Mike into the centre and in front of him I caught sight of the long blonde hair of what looked like one of the guards. I felt my chest tighten and bile flooded my mouth. I let out a whimper, before turning around and wheeling as fast as I could. I retched, not caring if vomit went on my clothes.

'What's up, Rachel?'

Mike was following me, but I couldn't reply, I wheeled to the back of the centre and parked myself in a tight spot between two cars.

'The woman, who just went in, long blonde hair, plump.'

'Who is it?' Mike bent down to look at me.

I put my head down onto my lap and wrapped my arms over my head. After a second, I lifted my head up. 'Mike please, just see if she's got a mole by her nose. Don't tell anyone anything. Please.'

'What if she does have one? Do you want me to get anyone? You're not really making sense.'

'Please Mike. Just see if it's who I think it is.'

Mike limped back towards the centre.

I could picture the guard as she gathered the group members together to tell them who I really was, and could almost hear the reaction her revelations would invoke. Mike still hadn't returned and this confirmed my worst fears.

I lifted my head back up when I heard footsteps.'

'She hasn't got a mole; look there she is, leaving now'

I looked up and used my hand to block out the sun. If I squinted, I could just make out the woman as she walked away from the centre. She was perhaps slimmer than the guard, but in every other respect, the resemblance was uncanny.

'You're sure she didn't have a mole? What did she do when she was in the hall?'

'She just wandered around like everyone else and didn't buy anything. Rachel, you're shaking something rotten. Here have a ciggie, calm yourself down.' Mike passed me a cigarette. 'Who did you think she was?'

'Rachel, Mike,' Kate called out.

'Over here,' Mike shouted.

'Are you two coming in? Oh, gosh, Rachel what's happened?'

'She was worried about some woman who just went into the centre. She thought she knew her,' Mike said.

'I'm alright,' I croaked.

'So, who did you think she was? You're not going to tell us you've got some deep, dark secret lurking in your past, are you?'

Kate said with a wink.

'Don't be stupid,' I snapped angrily.

I saw Kate raise her eyebrows to Mike. A shared glance, I wasn't meant to see.

'It was just a woman I wanted to avoid. She's nothing special. She would be nosing around, so I just wanted to get out of her way. There's nothing wrong with that, I don't think so anyway.' I was giving a nervous, long-winded answer and stopped when I saw Kate and Mike glance at each other again.

'Shall we go back in?' Kate looked down at me and mouthed, 'are you sure you're OK?'

I replied with a quick nod.

'I've got to get off now.' Mike rubbed his back, and after another glance at Kate then me, he started to walk back to the centre.

Kate waited for me to get out from between the cars. In silence we made our way back around the centre. At the main doors, Kate bent down; with one hand she rubbed the top of my arm.

'You do know you can talk to me, Rachel? Anytime.' She gave a sad lopsided smile.

'I'm sorry; I'm just tired and a bit fed up today.'

Kate stood up and waved me into the centre first.

Inside, Mike was writing a message on the back of the painting he was going to give me. I saw him put the painting of the Labrador into a carrier bag so while he was writing I put twenty pounds into the bag.

'Here you are then. I don't want any money, take it as a present.' Mike handed me the painting.

'Thanks Mike. I can't wait to put this up when I get back home.'

Mike blushed, picked up his rucksack and the carrier bag. 'See you later.'

'Where's young Mike going?' Eddie boomed as he walked

towards me.

'He's not well,' I said when Mike had finally left the hall.

'Well? Who's not well?' Anne demanded as she walked into the hall with a mug in her hand.

'Young Mike. So what's he doing about his paintings, Rachel?'

'He said to me if we could look after his table and keep his paintings in the store cupboard until Wednesday.'

Anne made a scoffing noise. 'So he goes off home, leaving us to sell and then store his paintings? What a cheek. I can't guarantee they'll be safe in the cupboard–other people use it. I hope he isn't expecting us to pay out if something gets taken or damaged.'

'He was travelling by bus and he doesn't feel well.'

Anne glared at me but I held her gaze until she walked away.

I smiled as I read back of Mike's painting, he'd written: To my friend Rachel, love, Mike xx

For the rest of the afternoon, I kept checking the window behind me, where I could see who was coming in or out of the car park.

After dinner, a group of three women who had no connection to the group turned up. They took a long time looking at each table, and when they arrived at my table I realised why. All three of them were amateur artists on the hunt for ideas and techniques.

'Hello, I'm an artist too and I was wondering how you did that?' One woman said. She touched a painting on my table; I couldn't see which one she meant.

'Can you just show me, please?'

'She can't see it, Emily.'

'This one here.' Emily held the painting up and was pressing her finger on the glass. 'How did you do this bit of sky?'

'I painted it wet on wet, then covered it with diluted Naples yellow, adding ultramarine blue before putting a touch of alizarin crimson to blend it together. When it was dry I then added a bit of definition around for the sh...'

I stopped talking when I realised two of the women were staring down at me. As they continued to stare I wanted to stick my tongue out or pull a face.

'What's wrong with you, love? Were you in a car accident?'

I moved my arm towards my body, and all three women moved closer to me. 'I was knocked over by a truck and then run over by a car on the motorway and left for dead.'

'Oh, Lord,' said Emily. She stood up and made a brief staggering movement as if she was going to lose her balance.

After spending the best part of an hour in the centre, the three ladies left without buying any artwork. Anne let out a very emphatic sigh and wandered over to the window.

'Maybe we should have left it for a bit, until we'd more members?' Anne said to nobody in particular.

'I just wonder whether we're placed in the ideal spot,' Kate said. 'I mean with the library shut, the police station closing, the health centre is shut on a Sunday, so who would walk down here?'

There were murmurs of agreement at this point.

I looked up at the clock, then at my watch. I wanted to go home but ideally I didn't want to be the only one. I needed a human shield to protect me from Anne.

I turned in my chair towards Johan, who had one elbow on his table with his head resting on his hand. He stared blankly at me, and then gave a half-hearted smile.

'Johan, I'm planning to go at three o'clock,' I whispered. 'What about you?'

'You've read my mind; I was just thinking when I could escape.'

Anne marched over and stood next to Johan's table.

'What are you two muttering about? It's not polite to whisper in public, my mother always said that.' Anne turned on her heels and walked over to Eddie.

'You must be disappointed Eddie, with no sales?'

Eddie shrugged. 'You win some you lose some.'

'Win some and lose some? It's a lot of work you know, an awful lot of work, and this is all we get. I don't want the responsibility of doing another one, not if this is all we get, just a handful of sales.'

'I don't mind helping out, Anne,' Kate said.

Anne ignored Kate and carried on with her conversation.

'I don't think it helps, the article only focusing on a handful of people, it really should have had a group shot with all of us holding our painting. With the photograph of the group you could hardly see me and this is my group.' Anne then whispered something behind her hand.

'We're all artists and we're a group, we should all support each other,' Eddie replied.

'Support each other? You don't understand what I'm saying, Eddie.'

Kate tried again. 'I'll help you with the next art sale, Anne.'

'Next art sale? If, and I really do mean if, there's another one then yes, you can help.'

I heard a beep of a mobile and turned to Johan, who held up his thumb and then held up three fingers. I gave a smile of thanks mixed with relief; I didn't want to leave on my own after what she'd said about Mike. Kate saw this, and limped across.

'When are you leaving, three o'clock?'

'I'm going to start packing up then. It will take a while getting everything bubble wrapped and in the car.'

'Are you leaving then as well, Johan?'

Johan nodded. 'I'll start packing stuff up then.'

'Just tread carefully. You saw how Anne responded when Mike left.'

'If Mike was well and could drive then I'd understand, but he's travelling on the bus, with all of those paintings. He's got a lot on his plate at the moment; I'm surprised he even came in the first place.'

'All I'm saying is be careful not to aggravate the situation.'

Kate walked over to the window to have a brief look outside before she turned around and sat perched on the windowsill. When she limped back I signalled to her.

'If I go just after three o' clock, I'll try and wrap up as much of Mike's work as well. If you stay until near the end, could you make sure it gets put away OK, or would you prefer I did it when I go?'

'Don't worry. I'll get Eddie to help me.'

'What's this?' Anne called out.

'Oh, she's getting on my bloody nerves,' I whispered under my breath. I wheeled quickly outside, tears rushing up into my eyes.

Kate limped out and joined me.

'Hey, sweetie, what's the matter?'

'It's just been building up. I'm scared of having an almighty fall out, but the photo in the paper wasn't my decision. I didn't say to the reporter to put my photo there. Anne, in the car yesterday said the reporter must've felt sorry for me. I don't...'

'She said what? The only reason your photo was there was because the reporter felt sorry for you? That's awful, Rachel, if she says things like this you've got to defend yourself.'

'And have her go mad?' I rubbed my forehead, and momentarily closed my eyes.

'So, what if it causes an almighty row? Surely, it's better to be said rather than festering inside you. I know her responses can be facile at times and she can use out of date language and terminology but it doesn't give her the right to be so offensive.'

'If I pull her up she'll get defensive and there'll be so much tension. In many ways I need this group, I don't have much contact with anything else.'

'So, I understand what you're saying; its contacts and you need to meet people, but it really can't be at the expense of your emotions.'

'How would you tackle her?'

'I'd just try to get her to see it from your point of view. So that she knows what she said upset you. After all, she wouldn't like it if someone said the only reason people bought her paintings was because they felt sorry for her. Would she?'

'I'm not confident like you are, Kate.'

'You need to do something. You can't just leave it, or she'll continue to say things like this, and it's in here, you'll suffer.' Kate tapped my forehead.

'This is where you are.' Anne appeared at the door.

'Rachel's a bit upset, aren't you?'

I nodded.

'Why?'

'So, why do you think, Anne? You said something quite offensive to Rachel. The reporter obviously recognises Rachel's talent. Whether she's disabled or not is immaterial.'

'What've I done wrong? All I'm saying is the reporter had to judge out of all the photographs who to put on the top. Rachel's the only one in a wheelchair so it's obvious why she was chosen. I didn't mean anything nasty by it.'

'It's about time you had a think about why you're making such remarks.' Kate banged her crutch on the ground and then stood as if glued to the spot.

'What's going on?' Eddie called out, running to the door. His narrowed eyes jumped from my face to Kate and then back to me.

Anne stood slump shouldered and deflated. I could hear Kate breathing next to me.

'I'm sorry, Rachel, but next time if you think I've upset you, talk to me first without involving the world and his wife.' She turned to Eddie. 'I was being told off. Apparently I'm insulting them, despite arranging this and involving them in the group. I didn't have to do it, did I? Now I'm being put in my place.' Eddie put his arm around Anne and glared at us as he took Anne inside.

'Oh God, have I gone and made things worse.'

'It's OK, Kate, honestly, it's alright.'

I followed Kate back in. Eddie was standing by the toilets and he said he wanted to speak to me on my own. When Kate had gone back into the hall, he explained Anne had said to him what she meant, and she was now upset in the toilets. Faintly, I could make out the noise of someone crying, presumably Anne.

'You need to have a word with each other, in private,' Eddie said. He knocked on the door leading to the toilets and then opened it. Poking his head around, he called out Anne's name.

Sniffling, with a screwed up piece of toilet paper, Anne emerged.

'I'm sorry if I offended you. I'm trying my best for everyone in this group, whether they're young, old or handicapped.'

'Disabled,' Eddie said firmly.

'Yes, so I'm sorry if it came out wrong. I didn't mean it like that.'

The words from 'Whispers of the Beloved' flashed in my brain and seemed to reverberate around my mind, eventually making a connection with a random thought about loneliness. This switched on in my head a warning signal, in the form of a neon fluorescent sign: 'Alone you're blown in all directions.' I gripped the sides of my chair

'I know you've included us, but I'm not here just because I'm disabled. I'm an artist just like you two are and...'

Eddie interrupted me. 'We know that, don't we, Anne?'

'What? Yes, yes of course.'

Anne looked over my head at someone and Eddie was doing the same. I turned around and saw my mum in the doorway.

I blurted out quickly and quietly. 'I think Kate has packed Mike's stuff but it needs putting away safely. I promised him.'

'I'll make sure,' Eddie said. 'Now, kiss and make up you two.'

I looked up at Anne who turned away.

From behind, my mum rubbed my hair.

'Is everything OK?'

'No, I need to go home. Now, Mum.'

Sixteen

The post mortem of the art sale began three days later at the art group. Despite there being a few sales, the consensus reached was the art sale had been a waste of time. Kate led the discussion and she focused on three main areas. When we held the art sale, with Kate and others deciding Sunday was probably not the best day. Where we held it, as the centre was now between two buildings, one closed and one soon to be closed. Finally, Kate posed the question as to why we held it; would it be better to have waited until we were more established as a group? Or wait until we'd more members?

Through this discussion, Anne had remained silent. She sat motionless, her clenched fists on the table. The only movement noticeable was an angry pulse twitching in her clamped jaw.

'So all in all, you think I chose the wrong day. I chose the wrong venue. And I rushed us into having an art sale. Why hasn't anyone complained before? You can't blame me for everything,' Anne snapped, ending her silence.

Kate rolled her eyes. 'No one's blaming anyone. All I'm saying are these three factors should be considered so our next art sale has more of a chance to be successful.'

'Next sale? There's not going to be a next sale, not with me anyway. All this responsibility and then being blamed left and right. On Sunday, I was ready to stop this group, that's how upset

I felt.'

Anne stood up, her face flushed.

'Come on, Anne, you're right. All of us organised the art sale, so this is only a discussion about how we can improve things,' said Kate.

Anne shook her head, her lips pursed together and walked out of the room, prompting Lena and Marion to go after her.

Kate tried to speak again, but Eddie cut her off before she'd even said one word.

'Shush. I think she's quite upset.' Eddie walked out of the room, leaving Kate and Mike, Pauline, Elaine, Albert and me. After a few minutes, Albert got up and joined his wife. They were all huddled around Anne in the corridor and even though I hadn't joined in with the discussion, I felt guilty.

Kate leant across the table. 'Do you think I was too brutal? I wanted to raise points we could all talk about, not simply get at Anne,' she whispered.

'It was fine. God knows what's going on, but I'm getting fed up with all of this.'

'Histrionics, that's exactly what's going on.' Kate ran her finger along one of the deep grooves in the table.

Mike tapped on the side of my wheelchair and nodded his head towards the car park.

'Yeah, OK.'

We got our coats on, and Kate said she'd come out in a minute for 'a word.'

Mike held open the door for me and managed to clear the huddle of people around Anne so I could get outside. I was aware the talking stopped as we went past, starting up again as we made our way out of the main door.

'This is turning out to be a waste of bloody time,' Mike said, lighting up. He put a trembling hand through his hair.

'Anne was like this over the photo in the paper. She said the only reason why the reporter put the photograph of me and my painting in was because she was felt sorry for me.'

'Surely you told her where to go, didn't you?'

I hesitated. 'No, the problem is I didn't.'

Kate limped outside and leant against the wall. 'What a performance,' she said.

Mike was now pacing up and down, following a pattern of five paces one way, then a drag on his cigarette and then five paces back, looking at the ground as he did so.

'Is he OK?' Kate whispered, nodding her head towards Mike.

'The atmosphere in there doesn't help.'

'My intention wasn't to upset her or blame her. The other week, I asked her how much money we'd got in the kitty and her reply was, "Why? Do you think I'm stealing the money?" She gets so defensive and sometimes she's downright hostile.' Kate looked at her feet, her bobbed hair obscuring one side of her face.

'I think we'd better go back in.'

'So, before we do, Rachel, are you alright for half five, to go to The Richmond tomorrow?'

'No problem. Mike, are you coming in, get some painting done?'

The huddle of people inside had gone. In the hall instead of the usual chatter, there was a prolonged awkward silence. After fifteen minutes of complete silence, stilted and strained conversations began.

Anne, however, was quieter than anyone else. I watched her for a minute as she briefly looked across at Kate then at me. Our eyes met and I smiled cautiously. Anne, with great effort, twisted the corners of her mouth into a smile.

As for the group, everyone was still subdued and quiet. It made me concerned about what would happen if there was a real problem, or dispute.

Anne waved in front of my face. 'Rachel, Rachel.'

'What? Oh sorry, what were you saying, Anne?'

'You were deep in another world there. I was saying do you want to go home at dinnertime again today?'

'Sorry. Yes, thanks.'

I left the table to go to the toilet when I realised my worst nightmare had happened. I was wet and the urine had soaked through my pad onto my jeans. Why did it have to happen at the group? I was light headed and felt a disembodied sensation, where, from above, I could peer down see myself panicking but also I had sight the hall, where I could watch the reaction of the group members as well as back into my recent past where I could hear the guards laughing and making fun of me.

Lena knocked on the toilet door.

'Everything OK in there?'

A weight dropped into my stomach.

'Yes... um...No. Not really. I'm coming out now. I need to go home there's been a bit of a problem with my, um, with my bladder. Could you do me a favour and ask Anne to put everything into my art bag?'

'I can put all your art materials away.'

'Thanks, Lena, don't tell anyone else, please?'

'It's OK, don't worry. I'll have a quiet word with Anne, and get your art bag ready.'

I waited outside the cubicle in the bathroom. Being wet, brought back unwanted memories of the guards when they laughed at me and pinched their noses complaining about the smell of urine in the bungalow.

Footsteps brought me back to Carthom, after a few seconds, Anne knocked on the toilet door.

'What's happened?'

'I'm just a bit wet.'

'Wet?'

'Can we just go?' My voice sounded weak and pathetic.

'You'll have to sit on some newspapers.'

In the car, all she wanted to know was what was wrong with

my bladder. I attempted an explanation before I sat in silence for the rest of the journey. My head was resting against the passenger window with the newspaper crinkling and rustling under my bottom. It seemed to take an awfully long time to travel the two or three miles.

On my own again, my chin trembled and I started to cry. Nothing was ironed, and I would need to have another bath. My tears of chagrin, angrier than my first, developed as soon as I began to replay events in my mind. I was annoyed at myself more than anyone else.

Janine arrived to find me red eyed and still tearful. She dumped her bag near the front door and then with one arm put it around the top of my shoulders.

'What's up, Rachel? Have you been crying?'

That set me off crying again.

Janine crouched down, with one arm still around my back, the other hand placed on my knee.

'Come on, don't get upset. What's the matter?'

'I'm wet, my stupid bladder, I was wet in my art group. Nothing's ironed and I'm going to need to get another bath and...'

Janine interrupted me. 'I can run the bath for you, and while you get ready for the bath, I'll iron your clothes.' Janine jumped up, and pressed down her skirt. 'What do you want to wear?'

'There's a pair of jeans and the blue top, on my kitchen chair. I'm OK for underwear, it's all upstairs.'

'I'll go and run your bath.'

Janine darted up the stairs and I followed her in the stair lift. Her reaction had been practical, like Lena, no fuss, no questions just ready to assist.

'Do you want some Radox in?'

'A bit, thanks.'

Janine passed me my bathrobe and in my bedroom, I got undressed. She nipped back downstairs while I went into the bathroom, transferred onto the bath board, and started to sponge myself down, as well as check my pressure points for ulcers. Five minutes later I heard Janine dart back upstairs. From the bathroom I called out to her.

'Nothing seems to faze you, does it?'

The bathroom door was open, Janine stood on one side of it, with me on the other side still on the bath board.

'I suppose not, no.'

'When I was in Weston, I had these awful people who wouldn't be like you, giving me privacy. Instead they'd sit staring at me while I had a bath. In fact they even took the door off the bathroom at one point.'

'Why? God, that sounds bloody awful.'

I shook my head slowly. 'I really don't know why. At one stage, I just accepted it, even thinking it was in my best interest but as time went on I realised it was just them trying to make my life…well, unbearable.' I dangled my fingers into the lukewarm water.

'You don't talk about it much. Were they carers like me, from an agency?'

'No, they weren't like you at all.'

'I would've complained, didn't you?'

'I complained, my mum complained. Even my brother complained. We worked out in the end they were all landing on the same desk, and then probably all thrown in the same bloody bin. Take it from me; they were a really nasty bunch.'

'I believe you, Rachel. It reminds me of how the nurses treated my nan when she was in hospital. One time, there was this old lady stark naked with the door open. It was nearly visiting time. None of the nurses shut the door, so I did. Next thing, this nursing assistant, she wasn't even a proper nurse, took off on me, and I mean, really shouting. I thought to myself you shouldn't be in this job, you should be a prison officer.'

'It's strange isn't it? Most people in the caring professions do it because they do care. Others seem to like the control. They don't see patients as human beings, and if there's more than one of them, all with the same mindset, well that's when it can get really dreadful and damaging.'

'I had this manager once, when I first joined Concerned about Care. She told me not to show sympathy. Not to feel sorry for people. Instead, she said, we should show empathy and see things through the client's eyes. Like, I don't know what it's like for you being like you are but I can listen to you and try to put myself in your shoes.'

I found myself smiling. 'You're spot on, Janine. Spot on.'

'She's a social worker now.'

'Wouldn't you ever like to do something like that? You're more than capable.'

'Do you really think so?'

'Of course. I mean, you might need some extra training, but you've got a caring nature. Not everyone has this. If you're working in social care, a caring nature can go a long way.'

'What I really want to do is run my own agency, like this one. Are you ready to come out now?'

'Yeah.'

'Are you OK transferring?'

I started to swing over to my wheelchair.

'I'm OK, just will need a hand with my clothes.'

Back in my wheelchair, I wrapped the robe around me before wheeling into the bedroom. Janine had laid everything out, including my underwear.

As she was helping me get my clothes on, I sighed.

'What's up?'

'I wish you'd been around when I was in Weston.'

Janine smiled. 'I'm nothing special.'

'I'm not sure if you know what a difference you've made to my life already.'

Janine blushed. 'Do you fancy a cappuccino? I'll make it, then I'd best be off. My next client will be phoning my supervisor if I'm not there on time.'

By the time I got downstairs, a mug of cappuccino was on the kitchen table.

'Are you sure you can't have one?'

'I've only got a couple of minutes, sorry, Rachel. So I'd better not. What are you up to this afternoon?'

I screwed up my face. 'Nothing much, I'll read my book and probably listen to music. Oh, that reminds me, it's still in my art bag.'

'Shall I nip and get it?'

'Cheers, it's called The Studio Game.'

Janine walked back into the kitchen a couple of minutes later without my book, instead carrying a white sheet of paper in a plastic wallet. She placed it in front of me.

'Did you do this?'

Sketched in pencil was my portrait. In the corner of the paper in ink was Johan's signature, which looked like a squashed spider. I tried to register the fact he'd drawn such a tender, lovely portrait, and had slipped it into my bag without telling me, and without me noticing.

'Oh my God, no, no, I didn't do it. That's Johan's signature. He must've done this at the art sale. I love it. How on earth did he get this in my bag?'

'It's lovely. Can I have another look?'

I stared at it again, and couldn't stop smiling, before I passed it back across the table.

'It's gorgeous and you never knew he'd drawn it?'

'No. I can't quite believe it. I don't even have his phone number or address to thank him. Anne probably does but I don't want her to know, she'd end up telling everybody.'

'What's he like this Johan? Do you er..? Do you like him?'

I pulled out my phone, and showed Janine the photo I'd taken while at the exhibition, which showed Johan talking to his mum.

I was aware I felt hot, and out of the corner of my eye, could see part of my nose was a deep red.

Janine smiled, as she looked up at me. 'You like him, don't you?'

I lowered my eyes but grinned at the same time.

'Aw, that's lovely, really lovely. Hate to say this but I must get off. You should frame this.' Janine was throwing her car keys up in the air and catching them. She was like a tennis player about to serve. Up they go, followed by a quick swipe

'No problem and cheers, Janine, for everything.'

Janine, grinned, and had a gleam in her eyes, as she waved goodbye. When she was gone, I spent a few minutes sitting smoking out of my back door. I was interrupted by a phone call from Kate.

'Listen Rachel, I didn't know whether to tell you this, but when Anne got back from dropping you off, Eddie asked her if everything was alright. She replied saying you had an accident.'

'She didn't, did she? Did everyone..?' I felt my mood, which had soared due to the portrait, suddenly dip, before it crashed down and disintegrated before me.

'Most people would've heard. I felt angry on your behalf.'

'That makes me feel mortified. In a way, I wish you hadn't told me that.'

'I just thought you should know, Rachel. Sorry to be the bearer of unpleasant news.'

'It's not your fault Kate, and it's probably better I do know about it. Anyway, I've got good news. Guess what I found today, in my art bag?'

'What was it?'

'A portrait of myself. Just in pencil but it's really lovely. Johan must've drawn it at the art sale.'

Wow! That is rather special. Try to think of that, and not Anne and what she said.'

When I finished on the phone, my delight at finding the

portrait was tempered by the embarrassment and anger I felt after hearing what Anne had said.

I was perplexed as to why I'd been so riled by her behaviour considering what I'd put up with from the guards. It was then I realised when I lived in the bungalow, humiliation and trouble-causing by the guards had been a daily occurrence. The guards were the ones responsible for calling me a 'spas' and 'cripp'. It happened so often I began to see it as almost normal. My outrage at Anne's behaviour was perhaps a sign my circumstances and confidence had improved.

The following day, I had only three items on my to-do list. Frame Johan's sketch, ask the social workers to reduce my care arrangements and go to The Richmond in the evening, with Kate.

The first item went smoothly. I framed the portrait and stood it up near my television. Each time I examined the sketch, I hoped he'd drawn my portrait because he liked me. That his intelligence meant he didn't see my wheelchair or disability as a problem. I told my mum about the sketch, and she wanted me to ask Anne for his address so I could thank him, but one thing I was certain about was I didn't want her to know.

The second item was more difficult. During the night before, I'd decided to try and take out the early evening visit from the care agency. The verdict, when I finally managed to speak to someone from the council, was I had to wait until a review meeting in six months. Even though I was ready to take the next step, I wasn't allowed to make the decision.

It reminded me of the lack of control I had at the bungalow, where decisions were made for me, and my opinions or wishes were disregarded completely.

By the time I got to the third item, I was ready to scream and felt a rush of relief when Jonathon and Kate arrived to take me to The Richmond.

Jonathon helped me into the car.

'So you're looking exactly like how I feel,' Kate said, when I got in the car.

'Just had a day from Hell.'

'My day in the office has been the same. So I think we're all in a bad mood,' Jonathon said.

'Great,' Kate murmured from the back of the car.

'I've been trying to sort out my support arrangements, and cancel one of my carers.'

'You're my carer, support worker, lover and best friend all rolled into one, aren't you sweetie?' Kate tickled the back of her husband's neck, making him smile.

I half turned in my seat towards Kate,

'What paintings have you brought for here?'

'You've seen them all before. It's paintings that didn't sell at the art exhibition.'

We pulled up outside The Richmond and were surprised to see it was full of customers and most of them were standing up. Jonathon read the a sign on the door telling us the singer had been on a reality TV show and that today he was promoting his new album. Jonathon held the door ajar, so we could hear him sing a few lines of a song, which sounded vaguely familiar.

'We're going to have to come back another day. I don't fancy going in there,' Kate said. She screwed up her face up, so her nose wrinkled.

'Do you want to come back for a coffee or anything?'

Jonathon with his eyebrows up, gave a little nod to Kate.

'Cheers, Rachel, Jonathon's got to nip to the office to pick up some files. Only for fifteen minutes though, I'm afraid, as getting home this time of day can be a nightmare.'

'I'll drop you both off. Come on, time's ticking, otherwise the office will be closed.'

'Jonathon, we're coming, don't nag.'

When we were inside my house, Kate asked if it was alright if she had a look around. Before I'd even agreed, Kate was making her way around the living room followed by the kitchen and the downstairs bathroom and toilet.

'So, from outside, you'd think this was tiny, it looks like a two up, two down house. Your kitchen; this is so much bigger than ours. Loving the fact your sink and most of the cupboards are at your level, even the plugs.' Kate pointed towards the ceiling. 'Can I have a little peek upstairs?'

'Sure. If you're walking up, watch out because of the stair lift, but if you want to go up in style, use the lift. What do you want to drink? I've got cappuccino.'

'Lovely, thank you.'

I heard Kate move around upstairs. By the time she came down, the kettle was just boiling.

'It's a lovely house, and so accessible.'

'I know I was lucky finding it. Here you go.' I handed Kate her drink and we sat opposite each other at the kitchen table.

'What about your place, Kate, is it fully accessible?'

'It needed a few adaptations when we first bought it.'

Kate took the newspaper that was folded on my kitchen table, and started to draw a plan on it, with the pencil I'd been using for the crossword.

'So, downstairs, we've got a kitchen, split like this one, so we use it as a kitchen and dining room. At the back of the house just here.' She indicated a spot with the pencil. 'This was a study when we bought it. We've made it our bedroom and added onto it an en suite. This means Jeremy's bedroom is upstairs as is Jonathon's study and I use the shed, which we converted into my studio.'

'Sounds lovely, though isn't it a shame there aren't more accessible houses around.'

'There's not enough access full stop – to property, jobs everything.'

'They didn't want to have me as a tenant here because I was on Benefits. It was only when Mum explained about my disability and acted as guarantor did they finally agree.'

'I've seen that a lot on adverts for rented properties. They put no pets, no smoking and no Benefits, as if being on Benefits was akin to destructive animals and the potential damage caused by smoking or fire.'

'Here, they didn't say I couldn't smoke, or have a pet. The only stipulation was I couldn't be on Benefits.'

'Love to know who your landlord is then, though sometimes these decisions are taken by agents. Of course, it could be just they're ill informed.'

'Like Anne.'

'Exactly. What she said about your bladder and the reporter and your photograph, just makes me want to clutch my head and scream.'

'I think she might be right regarding the paper. Maybe the reporter did put my photo there because I have an obvious disability. You know how some people can be? When they see a wheelchair all normal sense goes out of the window?'

Kate shook her head. 'Sweetie, her boyfriend bought your painting because she liked it. That's probably the reason why your photograph was there. I'm really sure it had nothing to do with your disability. If that was the case the photograph would very clearly show your wheelchair, but it didn't, not at all.'

'She did put I was disabled.'

'So, sweetie, that just relates to the piece. Honestly, it won't be that.'

'I'm not sure and as for Anne, I really don't know how to deal with her.'

'In the past I've managed truculent staff and it wasn't the easiest job in the world to try and get them to accept other views and possibilities.'

'I suppose it'll be like that with Anne.' I nodded slowly, and sipped at my coffee, 'Sometimes I get so cross at her language, but then I suppose some of that is her age.'

'Sure, it could be. Usually, I find if someone has life experience of disability, either personally or through a friend or family member then they're generally more up to date, regarding disability matters.'

'Like Lena–her husband was disabled,' I offered.

Kate nodded. 'Language can make such a difference. So, the other day, Jonathon and I were talking about all the phrases that include references to walking or standing - like best foot forward.'

'Or stand up and be counted,' I said laughing.

'If you think about it, there're lots of examples. We're living in an able bodied world, and it's going to take a long time, before it's more inclusive.'

'I hope you don't mind me asking, Kate, but do you find any of what's going on now difficult, y'know the scroungers/skivers rubbish?'

Kate stretched out her legs, and carefully massaged her knee. 'It does worry me. When I was working, I could almost kid myself I wasn't disabled – by being busy, lots of staff under me, and quite a big budget with lots of responsibilities.'

'I can relate to...'

Kate interrupted me. 'So, it really worried me that I was trying to pretend I wasn't disabled. I wondered why I was feeling ashamed of being disabled. I never used to be.' Kate shook her head. 'So, I do think it's got a lot to do with how disability's now viewed in the media and the effect this debate is having.'

'I know what you're saying, Kate. You can't escape it at present. The television, radio, newspapers all making out its disabled people's fault.'

Kate nodded. 'It's pernicious, it really is. When I hear Jeremy, he hardly ever tells anyone I'm disabled. He says I'm an artist, but leaves my disability out completely. I keep telling him, it's nothing to be ashamed of, that anyone can be born with a disability and that it only takes a split second for someone able bodied to become disabled. I also try to stress how difficult it is for someone with a disability to find work, but it doesn't seem to be sinking in yet.'

'I would've thought that age group would be more switched on regarding disability.'

'Sweetie, you know in the group we get annoyed at some of the comments from the older member? Well, you should hear kids who're around the same age as Jeremy. All they've grown up hearing is the demonization of those disabled who're using Benefits. A lot of them think people on Benefits who they call scroungers are the lowest of the lows.'

I stared out of the window. 'Since all the scrounger business, I've felt embarrassed and guilty about my disability, a lot more than I did before. I feel now I have to justify myself a lot more than I've done before.'

Kate held out her palms. 'So if this is what we're feeling, sweetie, imagine what somebody without a disability is thinking. It's scary isn't it? It's going to lead to some people simply not claiming benefits, not getting the money they really need, because they're frightened of the stigma or of being labelled a 'scrounger".

I nodded.

'Anyway, I want to know more about this portrait?'

'It's next to the television in the living room.'

Kate limped into the living room, while I watched at the door.

As she picked up the frame her mouth dropped like an 'O'. 'This is super, you lucky thing. He's a lovely guy, isn't he?'

I blushed and Kate grinned.

'I daren't say it out loud,' I whispered.

Kate held out her palm. 'What?'

'In case he doesn't like me in that way.' I glanced across at Kate. 'Can we talk about something else?'

'Don't feel embarrassed, sweetie.' Kate eased herself up and put her mug in the sink. 'OK, something different. Have you got any plans for this week?'

'Mum wants me to do a painting of her garden, and I'm going to buy back another book at the weekend.'

'Buy back?'

'I lost a few books when I moved so my favourites I've been buying again.' I felt my face burn red again. 'Can I be cheeky? Would you mind putting my paintings up for me at The Richmond? It would save you having to come to me first.'

'No problem. So, are they all in there, with price labels on?' Kate pointed at the large carrier bag propped up against my fridge. Her eyes narrowed. 'So how did you lose your books?'

'Was that a car?'

Kate limped through into the living room and over to the window. She leant on the windowsill straining to see Jonathon. After a tense minute, I heard a car, this time for real.

'Here he is. Thanks for the cappuccino, Rachel. I'll see you next Wednesday. Could you just bring your paintings to the door?'

When they were ready to drive away, I waved and went back inside. When I first moved to Carthom, all I wanted was a friend like Kate, yet talking to her made me feel guilty, ashamed and increasingly nervous. I knew a time would come when I couldn't keep the pretence up any longer, a time when I would have to reveal my true identity and past.

Seventeen

While Anne chatted away, I squinted out of the car window, my left hand shielding my eyes from the sun. Spring had definitely arrived. It felt much warmer and people who were out and about in Carthom blossomed with lots of smiles and pastel coloured cotton clothes. Anne seemed brighter in her mood as well, though I didn't know whether this was due to the change in weather or whether it was more evidence of her mercurial moods.

I was still seething about the comments Anne made to Eddie so my plan was just to go and paint for an hour, mainly to make sure they didn't start gossiping about me.

After the art group was the Information Day at Inspire and Support, and I was all prepared for it. I'd even put my suit out ready to change into and packed a bag.

'Rachel, are you listening?' Anne momentarily turned her head to face me. 'I was saying, I'm going to ask everyone today to write down if they want to see a demonstration. Like someone showing how they do screen printing or oil painting.'

'Good idea,' I muttered. My nose wrinkled up and I sniffed. The car smelt rank, like she'd left a bag of fish and chips in the car for a month or two. I peered down at my feet. I lifted up my left leg, with both arms. I couldn't see anything. I did the same movement with my right leg and still couldn't see anything. I then glanced behind me. On the back seat was a white carrier bag.

'What's the matter? You're a fidget bottom today.'

'Nothing, just looking at what's on the back seat.'

'In the back? Oh yes, I found that bag near the recycling tip. It was just balanced next to a skip and when I peeked inside there were lots of plastic boxes, packets, which just needed a wash. Always worth keeping things like that as you never know in a few years you might need them.'

I gave a half nod, though I didn't understand Anne's hoarding compulsions. I suppose she wasn't strictly a hoarder; it hadn't completely taken over her life. The only real problem area was her spare bedroom but I still couldn't work out why.

When we arrived at the centre, I immediately went to my

place and got out my art materials. I wanted to finish a painting of the Cumberland hills, but needed to concentrate as it was important to get the different tones right for the trees and hedges. I'd just started to paint when Eddie, Pauline and Elaine arrived. I didn't respond to their chatter and tried to concentrate.

'Not like you, Rachel, to be sat here painting before ten o'clock?' Eddie boomed.

'I'm only here for an hour today, so I just want to get on with it.'

'And you're OK after last week?'

I pretended not to hear, my burning cheeks my only reply.

Minutes later Kate arrived. When she sat down I lifted my hand for a silent 'hello'. Kate nodded and pointed her finger at Mike's empty seat with a shrug of her shoulders and a raised eyebrow. I mirrored her actions as my reply.

At ten o'clock everyone had arrived apart from Mike. Albert was in the middle of telling a joke. I hadn't heard the first bit but when he finished only Eddie and Pauline laughed. Lena gave out a groan, and Marion shook her head at her husband.

When there was silence, Anne cleared her throat. 'I was chatting to Lena and we thought it would be good every month to have a demonstration. For example someone could teach us how to do screen printing. So if you want to learn how to do something or you can give a demo yourself, then put the details in the notebook on the hatch.' Anne pointed towards the kitchen.

'Mind, if you want to give a demonstration, you must be good at it yourself. I thought Johan could do one. His caricatures and portraits are great.' Anne paused to peer around the table.

'Instead of calling out names, can you just come to me with your money and I'll tick you off the register.'

Anne glanced across the hall and frowned as the hall door opened and Mike stumbled in. His shirt was soiled and generally he appeared dishevelled. With a slight nod to acknowledge Anne he limped over to his chair,

'Well, this is all I wanted to say,' Anne said. 'So don't forget the register and this notebook on the hatch, OK?'

I turned my head around to face Mike. 'Are you alright, mate?'

Mike slowly shook his head.

'What's up?'

'They've said...They've said they're going to stop me money.' Mike gripped his head in his hands. 'I've tried to get an appointment at the welfare rights centre, but they won't take any new cases. The C.A.B. has closed. The only place where I've managed to get an appointment is on the far side of Weston and they won't see me until three weeks time.'

'Phone up the job centre or whoever's dealing with it and explain,' advised Kate.

Mike lifted his head to look at Kate. 'That's what they said. So, I phoned to say I needed another appointment to give me time to see these people from the welfare rights place.' Mike stared gloomily back down at the table. 'I got this shirty woman on the phone who said they couldn't postpone it and if I don't attend, I'll be taken off them. She said something about sanctions as well. I really can't take much...'

Someone started to tut. I immediately turned and saw it was Elaine.

'Why are you doing that?' Mike demanded. 'Come on, why?'

Elaine looked disgusted and turned to Pauline.

Pauline sneered and with one finger pointed directly at Mike. 'That's the reason the economy is in such bad shape. If people like you can't be bothered to turn up to an appointment, then you shouldn't get Benefits. It's like you want something for nothing.'

'The reason the economy's in such bad shape is because of the bankers,' Kate snapped, both her fists clenched on the table.

Eddie held up his hands into a 'T' shape. 'Time out, please...'

Pauline ignored Eddie and continued, as if she hadn't heard

Kate. 'It's something like three out of four pounds goes on welfare, so there does need to be cuts.'

'There are some people who need Benefits,' Elaine added. 'But then you've got the bad back and stress brigade who've been on Benefits for most of their lives. I think the government needed to put their foot down and weed out this lot.'

Pauline nodded. 'Most of them drink, smoke and gamble with tax payers' money. Working people can ill-afford such luxuries. What's fair with that?'

'Don't be so insensitive.' Kate remonstrated. 'Vulnerable people are being taken off Benefits. Just remember that.'

'Vulnerable people?' Anne replied. 'Most of the people being taken off have been filmed; you see 'em running marathons or playing football. These are the scroungers we're talking about.'

Kate swiped the air with her hand. 'Fraud is really low, it's no more than 0.7% of the whole Benefits bill.'

'That's only because they haven't caught them yet,' Marian muttered.

'You don't work percentages out like that, Marian. You take the figure for...'

Pauline interrupted Kate. 'Just in my road alone, there must be at least ten people who I reckon are scrounging. I look at them, they've got loads of kids, yet they go on holiday each year, and I'm not talking about a week in Wales, I'm talking about a foreign holiday. Where do they get the money? The answer is as clear as day; it's Benefits and they're scroungers.'

'The bloody State Pension is a Benefit, so would you call yourself a scrounger?' Mike shouted. His face was deep red, and his body was shaking.

Albert had been watching Mike, like a predator. He pointed at him with his hand trembling.

'I want you to know, young man, I've fought for this country and I could've died for this country. After the war I worked in whatever job I could find. I've never accepted a hand out in all my life and I don't intend to either. The pension's what you get for your work when you're younger. It's not a bloody Benefit. I want to know why you need advice. All they're asking you to do is turn up. I bet you want to know how you can get round it. Well, I'll tell you what you need to know now for free. Our pensions are not, and I'll say it again, they're not Benefits.'

'Come off it, the state pension is a Benefit but where's the problem in that?' I shouted. I was aghast at what was happening. To my disgust, some of the members, including Anne, appeared to be rapt, as if they were enjoying the argument.

'How dare you, how dare you?' Albert lifted his clenched fist up; he was scowling with his dark slug-like eyebrows meeting each other. I could imagine him in his younger days, combative and provocative. He'd be full of bluster, and despite his diminutive frame, prepared to be belligerent and belittle anyone who'd dared to stand in his way.

'Albert's right, what we get isn't a Benefit or Welfare.' Anne prattled. 'In our day, you didn't get all these people not working.'

I could hear both Kate and Mike groan.

'Don't forget nowadays, lots of illegal immigrants get Benefits now as well,' Marian said. Although calmer than Albert, Marion's eyes were dark and cold casting a visible shadow of displeasure across her face.

'Illegal immigrants can't get Benefits,' Kate said. 'The largest group claiming Benefits are pensioners.'

'All those Romanians and Polish people can get Benefits,' muttered Marion.

Kate raised her arms up. 'They're not illegal immigrants. If you decide to retire to Spain, you'd get Benefits.'

'That's totally wrong, The Daily Mail said pensioners...'

I interrupted Anne. 'Oh yeah, if it's in there, it must be right.'

'So, my dad's a pensioner.' Kate said. 'Even though he's nearly eighty-five, he knows it's a Benefit. Where do you think the money comes from? The trees? So, if it comes from the government it's a Benefit.'

Eddie stood up and started to rap his knuckles on the table until everyone was quiet. 'State Pension's a Benefit, course it is. However, can we calm this down? Everyone must respect everyone else. Jesus said 'Love thy neighbour as thyself', so please respect your colleagues.'

As he sat back down, Pauline, for a second closed her eyes. When she opened them, her eyes were trained straight at him. 'Eddie, don't you dare tell me what I should do. This isn't your bloody business.'

Lena put up her hand. 'Now come on, this doesn't help, using this kind of...'

'Don't you start now,' Pauline growled.

There was a moment of silence until Mike kicked out his chair and stood up, one hand rubbing his eye. 'I came here thinking you lot were me friends, well now I know the truth.'

'I'll tell you the truth. At this end of the table you've got folk who were prepared to die for this country. So even if we do get a pension, at least we've contributed to the country. What exactly have you done? Come on? What've you done? Nothing? What a surprise.' Albert smirked in a long drawn out way, like a person who thinks they're always right.

'Quite right,' Pauline barked.

'Let's go for a cigarette, Mike. Ignore them, they're just talking rubbish, come on.'

'What a bloody cheek. Talking rubbish? They can hardly talk,' Pauline said to Elaine who nodded.

I ignored Pauline and put my trembling hands out in front of me.

'I'll come with you. I'm absolutely disgusted by this,' Kate muttered.

I pushed myself away from the table and waited for Mike. Midway through the morning and Albert was still on his feet, one hand on the table, the other still clenched into a fist. Elaine was scowling, Pauline was shaking her head and nobody was painting at all. I was appalled at how quickly the composure of the group had disintegrated into mutinous factions.

Mike had his coat half on and was putting his art materials into his rucksack.

'You aren't leaving now, Mike, it's only early? I just meant we have a ciggie, not leave.'

'Thank God, maybe we can get some art done now,' Pauline said, with her lips curled, and eyebrows narrowed.

'I thought you lot were me friends,' Mike repeated.

'It's OK, Mike,' I pleaded. 'I'm your friend, Kate's your friend.'

Eddie coughed and put out his arm towards Mike. 'And I'm your friend.'

'Whose bloody side are you on?' Albert shouted. He banged his fist on the table, which made the water in Eddie's palette spill onto his paper.

'Now, look what you've gone and done' Eddie cried out. Lena dashed to the kitchen and ran back with a piece of kitchen paper.

'Don't you dare do that again,' Eddie threatened, as he dabbed at his painting with the kitchen towel. 'Or you won't know what's hit you.'

Lena leant back in her seat. 'Mike I'm your friend too.'

'Another bloody idiot,' Albert yelled. 'We're all pensioners this end of the table.'

'No, we're all in the same group, pensioners and disabled all in one group,' Lena replied. 'Don't you dare raise a fist towards me otherwise I'll go.' Lena half stood facing Albert. 'For that matter you can stop swearing too.'

'Well said, Lena. I can't believe he,' Eddie pointed at Albert, 'hasn't even bothered to say sorry to me yet.'

Mike squeezed past me, with his head down as he limped out of the hall. I followed him and shortly afterwards I was joined by Kate. Outside, Mike was sitting on the small wall of the car park.

He was smoking very fast and was uncommunicative.

'Are you alright, Mike?' I said, fearful of the answer.

He lifted his head up, his eyes squinting in the morning sun.

I persevered. 'They don't mean it, and it's just...'

Mike was inhaling hard. I turned my head towards Kate and shrugged.

She gave a nod. 'They don't mean it personally. It's hard for them to understand.'

Mike sighed deeply. 'I won't be back if this is what it's going to be like.' He stood up, one foot squashing his cigarette, before he fished another cigarette out of his packet and placed it behind his ear. He pulled up his jeans and adjusted his rucksack all without making eye contact, and limped off down the road.

'Mike,' I called out, but he carried on walking.

Kate put a hand on my shoulder. 'Leave him, Rachel, he'll need time to cool off. He'll be back next week.'

'Would you come back after that?'

Kate shrugged her shoulders, and slowly shook her head. 'I don't know, Rachel. I really don't know. So, I feel like going home myself, but we can't let this row affect us to the extent that all three of us no longer attend. We need to go back in and paint.'

'Go back in there, now? I don't think I can, I really don't.'

'It'll make it incredibly hard to continue, if we don't go back in.'

I looked down the road, and tried to block out the sun with my hand. I couldn't see him at all.

'I can't do it, Kate. They were awful in there, really awful. I'd feel as if I was letting Mike down.'

Kate sat down on the bench. 'If you're not going in then I won't. I must admit, I wasn't exactly looking forward to going back in there.'

'What about our bags?'

'Do you want me to get your things together?'

'Nah, I'll get mine, you get yours.'

I followed, Kate in but before going into the hall, she placed her hand gently on the top of my back. As we made our way to the table there was silence. I grabbed my bag and jacket, and followed Kate out of the hall.

Anne cleared her throat, as I was just by the double doors.

'Do you want a lift back?'

'No,' I muttered.

'Don't forget its Easter next week, so there isn't an Art for You meeting on Wednesday. We're back the following week.'

I inwardly groaned. 'Does Mike know? Somebody will need to tell him.'

Anne's face clouded. 'I'll give him a ring. Where are you off to now?'

'Home.'

Despite the frostiness inside the centre, outside, it was turning into a gorgeous day. I lifted my face up and felt the warmth on my skin. In the air was the smell of cut grass, mixed with the ever present smell of manure. A new season full of hope and possibility, but all I could think about was Mike.

'Do you want a lift?' Kate was rubbing her forehead and she looked weary.

'I think I'll wheel home, thanks anyway. Are you OK?'

'I just need a rest.' Kate gestured towards the centre. 'All this has made me thoroughly exhausted and fed up.'

'It's a mess, isn't it?'

Kate nodded.

It felt strange, going from the fracas at the group to the silence of my home. I tried him on his landline as well as his mobile but all I got was his answering machine. If it was me instead of Mike, I wouldn't want to go back. It was obvious there were deep divisions in the group and I couldn't see how we could ever go back to how we were before.

Janine arrived and I asked for help in getting ready for Inspire and Support.

'What's up? You seem awfully quiet.'

'There was a nasty row at the art group. I can't see how I'd ever go back. If Mike doesn't go back, then I'm not.'

'How do you mean?'

'I don't think I can go back. They were really appalling with Mike. I don't feel like this today.' I indicated to the stairs. 'Do you want to go up and I'll follow you?'

'I thought you didn't want to do this voluntary work. You were talking about it when we first went to the pub.'

'I didn't and part of me still doesn't. Though, after the row today I might need to find something else to do. It's not an interview. It's just to find out more about it.'

'So, what are you wearing?'

'Over the chair there's a blue trouser suit and on top a white blouse.'

Janine put the blouse on my bed, and held up the suit. 'This is nice, is it new?'

'Nope, it's years old.' The suit was one the few items of clothing put into a bin bag by the guards.

When I came back from the bathroom, I transferred onto the bed, and pulled off my jeans. Janine put them on my wooden chair, and helped me put the navy blue trousers on. I peeled off my top and put on the white blouse, Janine straightened it out at the back. She then helped me put my boots on and finally the jacket.

'Gosh. What a change.'

The last time I'd worn the suit was when I worked for the Council. As well as being busy, for the first time in my life I lived on my own. I moved into a flat near the office and with the help of carers was independent. When the scheme folded it set off a series of events, like dominoes falling. At one stage I thought I'd lost everything, before losing my freedom, my sense of who I was and my sanity. The next one on the list would've been my life, and frankly when you lose everything by the time it comes to your life, you don't care if it goes. I was just thankful my mum and my brother had my back before that happened.

I sat in front of my mirrored wardrobe and smiled at Janine who was standing next to me, preening her hair and smoothing down her tunic. Having lived so long in my uniform of jeans and a top it was strange to see myself dressed up. I put the sleeve of my jacket up to my nose and could almost smell the remnants of the perfume, 'Obsession' by Calvin Klein, I used to wear.

Going to the scheme with the Council gave me such a sense of purpose. I felt I was on the cusp of a new, exciting career. I'd return home each evening feeling I'd contributed to society, only for it to be crushed when the scheme folded. I stared again into the mirror; who was I now? As emotions bubbled up, I turned away to make my way downstairs.

'And here's the business lady,' Mum said with a smile when she arrived. 'I'm a bit early, but we might as well make a move if you're ready. Oh, is this the portrait? Isn't that lovely. Have you thanked him yet?'

'No, because I don't want to have to tell Anne. Course, if this group falls apart I mightn't see him ever again.'

'Why would it fall apart?'

I pulled a face. 'I'll tell you in the car.'

'Rachel, shall I do a quick tidy and post your keys through the letterbox when I'm done?'

'Great thanks, and thanks for helping me get ready.'

'OK, have a good time.' Janine turned to my mum. 'Goodbye Mrs Aspinhall'

In the car, I started to tell Mum about the argument, before I'd finished she interrupted me.

'There's an awful lot of ill-feeling about. I think it's exactly what the government wants, but for now, Rachel, you're just going to have to put it out of your mind.'

'That's easier said than done.'

When we arrived in Weston, Mum asked me to turn the

radio off.

'There's something you need to know. I don't want you to get worked up, but a while ago, when I was worried about what was happening at the bungalow, I had a quiet word with Brian about you, just to ask his advice. He was a solicitor, specialising in human rights, before he set the charity up.'

My stomach churned. 'When? What are you saying?'

'I'm saying he knows about the guards and your history. I didn't tell you earlier in case you wouldn't come out of the house.'

'He knows about everything?'

'I knew you'd be like this. Don't you understand? They still want to see you, regardless.'

'You've not gone and cooked this all up between you, have you?'

'Of course not. Anyway, Brian came to me, not the other way round. So you see, they know all of it, but they'd still like to have you involved.'

'Mum, it was you who said my move to Carthom was a fresh start, for me to hide my history. Now, you've gone and done the opposite.'

'Oh darling, he isn't bothered, he wanted you to apply. Come on, don't be silly. And, anyway, how could you do this, if you weren't going to tell them everything?'

'Why didn't you tell me earlier, instead of now, just before I'm going in?'

'So, you'll go in?'

'I don't know. I suppose I'll have to now.'

We pulled up by Inspire and Support. A small gold plaque by the main door was the only visible sign a charity was inside the anonymous red brick building. I peered at it from my car window, and reluctantly unclipped my seatbelt.

I wheeled in and was first met by a receptionist. I was instructed to sign in and then for a tense five minutes waited in the reception area. Eventually, Andrea Mulligan, Brian Taylor's assistant, met me. Despite being only a young woman, she looked serious and stern. She was very thin, and walked with a straight back and wore her hair in a tight bun.

She led me through a myriad of corridors until we reached the back of the building that housed Inspire and Support. An outdoor path linked the older building to a more modern section. After I wheeled down another corridor, Andrea eventually deposited me in the large room, used for the Information Day.

Around the perimeter of the room were various stalls. Apart from the people behind the stalls, I was the only visitor. The first table had a clipboard on it and nothing else; whoever was meant to be sitting there had disappeared. I moved onto the next stall, where a deaf woman with a friendly smile gave me a small goody bag which had a stress ball with Inspire and Support printed on it, a bookmark and half a dozen leaflets inside. On her table there was an A5 flyer with a quotation printed on it:

'Happiness is not a matter of events, it depends upon the tides of the mind.' Alice Meynell.

I found myself staring at this quotation, and read it over and over again.

Behind me the door opened, making me jump. Brian Taylor, who I instantly recognised, walked up to me. He crouched down so he was at my height.

'I'm so pleased to see you here, Rachel. Now, I know that in time you might want to be involved in joining our befriending service, so I suggest you go over to the table in the corner.' Brian pointed over to where a man and woman were seated, one on crutches and one in a wheelchair. 'Tracey is a befriender and Jimmy a client.'

After a tickle in my throat turned into a cough, I managed to splutter, 'Yes.'

I followed him as he walked to the corner of the room. It seemed strange that the C.E.O. of the charity was the only able bodied person in the room and made me curious about why he'd started the charity up.

'I'll leave you in Tracey and Jimmy's capable hands. If you want to speak to me, Andrea will be milling about, just ask her. OK, Rachel, hope to speak to you again soon.'

Tracey was a pretty long blonde haired woman who was paraplegic as well and had been volunteering with Inspire and Support for two years. One of her first clients had been Jimmy. She first met up with him when he was leaving hospital.

Jimmy cleared his throat. 'Tracey literally showed me how to get support at home and how to apply for Benefits. She knew what I'd been through and helped me get to the other side.'

Tracey smiled. 'The beauty of the scheme is I definitely didn't know everything but through Jimmy I felt my knowledge and my own perception of who I was, including my situation improve. I'd strongly recommend you go on the training course at least, and then see how you feel before you make up your mind.'

'If I did decide to do it, would I sign up here?'

'Tony on the table near the door can sign you up,' Jimmy said. He pointed at a bearded man who was transferring from his wheelchair onto another chair behind the table with the clipboard. 'You can do it online too. Any more questions, feel free to come back.'

'Thanks. I'll come back once I've had a look around.'

I began to wheel around the hall, and was offered a chocolate cupcake, as well as more leaflets.

Jimmy had left the hall, so while he was gone, I made my way back over to Tracey.

'Are you any closer to making a decision, Rachel? It is Rachel, isn't it?'

I nodded. 'The thing is I'm not really used to talking about my disability, and how I became disabled.'

'You don't have to give lots of personal reasons. Basically, you're there to help the clients; discuss what has happened to

them. What they think about what's happened to them, tha
of thing. So they can talk about how they're feeling and wⁱⁱaι
they're worrying about. What I was saying before, this service
aims to help the clients but there are knock on benefits for us,
the befrienders. Do you understand?'

'Yes, I think so. I just don't know I would be the best role
model.'

Tracey held out her hand. 'You're here aren't you? It shows
you want to help others. I know it can be difficult. For me, I was
on and off depressed for years after this happened. Some days I
just wanted to hide, to be invisible, but you must know what it's
like, everyone seems to stop and stare. Some days you wish you
could just be unnoticeable, but then you can be totally ignored.'

'Yeah, I know that feeling.'

'Through the course I realised it was my view of myself
holding me back, nothing else. Furthermore, with Inspire
and Support they help you become proud to be visible and
encourage you to contribute to society by helping other people
with disabilities.'

Tears welled up in my eyes.

'You see, what really matters is not how other people treated
me or thought about me but rather what I do and think. Some
days I still think like this, don't get me wrong. What I'm trying
to say is doing things like this, knowing other people need you
to be strong for them, all helps. Sorry, I'm rambling.'

'No, you made a lot of sense, you really did.' I smiled at
Tracey and she gave a cautious smile back.

'If I went on this training service, I could still say 'no', could
I?'

'God yes, I think it was only about two people out of five
who joined when I did my course. Even if you decide to take it
no further, you'll find it useful. It's an incredibly life affirming
course. I wish I'd been on it when I first was injured.'

'How long does it go on for? The course, I mean?'

'It's only a short course, ten days in total. As soon as they get enough people interested they run the course. So, it could be a bit of a wait or very soon, it's just how it works, I'm afraid.'

Jimmy came back into the room with a small bottle of water. 'Ten days doesn't seem long.'

'If you decide to be a befriender after the course, you then shadow someone more experienced for a few months. There's also ongoing support, so if you've been asked about something you're stuck on, you can just phone in or email.'

I glanced down at my watch. 'You've been really helpful, and I do think I might give it a try. I'd better go, my mum's waiting outside.'

'I'll show you out,' Tracey said. 'It's a bit of a rabbit warren this building.'

In silence I followed Tracey through the corridors until we were at the entrance. She banged on the green button and slowly the front door opened.

'Listen, I do know what it's like. If you ever fancy a chat, or just someone to moan with, this is my card. Here put it in your goody bag,'

'Thanks Tracey, you've been a real help.'

I wheeled down the ramp aware Tracey was still sitting at the open door. When I got down to the bottom, I turned to wave. In that hour, my views about Inspire and Support had shifted further to the point where I now, with all the hostility and antagonism in the art group, was tempted to do the course and leave the group completely.

Eighteen

Five years after my dad died, my mum came up with the idea of putting all the newspaper cuttings, photographs of him and The Butterfly Collective into one scrapbook. There were reasons why I didn't want to do it, and I thought my mum was probably the same, as each year, although the scrapbook was mentioned, it wasn't actually completed. Mum usually brought it up around Easter time, and this year was the same. She dropped in at my house, the Monday after Easter Day, but this time, along with the scrapbook, there was glue and scissors plus all the photographs and newspaper cuttings.

'I know I've said this before, Rach, but would you like to put it in order?'

'Yeah, same answer I said last year, and the year before that and so on.'

'Don't be sarcastic.'

I rolled my eyes. 'You do say this each year, though, don't you? The answer's yes, it'll give me something to do.'

'I might say it each year, but this time I've got it all ready.'

'OK, OK, I'll do it.'

Mum stood up, and put her bag on her arm. She shot me a sideways glance.

'What plans do you have this week?'

I groaned. 'If I'm not going to the group, the only thing I've got to do is going to The Vines for a coffee with Kate tomorrow.'

Mum frowned. 'Really hope all this with the group can get sorted out.'

'So do I Mum.'

I was praying that, Kate with her calm manner would help me make sense of what had happened with the group and this in turn would help with my anxiety.

The next day, Janine helped me get into The Vines. Inside, I scanned around the pub. The bright sunlight outside leaked into the pub and produced a shimmering, multicoloured light across the carpets. In the distance, a radio was playing undistinguishable dance music. Apart from a man in a flat tweed cap, wearing green wellington boots who was sitting on a bar stool, and a bar maid who was texting on her mobile, the pub was empty.

'Are you OK now? Do you want me to wait until Kate comes?' Janine peered down at her watch.

'No, you go and get your bus, Janine. See you tomorrow.'

A minute or so after Janine had gone, the door of the ladies' toilet swung open, with Kate hobbling out.

'Sorry, sweetie, have you been waiting long?' Kate hooked her bag handle over her shoulder.

'No, just arrived.'

We started to make our way in the direction of the bar, when the man in the cap turned towards us.

'Cor blimey, what's happened? Have you two been in a fight?' He leered at Kate then at me.

'Just ignore him,' Kate whispered to me.

'I said, what's happened to you?' He persisted, this time his voice was louder.

'None of your business,' snapped Kate.

The man stood up with a wobble and held up both hands as if in mock surrender.

'Eh, stop being shirty with me lass, keep your wig on.'

'Rachel, let's go over there.' Kate nodded towards the far corner of the pub, not far from the kitchen and courtyard.

We made our way to the back of the pub, and sat at a table usually reserved for those having a meal.

Kate picked up one of the soggy beer mats, and smiled across at me.

'What do you want to drink? Or do you want something..?'

'I'll pay,' I said, interrupting Kate. 'I just want a cappuccino.'

Kate whipped out her purse. 'Sweetie, I'll pay for mine. You pay for yours.'

Kate tried to get the attention of the barmaid but without success. Eventually, we spotted Sue walking past the kitchen and signalled to her.

Sue walked over to us.

'The barmaid told me you had trouble with that chap at the bar. When Matt gets back he'll be getting thrown out on his ear. Drinks on the house as we've got to keep you ladies sweet, After all, we've got our famous, resident artist here.' Sue grinned at me. 'So, ladies what would you like to drink?'

Kate smiled across at me before she looked up at Sue.

'Could we have two cappuccinos please?'

'Coming up, ladies, I'll get Sarah to bring them over.' Sue indicated to the barmaid behind the bar who was still engrossed in whatever she was keying into her mobile.

Kate tapped the table with her forefinger. 'Have you heard what Anne has said?'

'No.'

'She said she's rung Mike and everything's alright.'

'I don't know why Mike would've said that, though I suppose if she spoke to Mike, he might say he's alright, even if he wasn't.'

'No, sweetie, she said everything's alright. Her exact words were - I've rung Mike and everything's alright.'

'At least she got through to him; he's not picking up when I call.'

'So, you've got his landline number?'

'Nope, I've only got his mobile, that's all. It keeps on going straight to answer machine. He's not picking up.'

Kate nodded slowly; she screwed up the paper serviette and wiped her mouth.

'I don't know about you, Kate but over Easter, I was wondering whether this groups suitable for me?'

'So I know this may sound strange, Rachel, but I think if we can get the group sorted out, it would be something valuable to be part of. I know it's a mess at present, I don't even think we've ever been a proper group, but I do think we could salvage it and work through some of the problems we've been having. We'd all need to be completely honest with each other.'

'I'm not sure, I keep on picturing them arguing with Mike.'

Kate folded her arms on the table and leant towards me. 'That's why we need to work through some of these problems. I just think it's worth a shot. As for tomorrow, we're just going to have to see how it goes.'

'So, you're definitely going tomorrow?'

Kate nodded. 'What about you?'

'If you're going then I suppose I will. Just to see if Mike is there, that's the only reason.'

Sarah came over to our table, and plonked down two cappuccinos with considerable force, making some of the liquid slop onto the table.

'She doesn't seem very happy?'

Kate grinned. 'Must be such a boring a job at times.'

We both began to nibble on the chocolate mints that accompanied our drinks.

I put my head in my hand. 'Have you heard anything from The Richmond?'

'No, nothing at all. It won't be that long before we have to put fresh paintings up.'

'When I'm...' For a moment I struggled to find the right words. 'When I'm stressed, I just find painting so difficult.'

Kate nodded. 'Hopefully tomorrow won't be too bad. If we have more commotion, then we're going to have to have a serious think about what we do next.'

I stared across at her. 'Do you think that's likely?'

Kate shrugged. 'I can't predict what'll happen, sweetie. I'd hope that in the time since the argument, some of them have thought about their behaviour.'

I tipped my mug to drink the dregs of my cappuccino.

Kate glanced down at my watch.

'Are you ready to make a move?'

'When you're ready, sweetie, there's no rush.'

I checked my bag on the back of my chair was in place and wheeled so that I was adjacent to the table. 'God. No way. Is Matt, the landlord a twin?' I rubbed my eyes and stared again at the two men.

Matt was behind the bar, and his twin was on the other side leaning on the bar. Both were wearing check shirts, battered jeans and brown ankle boots.

Kate arched her back. 'Didn't you know? So, both of them are landlords, Matthew or Matt as he prefers to be called and his twin is Mark.'

'There isn't a Luke and John at home by any chance?'

Kate smiled.

'What pub does Mark have?'

Kate glanced over to Matt and Mark. 'He's not that type of landlord. According to Jonathon he's got quite a portfolio of different properties, spread over a large area, lots in Carthom, apparently. So, wealthy, very wealthy indeed.'

Kate pulled herself to her feet, using the table for support and slowly straightened up. Her face was at first pink, and then it turned pale, before finally turning into a deathly grey colour. She placed one hand on her lower back, and made a low moaning sound in her throat.

'Bloody pain. I get stiff and then when I get up I pay for it.'

I held out the palm of my hand. 'Kate, it's a pleasant enough day, I'll make my own way back.'

'Are you sure?' With her spare hand, she ran her fingers through her hair.

'Sure.'

When Matt or Mark had helped me down the steps, I turned

to face Kate and we hugged outside The Vines.

'Try not to worry, sweetie. See you tomorrow.'

'You too, Kate.'

I started to wheel home. As I approached the pedestrian crossing, I saw a group of around five or six, elderly residents who were gawping over the road; some were pointing as well.

I stopped to look. Near the new shop units, was a queue of about twenty people all in a straight line.

A plump man, with a bloated face, grey goatee beard, and a collie dog on a lead bent over me, his hot and boozy breath in my face.

'What do you think, eh?'

I screwed up my face.

'The food bank over there.' He pointed at the queue.

'Run by the council?'

'Sit,' the man suddenly barked and the collie dog sat with his head resting on my knee, his doleful eyes staring up at me.

'What were you saying, love?'

'Who runs it?'

'The Catholic church, so I'm told. They're using one of the empty shop units for it. I've nothing against them, but anyone driving through Carthom will now see this food bank, it's not exactly adding to the natural beauty of the area, is it?' The man pulled the lead and the dog stood up. He wandered back to the group of residents.

I wheeled quickly past the group and crossed the road. The queue of people seemed to be getting longer. A large proportion of the group were elderly and nearly everyone seemed to be holding a white slip of paper. I saw the reaction the people in the queue were getting from residents who either averted their eyes, or like the group across the road, who were being openly hostile. I wheeled past them, and tried to make eye contact and gave what I hoped was a supportive smile.

I was now at the top of my road. It was a long stretch of

pavement, with no obstacles to negotiate that would impede my journey. I started to pick up speed. The long arm movements needed for wheeling and the rhythmic motion had the power at times, to get me into 'a zone' where I could think through problems, and churn out solutions.

I thought again about the argument. I knew when I was fearful, I could get angry, and so understood Mike's outburst. However, I'd been blinkered with regards to the other side, in that I hadn't considered what life would be like for older people on pensions. No doubt, trying to manage on a meagre pension was just as precarious as being on other Benefits.

Nineteen

It was a glorious, sunny morning, but the first thing I did was groan. Any charitable feelings I had towards the group had vanished. I knew the only reason I was going to the group was to see if Mike was there, that was it. The group no longer appealed to me at all. Excitement had been replaced by dread. Anticipation was replaced by foreboding. As I waited for Anne to pick me up, I could feel my forehead muscles getting tighter, my jaw aching as my teeth were clenched together and my nails were digging into the palms of my hands.

I wheeled through into the kitchen to have a cigarette but had only just opened the packet, when I heard Anne rapping on the door.

'OK, Anne, hang on, I'm coming.'

'You seem quiet.' Anne said as she walked alongside me towards her car.

'It's just my sleeping is a bit up the wall at the moment,

making me feel rough.'

Anne put my wheelchair onto the back seat. 'Rough? I don't feel great either. Flipping back pain's getting worse.'

She drove up my road, and after a short wait turned onto the main road and past the food bank.

Anne tutted under her breath. 'Did you see that we had a food bank now? Big long line of people yesterday all wanting free food.'

'They shouldn't have put it somewhere so obvious. It must've been difficult for those in the queue.'

Anne snorted. 'It should be somewhere obvious. If they want free food, then let everybody see who they are.'

'There were a lot of elderly people in the queue.'

Anne glanced at me. 'Times are getting hard for us pensioners.'

We pulled into the centre and parked. For a minute neither of us moved nor spoke. Eventually Anne turned to me.

'I hope its quieter today. Maybe the week off has helped.'

'Maybe.'

'Let's get you out then.'

I had a cigarette outside the centre in an attempt to get my nerves under control. Eddie walked behind me and made me flinch.

'Sorry kiddo, did I frighten you then?' He crouched down in front of me. 'Are you feeling alright about today? Is young Mike coming too?'

'Anne's spoken to Mike and she said everything's alright, so yes, he might come today.'

'She left a message on his answer machine, as far as I know she didn't actually speak to him.'

'Was my name mentioned then?' Anne said, as she walked out into the car park.

'You didn't speak to young Mike; you left a message didn't you?' Eddie straightened up and half turned towards Anne.

'A message? Yes, you told me to leave a message. All the things you asked me to say I said. Come on, let's get inside.'

Eddie and Anne walked ahead of me into the hall. Anne went straight ahead into the kitchen while Eddie stayed in the doorway of the kitchen, his legs wide apart with each foot touching either side of the doorframe, which prevented me from entering. I couldn't hear what they were whispering about, so I turned into the main hall.

I looked up at Mike's painting of a black Labrador retriever and hoped he'd got the message and was alright.

Next to arrive were Marion and Albert who were closely followed by Pauline, Elaine and Lena. Marion and Lena walked straight into the hall, while the others made drinks or talked in the foyer with Anne.

Usually, there'd be chattering as well as laughing and joking, but instead there was a distinctly subdued atmosphere.

I smiled at Marion and she responded with a cautious smile.

Lena walked over to me and perched on the table.

'Are you alright, Rachel? Glad you've come today. Do you know whether Kate and Mike are coming?'

'Kate's coming, but I don't know about Mike. I thought Anne had spoken to him, but all she was able to do was leave a message. I just hope he's alright.'

'There was no need for that nasty business the other week, no need at all.'

Lena eased herself up, and placed her warm hand on my shoulder, before she walked back to her seat.

Eddie strode back into the hall with a small plastic bag. He emptied the contents onto the table and began to organise the ink pens according to nib sizes. When he'd finished, he turned towards Lena.

'Sorry, couldn't give you a lift today, Lena,' he said. He stood up and winked at me before he disappeared back into the kitchen where Anne was now chatting with Elaine.

It was ten o'clock, with no sign of either Mike or Kate.

Anne walked into the hall with Elaine, Albert and Eddie. Down the table I stared at Elaine and Pauline; turning back to my art pad when they looked back at me.

I glanced up again at Mike's painting silently pleading with him to turn up.

As members started to paint and draw, Anne talked about a story line in a thriller she'd watched on TV. I half listened as I watched the door. Eventually, after a long ten minutes, Kate arrived and apologised for being late.

I felt myself breathe again. She limped up to her space opposite me and mouthed 'sorry' to me.

I pointed to the empty seat next to me and shrugged.

As time went on it became obvious Mike wasn't going to come. I wheeled out for a cigarette and pulled out my mobile from my pocket. With my finger shaking, I scrolled down to Mike's number and tried to ring. It went straight onto his answer machine. I then sent a text:

Hi Mike, we've missed you today at the art group, hope to see you soon, Rachel x

I wheeled inside, but instead of going into the hall, I held back and watched everyone at work.

Anne stood up and after looking around the hall, she squinted in my direction, before walking briskly towards me. I quickly picked up a leaflet that was lying on one of the tables opposite the toilets and pretended to be reading it.

Anne snatched the leaflet from me. 'Male incontinence? Why are you reading about that?' Anne frowned, her eyebrows knitted together in a 'V' shape, touching the bridge of her nose.

'You know me, I'll read anything.'

Anne huffed as she shook her head again. She opened the door for me with an audible sigh.

Kate was painting and after a few minutes, I got back into the drawing I'd brought with me of the Methodist Church in

Carthom.

Twenty minutes later, Kate passed me a note asking me if I wanted a drink and a chat in the kitchen. As she got up and set off, I waited for a few seconds before following her in. With one eye on the main hall we chatted.

'It's a shame Mike didn't come, isn't it?'

'Anne didn't speak to him, Kate. She left him a message on his answering machine, that's all.'

'So that means nobody from our group has spoken to him since the row. I was sure Anne wasn't being completely honest with me.'

'I just hope he's alright, and not sitting at home brooding or depressed.'

'I hope so too.' Kate held open the kitchen door for me and we both went back to our places.

As we were starting to paint again, Lena got up, and walked slowly around the table. She made polite comments about everyone's painting or drawing. When she eventually walked to our end of the table she crouched down, on my right side, so she could speak just to the both of us, but was hidden from the rest of the group.

'Dreadful business last week, truly dreadful. Is Mike OK?'

'We don't know Lena; he hasn't been in touch at all. Rachel's been texting him, but so far hasn't been able to reach him.'

'If you get to speak to him,' Lena said. 'Can you pass on my love and my best wishes, please.'

We both nodded.

Lena stood up, and spent a moment examining Kate's painting, and commented on how original and well executed it was. She pointed to an area of azure sky and mumbled a comment I couldn't hear. She passed her watercolour pad over to Kate, showing her what she'd painted. Kate pointed out a few things and they talked quietly.

Eddie coughed loudly, and scratched the bald centre of his

head. 'It's sad we don't have young Mike with us today, isn't it? Hope we haven't lost him, due to that nasty business a couple of weeks ago.'

'Eddie, it was actually Mike who started the whole business, who shouted out that the State Pension was a Benefit,' Albert snapped, his fists clenched on the table.

Anne lifted her hand in the air and Eddie signalled for her to speak with a nod.

'All my letters about my pension are in the same file. So the State Pension comes from the Department for Work and Pensions, the same place Benefits come from. Mind, a private pension is different, that's not a Benefit, but if it's the state pension, then it is.' Anne paused, her face flushed. She stared down at the table. 'So when Mike comes back, I think we should say sorry to him.'

Kate arched her brows.

Lena nodded. 'We do owe him an apology.'

'Well, I'm sorry, but I found him, like Albert said, very confrontational. So if we have to apologise, so should he.' Pauline said, spreading her fingers out on the table.

'If he comes back,' Kate muttered.

'It's not just what he's said; it's how he said it, that's what my objection is,' Albert snapped.

Eddie made a swift movement with his hand. 'I don't want us to spend any more time on this, but we'll lose good people from this group if we don't start to respect each other. We only get one chance on this earth, so please; I don't want to hear another word on the subject.'

Albert, Marion, Elaine and Pauline muttered to each other, their irritation obvious.

Kate was biting her lip, lost in deep thought. I thought about Mike and how it felt like I was betraying him by being in this group, even though it seemed like half of us now supported him.

I tried to paint the churchyard, but it wasn't going well as I made mistake after mistake. After what felt like a long hour, I glanced at my watch. It was nearly midday, so I started to pack up my things.

I wheeled out for a final cigarette and this time I went around the corner so I could try and get through to Mike on the phone but it went straight to voicemail.

A few minutes later, Kate poked her head around.

'Are you OK?'

'I've been trying his mobile, but I've not been able to get through. He was so down about his money and his Benefits, I ...'

Kate interrupted me. 'Maybe we should think about pooling our resources and look for him.' She paused and leant against the wall, flexing her hand. 'Also, sweetie, when you're texting him, I think you should try and say something that'd make him have to respond. I'd put something like; we're getting really worried, Mike. If you don't reply we'll have to report it to the police.'

'And do we? Report it to the police, I mean?'

'No, but don't let Mike know that. What if I come over to your house after the group? We can think about how we're going to tackle this; draw up a plan.'

Kate put her finger to her lips when we heard the centre door shut and someone walking towards us.

'What are you two talking about?' Eddie said poking his head around the corner at us.

'Mike. We're both going to go in a minute.' Kate glanced at me, and I nodded.

'Will we see you next week?' Eddie asked.

Kate gripped her crutches and moved away from the wall. 'I can't come; I've got an appointment with my son at his school.'

'I don't know, Eddie. I just don't know,' I said grimly. I turned to follow Kate back into the centre, where we said our goodbyes after grabbing our bags. As we were making our way out of the hall, I took one last look at the group and wondered if I ever would be back.

In my house, Kate settled down on the sofa while I made her a mug of cappuccino. She'd kicked off her shoes, and in one hand was her iPad, in the other a notebook and in her mouth a pen.

'I think we need a strategy so we cover all the bases. On the Windmill Estate all the roads are named after trees, which will help us spot his address in the online phonebook, if he's in there. Though the first thing we should do is change the nature of the texts.'

'I can start doing that today.'

'I know this sounds rather obvious, but he wouldn't be on holiday, would he?'

'He didn't have the money, Kate.'

'What about his family, would one of them take him away?'

'He didn't really talk about them, but I really doubt it.'

Kate was silent for a moment, her hand in a fist over her mouth. 'Rachel, you may have to brace yourself because it may be bad news,' she said eventually. 'He may tell us to stop harassing him and say he doesn't want anything to do with us.'

I nodded slowly.

She scribbled in her notebook. 'Now, I can start ringing any M. Greaves who lives on the Windmill Estate. If by next Thursday, we'd had no joy, the only other thing I can think of is to visit the estate. Maybe visit it by day and by night.' Kate stopped writing and glanced across at me. 'Mike's fairly easy to recognise, so I'm sure someone on the estate will at least know him by sight.'

'I don't know much about this estate. I'm just thinking two disabled women, we...'

'We'd go by car definitely and yes, I'll ask Jonathon to come with us. Now, if this doesn't lead us to Mike, I think there's only two other options available, and that's phoning the hospitals and as a last resort, report it to the police.'

'I'm worried he might have had a seizure and be badly injured somewhere.'

'Does he have regular seizures, sweetie? It's a pity the group didn't know about this. I know Weston General has quite a large neurological department so that's one number we should try.'

'He also was...' I couldn't get the word out as it gave me an uneasy feeling.

'He also was what?' Kate narrowed her eyes.

'With all the Benefits stuff he was getting quite down, I wonder if we should, um...'

'...ring the psychiatric hospitals? I've got a few colleagues in the NHS who may be able to give me a hand with it.'

'Thanks, I've not got any numbers or anything here.'

'I'll check the phonebook over the weekend, you try texting him. If we get no joy there, we visit the estate. Then if we've not found him, I can check with the hospitals.'

'And if there's still no luck, the police?'

'I'm sure it won't come to that. He might be back at the group next week. But if we still can't find him, at least we can say to the police we've tried. With the epilepsy and possible mental health issues; they'll have to take some form of action. If we both haven't got through on the phone or by text then I suggest we meet up on Thursday afternoon, and if still no joy we can come over on Friday afternoon and drive around the estate.'

I stared across at Kate, and after a gulp, slowly nodded.

Twenty

The search for Mike brought back memories of my dad. When I was ten or eleven I'd started to notice times when he was unusually quiet and almost detached from family life, coupled with occasions when he was missing, sometimes only for a few days, other times for as long as a month. At the time, I chose to believe my mum, who'd tell me he was absorbed with a tricky problem related to his artwork or at the last minute had decided to go to an exhibition abroad and was staying with his outsider colleagues.

However, it was only in my mid-teens, I found out the basics in that my dad went through phases of extreme anxiety and insecurity. This would lead to a period of introspection that, more often than not, precipitated the depression, which would follow. It usually started with him being picked up by the police for wandering around the streets or motorway and ended with him being hospitalised.

When I was nearly thirteen, he was well and on good form. The Butterfly Collective was getting positive attention and one exhibition had sold out on the first day. So when he missed a parents evening at my school, my mum wasn't too worried at first. However, as the evening progressed and there was still no word from him, she embarked on a frantic few hours phoning round his friends and colleagues and even left us at home to drive around the various haunts, pubs and places where in the past he'd been picked up by the police.

The call from the hospital came just after midnight. Mum woke us up and blurry eyed and hand in hand the three of us stumbled towards the relatives' room at the hospital to be told the worst news a young family could hear.

Although the rational side of me understood it was more than likely Mike was angry towards the group after the argument, my emotional side was connecting Mike's disappearance to the time my dad was missing making my anxiety levels soar.

All through Saturday and Sunday, I'd been calling and texting Mike with no response. Kate had also been trying to get through to Mike with no success, which meant the next course of action, was to visit the estate, to see if anyone knew where he lived.

I'd planned to go to the art group to see if Mike turned up, but as I sat and waited for Anne, I was aware my mood was dropping.

The phone rang; at first it sounded like a nuisance phone call, with the female caller asking for Miss Aspinhall. With one eye on the window, I asked who was speaking.

'My name's Jill Davies. I have a friend who knows Anne Wilby and she's given me your number. To get to the point, it's about Mike and...'

'...Is he OK?' I could feel my heart rate increase.

'I don't know. I was hoping you could tell me. You see, I've been trying to contact him, and I can't get through.'

'We've been doing the same. Do you know his address?' As I spoke I felt increasingly despondent. I turned in my chair and saw Anne outside my window. She was standing with her hands on her hips like a nightmarish apparition.

'Can you just hang on a minute, Jill?'

Using my wheelchair, I wedged the front door partly open and peered through the gap.

'Anne, I can't come at the moment. I'll make my own way up in a bit.'

Anne tried to open the door. 'Why, what's the matter?'

'It's the Council on the phone; I'll see you in a bit.'

Anne stepped closer to me and bent her body as she tried to peer into my living room. I moved forward and nudged her back into the path.

'I'm going to have to go, see you soon.' I banged my front door shut.

I took a deep breath before I picked up the phone again.

'Sorry about that. I was asking whether you know where he lives.'

I moved into the kitchen and sat by my kitchen table, in front of me were the scrapbook and envelope of articles Mum had given me.

'No, that's why I'm ringing. Now, he'd been texting me quite regularly as I was in a bit of trouble but I haven't heard from him for a couple of weeks.'

'Do you have any idea where he might have gone?'

'He's got family somewhere. But you see he'd still ring me, even if he was away somewhere, unless he's in a mood with me.'

'No, we've been trying to find it out as well. If he's not at the art group today, then a couple of us are going to try and find out a bit more.'

'I met Mike through an art group as well,' Jill whispered.

'Is that the group in Weston, connected with the hospital?'

'Yes, but it's closed down now. I joined just as it was winding up. The only person I really knew was Mike. He was so open and friendly.'

'Can I take your number? I'll ring you if we find out anything.'

I put Jill's number on the fridge and wheeled back into my living room. I noted how the sight of my art bag on the sofa made me tense up. In a short space of time, the group I viewed as the key to my independence was now something I wanted to avoid. I thought it was unlikely Mike would show up and the thought of having to sit and listen to more bigoted nonsense without him or Kate sickened me. I put my art bag, away.

After a morning of being too worried and too distracted to do anything else, Janine arrived ready to do the cleaning. While she was upstairs, I rang Lena to see if Mike turned up to the group.

'No, sorry, Rachel, he didn't.'

'Did the group go alright? What was the atmosphere like?'

'It wasn't like it normally is; instead I found it uncomfortable and tense. Albert and Eddie were sparring with each other and it wasn't pleasant at all. I've got a feeling Eddie might leave the group soon. If he goes and you three don't come back then I'm leaving as well.'

'Oh, Lena, you said how helpful it was with you living alone.

Please, I don't want you to miss out...'

Lena interrupted. 'I feel the same way about you, Rachel.'

'I just can't see myself at the group, Lena, I'm so angry with some of them.'

'I'm exactly the same. I'm annoyed with how they treated Mike.'

I stared down at the floor. 'I know; it could've easily been me or Kate coming to the group with a problem with our Benefits.'

'As Kate said we're all on some form of Benefit,' Lena mumbled.

I said goodbye to Lena and after I put down the phone, I held my head in my hands.

Janine trundled downstairs, with an armful of bedding ready for the washing machine.

'Is everything OK?'

'No. Lena, who lives on her own, is now saying she might not go to the group anymore.' I lifted up the brown envelope from the kitchen table, stuffed full of articles about my dad and The Butterfly Collective. 'It's like the group was this envelope all sealed up and now the arguments happened it's been blown open, and now we can see what really was inside.'

Janine pulled out the kitchen chair and sat down.

'I'm beginning to wish I'd stopped going to the group when I had chance.' I turned the envelope upside down, before laying it back on top of the scrapbook.

'It seemed to help you at first.' Janine said 'I mean when I first met you for months you hardly went out at all, except with your mum.'

'It did, and that's what I was saying about Lena, she said to me a while ago how going to the group was helping her, but since the argument, I can't see how it's helping anyone now. I really am tempted to say I'm not going anymore, but before I do that I need to make sure Mike's alright. I'm just hoping Kate can help when I next see her.'

'When's that?'

'Tomorrow.'

Janine used the kitchen table as support, as she stood up. 'I hope she can, Rachel.'

When Janine had gone, I stared at the scrapbook and envelope. I didn't have anything to do in the time before my next meeting with Kate, but I was still reluctant to complete it. Instead, I tried to carry on with my farm painting but I wasn't motivated at all.

All the time, I was getting more worked up about the group, so by the time Kate arrived, and I brought her a drink of apple juice from the kitchen, a torrent of worries and anxiety poured out from my mouth.

'Kate, I feel in such a state. I've got such a mix of emotions. I don't know whether to shut the door on the group? Don't know what to do about Mike? Don't know whether we'll keep in contact if..?'

Kate stretched out her legs. 'I know, it's so sad we couldn't as a group, work through these issues. I was thinking one of the problems is we don't socialise outside of the group. The obvious outcome is our failure to really know each other. For example, I was oblivious to the fact that Mike was epileptic. If Elaine, Pauline or Albert had known this, would they have attacked him so viciously? I think they only thought he'd a bad back.'

I shrugged and held out my hands. 'Even if they only thought that, they still shouldn't have attacked him.'

'I know that and you know that, but the climate's changed and there's been an active campaign to demonize people on Benefits. So, some of the group have only got The Daily Mail view of what a disability is about. If we met up socially, outside of the group, it would give us all a chance to find out more about each other. I'm not just talking about them finding out more about disability either, but us finding out more about their needs, worries and problems they face as well.'

'I'm just not sure I can cope meeting up with them anymore and Lena phoned me to say she and Eddie might stop going.'

'Well, we're not responsible for anyone else. It's up to each of us to do what we feel is right.' Kate pulled herself up in the chair to get in a better position. 'First thing first anyway, let's focus on finding Mike, go through the what, where, why and hows. So how many texts have you sent him?'

'Eight texts plus phone calls.'

'So as well as that, he's not been seen for three weeks and has missed two weeks of art.' Kate stopped writing and glanced at me.

'A friend of his, called Jill phoned me yesterday. She was at the Weston Art Group he used to go to, and she hasn't heard from him either. Though, Kate, I think he once said he left a group, I can't remember the reason, but I think he left it without saying goodbye.'

'I think we can only work with what we know now. He was stressed about the up and coming Benefit assessment. He was in trouble with debt. Can you think of any other problems he had?'

'He sounded alone, upset at his mother's death. Oh yes, and he says stress makes his seizures worse.'

Kate had her head down as she made some sort of a list using bullet points. 'We know he said he lives on the Windmill estate. Can you recall anything he might have said about the area where he lives or his neighbours?' Kate peered at me, her head on one side.

'The only thing I think he said was about a neighbour. I don't think she was well in herself. She was called Sandy, or was it the dog called Sandy? She kept an eye on him, said hello, that kind of thing.'

Kate lifted her head up, with her silver fountain pen poised in the air. 'Did she live next door to Mike?'

With my thumb nail I picked at another nail on the same hand. 'I got the impression he lived in a flat, and this woman lived not next door, but a few doors down. I think so, anyway.'

Kate started to cross something out. For a brief moment, she stared down at the paper, sucking the top of the pen before she wrote down another point. 'Right, I've got here,' Kate brought out from her bag a folded up piece of paper, 'all the numbers of the local hospitals and psych. units, so just to start off I think it's worth ringing them up. Can I go into your kitchen, with the phone?'

'You don't think something awful has happened, do you?'

'People don't just vanish into thin air. I'm sure there will be a perfectly rational explanation. We just need to find out what it is.'

Kate gripped the sheet of paper as she went into the kitchen. I followed her in. My worst fear was he'd cracked up and was in an awful psychiatric unit, or was seriously ill somewhere. As she started to ring each number I felt increasingly desperate. The first two numbers, Kate got swift replies. It soon became obvious that the fact we didn't have Mike's date of birth or the right address was holding us back.

Kate sighed, after being put on hold again, and held out the phone so I could hear the tinny version of Vivaldi's Four Seasons which was being played. She put the phone against her chest and whispered to me. 'I'm going to call in a favour from a colleague. You've not heard me do this, Mum's the word.'

I nodded and pointed into the living room. 'If you phone them from the living room, we can shut the door. I'll have a cigarette out in the back so I won't hear anything.'

We swapped positions. Kate took out her phone, scrolled down, copied out a number, and then shut the door.

After ten minutes, Kate came through into the kitchen. 'Right, I've spoken to an old colleague, she's going to ask around, to see if he's in hospital locally, and she's going to speak to the bed manager who covers the psychiatric wards as well. Now if they've not got anything...'

'He must be alive?' I interrupted.

Kate leant back on the kitchen chair. 'I'm sure he's alive, but we still need to know he's well. I think the only course of action open to us, is to visit the estate, and if we get nowhere, the police. So, are you alright if tomorrow, Jonathon and I pick you up about ten o'clock? Then it gives us time to go to the police if we have no joy.'

'I just hope it doesn't come to that.'

'I know, sweetie, I feel the same.' Kate picked up the scrapbook. 'This brings back memories, Jeremy used to have so many of these; he used to collect train tickets and stamps. What are you using it for?'

'Oh, it's just something my mum wants me to do. I've not started it yet, just finding it hard to get motivated. Same with painting, I had a go, but I made a right mess of it. I just can't paint when I'm anxious, stressed or worried.'

'I'm exactly the same, sweetie. All this will get sorted out. Don't worry.' She pulled out her car key from her bag, limped across to me and bent down, putting her free arm around my shoulder. 'See you tomorrow, Rachel.'

'Until then.'

That night I had a fitful sleep waking up in the early morning. Unable to get back to sleep I went downstairs and opened the envelope, full of newspaper articles, all onto my kitchen table.

Mum had assiduously collected any press mentions of the Butterfly Collective and some photos as well as articles about the outsider movement in general. I put all of it in the right order. The first one was a profile of my dad when he was still at university. It was years before the Butterfly Collective was formed, and there was no mention of outsider art in the article.

As a child I was shielded from most of my dad's illness and only found out the full truth after his death. This meant as I was growing up, I didn't fully understand the work of the collective. All I had now were fading vague memories and snippets from old, yellowing newspaper articles with which to construct an image of my father, someone I barely knew.

I found a review of an exhibition in the local paper, when the collective had just been formed. At that time, there were five members. My dad was the fine artist and responsible for booking venues. Peter concentrated on photography, and he organised the reports and reviews for newspapers. There was also David, who did sculptures. Another member, Jane, did textile work and her partner, Keith, did artwork using glass.

As I examined one of the photographs, I remembered how, even after his death I wouldn't talk about my dad. Just like, Jeremy, Kate's son, who didn't like to mention his Mum's disability, I was embarrassed about my dad's mental illness and would avoid talking about him or his art in case it would slip out.

This was one of the reasons I was reluctant to complete the scrapbook. I was aware of the judgements I'd made about my dad and the rest of the collective. I was so ashamed of the mental illness each group member had, I completely neglected their huge achievements as artists. The other reason why I'd been reluctant to do it was I didn't want to consign my dad to history. It felt like a final act, especially because all the members of the collective were now dead.

My dad and the other members of the collective were proud of their status as outsider artists and certainly weren't hiding the fact they each had a mental illness. Yet here I was, his daughter, hiding my true self, as well as my past.

Why was I so bothered about what other people might say? I stared at the picture and from it seemed to almost get a message from my dad. I felt like he was telling me to accept who I was and to open up. It was then I realised completing the scrapbook needn't be the final act. If I could take some of my dad's spirit, honesty and openness, his message would be living on.

With the last article glued into the scrapbook and I found

myself crying. I transferred onto the sofa and eventually fell asleep.

Later on in the morning, I waited for Jonathon's sleek car and was surprised to see him in 'dress down mode', wearing jeans and a pristine white t-shirt. As I wheeled to his car, he told me a 'police contact' had made some enquiries, none of which revealed anything.

'So he must be in his flat or with friends,' I said, as I sat in the passenger seat.

'The thing is, Rachel. We're not getting records of him at all. Our search hasn't revealed any snippet at all, almost as if he didn't exist. So, either we've got the area wrong; his name isn't right or something else. It's near impossible not to have a virtual footprint these days.'

'So, we're now not certain of the value in this trip. If Mike doesn't want to contact us, we may just have to accept that.' Kate commented from the back.

'We're still going, aren't we?' I picked at my lip.

Jonathon slid into his seat next to me, and after a brief glance in his rear view mirror he turned on the ignition. 'We're going.'

It took about ten minutes to get into the Windmill Estate, by which time I was totally disorientated. Jonathon and Kate both tried to explain how we'd managed to get there but this confused me even more. What surprised me most was the Windmill Estate was predominantly social and Council houses.

'Apparently, before this estate was built, it was a couple of big farms and on one of the farms was a windmill. This estate wasn't built until the sixties. It wasn't part of Carthom until the eighties. In fact, there were large street protests when it became under Carthom. You'll soon see why,' Jonathon said.

'Jonathon's into local history. If I hadn't married him when I did, he may've been lost forever as a train spotter,' Kate joked as she tickled Jonathon's neck and winked.

The houses changed from being detached or semi-detached

into rows of nondescript terraced houses with front yards. In some of them, the owners had obviously tried, with pots of flowers or hanging baskets, whereas others had overflowing rubbish or broken plastic toys littering the front.

I saw a row of boarded up shops with a gang of kids on bikes on the corner. The only shop open was selling cut-price booze. Behind these shops were four and five storey flats with washing hanging out in the front; one had a stained mattress hanging out from a window, another a large CCTV sign on their door. A number of windows had UKIP posters displayed.

'You're quiet, Rachel?' said Kate.

'You must be taking in the breath-taking views,' Jonathon smirked.

'I didn't realise it was this sort of area. It reminds me of where I used to live,' I whispered. It looked exactly like the area the bungalow was in, and for a moment I felt fearful and despondent just as I did when I was there.

The car went over a speed bump.

'Any ideas, anyone?' Kate said. 'Where shall we start?'

'Women, any respectable women, and then we stop,' replied Jonathon.

We crawled down a road and passed by a child who must have been around ten years old firing an imaginary gun into the car.

'Charming,' said Jonathon.

'Or shops that sell papers or cigarettes,' I blurted out. 'Mike smokes.'

'Jonathon, stop here, the lady opposite the one with the push chair.'

He pulled in. 'Do you want me to go and ask her? It'll be easier won't it?' ·

'Yes, you go.'

He got out and after a quick glance right, then left, dashed across the road. He stood for a few minutes talking to the woman. She looked as if she was giving him directions with her hands, which he then copied. She pointed in the opposite direction, shaking her head as she did so. Jonathon scooted back across the road and into the car.

'Right, there are some shops, if we go straight up this road and turn left. She hasn't heard of Mike but when I asked about flats, there are the ones we have just passed, or over the other side of the estate there are some flats for older people and possibly the disabled too. I reckon we take a look at these shops first.'

He pulled out from where he parked and soon we were going up into the heart of the estate. We passed a boarded up pub and then just as the woman had said, as the road veered to the left there was a row of four or five shops.

'Won't be long,' Jonathon said as he got out.

He came back after a few minutes, shaking his head. 'Sorry, no luck there. They seemed to recognize the description of Mike but not his name. Apparently, if we carry on up this road, on the left hand side are some flats.'

We crawled up the road until we came to a group of four storey flats which appeared to be newer than the other houses in the estate; sitting outside on a bench was an old lady with bags of shopping and an old golden Labrador.

'That woman on the bench, ask her,' I cried out.

'Can't stop at this moment, got a car on my tail.'

When Jonathon was able to park up, he sprinted back over to the bench.

'I should have said to him, to ask her if her dog was called Sandy.'

'He knows about it,' Kate assured me.

By craning my neck, I could just make out Jonathon bending down as he spoke to the lady.

'She's just patted the bench; Jonathon's now sitting down next to her,' Kate reported. 'Oh God, it looks like she's in tears.'

After a few minutes more, Jonathon walked back over to the

car, opened the door, sat back and loudly exhaled.

I turned to face him and Kate was leaning forward in the back seat.

Jonathon again half turned in his seat. 'Unfortunately it proved to be a dead end. I think there must be someone on this estate called Stewart who's Mike's doppelganger. That lady was a little bit mixed up, which didn't help. I tried asking if her dog was called Sandy but if I'm honest, I hadn't a clue what she was going on about.'

Jonathon glanced in the rear view mirror and then turned around in his seat, first to peer at Kate and then back at me.

Kate leant forward and tapped me on the shoulder.

'Rachel, if I keep in touch with my former colleagues in the NHS, and Jonathon gets in touch with the police and keeps checking their records, then I think we've covered all bases. It could just be Mike doesn't want to be found and he's staying with friends or family.'

'However, it's unusual he's not matching any records,' Jonathon said. 'You might have someone who's hiding their true identity. That would fit perfectly into a television drama or a novel, but not in an art group in Carthom. Something isn't quite right. Once we know what it is, everything will make sense. Until we know we're stumbling in the dark.'

'So what are you saying? We should stop searching?' I said, first turning to face Jonathon and then at Kate.

'We stop looking here,' Jonathon clarified. 'Instead we use the police and NHS contacts.'

On the drive back to the village, we all sat in silence. I peered at my reflection in my passenger window. I hadn't been honest about who I was, so it wasn't so unlikely Mike was the same.

I shut my eyes briefly and when I opened them I saw Mike waving at me from the side of the road. When I focused in, I saw it was simply a teenager waving to someone.

'He'll turn up,' Jonathon said, in an attempt to reassure me.

He proceeded to help me get out of the car.

As I was ready to wheel up my path, Jonathon crouched down. 'Try not to worry.'

Twenty-One

Janine was just finishing off her coffee in the living room. She'd been telling me about her boyfriend's job worries. He was a sales assistant in a large office supplies shop, part of a company with forty such shops dotted around the country. A memo had been sent telling all the staff to be prepared for possible redundancies as the company was looking for ways to streamline its operations.

'He's been in this job since leaving school. He's feeling really worried because if his job goes then we'll have to rely on my wages, which are pathetic,' Janine said, staring gloomily down at the floor, twisting the ring on her chain. She slurped another mouthful of coffee and wiped her mouth before staring across at me with her big brown eyes blinking slowly. 'There was no mention of this in his horoscope. I know we've talked about it before but I want you to tell me honestly, Rachel, if it's a mad idea, me and my fella starting our own business doing cleaning for disabled people?'

'I think it's a great idea.'

'So, do you think it could really work?'

'Definitely, but I would try and make sure you had people to clean for before you jack this job in. I also thought it might be better if you say you'd clean for anyone, not just disabled people. You'd then have a much wider group of people to sell your service too.'

'I suppose I'd have to tone this down even more.' With one

finger, Janine drew a circular shape in front of her face.

'Your make-up? I would. You'll be the face of your company and people do tend to judge by appearance. You know, Kate, from the art group, well her husband's an accountant for start-up companies. He may be able to give you some more advice.'

There was a knock on the door, Janine pulled herself up. 'I'll get it.' She walked out of the living room and I heard her thank the postman.

'You've got a letter and a parcel.' Janine held the letter in one hand, as she scrutinised the parcel.

After giving me the post, Janine carried on with her story. While she talked I examined my post. The parcel was a book on modern art, a late night impulse buy from Amazon. The letter was more interesting. My address was hand written in beautiful, green ink handwriting. I opened it up whilst trying to maintain eye contact with Janine.

'To be honest if he does lose his job, I'm going to see whether we could move in with his mum, to save on rent. I'm wondering if we can both work for the cleaning company. He's dead good at maths.'

For a moment I didn't reply.

'Rachel?'

'Sorry, I was just reading this. It's from Janet Riley. I met her at the art sale. She's invited me to a book group starting in the autumn. It's going to be in The Vines. Don't you think it's a bit strange, a book group based in a pub? The only thing I've seen in pubs is old men reading The Sun.'

Janine leant forward with an impish grin. 'My mate calls them dirty old men or DOM for short.' She winked at me.

'So reading 'Infinite Jest'. I pointed at my copy on the coffee table. 'Will be a change from gazing at infinite breasts.'

Janine stretched out her legs. 'Is there anything else you need?'

'I don't think so. I'll ask Kate if Jonathon can give you any advice about setting a business up. Oh, I'm sorry, before you go, you know the box I called the 'old Rachel'? You carried it upstairs for me a while ago.'

Janine nodded.

'You wouldn't mind just bringing the box back down for me?'

Janine eased herself up from the chair.

'I'm going to be a pain now, but could you also get the shredder from the cupboard under the stairs.'

'You want them both in here?'

'Yes, sorry to be a nuisance.'

'It's OK, but then I do really need to get off.'

Janine made her way upstairs humming to herself.

While she was up there I left a quick message on my mum's answering machine to tell her about the book group.

Janine walked into the room, her face flushed as she carried the box.

'Where do you want it?'

'Just put it back next to the blue chair please, Janine.'

After putting it down Janine fanned herself with her hand, before retrieving the shredder from the cupboard.

'I can help you with it another day.' Janine checked her mobile.

'You get going, Mum can help me.'

For a minute I watched Janine after she left my house. She raced over to the other side of my road and I thought about how she'd changed. When I first met her, she used to have her shoulders rounded and forward and often looked down as she walked. Now she had a much more confident stride, and appeared to be taller with her shoulders back and straight.

About half an hour later I heard the grinding noise of the brakes of my mum's car. I wasn't expecting her and my first thought was perhaps she'd picked up my message and was coming to talk about it.

'It's good news, isn't it.' I blurted out as soon as she was walking up my path.

'Rachel...'

'...I know, don't get too excited. I know, Mum.'

'No, Rachel. I need to let you know something. Come on; let's sit in the living room.'

I transferred onto the sofa. Mum usually sat on the blue IKEA chair opposite me, but instead she sat down next to me.

'Rach...'

I could hear an ominous tone in Mum's voice. 'What's the matter?'

'The man you've been searching for...'

'...Mike? What about him?'

'I noticed this article and the guy who's died sounds a lot like the one you're looking for.' She picked up her handbag from the floor and pulled out her diary. Inside was a folded piece of newspaper, which she placed on my knee.

My hands were trembling so much, Mum had to take it back and unfold it. A woman was holding a framed photograph of Mike, though in the article he was called Stewart Murray. I couldn't speak, and for a moment sat there, confused and in shock.

'It's him, isn't it?'

I stared down at the paper, and nodded.

She pointed to a paragraph in the article. 'It says here his name was Stewart but he called himself Mike, which was his middle name. His sister said he wasn't taking his medication either.'

'Stewart? That was the name everyone mentioned on the estate.'

Mum felt my hand. 'You're cold, Rach.'

My mind tried to take in this information. Could this really be right? Mike was dead? I glanced again at the article.

'The surname still doesn't match, and the age, Mike wasn't

thirty.'

Mum pointed to the article. 'But it's him in the photograph. I think you might be in shock, sometimes it can feel strange.'

'When did he die? Did we miss the funeral?'

'I don't know. There's going to be a memorial service next week, followed by a poetry reading by his sister and they're going to show his photographs and paintings'

'Photographs? Mike didn't take photos he painted dogs.'

Mum put her hand on my knee. 'It's what his sister says in the article'

She stood up and walked into the kitchen, bringing back my cardigan from the back of my kitchen chair. She placed it around my shoulders before going back and making a cappuccino.

I picked up the piece of newspaper. As soon as I saw Mike's sister holding a framed photograph of him, I felt a deep and painful ache inside me. I tried to read it but the words seemed to blur into each other.

'I can't believe this is actually our Mike, you know.' I glanced at my mum as she walked back into the living room.

'It's a shock, isn't it?'

'Why can't I cry? I really liked Mike, why can't I feel anything?'

'You will do, when you're ready you will,' Mum said.

I buried my head in my hands.

'Only thirty years old, so very young to die, just like your dad.'

Mum leant towards me, her arm around my back. For the next few minutes we sat there, my body shaking as I began to cry.

'Are you thinking about your dad?' Mum stroked my arm with her hand.

'Both of them.'

'I remember your dad's funeral like it was yesterday. The emotions still feel raw all these years later.'

'I didn't help.'

Mum held my hand. 'You were dreadfully upset but were so supportive to me despite only being young. I remember at the funeral you reaching for me when I was crying.'

'I seem to only remember before he died and the arguments. I thought I'd let you down when I became unwell.'

'Oh Rachel, you mustn't think like that. The arguments, the ones you remember, were connected with his art in so much as I didn't feel he was focusing on the family. I was worried he was defining himself by the illness, less on being your dad or my husband.'

'But he couldn't choose to switch on or off his illness, so why did you blame him for it?'

'I didn't blame him for being ill. It's just, before The Butterfly Collective, he focused on his art not his illness. By the time he met Peter and the others, your dad had become ill again. He met them all while he was in hospital. He called it an epiphany moment as they all discussed their various art projects. Out of something ugly something beautiful emerges.'

I nodded. 'I remember that.'

'I really believed when your dad was better he'd come back to the family and we would go back to normal.' Mum shook her head. 'Instead he spent more and more time away. Rather than his artwork focusing on beautiful things they all homed in on what it was to be mentally ill.'

I shrugged. 'That's what outsider art's all about.'

Mum caressed my hand. 'But, Rachel there were reports in the press and they all focused on mental health. I didn't want you or your brother to be bullied because of it, and you may remember at that stage I hadn't told either of you about his illness. I just wanted to protect you from all that. I was worried sick about it all and how it would affect us, as a family. It was something at the time, I didn't fully understand. That's when all the arguments started.'

I stared down at my knees.

'In essence part of it was my own insecurity and another part was to protect you two. I know when he died I tried to shield you both from what was going on. I should've been more honest with you. As time has gone on, Rachel, I've come to realise your dad was a master of reinvention turning what could be negative, like his illness, into something positive.'

I turned my head towards her. 'You were angry, Mum, when I first became ill.'

Mum nodded. 'I know and I'm sorry. I seem to recall I went off at the deep end. It was just because I worried and it was scary for me to see you so poorly.'

I picked at stray pieces of cotton on my jeans.

'When you first became ill, it wasn't because I was ashamed of your illness. It was because I just wanted the best for you. The best chance of as normal life a life you could have.'

'I've made a real mess of it, haven't I? My life I mean.'

Mum put her arm around my back and held me. 'Please, don't think like this, Rach. This year I've watched you grow after that awful time at the bungalow. You've done your best to join in with activities and be independent and you've made me feel proud, so proud.'

I started to feel tearful again.

'Think back a couple of years, you were with those awful people and frightened to go anywhere on your own. Compare that with now. And like your dad, you've got a chance now of making something out of that awful time. You could volunteer with Inspire and Support and help others who are in difficulty.'

A tear started to fall down my cheek.

'Rach, I know if your dad was here now he'd be saying exactly the same thing.'

'I feel sorry for Mike, Mum. He was so worried, so upset with all that was going on. If I'd opened up to him, he might be still here.'

Mum squeezed me. 'I think this would have happened regardless.'

I buried my head into Mum's side, and for a moment we sat like that; Mum holding me and stroking my hair.

I sat back up and picked up the newspaper article and attempted to read it again. I tried to wipe my tears away, enough for me to read.

Poet Blames Welfare Cuts for Brother's Death

Wallaston resident, the performance poet, Carol Greaves, believes the recent death of her brother Stewart was partly due to debt and Benefit cuts.

Stewart Murray, 30, from Weston suffered from sciatica, depression and epilepsy. On visiting his flat, following his death, Carol found a stack of paperwork detailing his serious financial problems and also discovered he had stopped taking his epilepsy medication.

Carol said, "Stewart, who often used his middle name, Mike, was such a talented young man, a keen photographer and artist– but he was also vulnerable, due to his disabilities. He died, hungry, surrounded by letters saying his Benefits would be stopped and Payday lenders threatening to take him to court.

"I would like to welcome all who knew Stewart or who feel a connection with his story to come along and celebrate his life at his memorial service.

"The memorial service takes place at St Andrew's Church in Wallaston at 10 a.m on May 31st followed by a small exhibition of photographs and artwork by Stewart. Carol's latest poetry collection, Degrees of Separation, will be sold after the memorial and proceeds from this will be split between two charities, details

to be given on the day."

'He was talented, very talented and we all let him down.' I wrapped my arms over my head. Mum put her arm across my shoulders.

'This article was only in my local paper, as his sister lives in Wallaston. Which means the others, people from your group, might not know about it. You'll need to let Kate know, and maybe see if Kate can let some of the others know.'

I unfolded my arms. 'There was also this woman who phoned up from the group he used to go to in Weston. I'll have to ring her.'

'Do you want me to stay with you while you do this? After your father died I found it easier to just let a few key people know, as then the word gets passed around.'

She put the newspaper article on my coffee table and spotted the letter from Janet.

'I left you a message about it, Mum. She's invited me to join her book group.' The excitement I had felt about the group had vanished.

'Oh, that's good. Sorry I didn't get the message; I saw this article and got straight in the car to come here. Try and get those calls done, Rach, and please ring me if you need me. Even if it's only just to talk, I don't mind.'

'OK.'

'Do you want another drink or anything?' Mum walked into the kitchen and picked up the phone, which she placed in front of me, on the coffee table. 'Are you sure you're going to be alright?' She cocked her head onto one side.

I stared down at the phone.

'OK. Well, I'll go. Let me know how you get on.'

I heard the front door bang shut and all of a sudden I felt scared. In the past, overwhelming emotions have tipped me over the edge. I didn't want this to happen again, but knew I'd little control over my moods.

Snippets of memory were bobbing up in my mind. One memory was when I first met Mike and he was showing me his paintings on his phone. Another was when he told me about his debts and about his family. I could also picture him giving me his painting at the exhibition and also how hurt he'd been when the argument broke out.

I picked up the phone and decided to ring Kate first. Jonathon answered and told me Kate was out with Jeremy. I told him Mike was using his middle name and in response I heard him sigh.

'This explains it then. When we went around his estate, all I heard was Stewart. If only we'd known. So when is this memorial? I'll make sure we both attend. Do you want a lift, Rachel, to go to it?'

I murmured my thanks.

Jonathon sighed again. 'Kate's going to be so upset when I tell her.'

'There's this one other thing. Do you think you or Kate would be able to tell Anne? It's just I've got to ring a woman who used to go to the art group Mike went to in Weston. I'd ring Anne myself but I don't think I can keep on saying this, before it really makes me break down.'

'Ring Anne? Yes, I'd better do it. I'm not sure how Kate will react to this. Which paper was it in again?' Jonathon asked.

'Wallaston News.'

I could hear Jonathon tapping and realised he must be either on a mobile or iPad.

'Alright then, Rachel, I'll tell Kate, and she'll ring you in the next couple of days.'

I took a deep breath after putting the phone down. I went into the kitchen and found Jill's number and called her up. She took a while to answer and part of me was hoping she wouldn't be in. When she did, I was thrown by the sound of young children on the line. I suddenly didn't know what I could say so in a roundabout fashion began.

'Hello Jill, my mum has just been round. Mike's sister who's a poet, she has written an article about Mike.'

'Thank God, I was getting really worried.'

I bit my lip. 'I'm really sorry, what I'm saying is he's dead. He called himself Mike but his first name was Stewart, which is why we weren't able to find him.'

'Oh God, was it suic..?' Jill's voice trailed off.

'It doesn't say in the article, but he'd stopped taking his tablets. It sounds like he just gave up.'

'Oh, poor Mike, he did suffer from depression and mood swings, you see, everyone at the Weston group had some form of mental illness. It was just Mike though, who had a combination of problems, his back, epilepsy and depression. Oh, I can't believe it. I'd only just started to get to know him.'

I could hear Jill whisper, 'Oh, no,' over and over again.

'I didn't know about the depression. It mentions it in the article but Mike never said anything about it.'

'He wasn't one to go on about his disabilities; he was such a gentle, lovely man.'

'If you want to come with us to the memorial service, you're more than welcome.'

Jill said nothing but I could hear her sniff and blow her nose.

I persevered. 'Give me a call if you need to?'

The phone calls done, I tried to do some painting but after about ten minutes it went in the bin. I tried to watch some TV but I couldn't concentrate. In the end I went upstairs to bed.

Before drifting off I peered at Mike's painting. The blue and white marble abstract took me back to the exhibition and also to the endless cigarettes we shared. I moved on to thinking about his memorial service in a week's time. I didn't know how I would cope at it. His death was so unfair.

Twenty-Two

On the day of Mike's memorial service, I was sitting on my sofa waiting for Anne. Donna, my morning carer, whizzed around the house tidying up and ironing. I felt as if I were in a bubble, separated from the rest of the world.

My Mum had been right, I'd only needed to phone a couple of people and the news of Mike's death and the service was passed from person to person until the whole of the art group knew. Thankfully, they were all going to attend, though Kate had asked if we could visit The Vines after the service rather than stay for refreshments at the church.

Carol Greaves had asked for two people from our group and from Jill's former group to say a few words about him at the service. Jill decided to do it on her own, and from our group Kate agreed to do it, and gently persuaded Anne to join her. I would've wanted to do it myself but I remembered when my dad died, I was meant to read a poem but as soon as I stood up at the front of the church emotion had risen up inside of me and I had to sit back down.

When Anne's car pulled up, I could recall waiting outside my home when I was twelve, my emotions in freefall as we waited for the cars to take us to my dad's funeral. Now in Carthom, I had the same feelings this time combined with guilt. I didn't want to say goodbye to Mike as there was so much more I wanted to say to him.

As I got my bag onto my wheelchair, there was a knock on the door, not her usual loud rapping, instead just one quiet, polite knock. Anne crouched down and we hugged. Her clothes were baggy and when she held me I could feel her ribs and spine.

'Have you lost weight, Anne?'

'A little. Are you ready?'

I nodded and followed her to the car. Kate had told me she thought Anne was depressed, and she certainly seemed more than sad. She was stooping forward as if someone were pulling her from a lead around her neck.

Anne drove to the centre, where we all were meeting up. When she'd parked, she sat in the car, not making any attempt to move.

'We can get through this today.' I rubbed the back of her right hand. She turned to me and I saw a tear edge its way down her cheek. She reached with her left hand and held my other hand, which she squeezed. For a moment we sat there in silence.

'Do you want to stay in the car, or say hello to the others?' Anne said eventually.

'I'll have a quick cigarette.'

Anne got out and walked towards Eddie and Lena. She'd forgotten about me. Eddie pointed in my direction and came towards me, tapping on the window:

'Are you alright in there, kiddo?'

'Can you help me out? I need a cigarette.'

'No problem.' Eddie put my wheelchair together but as I transferred over, my already bent foot plate fell off and I started to cry.

'It's alright; I've got some gaffer tape in my boot. I'm just around the back. Don't get upset. Do you want to stay here?'

'I'll come with you.' With my head down, I passed the others and followed Eddie to his car. I watched as he opened his boot and pulled out frames, canvas, easels and a dog bed before finally bringing out a blue plastic box which had the tape inside.

'How, are you feeling, kiddo?' He crouched down to put a final layer of tape around my footplate.

I looked down at his flushed face. 'I don't know really, Eddie. I just seem to cry for no reason. I'm a bit nervous about speaking to the others in case I get upset again.'

'How about we join the others together and if you're

struggling then I'll rescue you. Does that sound like a plan?'

'Yes.'

Eddie held onto the sides of my wheelchair and stood up. As he stretched, his shirt pulled up from his trousers. I turned my head away and felt the heat on my face.

Eddie crouched down again. 'Actually, while I've got you here on my own, I just wanted a quiet word about Anne.'

I started to bite my lip.

'Some of this you might know but if you don't know it, then please keep it quiet because Anne's very fragile, very fragile indeed. She's had an unbearable time, the worst a mother could have. Also, not having contact with the younger members of her family means she often doesn't keep up with changes, keeping her a bit old fashioned at times. Being around young people challenges us oldies to see the world through the eyes of young people. The second thing is...'

We both turned our heads as we heard Anne shout my name.

'I'll tell you the rest another time,' whispered Eddie.

'Are you ready, Rachel?' Anne said. 'Pauline and Elaine are coming with us.'

We set off and for most of the journey we were behind Jonathon's car. Pauline and Elaine attempted light conversation but as soon as we passed the sign for Wallaston, conversation dried up.

Anne was biting on her lip, and had a faraway look in her eyes.

'Are you alright for this morning?' I asked. 'Doing the talk with Kate?'

Staring straight ahead, Anne gave a slight nod.

When we arrived at St Andrew's church, Anne turned into the car park where a man with a high visibility jacket was standing in our way. She wound down her window, each movement accompanied by a creaking sound.

'Are you here for the memorial service?' The man glanced

down at his clipboard.

Anne didn't react.

'There's no free spaces in the car park now. You'll have to turn around and park on the main road. Put one of these on your dashboard.' He handed Anne a piece of paper, which she held in her mouth. As soon as we were parked, we joined the line of people waiting to get into the church.

Pauline and Elaine were behind me and Anne by my side, as we waited in the queue. There must have been at least ten in front of us. I was aware nobody was talking but as we got closer to the church I could hear music and a voice welcoming people.

Eventually, it was my turn to go inside. A service sheet was pushed onto my knees by an elderly man. There was a photograph of Mike with the dates of his birth and death. With my finger I touched his photograph, tears stinging my eyes.

I could smell a heady mix of perfume, sweat and aftershave and I think the music was 'Songbird' by Eva Cassidy. I was feeling hot with all these bodies so close together. I realised Anne and the others were no longer with me. I couldn't move any other direction apart from forward at a slow pace.

I decided to break away from where I was and tried to turn around. I moved to my right and caught a woman's ankle with my chair, she squealed before looking down at the offending wheel and then at me.

'Hang on. Are you Rachel?'

'Yes and you must be Carol,' I said, breathing out.

'Let me get you out of here, it's a much bigger turnout than we estimated.'

Carol took my handles and pushed me to one of the side aisles, where she found our group. Anne and Kate were on the front row, alongside what could be Jill and another man. The rest of our group were on the fifth row from the front.

'You can either sit in your chair in the main aisle or at this end? Or if you want you could sit in a pew; I don't know how you would manage this.' Carol pointed to the bottom of the pews which were raised off the ground by around ten centimetres.

'Is it OK if I just sit here?'

'Will you be able to see?'

I nodded.

'I just have to speak to the vicar. Are you staying for the exhibition?'

'Yes, but I'm really sorry we might not be able to stay for the food.'

Carol nodded. As I looked up I caught sight of her eyes. They were just like Mike's, a little sunken, but intense. She disappeared and when I saw her again, she was talking to a vicar who was checking his watch. In the chancel area behind the vicar there was an easel displaying a large glossy photograph of Mike. He was smiling broadly and looked relaxed. It struck me I'd never seen him like that before.

Jonathon had been slowly edging his way along the pew, with the other group members either having to stand up or sit sideways to let him get past. Eventually he got to my end of the pew.

'Didn't want you sitting on your own, Rachel.'

At that point the music increased in volume with Eva Cassidy singing, Over the Rainbow. When the song finished, a vicar stood in front of the congregation with open arms.

'Let us pray. Dear Lord, today we're here gathered in your name to remember Stewart, to give praise and celebrate his life and to offer comfort and prayer to his family and friends. I pray that those who take part in the service today may find peace and reassurance in your name. Through Christ our Lord. Amen.'

'Amen,' I whispered.

Carol walked over to our side of the church and stood in front of the lectern. She opened a large Bible. 'The Bible reading is taken from Psalm twenty-three, The Lord is my Shepherd. It can be found in the pew Bibles on page five hundred and twelve.'

Jonathon nudged me and mouthed, 'Are you OK?' just as a tear dropped onto my lap.

The reading had finished and I could see Carol pressing down her skirt with her hands as she walked back over to the vicar.

She stood in the middle of the steps and cleared her throat again. 'My brother, Stewart, endured much in his life. Born with epilepsy and suffering from sciatica he often was in so much pain he could cry. Instead of just passively accepting his lot he translated this suffering into photography and art with examples of his work being shown after this service in the church hall. As well as being involved in the arts himself Stewart often encouraged those around him to follow their dreams.

'He was also a very caring man and I know he'd be pleased if today we could raise some money for charity. I've decided to split donations between The Samaritans and the Epilepsy Action Group. There'll be people here at the end of this service collecting, as well as some in the church hall during the exhibition and poetry reading.

'In a few minutes we will hear from four people. Gary, who's from the photography group Stewart attended, followed by Jill who was at the art group in Weston with him. Finally, Kate and Anne from the Carthom art group will say a few words. Many people knew Stewart as Stewart but he tended to use his middle name Mike towards the end of his life.

'Before we hear from Stewart's friends I'd like to introduce his niece, Sara, the latest creative member of the family. She'll sing "Come Away with Me" by Norah Jones and Peter, here, will play the guitar.' Carol held open her arms as a serene looking, red-haired, girl walked up to the front followed by a bearded man carrying a guitar.

Sara sang a haunting and achingly beautiful rendition of the song. Her soulful voice sounded odd belonging to such a young girl but as I listened, I closed my eyes and soon was drifting away.

'Wow,' Jonathon whispered, when she finished singing. The clapping rippled into rapturous applause and the girl bowed her head in response.

Carol reappeared at the top of the steps and held out her left arm. Gary stood up closely followed by Jill. The three of them were looking in the direction of the front row. There was a short delay before Kate got up and hobbled to the front. I was craning my neck to try to find where Anne was, but didn't notice at first, she'd been moving herself on her bottom up to the end of the side aisle. She got out of the pew and hurried past me, with her head down. As Gary started to talk, I let Jonathon know what I was doing and wheeled towards the back of the church to try and find her.

At the back, there was no sign of Anne. The old man who'd given me a service sheet opened big wooden doors opposite the main door of the church and pointed up the corridor.

At the end of it, to the left were two toilets and to the right the church hall. The hall was empty as far as I could see so instead I quietly knocked on one of the toilet doors.

'Anne, are you in there?'

There was no response.

'Are you OK? Do you need any help?'

Again nobody replied but after a few seconds I heard the toilet being flushed.

Anne opened the toilet door. Her posture was saggy and she held on tight to the side of the door frame as if she would collapse if she let go.

'It was a lovely service, wasn't it?' I said.

'I've let everyone down.' She stared at the ground, her body shaking.

'Come here.' I opened my arms and she bent down with her arms by her side, as I hugged her.

Anne pulled back from me and stood limp, her back bent

254

and head down.

'Come on, let's try and see some of this exhibition before the rest of the congregation arrive.' I didn't know what to say to her.

I forced the door open with my chair and held it open for Anne. A man who had greying hair, one side of it pulled over his head to hide the baldness, was sitting behind the door in front of a table piled high with copies of the poetry collection by Carol called 'Degrees of Separation'. He had a clear, luminous, moon-like complexion that defied age and the wrinkles and lines accompanying it. I bought a copy of the book, and carefully placed it in the side of my rucksack.

'What about looking at Mike's photographs now?' I said to Anne. When I got no response, I moved over to the wall where there were about ten or twelve large framed photographs. Anne stood next to me and was staring at the floor.

The first photograph was a black and white scene outside a job centre with various people sitting on the wall and standing near the doorway. There was a girl in a wheelchair with her head down, and a man leaning with a stick. The photograph was taken through a gap in a fence.

'It's really evocative, isn't it?' I said.

'Does she blame me?' Anne replied, her expression inscrutable.

'Who?'

'Mike's sister.'

'Carol? No, of course she doesn't and she'll understand about today, you not being able to do the talk with Kate. Honestly, she'll totally understand. She isn't the type to go blaming people.'

'I don't mean about the talk,' Anne said gloomily.

'Nobody blames you.'

'Are you going to go to the pub after this?' Anne pulled her hands away from mine.

'Yes, are you?'

'I don't know. Depends who else is going.'

The doors of the hall were flung open and the congregation spilled into the room. Within minutes it was full.

I was separated from Anne and decided to leave the hall and get some air. As I made my way through, I saw some of Mike's paintings on a stage in the hall. Next to the stage was the door leading to the fire exit, which in turn led to the church hall car park. Here I found Carol getting a packet of cigarettes from her bag.

'It was a good turnout, wasn't it?' I searched for my lighter.

'Here, let me.' Carol crouched down and lit my cigarette. She tapped her own cigarette two times on the packet, before she cupped it in her hands to light it.

Carol stood back up and arched her back. 'I reckon some of the people here have no idea who Stewart was, it's my fault for putting an open invite in the paper. We only catered for about thirty people tops.'

'What was the turnout like for the funeral?'

'We haven't had one yet. Although it's plain to me he must've had a seizure, the post mortem was inconclusive, and one line of thought is that perhaps Mike had run out of rope.'

I screwed up my face.

'They think he could've taken something. He had only four pounds to his name and because it was in his bank account, and under five pounds, he couldn't even take it out. The only food he had was stale. He'd also put in neat piles all the letters regarding his Benefits.'

'Only four pounds in his bank account?'

'Yes, so they think stress may've made him kill himself. That's why we've now got to wait for toxicology results, but we're hoping they will release his body any day. We'll just have a private service at the crematorium, family only.'

I nodded.

'I wanted to have a memorial service as I knew he was involved in groups, so this was more about what he did, how creative he was. He was held back educationally due to his epilepsy and other problems, but he was such a talented man.'

'He was hugely talented and very kind. It was a lovely service. The girl who sang was brilliant.'

'She's my little brother's daughter.' Carol crouched down for a minute. 'Is your friend Anne OK? She seemed a bit upset?'

'I think she may be a bit down. The thing is, when Mike, sorry, Stewart, was with us, he was ever so worried about his Benefits. At one stage there was an argument about it. I just think some people might be blaming themselves.'

'Tell them not to be worried. Stewart was getting so stressed and at times short-tempered. I hope he didn't cause too much trouble.'

'Oh, it wasn't him causing trouble. It was the others having a go at him,' I said, looking at the ground. I turned to Carol. 'Why did he call himself Mike and use a different surname?'

'It's a bit complicated. I'm not sure how much Stewart told you about our dad.'

'He said to me that his mum had a bit of a hard time with him.'

Carol nodded. 'Stewart was his dad's name, which was why in the last year or so he started to call himself Mike, which was his middle name. Greaves was our mums' maiden name. He didn't change them formally, though I knew it was something he wanted to do.'

For a couple of minutes we were silent.

'I bought your book of poems,' I said eventually. 'Would you sign it for me?' I pulled it out from the side of my chair.

'Thanks – yes, pass it over.'

Carol positioned her leg to create a surface on which to rest the book; with a flourish she signed it. When she passed it back to me, she said cryptically, 'You're going to need this soon.'

'Can I just ask, why are you called a performance poet? Why not just a poet?'

'Good question. Obviously, rhymes, metres and metaphors are part of my work, just like any poet, but what I find more interesting is the experience of people coming together, to say out loud the poems. What emotional intensity it produces? What effect the spoken word has on an audience? So, I try to make my work accessible and about everyday subjects. It's hard to explain, but you'll see what I mean in a few minutes time.'

As Carol was talking I opened her book; she'd put the date as well as writing in purple ink, 'Dear Rachel, thanks for being a friend.' I remembered the message Mike had put on the back of the painting at the sale and the emotion seemed to rise up within me. I took a deep breath in and held it for a few seconds.

'Did you ever sit like this outside with Stewart when he was smoking?'

I nodded. 'I do miss him, you know.'

'I know, so do I.' Carol half crouched down and put her arm around my shoulders and squeezed.

'Are you coming back in? I'm going to read out a poem.'

As Carol made her way back into the main hall, I stayed by the fire door, the amount of people and lack of space in the main hall, put me off from even attempting to find the rest of the group. After a few minutes I saw Eddie push his way through to me.

'We've been looking for you, kiddo, where did you go? Oh, I know, tsk, tsk. You've been out having a fag, haven't you?'

'I was speaking to Carol; she's really lovely.' I tried to hide my cigarettes under my bottom.

'It's so packed in there, we're thinking of calling it a day in the next half an hour or so.' Eddie folded his arms and leant against the wall.

'What were you going to say to me earlier, about Anne?'

'It was only to stress how fragile she was. Anne keeps a secret. A secret that's devastating. It's something she very rarely talks about. Not only that, she's lost contact with her remaining family and was blamed for everything that went wrong. It's had a profound effect on her.'

'What's the secret?'

Eddie rubbed his forehead. 'I've probably said too much already. Just bear in mind, sometimes she behaves in a way that is all about what she has dealt with in the past.'

'I thought you felt angry with Anne about Mike and how she didn't stop the row?'

'It wasn't all Anne's fault. Yes, she could've tried to stop it when it started but who's to say the others would've listened? Also, it takes confidence to be able to wade in. Something she's not got. That's all I was saying.'

From the hall we heard clapping and then Carol's voice. She was thanking people for attending.

'The photographs you see in this hall are going to be put in a book alongside my poetry. Stewart often used to say we should do a joint project.'

'Now that's a really good idea,' Eddie whispered.

'Yeah, I'd buy it, definitely.'

'When Stewart died, I felt so angry yet powerless. In the early hours of the morning, I sat at the kitchen table and wrote this poem. It's very simple but I hope you can get a sense of the anger I feel, not at Stewart but at the government and how many deaths have been connected to recent policy. I thought it would be great if we could say the poem out loud together. It's called, Dear Coalition Government. If any of you have bought my latest poetry book it's printed on a loose sheet inside it and if not, people are now handing out some spare copies. I will give you a few minutes. Some of you might need to share.'

I pulled the book from my bag, and found the sheet of paper; Eddie walked over and crouched by my side.

'Are we ready everyone?'

Applause and wolf whistles were the reply and when it was silent, Carol began to read the poem, accompanied by a multitude of voices in the hall.

> *'Dear coalition government,*
> *This lament is for you.*
> *Through my anger, discontent,*
> *Others must hear it too.*
> *I am one of the walking dead*
> *And we are on our own,*
> *On wheels, depressed,*
> *On sticks, bereft,*
> *Out of sight, stuck at home.*
> *The money you gave us,*
> *Benefits, a dirty word,*
> *Gave us life, gave us hope,*
> *Included us in the world.*
> *Now it's cut, you don't care,*
> *If one dead here,*
> *One dead there.*
> *The country's debt*
> *Is your defence.*
> *You claim it makes*
> *Economic sense.'*

Eddie and I had read the poem out loud along with everyone else, but due to being in the hallway, our voices sounded separate from the crowd. It felt intimate. As we reached the end of the poem, we both wiped away tears before we turned to each other and hugged.

'If only Mike could hear,' I murmured in Eddie's ear.

Eddie pulled away from me, and grasped my hand. 'He can hear, he'll be looking down at us now, kiddo.'

I picked up Carol's book, and flicked though the pages. I underestimated Mike completely. Who else in the group had I misunderstood?

Eddie stood up. 'My guess is everyone will be ready to go soon. Are you OK waiting here, kiddo? I'll go and try and find out what we're all doing?'

While I waited for Eddie to reappear, I flicked through Degrees of Separation; the poems were all very literal and also very political.

A few minutes later Eddie was back. The rest of the group were going out through the church so he walked with me around the side of the church towards the main road. The ground was covered in hot gravel, which was sticking onto my wheels and making my hands sore.

'What I was saying about Anne, is sometimes you just have to think what it must be like for her. I can't stress enough how it affected her.'

'It must've been very traumatic.'

'I think us going to the pub and having a chat together will be just what the doctor ordered.' Eddie said between gasps. He stopped for a minute and leant against the wall of the church. With his hands pressed onto his knees and his head down, he gave a laugh. 'I've got to get back on my bike or one of these days it will be me who needs a memorial service.'

I stared at him, frowning.

'Sorry, that was bad taste, wasn't it?' Eddie smiled as he stood up, the colour draining down his face leaving his nose alone a deep purple colour.

Twenty-Three

Albert and Marion had managed to get the group a good spot

in a corner of The Vines. The pub was fairly quiet, with only two older men talking at the bar. While drinks were being bought, there was total silence in the group. The tension made me extremely nervous and concerned this meeting would result in another major argument. When everyone was sitting down and we all had a drink in front of us, Eddie cleared his throat before raising his glass.

'Now we're all together,' he said. 'I want you all to raise a glass or cup to Mike.'

Hesitatingly, the group murmured, 'to Mike'.

Kate cleared her throat. 'So, I know we've just come from Mike's memorial service but I think this is really important. Mike sounded like a lovely bloke and he would've wanted this group to grow and develop. So, if that's right, then I think we must learn from what's happened. Sitting in the service made me think, we didn't know Mike at all, and I think that's part of the problem. We need to get to know each other better.'

Eddie gave a slight nod. 'You're right, Kate, we almost need to start again, and spend a bit of time getting to know each other. I'm not saying how it was before was wrong. It's just we need to be working as a group. The only way we can do it, is if we understand each other's needs and abilities. We need mutual respect between members, whether it's a newbie like Rachel or Kate or somebody who's well known in the group and in the village.'

Marion frowned as she turned to face Eddie. 'So what are you saying? We need to do what?'

'I'm not saying major changes are needed. Just we need to understand each other better. How can we be a group if we don't really know each other? Do you get me?'

'I think so,' mumbled Marion.

'What do you think, Anne?' Eddie asked.

'Think? Yes, I think it's a good idea but I don't want to be left with more work to do.'

'I used to do this team building exercise at work. Now, in best 'Blue Peter' style I've come prepared.' Kate pulled up her bag and plonked it onto the table. After a quick rummage, she produced a notebook and pencils held together with a red rubber band.

'And what's this got to do with starting the group again?' Marion protested.

'It's just an ice-breaker to help us get to know each other.'

Marion pulled a face but kept quiet.

'So, if we can now pair up. Try and be with someone you don't know very well or you don't usually sit by. One group will have to be a threesome.'

Pauline turned to me and tapped me on the hand.

'Rachel, can I be with you?'

I gave a slight nod but wished Kate had warned me in advance so I could sit with someone I actually liked.

There was discussion round the table as people paired up. Albert and Elaine moved onto the next table, which allowed the rest of the group the space to move around. I saw Kate tear off paper from the notebook. She gave Lena the pencils and paper which were then passed around the group.

Kate raised her hand. 'So, what I'd like you to do, is in your pairings each person tell your partner one interesting thing about yourself, one thing people don't know, and one funny or curious thing. Write these down if you need to. Then swap over.'

I turned to face Pauline. 'You go first.'

'One interesting thing is that I once met David Beckham!' Pauline sat back smiling.

'Come off it. Really? When was that?'

'It was years ago, when he played for Manchester United. I took some of our clients to meet him. He was lovely, really lovely, kind as well.'

I leant towards Pauline. 'What about something people don't know?'

'I've got a degree in history.'

'I never knew that either.' I sat back in my chair and tried to think about what I could say.

'I don't really go on about it; I don't want to appear big headed. Right, a funny thing is, Elaine and me, we were nicknamed Morecombe and Wise. You can guess which one is Morecombe and which one is Wise.'

I didn't smile at Pauline, despite her grinning at me. After all, this was the woman who'd been so nasty with Mike and who'd argued with me.

'What are yours, Rachel?'

'I don't know what to say.' For a minute I tried to think about something of interest. My mind was blank.

'OK, an interesting fact is before my accident happened I wanted to go to Art College. Something people don't know is that when I was seventeen I'd a boyfriend who was studying philosophy. I can't really think of anything else?'

Pauline moved herself closer to me.

'These are interesting things, Rachel, but can I say something? They're about your life before your accident, aren't they?'

I tried not to scowl. What did she know about life for people like me? People like Mike? I couldn't get out of my head the image of Pauline sneering and pointing her finger at Mike.

'There must be things you can say about your life now.'

I stared down at my knees.

'Rachel, I do understand, I really do. I've worked with people with disabilities all my life and sometimes it can seem life stopped when you became disabled. Although that may feel like it's true, it isn't really. Look at you, you're living independently. I bet there are a lot of people with your level of disability who haven't taken that step yet. And what's more, you're talented, your paintings are lovely. I wish I'd a talent like yours.'

A tear started to make its way down my cheek. I sniffed and brushed it off.

'Weren't you doing some voluntary work? I think Anne told

me you were?'

I nodded and took a deep breath in. 'OK, one interesting fact is I may in the future be doing some voluntary work with Inspire and Support. One thing people don't know is that at one stage in my life I was told I'd never be independent. I can't think of anything funny so it's another thing people might not know and that's that my dad was once a professional artist.'

'That is interesting, what kind of art did he do?'

I chewed my lip. 'Outsider art.'

'Oh, I've not heard of that.'

I gave a half nod.

'Going back to your disability, if you compare your life now with your life before the accident, it will never be good enough. You've got to compare like with like. Do you get me? Look at me, I'm retired and if I compare my life now with when I was working I'll always be miserable . The truth is I've retired so I've got to make the most of it.'

I gave her a reluctant smile. 'Yes, that does make sense.'

Kate got up and squeezed herself between Anne and Marion before then coming over to me.

'OK, sweetie?'

'Yes, thanks. I'm sorry I missed you doing your bit at the memorial, I just didn't know how she would be.' I nodded my head in Anne's direction.

'Don't worry; I'm just glad you went out with her.' Kate perched on the edge of the table. 'This has worked in getting everyone talking. I was thinking about suggesting we go and see The Dream. It's a piece of public art in St Helens and I think it would be good way to keep this momentum up. Go to somewhere where we can chat, but away from our normal surroundings.'

'How would we get there?'

'I was thinking minibus; I'd make sure we get a wheelchair one. Do we have money left in the Art for You kitty?'

I shrugged. 'I don't know; you'd have to ask Anne.'

'If I suggest the trip, will you give me some support?'

'For you, yes of course'

She nodded her head in the direction of Anne. 'I'm still worried about…'

'Anne? Yes, I was watching her before. She isn't right, is she?'

'I'll try and speak to her before we go.'

'I'm just going out to the back, Kate; I'll be back in a minute.'

I wheeled through past the kitchen and into the courtyard. The warmth outside hit me, and as I sat there, I listened to the birds. On the table next to me was a tiny white feather.

When I wheeled back indoors I saw Matt standing in the direction I was heading. He made no attempt to move so I slowed down. In just those few minutes the numbers in the pub had increased. He held out his hand in a stop sign.

'I'm your landlord.'

I nodded, confused as to why he needed to tell me.

'No, I'm your landlord.' He pointed at me.

I pointed at my chest. 'My landlord?'

'Yes, I'm Mark not Matt and I am your landlord, at number four.'

'Oh, at my home.'

Mark leant against the wall. 'Usually I don't tell my tenants who I am. However, I really wanted to tell you when I found out that you were my tenant and you were the one who did this painting here. How are you finding it in the house?'

'I love it. It's perfect for me.'

'Great. What I wanted to talk to you about was your paintings. I'm in the process of buying a farmhouse on the edge of Carthom. Would it be possible for you to do two paintings for me? One to show how the farmhouse as it is now, followed by another one to show what it's like when it's been converted. Do you think you'd be able to do that for me?'

I gulped. 'Yes, that's no problem.'

He pulled a thick wallet out from the back of his jeans and passed me a business card. 'Give me a ring. We can discuss it further then.'

'I'll phone you soon.' I felt like giving him a big hug.

I slotted back in, next to Pauline. Albert looked across at me and gave a half smile which I returned. He got up and squeezed himself past Anne and Kate to stand next to me.

'Are you alright, Rachel? Do you blame me? I did think Mike was being argumentative, but I suppose I didn't know the full story, did I? I just want you to know I'm sorry and I'll try and think before I open my mouth again.'

I didn't know how to respond so murmured an unintelligible reply.

When he sat back down, I suddenly saw how old he was. I was aware as I got to know the older members of the group, their age or even appearance hadn't registered with me as much as it once did. This made me consider how the people in the art group now viewed me. I used to maintain people were just trying to be nice when they said they didn't notice my disability. What if it was true?

I suppose this had been what my mum had urged me to do. Not to focus or dwell on my disability, but concentrate on the positives and try my best to fit in. Only now the penny dropped.

'Sweetie, are you off in another world again? I've been talking to you or rather trying to talk to you,' Kate said.

'Sorry, what is it?'

'I've spoken to Anne about the trip. We've got plenty of money to hire a minibus and if we ask everyone to prepare something to eat, then we can have a picnic up...'

I interrupted, 'up?'

'Yes, it's a bit of a climb but we have enough people to help, as long as everyone comes, that is,' she whispered.

'To climb steep hills requires a slow pace at first.'

Kate stared across the bar for a second, her brow crinkled

before she turned her head back towards me. 'Shakespeare?'

'Yeah, my dad used to say it a lot. It's from Henry VIII'

'So appropriate and in more ways than one. To change the subject, privately, I've said to Anne she should try and see her GP because she isn't well by any stretch of the imagination.'

'By the way, guess who my landlord is?'

'Who?'

'Mark, Matt's twin brother.'

'Ah, I did have an inkling it may be him.'

Pauline had stopped talking and was staring at us.

'I'll just go back to my seat, and start the discussion about The Dream.'

'Now we're having lovely sunny weather, what do you all think about meeting up to have a picnic?' Kate paused as there were murmurs of approval. 'One picnic spot that combines great views as well as art is at The Dream in St Helens. What do you think, would this be something you would like to do?'

'I've heard of that. Wasn't it on TV one time? It's meant to be beautiful.'

'I think I've seen it as well, Lena,' Elaine replied.

'St Helens is quite a long journey,' Albert said. 'I reckon it would take it three hours I'd guess.'

'It's near to where Mike was actually born,' I said. 'He was from Birkenhead in Merseyside.'

For a moment, there was an uncomfortable silence.

'It's actually an hour and a half with decent traffic,' Kate said. 'We'd go by minibus. I was thinking next week, Friday or Saturday?'

Everyone felt that Friday would be best, mainly because of the increased traffic at a weekend.

'I think it's a great idea, I really do. How are we going to organise a picnic?' Eddie asked.

'If I just make a quick list of what we would need then if each of us can bring an item on the list.' Kate tore off a sheet of paper from her notepad and made a list, which was then passed around the group.

After putting my name down to buy crisps, I glanced over at Anne and watched her reactions to what was going on. Was she annoyed about Kate taking the lead here and also doing the planning for the trip to St Helens? If she was feeling put out she was doing a good job of hiding it.

Eddie half stood up. 'Can I ask for another toast, this time to Art for You?'

With more enthusiasm than the first toast, we all replied, 'to Art for you.'

The group was starting to break up. Pauline offered to take me home, and Kate did as well. I held out for going home with Anne.

Eddie patted me on the top of my back. 'OK, kiddo? All in all, today was not too bad. I think young Mike would have approved, don't you?'

'I think so, yes. Put it this way, I hope so.'

'What's this?' Lena said.

'Young Mike, he would have approved of all this.'

'Yes, I wish we'd more time with him,' Lena said. 'I'd no idea of the photography or his sister being a poet. No idea at all.'

'He was,' I took a deep breath in, 'incredibly talented.'

'Did you know about his photographs?'

I turned to Lena. 'No, to be honest I think I saw Mike as someone worried about money, someone in debt. Yet he was something else, a talented painter, gifted photographer and comes from a creative family. Just shows how appearances can be deceptive.'

'Very true,' Lena replied. 'Very true.'

'Do you want a lift, Lena?' Eddie said, his voice booming in comparison to Lena's gentle lilt.

'Yes, please.'

'Rachel?'

'I'm ok, thanks.'

Anne caught my eye. 'Are you ready, Rachel?'

I nodded.

I said goodbye to everyone and followed Anne out of The Vines, with the help of Matt or Mark. I could sense Anne wanted to say something but she waited until we were both in her car. She turned towards me with a pained expression.

'Kate did a good job today, better, I suppose than I could've done.'

'You do know that she's only stepping in now because you're not feeling great?'

'Not feeling great? That's the half of it. I feel so exhausted and useless.'

'You sound depressed, Anne.'

'Kate said I should go to my GP, but I'm not sure. I don't want to have to go into hospital or anything like that.'

'I'm sure it won't come to that. Your GP might be able to give you something just to get over this patch. You don't want to ignore it. If you don't do anything it might get worse and then you might well end up in hospital. So, it's better you go now.'

She turned her head away from me. 'Perhaps.'

At home, I was going to take Mike's service sheet upstairs when I thought about Carol's poem. I put into Google 'deaths as a result of benefit reform' and expected to see a few cases. Instead, I read about hundreds and hundreds of people who'd died by suicide or after being passed as fit to work. There were also many people who'd been sanctioned and died with no money, food and heating. It almost seemed as if there was an active campaign to wipe out the vulnerable, the sick and depressed. I couldn't understand why this wasn't being reported in the press.

Twenty-Four

Kate stood on my doorstep, wearing calf length beige Capri pants with a flattering white shirt. She leant on the side of her crutch as I looked at my watch.

She smiled. 'If you've got a better offer, we can do it another day.'

'It's not that. Lena called me last night; she can't go with Anne to the GP today so I'm going with her instead. Anne's going to be picking me up at around three-thirty.'

'I won't keep you more than an hour.'

'OK, where are we going?'

'So I was thinking about The Vines. They've got this wicked chocolate cake, and...'

I interrupted her, 'Give me two minutes.' I turned around and went back in to get my bag and a purse.

In The Vines car park, Kate pointed to the back of the pub.

'So, when we met here after the memorial service and you said Matt's brother was your landlord, it got me thinking. I was once invited to a leaving party for one of my colleagues, and this was the venue. If you see this section at the back of the pub, that's where the courtyard is.'

'Yeah, I can see that.'

'So, now look at the section to the left.'

'Is it where the kitchens are?'

'No, that's on the far side. Here, there are two function rooms. One could hold thirty-forty people, I reckon. The other room was smaller, maybe twenty to thirty people.'

I fidgeted in my seat.

'What I'm saying is, if we approached The Vines and said we needed a venue for a community art group and suggested a Saturday morning when they wouldn't normally be busy, they might agree. This way the group could be for everyone over the age of eighteen. Are you following me?'

'I'm following.'

Matt helped me get inside the pub. The bar and kitchen staff were all sitting around two tables they'd pushed together.

He waited until we were both settled before he strolled up to our table. 'Now, what do you two ladies want to drink?'

We'd decided since it was a one-off we would have a slice of Sue's 'triple dip chocolate cake' along with a chocolate milkshake to drink. When the cakes arrived they were dripping in thick, chocolate coloured cream.

Kate laughed. 'My other friend called this a coronary in a cake.'

We dug in with our forks at the same time and when we eventually finished we both had chocolate everywhere.

'So how's Anne? Is she well enough to come on the trip?'

'I don't think so.'

For a second, she stared towards the bar area and was completely still.

'I don't know whether we should cancel or postpone it to a later date?'

I stretched out my hand. 'Everyone else seemed to be really up for it, surely it would be a shame to have to postpone? We might end up losing more people as time goes by.'

'Yes, I know it's a risk but we really need Anne to be with us. The whole point of the trip is to get the group talking. Hopefully, the group as a whole will accept that we need to change and as a result, move on. If everyone in the group takes part in this change they will see it as being quite cathartic. I believe we can be a stronger, more tightly-knit group. They do say adversity is the touchstone of friendship.'

'I don't know about you, but I'm finding it hard to pretend everything is OK.'

'I know, sweetie. I don't think we can just go back to how it was, but if we managed to clear the air, and change the make-up of the group, then, yes, we can start again.'

'I just hope you're right. I also hope that the group start to understand the issues more. Since the memorial I've been thinking a lot about Carol's poem.'

'So have I. The poem was very angry, but rightly so. There are so many people who've died since the shakeup in Benefits.'

'I know, I Googled it after the memorial...'

Kate smiled and interrupted me. 'We did exactly the same. I was talking to Jonathon about it. So Jon said why don't we Google it.'

'I knew it was getting tough for some, but I never knew it was getting this bad.' My voice was getting higher and louder. 'Mike only had four pounds in total. Carol said he only had scraps of stale food. He died like that in this day and age. Worse still hundreds of people are dying like that, and the press ignores it completely. No wonder people think we're scroungers. The real truth is hidden away.'

'I know, sweetie. It is horrific and hidden from view. But we're not going to get the group to understand straight away. Primarily we're an art group, but if we meet socially, then there's a chance for us to get to know the issues they are dealing with as well as them understand our point of view.'

'That's if we remain a group.'

'Exactly. We need to bring people together to discuss the future of the group. That's why Anne needs to be with us. We also need to give everyone a glimpse of how it could be - meeting at the weekend and open to anyone.'

Sue strolled up to our table.

'Was everything OK, ladies? Would you like anything else?'

I shook my head.

Kate smiled up at Sue. 'No, thanks, that was lovely. We're just wondering whether we could view your small function room, please.'

'For a party?'

'It's actually a weekly group, a community art group.'

'Follow me.'

She led us through a set of double doors next to the bar, and into a room, which was a little bit smaller than the main hall at the centre.

Sue gestured towards the room in front of us. 'This is the smaller of our two function rooms. Was this the kind of size you were thinking of?'

'Yes, it's perfect.'

'When were you thinking of holding it?' she said smiling, her hand on her hip.

'Saturday morning. Say ten until one?'

'Mmm, mornings are usually quiet but come one 'o' clock, we often have parties, or wedding receptions, that kind of thing. So by one, you'd need to be out of the room.'

Sue waved her hand towards the chairs. 'Do you want to sit down?' Sue pulled out a chair for Kate.

'Cheers.'

'So, where did you used to meet?'

Kate leant towards Sue. 'The community centre next to the library, but it was pricey as well as not being in the best position.'

'How many were in the group?'

I cleared my throat. 'It used to be ten,' I said. 'But Mike, one of our members, died recently. There are potentially others who might be interested.'

Sue stood up and leant on the back of the chair. 'I'll just nip and get Matt so we can go through a couple of things.'

'I didn't realise you wanted to do this today. Isn't it a bit premature, Kate?' I whispered when Sue had left the room. 'What if, at The Dream, we all decide to stop the group?'

Kate shrugged. 'It's just so everyone knows we've got this option.'

The door creaked open as Matt and Sue walked back in.

Matt picked up a chair and swung it into position, in front of me, before they both sat down.

'For a while now we've been actively trying to get groups meeting here,' Sue said. 'Mainly due to the number of community venues disappearing so quickly...'

'And our customers evaporating,' Matt added, with a wink.

Sue nodded. 'As part of our plan regarding groups, we can help with the promotion and marketing of your group. Now, because we know each other we can offer it to you for twenty pounds for the morning.'

'We'd be delighted to have the group here,' Matt added with a quick smile. He stretched out his long legs, and put one foot on top of the other.

'After all, we're accommodating a book group which starts in the autumn,' Matt said. 'We also hold various church groups here as well as the Carthom Ramblers and Climbers. The very popular Fishing and Farming group has also just started to meet here. This shows how committed we are to holding group meetings here.'

'It sounds great,' I blurted out.

Kate put her hand on my armrest. 'I agree. We do need to go back and speak to everyone else, just to make sure everyone is happy.'

Matt and Sue stood up. 'OK then, if you do that and make sure everyone's in agreement. Then if all is OK, give us a ring and we can look at diaries and meet up before your group starts, just so we can make sure everything's on course. If you want us to make and print some posters and flyers then get the details to us ASAP.'

'Super,' Kate said, smiling down at me.

Sue and Matt left first; I was getting my rucksack straight on the back of my chair. While I was fiddling about, Kate leant against the wall.

'I can really imagine us in this room, getting on with painting and with each other.'

When my rucksack was straight, I glanced up at Kate. 'Can you? I can't. Each time I try to imagine them all I see is us all arguing with each other.'

'I suspect at this point in time not many of our group will be thinking anything favourable about the group.'

We passed the bar and on one of the tables there were flyers for the book group, I picked one up and showed it to Kate.

'I'm going to be at this group. Do you remember..?'

Kate took it from me. 'Janet Riley?'

'She was at our art sale.'

'Ah. I think I know who you mean.'

We both smiled at each other and for a moment I felt warmth in my chest, a tingling sensation in my hands, and a feeling of weightlessness.

'When do you need to go for Anne?' Kate asked.

'Oh heck, I need to shoot.'

'Do you want me to drop you off?'

'I'll just give her a ring. She was meant to be picking me up.'

My fingers were trembling as I fumbled about with the phone. Eventually I found her number and called her up.

'I've been trying to call you,' Anne said immediately.

'I can be with you in less than ten minutes. I'm just with a friend.'

'Who?'

'Kate. She's going to give me a lift.'

Matt walked up to me. 'Do you want a hand out?'

I nodded. 'You really should get a ramp.'

'If you're here each week, I'll make it a priority.'

Twenty-Five

We pulled up outside Anne's home. As I peered at her bungalow, I felt tense, an inner turbulence that made my stomach flip over several times.

'There's no sign of life in there. All the curtains and blinds are closed,' Kate whispered as she peered through my passenger window.

As soon I saw the closed blind in her kitchen, a memory hit me. It was when I was disconnected from life, at times emotionless, at times, full of despair. I shut myself off completely from the world and wanted to disappear.

'I'll wait until she's opened the door, Rachel, then I'll go, just in case she's nipped out.'

I wheeled up to Anne's door and knocked. As I did this, I saw the blind in her kitchen twitch.

Anne opened the door with the chain on.

'Who's with you?' she croaked.

I heard Kate's car pull away.

'Nobody. How're you feeling?'

Anne didn't respond. We'd only got half an hour to go before her GP appointment, but she was still in her slippers. She looked dowdy and unkempt.

In her living room, the curtains were only half shut, which gave enough light for me to notice her red eyes and pallid skin.

Anne sat down with her fists clenched upon her knee.

'How are you feeling?' I repeated. On her wall, nine hooks were visible where once her photographs were proudly displayed,

'Not good,' she muttered. 'I've made a right mess of things, haven't I?'

'Do you mean with Mike? If so you haven't, he was up to his eyes in...'

Anne interrupted me. 'Not just with him, I mean with the group, with my family and with my life. I don't know how I can continue.'

Her response and how she was presenting sparked memories of the weeks and months when I felt numb and unreal. There were times when I didn't want to even get out of bed, let alone drink or eat. I cut myself off and like Anne would only think of worst case scenarios, unable to see any positives at all. I wanted desperately to reach out to her, to let her know she wasn't alone.

'Oh Anne, you haven't let anyone down. You're just feeling down at the moment, when you start to feel better you'll feel more positive.'

'If I go in hospital, my spare key is under the gnome in the front garden. He may want to put me in hospital. Could you tell Dot as well?'

'Do you mean psychiatric hospital?'

She lowered her eyes. 'I've wanted to tell you, I'd a feeling you might understand. You see, with all the business with Andrew and M...Theresa, I... I...' Her voice trailed off and I saw her brush a tear from her face.

I waited for Anne to continue, but she sat staring at her hands. Eventually she slowly lifted her head.

'I did something awful. I tried to ki, ki...' She stopped talking as tears were tumbling down her cheeks.

'I've been depressed in the past, too.' As soon as the words left my mouth, I wanted to grab them back.

'That's what they said was wrong with me. I'm scared it's happening again. I can feel myself sliding down. Last time, I did something stupid.'

'Oh, Anne. Did you try to..?'

She nodded slowly as she sobbed.

I moved closer to her and held her hands.

'It was Dot who found me. I'd managed to have a few years where I wasn't too bad. Then when I moved here, I'm not sure how it started. I used to have two beds in the spare room, just in case Theresa and Katie turned up at my door. Over time I realised it was never going to happen, I started to put anything and everything in there but then felt guilty there was nowhere for them, if they ever did come to see me. I wasn't sleeping at this point at all. Going through my mind was all that had happened, all that I'd lost. I started to gather together all the tablets I could take.' Her body started to shake.

I moved closer and held her the best I could.

'Dot used to be a nurse, so when I missed a group, she said she had a gut feeling something was wrong. She knew where my spare key was and found me. She called the ambulance and even came into the hospital with me.' Anne glanced at me for a second, our faces only inches apart.

'When I found out where you lived, I thought, good, at least she's got a decent neighbour.'

'I tried, as well, Anne, when I was eighteen.'

'To kill yourself?'

I nodded slowly.

Anne held on to my hand and squeezed it. With her other hand she covered her mouth.

'When you were eighteen? With all your life in front of you?'

'You know what depression is like, Anne, it messes up with your emotions. Sometimes, no matter what age you are, depression can get the better of you.'

'What made you depressed?' Anne placed her other hand on my knee.

'I don't know. During the year, I just gradually got worse, until I thought I'd be better off gone. I felt like a burden.'

After a minute, Anne nodded. 'It does do that. I start thinking about who I've lost, and despair grips me. I can't seem to shake it off.' Anne looked into my eyes. 'I've wanted to tell you almost from the first time we met. I knew you'd understand.'

I squeezed Anne's hand. 'I've wanted to tell you too. You're the only one in Carthom who knows. You'll keep it to yourself?'

'Keep to myself? Of course I will, I won't say anything if you don't want me to. I know sometimes I can, well, speak out of turn, but, I know why you want it kept quiet.'

Her wooden grandfather clock chimed and I glanced at my watch.

'Anne, your appointment, we'd better make a move.'

I wiped a tear away, as Anne slowly got up and started to search for her shoes.

When we arrived, we were already ten minutes late. Anne had only just sat down when the harassed GP called her name.

She was in with him for a long time. While I waited, in an attempt to try and calm down, I examined the painting of a water mill on the wall and in my mind tried to name all the colours used in the painting.

Eventually, she came out, the green prescription sheet stuffed in her cardigan pocket. It was all making more sense, the hoarding, the Fluoxetine tablets in her bathroom, Dot comforting her and Eddie's talk about her fragility. It all seemed to fit into place.

In the car, she stuffed the prescription in her handbag. 'Antidepressants and he has referred me for some, um... bereavement counselling.'

'Bereavement counselling? Oh, because of losing touch with Theresa?'

'He said it might take a while for the counselling to start, and ten days to two weeks before the tablets kick in. I hope I can last that long.'

I turned to Anne. 'If you ever need me, I'll be over like a shot, or you can come to mine. Please, remember I've been through something similar. You know, Mike suffered from depression. If he'd felt confident enough to talk to us, we may have been able to help him.'

'I've found talking about it, is better than trying to hide it. I told you, Dot was a nurse. Well, over the years she's been a huge support to me,' Anne said. 'I did what you did for many years but I nearly had another breakdown just through having to hide it all. Dot helped me face up to it, and talk about it.'

'I know, at times I've felt like hiding it was causing more problems and not helping me in the long run. My dad, he suffered with depression too.'

'Depression? He didn't, did he? I mean he didn't...'

'No, he had a heart complaint. We didn't know about it until he died.'

'I often wondered whether any of my children would've been artistic. Theresa could draw well at school. It's really tearing me apart, not knowing anything about them.' Anne dropped her head as her eyes were filling up with tears.

'It must be. I can't imagine what it must be like, but Anne, you've got friends and we're all here supporting you, we're here holding your hand.'

'The counselling isn't just about Theresa.' Anne chewed on her lip and for a couple of minutes there was silence.

She retrieved a tissue from her sleeve to wipe away her tears.

'What is it, Anne?'

'We called him Mark; he was my first born. I thought I had it all, nice house, husband, baby on the way. Andrew was really excited and painted the guest room, which was going to be the nursery. But it all went wrong.' She rested her head against the window and looked down at her hands, as she tugged and pulled apart the paper tissue on her lap.

'What happened?'

'At seven months I realised he hadn't been kicking or moving. Part of me knew something dreadful had happened, but even in those early days I couldn't speak properly to Andrew. In the end, I had to go through a normal birth, but Mark he... he never took a single breath.'

'Oh, Anne.' I put my arm around her.

'I was put in a side room, and all around me were excited mums and crying babies. When I got home people would ignore me. Friends were embarrassed and didn't know what to say to me, not wanting to upset me. I got more and more isolated.'

'Oh, God, Anne, I'm so sorry.'

'Andrew's answer was to have another one, but I really wasn't ready, Rachel. When I did get pregnant, I was terrified of the same thing happening. Theresa was born, fit and healthy but I was still numb, I couldn't feel anything. If truth be known I couldn't bear to be with her. I couldn't even breast feed. I felt like a failure and wanted to curl up and die.'

'You could've had post-natal depression, Anne, as well as grieving.'

'In those days you just had to get on with it. Andrew got his mother to come and help me, but that made me feel even worse. Later on, when our marriage was falling apart, Andrew mocked me, and said I was an unfit mother. He told Theresa I'd not been able to care for her as a baby and as a toddler. So, when we finally split up, Theresa went to live with him and stopped speaking to me. I feel like I've lost them all – Mark, Theresa, and Katie, my granddaughter.'

I squeezed and stroked Anne's hand.

Anne put her elbows on the steering wheel, and held her head in her hands. 'I feel numb, just like I did then. I tried doing what you said, about taking the photographs down, but it just left me feeling even more empty.'

'You're still their mother, Anne so please put your photos back up. I didn't say you should take yours down; just I have difficulty looking at mine. Your photographs are lovely.'

For a minute or two, we sat in silence. Anne still had her head in her hands.

'Anne, will you come on the trip? You're the leader of the group. I know Kate's doing a lot now, but it's only while you're not well.'

She lifted her head up and glanced at me. 'I don't know. The group might be better with a different leader.'

'That's just the depression talking.'

For a while we sat here holding onto each other. Outside a car horn was sounding and people were walking in and out of the surgery but all of that was irrelevant as I held onto Anne. Afterwards, when we pulled back, I saw in her a vulnerability I hadn't seen before. I also recognised she was resilient. She'd dealt with a life changing situation, and was doing her best to cope.

The driver who'd been sounding his horn, got out of the car, and was gesticulating at the both of us, as he stood in front of Anne's car.

She wound down her window and he walked towards her.

'Are you deaf woman? Are going to bloody move, or what?'

'We're just going, sorry.'

Before Anne put her key into the ignition she glanced over at me.

'I'll think about it, about the trip.'

The short journey back to my house was in silence. When she parked outside my house, I turned to her while I was taking off my seatbelt.

'Anne, whenever you need to talk, just call me or come round.'

She nodded. 'Thanks, Rachel, you too.'

As she helped me into my wheelchair, I saw her glance across the road to Dot's house.

Anne gently put one hand on my shoulder, I could see her reflection in my door and her expression brought fresh tears to my eyes.

Twenty-Six

After my conversation with Anne, I found myself in a ruminative state. It was becoming clear I needed to be honest about my own situation and no longer hide behind lies and half truths.

Anne's openness helped me understand her behaviour and actions. As she spoke to me, I felt she was also holding a torch to illuminate a path I should take myself. On my coffee table was The Butterfly Collective scrapbook. The earnest faces inside had all been open about illness, and the result was a place in art history.

I put the radio on and after listening for five minutes was ready to turn it off. Just as I was finding the remote control the programme on next - a new six part series all on the topic of forgiveness - was advertised.

A woman in her late twenties from America was talking, along with a clergyman and philosopher. The woman was abducted when she was only sixteen, and for the next seven years held captive and abused by her two kidnappers. She escaped and now worked for a charity to help people in similar circumstances. She'd asked if she could visit her kidnappers in prison, where they both were serving long sentences, and talked about how she'd forgiven them.

The clergyman read out a quote from Hannah Arenet - 'forgiveness is the key to action and freedom.'

I couldn't imagine ever forgiving the guards but I'd already found out talking about my experiences could give me a taste of freedom. The freedom of not being ashamed of who I was and freedom from the guilt, the shame and the fear I'd been carrying around for years.

I picked up the scrapbook again and opened it up. My dad stared out at me from a newspaper photograph.

I knew I needed to talk to Kate. She'd been accepting of me and was someone I now considered a friend. If I was going to be honest with anyone it would be with her. I inhaled and slowly breathed out before reaching for the phone. It rang and rang before Kate answered. She sounded subdued and tired.

'Hi, sweetie. How's Anne?'

'She could be better.'

'So, what's the verdict about the trip?'

'She says she'll think about it. We actually had a good chat. We also talked about things I really should've talked to you about.' My mouth dried up.

'What kind of things?'

I tried to swallow. 'Things I feel I should tell you.'

'That sounds ominous. Jeremy's playing on the computer with Jonathon. I can't really talk. If it's important, I can pop round for half an hour now, would this be OK?'

'You don't mind?'

'No, of course not. You're alright, Rachel? You're not poorly or anything?'

'No, I'm OK. Can I tell you about it when you're here?'

Half an hour later, I heard Kate's car pull up. I opened my front door ready for her. A few minutes later, she limped in. My heartbeat was thumping in my ears. Kate was pale and looked worn out. The tense atmosphere was so different from when we met up at The Vines, and for a moment I felt this was all a terrible mistake.

'Do you want a coffee, Kate?'

Kate shook her head. 'I'm trying to cut out caffeine as much as possible, to try and improve my sleep.'

I rubbed the back of my neck. 'I need to talk to you, Kate. I'm not sure how to say it, or where to begin really. Just I've been thinking how Mike was really open about some of the problems he was having. Anne's just opened up to me about a few things. Even my dad, he was open about his illness. So I'm aware I've not been as truthful as I should've been, and I really want to be friends with you, so it shouldn't be based on lies and half truths.'

'Go on.'

'I suppose I should just spit it out.' I pointed at my legs. 'All this is my fault. It wasn't an accident. Instead I was...I was depressed.'

Kate looked at me with her brows knitted together. She eased herself up, limped across and sat next to me on the sofa.

'What happened, sweetie?'

'It was when I was eighteen, I'd just finished my 'A' Levels but instead of celebrating I was stuck in hospital.'

'Psychiatric hospital?'

I nodded. 'Problem was, they were hopeless. They put me on this new drug and yes, I did improve a bit. I didn't stay in bed all day, but going through my mind all the time was how I could end my life.'

Kate rubbed her finger on my hand.

'He discharged me, out of the blue. Mum thought that was it, I was better, when really I was still feeling awful. In fact, I was just waiting for a time when I was alone. Oh God, it sounds really selfish, but that's all I could think about.' I rubbed my temple.

'What happened?'

'My dad was an artist and suffered from depression too. He was ill lots of times. I've only had two really bad bouts, that time when I was eighteen the other when I was twenty-eight.'

'Rachel, you really don't have to tell me if you're not ready.'

'It's just I'm not used to talking about it.' I looked down at my knees. 'My mum went to visit a friend in hospital. As soon as she left, I called a taxi and asked the driver to take me to the station. It was really quiet and without much trouble, I got on to the tracks.'

Kate whispered. 'Oh no.'

'I think I just wanted to be finished off as quickly as possible. The tracks were just as deserted as the station, and I ended up walking for a long time. Suddenly I found I was on a railway bridge, I peered over the edge and did something that would change my life forever. It's something I've had to live with.'

Kate swallowed. 'Did you jump?'

'No, instead I simply stepped off. As I was falling, I saw the trees slowly pass by but at some point, I must've looked down because hurtling towards me was the ground. Next thing I knew, I was lying there, crumpled up and broken amongst the leaves.'

Kate turned in her seat and hugged me.

'I was there for a long time before a man walking his dog found me. He kept on telling his dog to stop licking my legs, and I couldn't stop sobbing because I couldn't feel the dog's tongue at all. I feel so guilty for what I've put my mum through.' I pulled my arms away from Kate and buried my head in my hands.

'I'm sure she's proud of you now. You're independent, and coping, aren't you? I admire you a lot.'

I glanced up at her. 'It's not admirable I was trying to kill myself, is it?'

'What I'm saying is I admire you for how you are now, for getting through it, for trying and not giving up.'

I nodded.

'You said you were ill again when you were twenty-eight. Were you in hospital again then?'

I groaned 'I got depressed again. The second time round the depression seemed to be deeper. This time, I was on a section three for six months.'

'Oh, gosh, that must've been hard.'

'It was a horrible place, Kate, really awful.' I turned towards Kate. 'Do you mind if I make a drink? Do you want one?'

'No, I'm OK. I can make it if you want.'

'It's alright, I'll do it.' I went into the kitchen and filled the kettle. Kate limped through and sat at the kitchen table.

'So, how long were you in there for? Was it the full six months?'

'God, I wish. No, at the end of the six months, I assumed I was going home, but I was put straight back on another one, for another six months. I lost my home as a result.' I put my mug onto the kitchen table and moved into my place, opposite Kate.

'So what happened? It sounded like a horrific place.' Kate had her elbow bent on the table, her head in her hand.

'There were three suicides on the ward while I was there, and I heard later that it had been closed in the past, due to one patient drowning in the bath.'

Kate stretched her arm across the table and stroked my arm.

'So when I was ready to leave, I was really relieved. I was going to be renting a place from a social housing association, because of losing my home. Then the psychiatrist said the best thing would be for me to have live-in carers. He said I'd be independent but if I needed help someone would be there. Well, naively I thought it sounded ideal. I left hospital, full of hope.' I buried my head back in my hands.

'What is it, sweetie?' Kate whispered.

'The care package meant two carers were with me twenty-four seven. At the start I just agreed to things because I didn't want to go back to hospital. So when they said I wasn't allowed to cook, I agreed. When they said they needed an office, then took the largest bedroom, I agreed.' I wiped my palms on my jeans.

'Are you OK?'

'You don't mind hearing this?'

'Carry on, please.'

'The next thing they did was they said my mum couldn't just turn up unannounced, they said she could come at the weekend, but they changed their minds and said the only time she could come was Saturday from one o'clock until three o'clock. So, she couldn't even take me on a day out.'

Kate put her head in her hands.

'It started getting really bad. They said I couldn't be in my bedroom or bathroom with the door fully closed. This was meant to be my home. One night, I wanted a bath so I banged the door shut. The next day a couple of guys came and they took the doors off completely. I kicked up a fuss and to show me what they could do, they put me in hospital for a month.'

'Oh, sweetie.'

'Well, this was their ace card, but that month in hospital was relaxing. It was the same horrific ward I'd been on before but compared to the bungalow it was relaxing.'

'How did they get you into hospital?'

'The team was an off-shoot from the hospital trust, so ultimately they were all employed by the hospital, so all they had to do was pick up the phone and ask for a bed. They even told me I was on a community section. Well when Mum was planning the escape, she found out that wasn't true. They controlled every area of my life and bullied me and mocked me.'

'It sounds terrible, truly terrible.'

'At first, I thought all of it, was just to keep an eye on me. As time went on, and the situation got worse, I realised they didn't want me to get better because I was an expensive patient. The number of guards, sorry, I mean staff, meant if I got better, they lost a big contract.'

'That's a huge betrayal of trust. Didn't you complain?'

'Lots of times, but because they all had the same employer, nothing happened. The only real response was the bullying went up a notch.'

Kate, with her right hand started to carve through her hair, holding it back and then releasing. As she did this, she glanced at me.

'It just upsets me, sweetie, to think of staff behaving like that. It really does.'

'The worst thing was they made me doubt myself. They made me think I'd self-harm or commit suicide. I ended up not trusting myself and my confidence seeped away. There was a long period where I just couldn't see an end to it all.'

I paused for a moment, and nursed the mug in my hands.

'One Christmas, I'd two minutes alone with Mum. She'd found out they'd got no legal right to hold me there. She started searching for somewhere I could live and found this place. One day, I told them I was going for a cigarette and wheeled out, leaving it all behind.'

'What about your possessions, your furniture?'

'Mum did go back to try and get some of it back. All there was, was a solitary bin bag with a few bits in. Luckily, all my paintings were at Mum's house. We could have made a formal complaint but Mum said it was better to leave it.'

'So when you moved here last summer, you'd just come from that, from those awful people?'

'Yeah, remember at the art sale I was a bit freaked out because I thought I saw someone? I thought it was one of the guards who'd seen the article in the paper and had turned up at the centre.'

Kate moved her chair next to mine and her arm around my shoulders. 'Sweetie, you know we've got a lot in common. Don't beat yourself up.' Kate put her finger under my chin and lifted up my head.

A tear fell down onto my lap.

'I always felt if I told you and Anne all of this, I'd be rejected or gossiped about. I can't believe your reactions; it means an awful lot to me.'

'If back when the group first met at the centre you made a big announcement then I think there may've been more of a reaction. We've got to know...'

'...each other. Yes, I think you're right.'

'Rachel, I've nothing but admiration for you in how you've handled your illness and your disability. Often folk say to me it's hard being born with a disability, but I think it must be difficult if, like you, you spent eighteen years able bodied for this to then happen to you.'

I nodded. 'I don't think it's easy if you're disabled full stop. Whether you were born with it, or acquired it. With me, it's all about loss of confidence, I think. It's also been so hard to find people who I can trust to talk to about what's happening and who don't judge me.'

'So before I met Jonathon I was floundering. I'd terrible issues with my self-esteem, and really struggled with how people viewed me.' Kate twisted her wedding ring around her finger.

'Was this when you were young?'

'No, it was when I'd moved away and started work. At times, I was very aware of my limitations so over compensated for them. I was determined to be independent and rejected all offers of help but in reality I wasn't coping and felt very conscious of my disability, and if I'm honest, I was terribly lonely.'

'It can be so hard, and so very lonely. Accepting my situation was the hardest aspect of it all.'

Kate nodded slowly. 'I think you're right. Accepting ourselves is the first step. In saying that, it's not a little step, or easily done, it takes a degree of honesty and maturity.'

I looked towards the living room, thinking about the box full of reports inside.

Kate followed my eyes. 'What is it?'

'When I was in hospital and then with those guards, I ended up with a pile of paperwork. Mum told me to keep it just in case we faced legal repercussions from the hospital trust. Now I know I'm safe I can get rid of the contents. I'm scared one day I might sit down and start reading it all, so I really want it shredded. I was wondering if you could help.'

'Course, where's your shredder and nearest socket? We'll need a bin bag too.'

'The shredder's next to the box.' I pointed at the sofa. 'There's a socket just at the wall by this end of the sofa, or by the kettle.'

'Why don't we sit on the sofa, do it in there. If you get a bin bag and I'll get the shredder and box.'

Kate dragged the shredder over and plugged it in. I came back in with a bin bag.

'Rachel, if you sit here next to me.' Kate patted her hand on the sofa next to her. 'I'll pass the papers up, any staples need to be out. Rip them out, and then pass to me.'

For the next twenty minutes we operated like a production line. Half-way through some paper got stuck in the shredder. While Kate pulled it out I turned over the report. It was a tribunal report from when I was appealing to leave hospital. I felt sick so quickly turned over the report and exhaled, counting to ten.

'Are you OK, sweetie?' Kate stroked my arm.

'I can't wait to get rid of this lot.'

We carried on for the next ten minutes until we got to the last report. I tore it up and felt a rush of emotion as I handed it to Kate and it was shredded.

She turned to me. 'You've got me crying now.'

As she began to tie up the bin bag, I reached into my back pocket, and brought out a squashed packet of cigarettes and lighter.

'Can you put these in as well?'

'Are you sure?'

'I only started smoking when I was in psychiatric hospital.'

'Good for you, sweetie.'

I smiled at Kate. 'My recovery has been thanks to you, the group and my mum.'

'Not forgetting your own determination to succeed. Going back to what we were talking about, I'll keep quiet about what you've told me. But people like you and me.' She pointed at me and then at her chest. 'We shouldn't perpetuate the idea that mental illness is something to feel ashamed about – we should challenge stigma, whenever we can.'

'I'm not too concerned about the stigma around mental illness. It's more to do with what people would think when they found out all this damage was caused by me, by a suicide attempt.'

'When people know you, they may look at your disability but what they see is you, Rachel.'

'Yeah, I understand that. When did you have your back surgery?'

'Oh, it's a long time ago now. Most of it happened when I was a child and a further operation when I was a teenager at Stoke Mandeville.'

'What was it like there?'

'It's just like any other hospital really. It was a lonely time. I'd been sold this idea my back could be fixed but while I was there, the surgeons told me this would never happen and I'd be disabled for life. In stark contrast, my parents were telling me everything would be OK. Reflecting back on it now, it was actually my parents who were right. Everything was and is OK.'

'What you say about your parents is just what I've come to realise. My mum was forever saying 'think positive' or 'it's your views that need changing.' I never believed her, but she was right.' I flexed my hands. 'I do hope the trip works.'

'I do as well. I think it was Marcel Proust who said, 'It's only while we're suffering that we see certain things, which at other times are hidden from us.' What I think it means for us, is through Mike's death and the breakdown of the group, we all might be able to see that we face similar problems and struggles in life. We could, if we get through this patch, be a well-functioning group.'

I nodded.

'I'm wondering whether on the trip you'd be able to say a few words, just about how the group helps you. I'm just thinking if the group hears that we have similar problems.'

'Yeah, that's OK, as long as I don't have to quote Proust. I'm feeling rather inadequate here.'

'So says the girl who quotes Shakespeare!' Kate winked at me. 'Anyway, I hate to disappoint you but the quote was in one of my management textbooks. That's not to say, I don't enjoy reading, because I do. After art, reading's one of my main interests.'

'Why don't you come along to Janet's book group, then?'

'I might just do that.'

As we hugged again, I was aware my prison walls were finally starting to crumble. I now had an opportunity to be free.

Twenty-Seven

The meeting point for the trip to The Dream was at Carthom Community Centre's car park. Kate had been unable to get a minibus with wheelchair access so rather than having a minibus and a separate car for me, Kate and Jonathon were both going to drive, along with Eddie. It meant we all had plenty of room and space for the picnic, as well.

I'd been in touch with Anne, and she'd been adamant she wasn't going on the trip. However, my visit was followed by visits from Eddie and Lena and eventually, with two days to go before the trip, she'd changed her mind.

Due to being on her antidepressants, Anne couldn't drive so I set off on my own on the morning of the trip. I'd watched the weather forecast the night before and although it was still going to be very warm there was meant to be a slight north-westerly breeze.

Eddie gave a wave as I wheeled up to the centre. As I got closer, I saw Albert sitting on the bench next to Marion, wiping his brow with a large white handkerchief. As I entered the car park, Eddie, who was wearing a khaki suit made up of shorts, shirt and a matching hat, walked towards me with a beaming smile.

'Hello kiddo, the Lord has blessed us with another fine day.' His salutation was accompanied with him holding his hands aloft, as if to catch the rays of the sun.

'Bertie, do you want some water?' Marion asked as she put her picnic basket onto the bench, next to Albert. 'Rachel, Eddie, do you want one?'

Eddie stretched. 'I'm spitting feathers here, Marion.'

Marion brought out four mini bottles of water. For a moment there was silence apart from the odd 'ooh' and 'lovely' from Eddie after each gulp of water.

Jonathon's car purred in from the exit side of the car park, and once parked up, Pauline and Elaine spilled out, chatting together, followed by Jonathon.

'Do you want to see my baby granddaughter, Rebecca? She's turning into right bonny lass.'

Pauline pulled out her mobile and after finding the pictures, showed them to the group. A few minutes later there was a honk from Kate's car as she drove into the car park. She'd given Anne a lift and a last minute pep talk. When they both were out of the car, the group formed a circle.

Anne stepped forward into the middle and cleared her throat. 'Who's going in what car?'

'There are ten of us between three cars,' Kate replied.

'Do you want to come with me, Rachel?' Anne said.

Jonathon pointed first at me, followed by Anne. 'Do the two of you want to come with me?'

Marion and Albert decided they'd travel with Lena, and Eddie would drive. This left Kate, who took Elaine and Pauline and the picnic items. We split off into our groups. Anne helped me into the passenger seat of Jonathon's car and she bent down to take off my footplates.

Jonathon lifted the wheelchair frame from Anne in one hand and with the other shut my door. Anne climbed in behind me and shuffled herself up so she was behind Jonathon's seat.

He got in, checked his mirrors and after a few minutes followed Eddie's car, which in turn was following Kate.

'How long will it take us to get there?' Anne asked.

Jonathon peered at Anne through his rear view window. 'At this time of the day, I'd say a good couple of hours, it's quite a journey. Shall I switch the radio on?'

'Go on, yes,' I replied.

Jonathon turned on the radio; it was tuned to classic FM. The adverts included ones from a loan company as well as payday loans.

I glanced at Jonathon. 'Would you be able to give advice on how to start a business?'

'For you? Are you..?'

'No, my cleaner and her boyfriend, they want to set up a cleaning company.'

'Setting up any business in this climate is risky. I can give them a couple of numbers. One is a philanthropist who often gives grants to small businesses. I'm not sure if he would help, but it's worth a shot.'

'Thanks. I don't think she's got much business background, but she's bright and more than able.'

'Are you looking forward to today, Anne?' I half turned in my seat and caught Anne's eye.

'Today? Yes, I'm a bit nervous to today, not sure it will work.'

'Why?'

'There's so much to sort out, that's all I'm saying. I don't know whether it can all be sorted out today. I'm looking forward to seeing this sculpture, though.'

'So am I,' Jonathon replied.

Anne seemed to be less tired. I didn't know whether she'd started the counselling, but wasn't going to bring it up in front of Jonathon. The traffic seemed to ease off a little. Another half an hour passed; I saw the sign for the Leeds connection and sighed. There was still a long way to go.

Telling Kate and Anne about my suicide attempt, my time in hospital and about the guards made me feel a lot less conflicted and as a result, more settled. It was almost like a rebirth and I felt I could get on with living my life. It almost didn't matter whether the trip went well or not.

I glanced again at Jonathon; I'd presumed Kate had discussed my history with him. Not that it mattered. It was time to accept who I was. To concentrate on the present day, my future, and to break free from the past that had held me back.

I rested my head against the car window. A combination of the lack of conversation, the gentle classical music, the warmth and general tiredness soon sent me off to sleep.

When I woke up, I put my hand straight to my mouth. I'd dribbled; a slight crust had formed under my lip. With my finger I picked it off and tried to position myself so I was straight. In the back, Anne had her head down as if she was asleep. Outside, we were still on a motorway. The sign said we were on the M62 but I didn't know where we were. I peered at my watch; I couldn't believe I'd been asleep for an hour and a half.

'You're awake, then, Rachel,' Jonathon said. 'You told us all your secrets while you were out for the count. Didn't she, Anne, didn't Rachel talk in her sleep?'

I turned to Anne who lifted her head and smiled.

'We should be able to catch sight of the sculpture soon. It's a bit like the Angel of the North, in that you can see it from the motorway. A giant sized child's head.'

Jonathon drove; every now and again he turned his head to peer out of his window.

'There it is, look out of my window.' Jonathon said.

All I could see was a hill surrounded by thick trees.

'Oh Lord, I never expected it to be so big,' Anne exclaimed.

I still couldn't see anything but trees. A few miles later, I got a quick view of the sculpture. The white stone glistened in the sun; a sculpture of a girl's head, her eyes firmly shut with clouds passing over her head. She disappeared again, and each time I saw her I saw a different perspective.

'It's high up, isn't it? Do we have to climb all that way up?' Anne said.

'There's a path which takes you up, plus benches along the way,' said Jonathon. 'I've only seen this through an App. It's impressive isn't it?'

'It's, it's...' I struggled to find the right word. 'It's bold.'

'You're right, it is. I think it's about twenty metres in height.'

'I'm not one for modern art, but this is different,' remarked Anne.

'Is that Eddie's car, Jonathon?' I pointed to the car in front.

'It is indeed.'

The symbol of a fish was on the back of Eddie's car along with a sticker with, 'Jesus loves you, so do I' in large red letters.

Jonathon tapped into his Sat. Nav. and said for a moment he'd need to concentrate. We moved into a different lane and passed a sign for St. Helens.

With The Dream in my mind, I thought how I'd started life in Carthom with a dream, just to feel included and accepted. It was through the group this had happened, slowly and steadily. Each week I was growing in confidence - most of the time without me even being conscious of it. Through individual members, who learnt to accept me, and offered their friendships, I felt I'd regained trust and hope for the future.

After a few minutes, Jonathon pulled into the car park. Kate was already parked up. Pauline and Elaine were standing chatting, while Kate was drinking from a bottle of water, her tanned long legs dangling out of the car. We parked up beside her. When I opened my door, she gave a slight nod. Her face was grey and for the first time, she seemed older than her age.

'Good journey?' Kate asked.

'I fell asleep for most of it. Are you OK?'

We both turned our heads as we heard another car purr into

the car park. It was Eddie, with Albert, Marion and Lena.

'Everyone's here,' Kate whispered under her breath.

I suddenly was aware of Kate's anxiety. She'd put all her faith in this trip to try and get the art group back together.

'Are you OK, Kate and Rachel?' Eddie called out. He was limbering up as he prepared himself, ready for the ascent. He stood with his legs apart and first leaned to his right and bent his knee, followed by the same movement to his left. Finally he bent forward his fingers not quite reaching the ground. There was a deep groan as Eddie straightened back up.

Kate stood up and brought us all together into a huddle.

'Now there's a bit of a trek as we walk up to where the first benches are. We might decide just to stop there for a bit before moving on and picnicking under the statue or we might have had enough walking and have our picnic there,' Kate said. 'Either way we need to team up as we're only going to get to the top if we help each other. Can somebody who is fairly fit help Rachel by pushing, if that's OK Rachel?'

I looked up at the hill and nodded; thankful she'd brought it up.

Eddie and Pauline both raised their hands.

'OK, Jonathon and Elaine,' Kate said. 'Are you OK, coming with me?'

The others paired up, Albert with Marion and Anne with Lena.

Picnic items were also shared around the group. I was given the cool bag to put on my knee.

Kate clapped her hands together twice. 'Be careful folks as there are some small stones underfoot, and take your time. Rachel reminded me of a quote earlier, which says, 'To climb steep hills requires a slow pace at first.' So let's heed that advice and take it steadily.'

The first section of the path wasn't very steep so I pushed myself up. We went along a tree lined path; here we saw iron gates which were the original Sutton Manor Colliery gates, which Jonathon told us opened in 1906 and only closed 1991.

'Imagine going to work each day down in a pit,' said Kate.

'It's what people did to put food on the table. I think the town of St Helens grew from this colliery, didn't it?' Albert said, glancing across at Jonathon.

Jonathon nodded.

Kate, Elaine and Jonathon let our group go in front as Kate was conscious about how long it might take for her to get up, and didn't want to slow anyone down. I was now out of breath so Pauline took over with Eddie walking by my side.

There was woodland all around us, along with a triumphant display of vibrant coloured wild flowers lining our route. When the sun rays were breaking through the canopy of foliage, the candescent, vivid hues and tones of the flowers and ferns, encouraged us all to stop for a moment and whisk out cameras.

We carried on slowly climbing but after only a few minutes we had to stop again.

'Ouch,' Anne cried out. 'I've got a stone in my sandal. Hang on, wait up a minute.' Anne held on to Lena's arm as she wobbled precariously and tried to fish out the stone.

Marion turned to Pauline. 'Aren't these purple orchids just lovely?'

'They're beautiful, and I'm sure I heard frogs earlier,' Pauline replied.

'Just listen to those birds,' Albert said with his eyes closed. 'Is that a willow warbler I can hear?'

'Look up now, Albert,' Eddie pointed in the sky. 'There's a swift, oh and there's another.'

'I can distinctly hear a chiffchaff as well,' Albert replied.

'Are Albert and Eddie having a bird spotting competition?' Pauline whispered in my ear.

I smiled to myself. The birdsong seemed to be the loudest sound, louder than our footsteps or our breath. It was unbelievable, considering how close we were to the motorway. We could see the traffic below yet it was still only birdsong we could hear. We hadn't yet passed anyone else.

Eddie took over from Pauline, but after about five minutes we all ground to a halt. Kate had stopped, needing a short rest, and she asked if we could go on ahead.

'Oh my God,' Pauline said, as we saw our first glimpse of the sculpture. We all stopped again, allowing Kate, Jonathon and Lena to catch up. Even though it was only a partial sighting of the sculpture, digital cameras and phones clicked away. As we set off again, the wheezing and panting sounds increased, as the group were getting tired.

We passed by a spot where we'd a bird's eye view of a town below us.

Jonathon stood bent over, his hands on his knees. He straightened up and pointed across at the view. 'If you look over there, those buildings with the big chimneys are Fiddlers Ferry power station in Cheshire, so further on must be Chester and Wales.'

'I need to sit. Take the weight off my feet,' wheezed Marion. She was bent double and red faced.

The ground underneath was rocky, and unsuitable to sit on.

'If I put my brakes on, you could lean on my chair for a bit. It won't take the weight completely off, but...'

'Are you sure, Rachel?'

'Course I am.'

While Marion recovered, the other members were taking photographs of the view and talked about the sculpture.

'Why did they choose a girl's head?' Pauline asked. 'Why didn't they use something to remember the miners and the pit?'

'I think they wanted it to be a sculpture that everyone could use. The girl has her eyes closed, so she could be remembering, or she could be dreaming about the future,' Jonathon replied. 'I think they've done a great job, as it's a place where people come to reflect, get away from things, or just have a pleasant walk.'

'It's super considering it's on the doorstep of the folk here,' Elaine said.

'You've just taken the words right out of my mouth,' Pauline said, and smiled across at Elaine.

Kate called over to Jonathon. 'What's the artist's name again, I've forgotten his name?'

Jonathon peered down at a piece of paper he'd retrieved from his back pocket. 'He's Spanish and called Juame Plensa. He's actually a world-renowned artist and works a lot with size and shape as well as light.'

We all peered down below. It was so still, so quiet apart from the sprinkle of birdsong.

'This is simply breath-taking,' Anne whispered.

Jonathon put his hands on his hips. 'We've not much farther to go until the next bench and a spot where we can have a picnic,' he said. 'Just a bit longer.'

The group plodded on, with Marion now by my side. Exertion and tiredness was marked on all the faces around me.

'We're at the bench,' cried out Albert. 'Come on, the rest of you, best foot forward.'

I turned my head to Kate and she winked back.

'The artwork on these benches, it's so intricate,' said Anne. 'I think they're iron, aren't they?' She paused to recover her breath. 'That's a canary, on this bench, isn't it?'

Albert stood up straight and stretched his back. 'Canaries used to be taken down mines because they could detect gas.'

The group members collapsed onto a large checked rug put on top of the grass. Anne, Kate and Marion sat on a bench and I sat next to them. From this spot we could see most of the sculpture and the town below.

There was silence as everyone recovered from the climb. Marion took off one of her sandals to reveal a bright burning red bunion on her toe.

'That looks sore, haven't you got anything to put on it, to protect it.'

'The dressing must've come off.'

Kate bent down and from her bag brought out an assortment of plasters, antiseptic cream and larger dressings. She passed one over for Marion, and Lena helped her put it on.'

'Are those swallows?' Jonathon said as he squinted at the sky.

'Majestic, aren't they?' Albert agreed. 'And I'm sure I heard reed warblers earlier.'

Pauline turned to me and grinned.

'It just feels as if we're one with nature, the flowers, the birds,' Lena said.

'I think the landscape has been developed to encourage the wildlife,' Kate replied.

'I wonder what she's dreaming about,' Anne whispered as she looked towards the sculpture.

'What Jonathon said about thinking of the past and dreaming of the future,' Eddie said. 'Sounds just right, and could be a slogan for our group.'

Kate nodded. 'I think you're right and as a group this is what we need to do now, think about what's happened this past year and then think about what our dreams are for the group as we move on.'

Kate paused for breath. 'We've all been through quite a journey already.' With one hand she held out three fingers. 'We have three choices in front of us. One, carry on, but in a new venue and open up the membership of the group so more people can be part of it. Two, stop the group now. Or three, we split the group up and the older members form a group on your own.'

'Oh no, we shouldn't just have a group for oldies,' cried out Eddie.

Lena held up her hand. 'Personally, I just want to say although we've been through a difficult time, we've got lots of things in common. It would be such a shame if we ended the group now. And I just think it wouldn't be right, not including you and Rachel.'

'I agree,' Elaine said.

'I do as well.' said Pauline. 'It'd be a shame if the group ended. I don't think it would be right, splitting off and just being a group for older people.'

Marion, Albert and Anne nodded.

'Well, Rachel and I went for a drink at The Vines, the other day. While we were there I remembered they had function rooms at the back of the pub. I knew different groups are meeting at the pub, such as the book group and a rambling group. So we asked if the art group could be based there.'

'Go on,' Pauline whispered. 'What was the verdict?'

'They said we could meet there on a Saturday morning, but really we'd need more coming. On my radar to invite would be the likes of Fiona and Johan but also Jill and any of the others who used to go to the art group with Mike in Weston.'

'There's a problem with this, we can't hold it in a p-u-b,' Anne whispered, her hand in front of her mouth.

'Why not?' Kate asked frowning.

In a low voice, Anne turned to Kate. 'Certain people have a problem, you know, in a pub, with,' Anne nodded her head in the direction of Eddie, and pretended to drink from a glass.

'Are you talking about me or Fi-Fi? Do you realise I haven't had a drink for four hundred and thirty four days? Fi-Fi hasn't touched alcohol for even longer. We're not going to suddenly start drinking just because the group's held in a pub.' Eddie's face was red, his voice was getting louder and his fists were clenched.

'Well done, Eddie. Well done,' Lena said quickly.

'I didn't know, did I? I was only thinking about you,' Anne protested, her face flushing as the colour rose under her eyes.

Kate defused any possibility of an argument by quickly discussing the arrangements.

'The Vines would help us with advertising and would supply

tea and coffee. So there is a possibility of us carrying on in a slightly different manner. If we'd regular social events like we're doing today, I think it would help us grow as a group. What do you think?'

· 'I think it sounds like a great idea,' Eddie barked. He still seemed cross.

'Anne, what about you?' Kate asked with her head on one side. 'After all you're the leader of the group.'

'The leader? It doesn't feel like it.'

Lena reached out to Anne. 'You're the reason we're all here today. Kate's just helping out. Aren't you, Kate?'

'I've no intention of running this group. You're the leader, Anne, and...'

Marion interrupted. 'Sorry to interrupt Kate, while we're chatting, would it be possible to start the picnic. It's my diabetes, you see.'

We all started to unpack the picnic items. Lena took my art bag from the back of my chair and brought out the crisps. Other members put out their contributions and soon a feast was laid out in front of us.

While this was happening, I could hear Elaine whisper to Pauline, 'The Vines is a good idea.'

'Definitely,' Pauline replied. She passed Elaine a paper plate with sandwiches and a scotch egg.

Lena overheard Elaine's comment and murmured to nobody in particular, 'It's such a relief. Isn't it?'

Pauline, Elaine and Marion all nodded in agreement.

Lena passed me a packet of crisps and I asked her to also get the book, my copy of Whispers of the Beloved, out from my bag. As she did, a small folded piece of paper fluttered out of the bag and landed by my wheel. I picked it up and put it on my knee.

'What's this - a secret love letter?' Albert asked with a toothless grin.

I unfolded it and was skim reading the contents. 'It's actually

Anne's speech, the one you were going to say when we first started. I think you'd forgotten your glasses which is why you never read it out.'

'I've not got my eyes today either. What did I write?'

'You put that the group was made up of lots of different people with very different backgrounds yet we are one group, united through the love of art and the urge to create.'

Marion and Albert nodded along with Lena.

'That's so true,' said Kate, who smiled across at Anne.

For a moment, there was silence as the group finished off their drinks and food. Kate winked at me and gave a nod. I picked up my book from my lap and held it up with my piece of paper and Kate nodded again.

I gulped and fiddled with the paper, folding and unfolding it.

'I hope you don't mind, but I'd like to read out a few lines I'd prepared for today.' I looked around the group as most of them nodded.

'It's been a year almost to the day when I first moved to Carthom. I'd had a bad experience where I was before, and all I wanted when I came here was to feel accepted. At certain times in my life I've felt as if I was blown about from one crisis to the next. So when I read this passage from 'Whispers of the Beloved' by Rumi, it reminded me of myself but it also reminded me of Mike. It says:

With friends you grow wings
Alone
You are a single feather in disgrace
With them you master the wind,
But alone
You're blown in all directions.

I think Mike was very much alone. His mother died a year before we first met him. He desperately wanted to give her a decent funeral, but he didn't have enough money. He turned

to money lenders but it wasn't long before he was swal
up with mounting debts. He wasn't in debt due to spending his
money on gambling or booze it was just so he could pay for
his mum's funeral. When he thought he'd lose his Benefits he
grew very scared, and I think that's why he got defensive when
the argument happened. His sister told me at the memorial,
that in total all he had was four pounds and all the food he had
was stale.' I paused, wondering how the group would react to
what I was going to say next. 'He wasn't saying anyone was a
scrounger. In fact all he was saying was that we all need help
from the Government sometimes, whether it's the state pension,
tax credits or disability benefits. We're all struggling in one way
or another.'

There'd been no discernible reaction from the group, which
I wasn't sure if it meant they weren't listening or had accepted
what I'd said. I tried to moisten my lips with my tongue and
continued, this time without reading from my prepared speech.

'Since I've been disabled, I've been like the single feather
but getting to know all of you, knowing I've got you as friends
has helped me feel protected and secure. I was wanting to be
accepted but really I needed to feel I belonged and had friends
and it's through all of you I've got that. This group is like a wing,
made up of lots of single feathers. On our own we might be
vulnerable but together we're strong.' A tear started to fall down
my cheek.

'We never knew about Mike and struggling to pay for his
mother's funeral, or his epilepsy. No wonder he was a bit...Well,
if we'd known we...' Albert whispered.

'...would've been more understanding,' Marion said. 'I think
we all could have done things differently, but as you said, Kate,
we didn't get much chance to really know each other.'

Eddie stood up and walked to the edge, admiring the view,
so I wheeled over to join him.

'Regarding young Mike, I think that's why we need to get to

know each other, because, well, we only had those few hours and most of time we were just chit-chatting and painting. If all of us had known young Mike's predicament I doubt the argument would have happened.'

'Rachel,' Albert called out. 'Before we met you, we never really knew anyone young in a wheelchair before, did we, love?' Albert turned to Marion who shook her head. 'My father was disabled, but he used sticks.'

Eddie and I rejoined the group.

Kate turned to Anne. 'What do you think, Anne?'

'What do I think? No, I don't think I want to be in a group just for pensioners. If the pub is willing to do this, then maybe we should give it a go. As long as everyone wants to do that.'

Eddie puffed out his chest. 'Who thinks we should carry on, move to The Vines on a Saturday morning, open the group up and have regular social events? A show of hands please.'

Everyone put their hands up.

Jonathon, in one movement, jumped from a seated position to crouching down. He then lurched forward onto his straight arms, and pushed his legs out, before springing into a standing position.

'Who wants to go up and view the sculpture with me?' He said, a little red faced from his gymnastics.

Eddie, Jonathon and Albert all decided to go on further.

Once they had set off, Kate stretched out her legs and massaged her knee.

'I can't get over how calm it is up here.'

Marion nodded. She grasped an empty paper cup and turned towards me.

'Rachel, when you read that passage about the feather, Simon, my son, came to my mind. I've missed helping him, being part of his life. He has been blown all over the place. Sometimes it was his own fault, but even so, I'd still like to be in touch with him. He doesn't even visit, or telephone because Albert has taken such a hard line with him.' Marion's bottom lip quivered and the paper cup was crushed in her hand. 'I think I'm going to make the effort and go and see him from time to time.'

'Albert will understand and I'm sure Simon will really appreciate it,' Lena said and placed her hand on top of Marion's.

'I just wish I could be part of my daughter's life. If Theresa was around I'd want to help her, so I think you're right Marion.'

I nudged Anne. 'Did you find her on Facebook?'

For a moment Anne's face lit up. 'Not Theresa, but then I put Katie my granddaughter's name into it and I found her almost straight away. She's beautiful, really beautiful. She looks so much like Theresa did at that age. Mind, it winded me when I first saw her. I thought I couldn't breathe. What I did spot was she wants to do an 'A' level in art.'

'So have you sent her a message or letter?' Marion asked.

Anne shook her head slowly.

'We'll all support you in this, Anne, whatever you decide,' I said.

'Oh yes,' Pauline agreed. 'We'd give you any help you needed.'

Anne nodded. 'This is such a peaceful, beautiful spot, isn't it? I feel I could stay here all summer.'

Lena nodded. 'It's like below us the world is being busy, while up here time is stretching out and slowing down.' She tugged on her cross and chain. 'I'm thinking of my Jim. He would've loved it up here with all the birds; he used to be interested in bird watching. Then I think of Mike. I can just imagine him taking photographs.' A tear fell down her cheek.

'Yes, he would've loved it,' replied Kate.

'If I'd known he was in such trouble I wouldn't have...' Pauline pulled off her glasses to wipe her eyes. 'I just feel awful, really awful.'

'That's why we need to do things like this, so we get to know each other better,' Marion said and put her arm around Pauline. 'We all could've understood him more if we knew his background. That's why I want to try and mend bridges with Simon; I don't want to leave it until it's too late.'

Anne cleared her throat. 'All I wanted was to be a good mother and artist. I feel like I failed at both. I don't even know if you want me to carry on running the group?'

'You're definitely both Anne,' I pleaded. 'In art terms, just think about what you've done. You started this group. Yes, we hit a rocky patch, but we're here today. We all want you to carry on. Don't we?'

Everyone nodded or said 'yes'.

'At least you've got your work in and around Carthom, like in The Richmond,' Anne said glancing first at me, then at Kate.

'More people might be able to do this later,' Kate said. 'Gary just wanted two of us at first.' I felt myself blush I didn't know Anne knew about our arrangement at The Richmond.

Lena seemed to sense our discomfort. 'Do you think we should still be called Art for You? I think if we're having a fresh start then maybe we should call ourselves something different.'

'If we were Art for You, why not call ourselves, Art for Everyone? If we meet at The Vines, on a Saturday, it means everyone can come along.' Marion said, smiling.

'Art for Everyone? Yes, it's good idea.' Anne replied, with a nod. 'I wonder what the others will think.'

'Could we have the dog painting of Mike's on the front of the flyer?' Lena asked. 'We could even send one to his sister. If we invite the people from the old Weston group, they might appreciate it too.'

Anne nodded. 'I don't see why not. Johan won't mind.'

In the distance, we could hear voices and soon we saw Jonathon gingerly make his way down to the bench. Eddie followed with Albert on his arm. While they were having a drink, Lena told them about the idea to change the name and flyer.

Eddie and Albert were all in agreement and for the next few

moments we all sat there in silence.

'Right, so this is the plan. We're going to meet on Saturday mornings, call ourselves Art for Everyone, use one of Mike's paintings for one of the flyers, and have monthly social nights or trips,' Anne announced. 'Does anyone not agree?'

There was silence.

'OK, I think we're onto to something good. Here's to Art for Everyone.' Anne lifted up her empty, plastic cup.

'Art for Everyone,' we all replied. Those who had drinks raised them up for the toast.

'Hear, hear,' said Eddie.

I gazed around the beaming faces of the group and felt like hugging them all.

Jonathon clapped his hands together. 'I'm sorry to have to say, but we now have got to get down this hill. We've got a lengthy drive ahead of us.'

Pauline adjusted her sandal straps. She straightened up and turned to Elaine.

'Just think we climbed up this hill, not knowing what would happen, and we're...'

'...coming down as a group,' Pauline and Elaine said in unison.

Epilogue

It was a grey October day, but the dark clouds, although ominous had bright patches of blue sky behind them with the promise of some late autumn sunshine. Across the road, Dot was putting some rubbish in her recycling bin. She spotted me and waved, before crossing the road to talk to me, still in her fluffy pink slippers.

'Are you off out, Rachel?'

'Yeah, it's the first art group at The Vines today. How did you get on with Janine?'

Janine and her boyfriend had started their cleaning company, Janclean Services, with the help from a grant from a philanthropist Jonathon had mentioned, who regularly assisted fledgling businesses. After advice they'd also taken out a small loan to rent office space. To give my support I moved my dinnertime slot from Concerned about Care, to Janine's company and tried to pass the word around about her business. Dot was the first person I told. She'd connections with the local church and had even put an advert in the church magazine about it, free of charge.

'I do like her; she's a lovely girl, isn't she? She even cleaned my windows. I was thinking about asking her to see my friend, Mary. She's like you, in a wheelchair, though she's not as independent as you. Do you think Janine would see her to discuss it?'

'Yes, I'm sure she would, just ask her.'

'I was going to ask about your paintings. The one in your window is super. How much do you charge?'

I half turned to my flyer in my living room window, which advertised my services as an artist. 'It depends on what you want, Dot, but I rarely go above thirty-forty pounds, and considering all you've done for me and Janine, I'd knock some off.'

'It's for a present for my daughter, as a moving gift, something to go in her new house. By the way, I love your new hairstyle. You look like a new girl.'

I smiled. Since the trip to The Dream, I'd started the course at Inspire and Support. Tracey had been right; it was a life-affirming course. Brian, the chief executive of the charity had spoken at the first session about why he set the charity up. His daughter, Isabel, was in a traffic accident when she was sixteen and as a result was paraplegic. She was depressed after it, and Brian realised it was a common problem so set the charity up to support people with disabilities following trauma.

He wanted us to focus on life now and look at the positive aspects of our lives. It helped me to think differently about my situation. That course and my first year in Carthom had all contributed to my feelings of renewal, and revitalisation.

I still spent a lot of time on my own, but the ache and pain of loneliness had gone. Instead, I was more self-aware and this led me to enjoy the company of others but equally enjoy the time I had when on my own.

To accompany my change in mood, I'd treated myself to a trip to the hairdresser. As well as a pixie haircut, I had blonde highlights put in. To complete my new look, I was also wearing a new long skirt, fitted blouse and scarf.

Dot padded back over to her house and gave a wave before she went inside. I checked my watch again and glanced up the road to see if I could see Anne's car. I knew Anne was nervous about today and was setting up with Lena before she picked me up. Matt and Sue had managed to get ten names from pub goers who were interested in coming to the group. We'd thirteen names ourselves, which included Fiona, Johan and Jill from the Weston group.

At nine-fifteen, Anne arrived. Since the trip to The Dream, she'd gradually picked up and on this day there was no sign of the depression that had dogged her for most of the summer.

'Cor, you're looking nice.' Anne examined me from my feet up to my head. 'I like your hair like that,' she added.

You're looking good yourself, Anne.'

'Two people turned up at nine o'clock. That's eagerness, isn't it?' Anne called out, as she plonked my chair in the boot. She came round to her door and got in, slamming it shut. She turned to me.

'Right, let's get our skates on.'

'Are you still OK to help me do the Facebook message for Katie?' Anne asked as we waited to turn onto the man road.

'Have you written something down on paper yet?'

'I've got most of it down. I just don't know how I'm going to end it. What should I call myself? Granny? Or just my name?'

'I could come for an hour after the group, if you think it would help?'

Anne nodded. 'Thanks.'

Matt, true to his word, had put down a temporary ramp. The pub was deserted, apart from the bar staff who were busy polishing glasses and Sue who was busy vacuuming under a table. As we got closer to the function room, I could hear the buzz of conversations taking place inside.

Albert, Marion, Lena and Eddie were chatting with six new people. It was an odd feeling not being the new girl anymore and hard to assimilate that at some point during the past year in Carthom, I'd emerged, almost imperceptibly, from being an outsider to an accepted member of the community.

Hanging on the wall was Mike's painting of the black Labrador. The Vines had used this image for the flyers advertising the group. I could almost feel him tug my sleeve wanting to pop out for a cigarette.

The toxicology results showed there wasn't any epilepsy medication in Mike's system. That, combined with the head injury pointed towards him having a seizure, but the final verdict was left open.

I was finding a place to park when the door opened. Jill walked through and gave a quick, nervous smile. She was followed by Pauline and Eddie, and Kate who was carrying a painting. As soon as the door swung back shut, it was opened again, as Johann strolled in. I'd really missed him. Before doing anything else, he looked at me and beamed. In the past, I might've checked from left to right and behind me, to make sure the smile was intended for me but after his portrait I wasn't in any doubt.

I slotted in at the table and introduced myself to an older man called Sebastian on my right and said 'hello' to Lena on my left, before getting out my art materials.

Kate crept up behind me, making me jump as she tapped gently on my shoulder. She placed her canvas in front of me. It was a beautiful, fragile and intricate white feather in acrylics on a black background.

'A present for you, sweetie. Put it on your wall and if you're ever down, remember this is what you were but your life is different now.'

'Come here.' I turned in my chair and held out my arms.

Kate bent down and we hugged.

'It's perfect, thanks,' I whispered in her ear.

'I love your hair,' Kate whispered. 'You must give me the number of your hairdresser.'

The door opened again, with Fiona walking in, followed by four more new members.

Sebastian leant over me and peered at the painting; his round, John Lennon style silver glasses now perched on the tip of his nose.

'Why a feather?'

'Oh, it's a bit complicated.'

Anne pulled her chair out, and stood up. 'I want to welcome you all today. This is the very first meeting of our new group. When we met at the Carthom Community Centre, we were called Art for You. Mind, we only ended up having older and disabled people in the group because of the time and day we used to meet. Thanks to Sue and Matt, we've been able to hold the group here, so our new name is Art for Everyone.'

'Hear, hear,' Albert called out.

Eddie started to clap and we all followed his lead. Anne blushed and raised her hand to indicate to us to stop.

'Thank you, everyone. Now, when the group was meeting in the community centre, we were going to hold a demonstration once a month, but, erm...' Anne stared down at her little piece of paper, her face flushed.

Eddie cleared his throat. 'What do you mean by demonstration, Anne, just so the new people know?'

'Somebody might want to learn about landscapes or how to use acrylics. So, next to the tea and coffee,' Anne gestured to the corner of the room, 'I've put a notebook for suggestions to go in. For the first one, Johan's going to show us how to do portraits and then how to develop them into caricatures. I think that's all. Oh, hang on, because there are lots of new faces, can we just use the stickers going around, and write your name on it. Have fun, everyone.'

'Are you going to tell me about this feather business?'

I glanced across at Anne. 'You'd have to hear it all really. It's all to do with this group, and my first year in Carthom. It's also just how I see it, others might see it differently.'

'Is it about your disability?'

'In a way, yes.'

Sebastian looked confused.

The door opened, and Sue slowly walked in, gingerly holding a huge fruit cake on a tin foil board. She was followed by Matt and two bar staff all carrying small plates, napkins and forks. Sue put the cake down and, wiped her hands on her jeans before joining Matt at the top of the table, not far from Anne.

'Hi everyone; it's great to see such a lot of people. On behalf of The Vines we'd like to welcome you all,' said Matt. 'We hope you enjoy the cake and our partnership with you is long and fruitful. If you need any more plates or napkins, give us a shout. Now, Anne could you cut the cake? If you don't mind we'll take a photograph for The Carthom News.'

Anne stood up and with a proud smile she cut the cake and posed for photographs. I was pleased she might eventually get recognition for all the work she'd undertaken for the group.

Conversations and laughter filled the room, as plates, each with a generous slice of cake were passed around.

Sebastian, with a finger pushed his glasses up to the bridge of his nose.

'Go on, then.'

Kate leant forward and tapped the table. 'What's this about?'

'The business with the feather,' Sebastian said.

I'd come such a long way, in terms of friendships and my overall situation. So why not tell Sebastian? After my slice of cake, I brushed the crumbs off my mouth and took a deep breath. I gazed into his grey-blue eyes as I started to share with him, my story of The Single Feather.

'Finally a book with a disabled protagonist, which isn't either 'woe me' or 'gawd bless us everyone'. Instead it's an honest portrayal of what it's like to be disabled in the 21st Century and is simply outstanding.'

A.Babbs

'The Single Feather is a dispatch from the hidden front-lines of austerity England that should be read by a wide audience.'

Rick Burgess (New Approach, Manchester DPAC)

'R.F.Hunt is an insightful writer, honest and does not shy away from difficult subjects; that she also writes with humour and sensitivity makes this debut novel both very readable and endlessly thought-provoking.'

Anne Hamilton (A Blonde Bengali Wife)

'I highly recommend this book to anyone who wants a real perspective on mental health and disability and anyone who wants to meet genuine characters between the pages.'

Rosie Claverton (The Amy Lane Mysteries)

'This is a fabulous book - engrossing, absorbing and warmly humane.'

Anthony Trevelyan (The Weightless World)

'In giving a central voice to those who have either been ignored or treated as mere victims in most works of fiction, this is s welcome and mould-breaking debut novel.'

Paul Simon (The Morning Star)